Dead Man Walking
A Wild West Omnibus

John Russell Fearn

First published in 2017 by Pioneering Press

Thunder Valley

John Russell Fearn

Chapter I

The dense cloud of dust rising into the spring Arizona sunlight drifted gently in the hot wind and then the glowing afternoon returned to its habitual unshaken calm. The stage coach, the cause of all the commotion, had halted at the station in Thunder Bend. There was a jingle of bits and bridles, the scrape and thump of boxes and trunks being dragged and dumped on the boardwalk, and the mixed conversation of the city dweller and rural denizen.

It was a moment or two before the man with the bedroll roped across his broad shoulders emerged from the shadow of the coach into the hot sunlight. He took a few steps and then stopped to contemplate the surroundings. Thunder Bend? Well, at least nobody had had the impudence to call it a city, though in this fairly deserted region of Arizona the inhabitants were reasonably proud of the place.

To the stranger it seemed to be all main street. Here and there a horse was tethered to a hitch-rail; a buckboard and team stood outside the general stores. At the far end of the main street from where the stranger stood were more familiar signs — the notice board of an assayer and agent in real estate, and a much bigger board proclaiming the Yellow Nugget Saloon. There was also a tabernacle of sorts with a shaky-looking wooden spire pointing a judgment finger to cobalt heaven. The stranger grinned to himself, either because he was making comparisons with a real Western city or else because Thunder Bend in itself amused him. He hunched his bedroll a little farther round on his shoulder and began to walk through the powdery dust of the high street. He was by no means a dude. Two days' growth of stubble hid his jaws, a faded, black sombrero put his high cheekbones and agate-blue eyes in deepest shadow.

He moved easily, as though his joints were on swivels. His attire — a check shirt, tight and dusty black pants, and worn half-boots stamped him as either a hobo or else a rancher who had taken a sudden dive down the social ladder.

As he progressed, he gazed. The place was not quite so deserted as he had at first thought for men and women were moving back and forth along the boardwalks, most of them avoiding the sunlight. The women in the main looked like housewives, the men like cattle-punchers or cattle owners, according to their attire and manner … Outside some of the buildings men sat on the hitch-rails, smoking, gazing out lambently into the afternoon. They did not regard the stranger with any particular interest — unless it was to notice that he didn't carry a gun. In any case one hombre more or less in Thunder Bend made no difference.

The stranger stopped when he came to the Yellow Nugget saloon. Outside its batswing doors a man with a round, wet face sat on a chair, his feet on the hitch-rail and the chair on its hind legs. A cigarette drooped out of the man's thick-lipped mouth and perspiration had flattened the black hair on his bullet head.

The stranger walked up the three steps to the boardwalk and the hollow sound his boots made caused the lounging man to glance up sharply.

"If yore lookin' fer a drink, feller, yuh'd better be lookin' someplace else," he observed. "We're not open 'til evenin'."

"It can wait," the stranger answered him. "I'm not dyin' of thirst — yet." He had a surprisingly quiet, gentle voice, yet it had assurance in it. "All I want to find out is where I can bunk hereabouts."

The man in the chair took the cigarette from his mouth and considered it.

"That depends. How much d'yuh reckon on payin'?"

"As little as possible. I've got some money — but not so's I can throw it around. That's one reason why I'm here — to do a little prospecting."

"Yuh'll make precious little washin' dirt around here, pardner. I know. I tried it once." With a thump the chair settled back on all four legs and the man got to his feet. He was plump and shortish. He held out a chubby hand. "So yore a stranger in town, eh? Wal, at least I c'n make yuh welcome, I reckon. Jeff Willard's the name. I'm th' barkeep in th' saloon here."

The stranger nodded, gave his infectious grin, and then shook hands.

"Glad to know you. I'm Brad Morrison — but there doesn't seem to be much to me except the name. I'll have to make that do."

"An' yuh want a place to bunk?" The black, pensive eyes of Jeff Willard ranged the lean, stubbled face for a moment. "The Yellow Nugget ain't the place fer yuh, that's certain. Too expensive. Joe Rutter — he's the boss — likes fancy prices fer rooms here, prices that wouldn't be t'yuh likin', I'm thinkin'. So, let's see. Mebby I c'n help somehow."

5

The barkeeper went into cogitation, drawing hard on his cigarette and contemplating the boarding at his feet. Brad Morrison waited, viewing the scenery meanwhile.

Thunder Bend lay at one end of Thunder Valley, with the steep, saw-toothed mountains rising to either side of it so that the ramshackle habitations looked as though they were in the jaws of a gargantuan bear-trap. The mountains themselves, separated from the town by pasture land and the vast expanses of the mesa, were hardly visible at this time of year. Scarlet ocotillo laced in and out of the greyness, relieved by the delicate salmon and vivid orange of the chollas and opuntias. In other directions the hues changed into the silver-white of the Apache plumes and the lilac of the loco-weed ...

"I reckon Old Timer might be able t' help yuh," Jeff Willard said finally.

Brad Morrison took his attention from the enthralling magnificence of Nature.

"Old Timer?"

"Yeah. Matter o' fact I don't know his real name. Nobody does around here. He's bin Old Timer as long as yuh c'n remember. An' he's a prospector like yuhself." Jeff Willard gave a faint grin which revealed yellowed teeth. "I don't want yuh t' take it to heart, pardner, but Old Timer's bin pannin' and lookin' fer colour fer th' past fifteen year an' he ain't found so much as a nugget! But he still goes on thinkin' he'll strike a bonanza lode one day."

"You never can tell what you'll find if you look long enough," Brad Morrison answered ambiguously. "Beginner's luck, remember. Anyway, how much good can Old Timer do me?"

"He's got a cabin down by the creek — 'bout five mile from here. He's been hankerin' after gettin' a pardner to share th' place with him. Mebby he's gettin' old or somethin' but he don't sorta like livin' alone as much as he usta."

"Sounds as though he'll do for me," Brad agreed, reflecting. "How do I find him?"

"There's only one place yuh'll ever find Old Timer — an' that's at one end of th' creek or th' other. That is while the sun's up. He pans down there every day, 'cept when the creek gets too full in the winter rains ... Some folks around here think he's loco. Not me, though. He's a mighty fine teller is Old Timer." Jeff Willard nodded his bullet head in slow confirmation of his own words. " Anyway, yuh don't need to go searchin' fer him. Fer one thing yuh've no horse … Mmmm, ain't got no gun neither. I reckon yuh oughta have one in these parts, pardner. Never can tell what's goin' to happen."

"I did have a six," Morrison said, "but I sold it back in Drew City to help scrape together my fare to get here. I heard there might be some gold lying around. If you know where I can get another gun cheap —"

Jeff Willard glanced about him arid then jerked his dark head towards the saloon's batswings.

"What yuh want t'do, pardner, is come inside and I'll fix a drink fer yuh. Against rules, I reckon, but I break 'em when it suits me. Yuh can't sit around an' wait 'til the place opens: won't be fer a coupla hours yet. By then Old Timer should be along. He ain't never missed a drink fer fifteen year … Mebby I can fix yuh a bite to eat, too. I live in this place at th' back and that sorta makes it easier."

Brad Morrison smiled at the friendliness of the man and followed him into the wide, gloomy expanse of the saloon. It was tidy enough, ready for the evening, but having smallish windows and no lights on there was a funereal aspect. Brad had a glimpse of shiny-topped tables with chairs tucked under them, of a distant platform with a piano, fretwork-fronted, immediately below it, of poker and pool tables, of gleaming mirrors and rows of bottles at the back of the bar … Then he pursued the barkeep across what seemed like a ghost saloon and through a rear doorway, and so into a neat little back room where the afternoon sun blazed through an open window.

"It ain't much," the barkeep apologized, "but it's better 'n nothin'. Take a seat. I'll fix a drink an' some sandwiches fer yuh."

"You're giving me more service than I rightly deserve, Jeff," Brad told him.

"Aw, it ain't nothin'."

The barkeep hurried out again into the gloom of the saloon and Brad Morrison pulled off his faded sombrero and threw it down in a chair. His bedroll and contents he dumped on the floor …

Black hair was revealed now, thick sloe-black, gleaming richly not with oil but with sheer good health. Brad Morrison had the burned-in brown of a Western outdoors man. He moved with his easy, gangling legs, ignoring the invitation to take a seat, and stood looking through the window, his thumbs hooked on to his pants belt.

Just for a moment the look of a hobo and wanderer left his lean face. It became hard and eagle-like as he gazed towards the mesa and mountains — then he turned as the perspiring barkeep came in once more with a bottle, two glasses, and some hastily contrived sandwiches loaded on to a tray. He set it down, and then beside it laid a gun belt, in the holster of which was a well-used but still highly serviceable .45.

"Why the hardware?" Brad asked him, settling down and filling the two glasses from the bottle.

Jeff Willard grinned with his yellow teeth as he sat at the opposite side of the table.

"That's fer yore own use, pardner. This town ain't as peaceful as it looks. Fer one thing this is a halt station an' it brings in more roughnecks than it does dust. They c'n make life mighty jumpy sometimes. Then there's Black Joe himself — he's the boss of this saloon, and most of th' town too, I reckon — an' his boys. They ain't too pleasant sometimes."

Brad picked up a sandwich and munched at it. Not by so much as a glance did he reveal what he was thinking.

"I take it," he said presently, "that Black Joe is pretty much the be-all and end-all around here, then?"

"Yeah. Got cause, too, I reckon. He's a cattle king." Jeff Willard reflected for a moment, his black eyes on the liquor in his glass. "He owns the Double-G spread at Arrow Point, round back of th' mountains. Got one of th' biggest herds around here, too. But I'll stake all I've got that he didn't come by it all honest like. Thur's lots of unexplained things about Black Joe, but naterally y' can't get anythin' outa his boys. Thur's two of 'em — 'Lefty' Wilmore and 'Rod' Jenkins. Gun hawks, both of 'em. I'm warnin' yuh, pardner, don't ask Black Joe too many questions or cross him up. Yuh might get bushwhacked."

Brad went on with his sandwich, lean jaws working smoothly under the stubble.

"You don't suppose," he said finally, "that Black Joe owes a good deal of his success and power to illegal gold, do you?"

Willard shrugged, "How'd I be knowin? Ain't I just told you he never tells me nothin'? Might be gold at that." The barkeep mused for a moment. "Thur's lost gold mines all over Arizona if it comes t' that. Mebby he happened on a bonanza and opened it up — but we ain't ever likely to find out about it. Joe Rutter ain't the talkative type."

There was a pause. Jeff Willard finished off his drink and then asked a question in some surprise.

"Listen, feller, how come yuh asked that question about him findin' gold? D'yuh know somethin' about Black Joe?"

"Not a thing," Brad answered amiably, shrugging. "Never heard of him in fact. But I *have* heard that gold is going out of this town — and pretty freely as well as illegally, so I thought I'd blow along and see if I couldn't dig some up for myself somewheres."

He finished the sandwiches and drink and then picked up the .45 and examined it.

"And you want me to protect myself, Jeff?" He smiled gratefully. "That's mighty nice of you. I appreciate it."

"Ain't nothin'. I just don't like t'see a young, strappin' feller like you riskin' gettin' hurt, that's all." Jeff Willard looked uncomfortable and perspired more than ever. "I s'pose I'm a bit of a sucker but I just can't help it."

"Generosity never made anybody a sucker, Jeff," Brad told him. "How much for the gun and belt?"

"Nothin'. Leastways, not now. You c'n pay me somethin' when yuh can afford it. I've two other forty-fives I use, when I need — which ain't often. I'm known around here. 'Innocent' Jeff Willard they calls me."

Brad looked at him earnestly and then nodded.

"Much obliged. If ever I can do you a favour don't forget to let me know."

Brad stood up, strapped the belt about his waist and then twirled the gun swiftly in his fingers and dropped it neatly into the holster. Jeff Willard watched the action and grinned appreciatively.

"It ain't th' first time yuh've monkeyed with a gun, I reckon," he commented.

"No," Brad admitted. "You're quite right." There was silence for a moment in the hot, sunny room, then Brad walked to the window again and glanced outside.

"Tell you what I'll do, Jeff. I'll take a look at this town and come back when the saloon's open. By then Old Timer may have arrived. Mind if I leave the bedroll and belongings here?"

"Not a bit." Jeff Willard-surged to his feet. "It might be a good idea fer yuh to nose around an' see what yuh think of the place. If yuh don't like it, I shan't blame yuh. It's one hell-fried spot, believe me …"

*

It was some hours later when Brad Morrison returned to the Yellow Nugget saloon, and for a moment the barkeep didn't recognize him. In the interval he had evidently visited the barber's amongst other places, for the stubble had gone now to reveal the smooth leanness of jaw and firmly set but half-humorous mouth.

The face which had been shadowed by two days' growth was now one that unconsciously drew attention because it was so different from the leathery visages common to Thunder Bend. It was young, flexible, and yet it hid a boundless good nature and easy assurance. It made the men and women at the tables look after him as he strolled across to the bar, the .45 Jeff had given him now holstered low down on his right thigh.

"Snakes alive, I didn't know yuh," Jeff Willard murmured, pouring out a drink. "An' look — go easy on spreadin' it around what I done fer yuh, eh? The boss mightn't think it was such a good idea at that."

"Okay, Jeff, you don't have to worry. Your secret's safe enough with me."

Brad planked down his money for the drink. Then he turned to survey the gathering, cuffing up his faded hat on to his forehead. The gaze of the men and women directed towards him turned away. For some reason he didn't look like the kind of man who'd welcome any questions.

After a while Brad's nostrils wrinkled at the atmosphere and noise of the place. The gloom of the afternoon scene had been banished now by the light from glassy pendant lamps swinging from the beams overhead. The glow penetrated into the deeper corners, out to the far side of the saloon where men and highly rouged women danced to the discordant thumping of the fretwork-fronted piano and scrape of an archaic violin.

In the nearer scene were the pin-tables and poker layouts with their rattle of chips. There was, too, an overall smell — of vulgar perfume, strong cigar fumes, cheap cigarettes, liquor, and perspiration. It was a stench all the more repulsive after the clean outdoors and the spring night breeze from mountains and mesa. In here the air was deep blue with tobacco smoke, and the lamps had haloes round them.

10

"Old Timer come yet?" Brad asked, without turning to look at the barkeep.

"Not yet. Be here soon, I reckon."

Brad finished his drink, hooked his thumbs in his in his pants belt and still contemplated the scene. The dancing finished presently and there was the shuffle and scrape of heavy boots and light shoes as the men and women drifted back to their tables. The "violinist" put down his fiddle and dived towards a glass of beer, leaving the pianist below the platform. He seemed to be waiting for something, and it wasn't long before Brad saw what it was.

From the back of the saloon, through faded draperies, came a girl. She was dressed in a dark sequined gown far too mature in design for her years, even though it did make her white shoulders and the upper part of her smoothly developed bosom appear more attractive by contrast. Her hair, a mass of honey-coloured coils and waves, was piled on top of her dainty head in far too middle-aged a fashion.

She moved with lithe grace, pausing finally when she had reached the centre of the stage above the piano. At his distance from her Brad could only distinguish that she was a blonde of average height with a small-featured face. He found himself wondering if the rest of her figure, hidden in the clumsy gown, matched the revealed portions.

"Who is she?" he murmured to Jeff Willard.

"Her?" The barkeep polished a glass and talked to the air. "She's Betty Tarrant. Too nice a kid for this dive, I reckon. Got a swell voice, too, as yuh'll hear — an' don't get any ideas, feller," Jeff warned, cocking a dark eye. "She's already earmarked. Black Joe's gurl."

Brad Morrison only smiled. He rolled a cigarette, put it between his lips, and lighted it. By this time the girl had commenced singing and the rattle of poker chips and shuffle and scrape of boots and murmur of conversation ceased. To Brad, at least, there was nothing remarkable about this. The blonde-headed Betty Tarrant had a voice with magic in it; it had purity, sweetness, and an appealing innocence. In a den like this it was like the voice of one crying in the wilderness. Though the song was ancient and made little sense she sang it like a prima donna and finished with a flawless high C which faded into silence.

"Yeah," Jeff Willard murmured, amidst the banging of feet and clapping of hands, "that kid has a voice. No doubt of it!"

Brad watched the girl bow her dainty head in acknowledgment and then turn to leave the platform. Suddenly he made up his mind. With swift movements of his long legs he crossed the saloon between the tables and caught up with her just as she was about to vanish between the draperies.

"If you don't mind, miss …" He removed his sombrero and smiled intriguingly. "I'd like to thank you. I mean personally — not with my clapping mixed up with the noise of all these hoodlums. I'd like to show my appreciation in a more practical way … A drink, maybe?"

She hesitated. She had very blue eyes, emphasized by the faint shadow of mascara. Her lashes were long, curled at the ends, and her glance half frightened.

"A — a drink? she repeated, and cast a hurried glance about the smoky saloon.

"Why not? It's the appropriate place, isn't it?"

She gave a slow, even troubled smile. "You're a stranger here, of course. Otherwise you wouldn't offer such an invitation." She drew herself up a little, serenely dignified despite the ill-becoming black dress.

"I'm so sorry," she said gently.

She turned to go, but Brad's next two words just caught her ear when she was half-way through the draperies.

"Or afraid?"

That brought her back to his side, sharp inquiry in her blue eyes and her firm, rounded little chin set.

"Afraid? Who's afraid?"

"If you're not, what are we waiting for?"

He took her arm and in spite of herself, she went to a near-by corner table and settled before it, regarding him perplexedly. Brad glanced up at the waiter as he came shambling across.

"I don't drink," the girl said hastily. "Never touch the stuff."

"Make mine a double whisky," Brad said, and thrust the crown of his sombrero on to the knob of his chair. He smiled a little and proffered a cigarette packet. The girl hesitated, took one, studied him as he lighted the weed for her.

"I don't blame you for not drinking," he said, over the match-flame. "But I'm glad you smoke. Makes it more sociable. If you don't like that weed I'll roll you one of my own."

"Suppose," she said, settling back and considering him through the smoke, "you tell me what this is all about? And who you are?"

Chapter II

"The name," Brad said, after a pause, "is Bradley Morrison — Brad for short. And my occupation's — well, I guess you might as well call me a prospector and leave it at that. As for what this is all about, that's simple." He shrugged and smiled. "You are the only person I've seen so far in this town of saddle tramps and hard cases who looks as though she knows what class really is. You may have noticed, Miss Tarrant, that I'm not without education myself."

"You know my name, then?" She did not sound indignant; only wondering.

"You can't get up on a stage and sing like you do without your name being known."

She meditated over this while the waiter brought the double whisky and then retired again. Finally, the frown returned to the girl's smooth forehead with the wisps of blonde hair fluffing down it.

"You just wanting to speak to me doesn't mean a thing," she said finally. "Surely you had something more than that behind it?"

"Oh, sure." Brad drained his glass and set it down. "I couldn't let a girl as pretty and refined as you out of my sight without sayin' something. After all, I'm supposed to be a man, and I'm only human. And don't get sore," he added, as the rouged little mouth tightened.

"What do you expect me to do? Give you a kiss?"

"I hadn't thought of that, but it's an idea."

"Why, you!" The girl half rose, but Brad's lean hand closed on her wrist and tightened. In spite of herself she sat down again slowly.

"I repeat, you're educated," Brad said. "I've reason to know that there's gold around here — and that's what I'm doing in Thunder Bend. I told you I was a prospector, but I don't think I'm ever going to learn anything worthwhile from the kind of folks there seem to be around here. So I thought, you being the sort of girl you are, you might be able to help me."

"Did you though?" She smiled cynically and smoked quickly for a moment. "If I knew where there was gold around, Mr. Morrison, do you think I'd be singing here?"

"I dunno," Brad answered, shrugging. "Where *would* you be singing?"

14

"In New York, London, Paris — not here! It's only because I have no money worth calling money that I'm in this … dive!"

She folded her rounded bare arms and looked angrily round the saloon. Brad continued to study her as he smoked lazily, then at length he seemed to come to a decision.

"Y'know something, Miss Tarrant? I can't place your accent. Which State do you come from?"

"I don't come from any State," she retorted. "If you must know, I'm British. London born."

Brad shook his head. "Well, think of that. You're ways off trail, Miss Tarrant, if I may say so"

"I think you've said quite enough, stranger!"

Brad and the girl glanced up simultaneously. Neither of them had noticed the man in the black suit and wide-brimmed black hat who had come up behind them. He was massively built and quite six feet tall, with darkly suspicious eyes set in a bulldog face.

His hands in his trousers pockets pushed back the black jacket he was wearing so that twin Colts were revealed on his thighs.

"Joe!" the girl ejaculated, with a little gasp. "I — I didn't hear you come up."

"So I figgered — and put that cigarette out. What are you tryin' to do — ruin your voice … ? Who's this hobo, anyway?"

"The hobo," Brad said easily, considering his cigarette, "can speak for himself, Mr. Rutter."

"Howd' you know who I am?"

Brad shrugged. "Miss Tarrant called you 'Joe' — and I'm told that 'Black Joe' is a pretty dirty character around these parts. You look as though you might fit the part, and so there it is."

A vein swelled slightly in Joe's bull neck. Suddenly the myriad sounds of the saloon seemed to have become muted. Even the bar-keep had stopped half-way in the act of polishing a glass.

"I don't like that kind of talk, stranger," Black Joe said at length.

"Come to think of it, there's something I don't like, too."

Brad put his cigarette back in his mouth, then suddenly his hand blurred to his .45 and whipped it up. It looked as though it exploded deafeningly in Joe's face — but the only effect was for his big black hat to fly off his head as though somebody had kicked it. By the time he had discovered what had happened, Brad was on his feet, the .45 cocked.

"Sorry, Joe," he apologized. "It just happens to rile me when I see a man stand near a lady with his hat on."

Black Joe swallowed something and behind him one of his swarthy gun hawks handed the hat back to him. He kept it in his hand, passed his fingers over his rich dark hair.

"I don't know yet who you are, feller, but I'm aimin' to find out," he said at length. "When I do — if not before — you'd best get movin'. And keep clear of this lady, too. Ain't healthy to be seen with her. She's mine, see?"

Brad only smiled, and Black Joe breathed harder through his broad nostrils — then he jerked his head to the girl. She shot Brad a troubled glance and escaped through the draperies. Joe turned and followed her, and for a moment Brad seemed to consider whether he should do likewise. Finally he eyed the two gun hawks who were watching him narrowly. He slipped his gun back in the holster, snatched up his hat from the chair-back and put it on the back of his head as he returned across the saloon to the bar.

"That's one thing yuh shouldn't've done," Jeff Willard told him in a sober undertone. "Gettin' yuhself in bad with Black Joe is just plain askin' fer a pill yer belly can't digest."

"If Black Joe wants to play games I can let the wind out of him any time he likes," Brad retorted. "And anyway, it was worth it. I got to know the girl."

"Yuh don't mean yuh went through all that just to get to *know* her?"

"Sure. Why not? Once you let a chance slip in this life" — Brad snapped his fingers — "it stays slipped. I'm not the kind who can do that … That girl's no right to be here, Jeff. I'll have to think up somethin' better for her."

Jeff Willard sighed and shook his bullet head, then he suddenly pointed a shirt-sleeved arm. "Here's Old Timer. Bit late tonight."

The batswings had just opened and shut before a small-built man in a flannel shirt, a shaggy wolfskin coat, worn riding trousers and dusty half-boots, and a round coonskin cap pushed back on grizzled grey hair. His coat was flowing open so that there was just a glance of a .38 swinging loosely on a slack cartridge-belt. The man was obviously old, though he moved with decided energy. He had a seamed, leathery face burned deep

16

brown. It looked somehow fierce and yet also benevolent, as though his bark were far worse than his bite.

"Gin," he said briefly, to Jeff Willard, and then he leaned his arms on the counter and considered his reflection in the mirror. "Gittin' older every day, I reckon," he observed morosely. "I'm a-gittin' grey in me hair an' me bones crack as I walk around, an' still I don't find no bonanza. It sorta leaves me a-wonderin' if I'm plain loco or whether the stories o' lost gold mines scattered around these parts is jest a lot o' wimmin's talk."

He swallowed his drink and ordered another one while he brooded over his misfortunes.

"Perhaps you're just plain unlucky, pardner, that's all," Brad said, smiling. "At least I hope you are. I'm on the same track as yourself."

"Huh?" Steel-grey eyes peered with intense brightness from the exposure-hardened face. "You a prospector, son?"

"Yeah. And I'm looking for a place to bunk. Jeff here said we might be able to do a deal over your cabin."

"He did, huh?" Old Timer swallowed his second drink and pulled out a short pipe. It crackled and smelled abominably as he lighted it. "An' why 'ud I be a-wantin' to share the peace an' quiet with a lusty young hombre like you, huh? Tell me that!"

"Yore as lonely as a prairie wolf, Old Timer, an' yuh know it!" Jeff Willard said flatly. "Here's a feller willin' to do all the back-achin' work an' it just ain't plain decent to turn him down."

Old Timer was silent, but his bright grey eyes remained fixed on Brad's tall, rangy figure. The eyes moved up and down him, from his face to his sinewy hands, to his lithe hips, his feet. Finally Old Timer spat sociably at the cuspidor and rubbed his bristly chin with the stem of his pipe.

"Wil, now, this takes thinkin' about, son. Where yuh from? Who *are* yuh?"

"Brad Morrison. I'm not from anywhere in particular. Just a roamer."

"Not five minutes back," Jeff Willard said softly, "he shot the hat from off th' head o' Black Joe. It wus that quick yuh'd ha' missed it if yu'd blinked."

Old Timer assumed a sudden and serio-comic dignity.

"Half o' my cabin is yours," he said. "Don't say no more. Any man who does that to Black Joe should have th' *whole* cabin by rights, but I reckon I've got to park these old bones of mine some place."

"Thanks." Brad smiled and gripped the gnarled hand. "How much?"

"Er — ah — I reckon we don't need to go into that right now. I'll see yuh get your share o' hard work, don't yuh fergit it."

"I'm going to buy you a drink, anyway!"

Old Timer grinned for the first time and revealed he had two teeth in the top jaw and no more. He swallowed his third gin without seeming to notice he'd had it.

"Mind yuh," he went on, as he set the glass down on the counter, "I figger yuh must be plumb loco to come prospectin' in this perishin' prairie. There ain't nothin' in it but sand and water — an' sometimes water an' sand. More often than not there's jest sand. In fifteen year I ain't got th' smell o' gold dust … If I weren't so fallin' apart I'd hit the trail an' go to a city or someplace — but somehow, dog-gone it, there's a-somethin' about this part o' th' world, a-somethin' about the creek an' th' hills an' th' night winds thit makes yuh — Hun! Reckon I'll be goin' on a-pannin' fer dirt until I crack up. But it don't make sense fer a jigger like yuh to be a-doin' it."

"I heard there was gold around here, Old Timer," Brad said, keeping his voice low so that only the decrepit old prospector could hear him. "In fact I know there is. Hefty amounts of it keep arriving in Drew City. It was seeing it coming, and from here of all places, that made me think this might be a place worth drifting to."

Old Timer frowned and smoked furiously.

"Reckon I exaggerated a bit, son. There is gold — sure, but it ain't no more than dust. I said I ain't had no smell of it, but thit wasn't quite th' truth. I've found dust, and sold it. I can't keep a-goin' any other way. But I ain't never heard nothin' about it bein' in any quantity"

Old Timer broke off and watched as a girl came through the batswings. She was dressed in grey riding trousers and half-boots and despite the coldness of the night air outside wore only a soft silk shirt open at the neck. She was small, intensely dark, with a reddish-brown skin. Her long black hair clung like night about her slim shoulders. Moving soundlessly she went past Old Timer and Brad and stopped a little farther away at the counter.

Brad's eyes followed her, chiefly in curiosity. There was a smouldering, dusky beauty about her which insisted on being noticed. She ordered a drink but sipped it slowly. Then at length her slightly oblique eyes rose to meet Brad's — coolly, inquiringly. He realized he had been staring and shifted his gaze back to Old Timer.

"What race is she?" Brad murmured.

"Aztec. Pure bred."

"Know her?"

"I reckon so — or sort of. Ain't many in this town as don't. Only th' more yuh know about her th' less yuh seem t' find out. Her name's Nariza. She's got some other name but I'll be durned if I know what it is. She's pure Mexican Aztec, she says. In a direct line or sump'n. Seems sorta proud of it. Sometimes she goes off on one of her ceremonial fits an' does some wailin' ways up in th' mountains." Old Timer sighed reminiscently. "Dog-gone me if I wouldn't sooner hear a coyote! There ain't nobody seems able to find where she lives. In th' mountains some place, I reckon."

Brad frowned. "In the mountains? But she's got style. She looks like a city girl."

"Thit's all I know about her, son." Old Timer shrugged. "She first turned up about two year back an' she comes in here some nights, jest fer a drink."

Brad's eyes strayed back to the girl. He noticed more detail on her face now as she considered her drink. She had a curved nose, rather large but expressive mouth, and though her features were regular they were also broad. Then she drained her glass and set it down.

"So the stranger finds me interesting?" she inquired, glancing — and Brad realized she had been watching his scrutiny by means of the mirror. The richness of her voice surprised him.

"Take it easy, son," Old Timer murmured. "She c'n scratch like a polecat when she's nasty."

Brad smiled and took off his hat. "A beautiful woman isn't something you expect to see twice in an evenin'," he answered.

"Twice?" The Aztec girl moved towards him, her heavy dark brows lowering a little. "What do you mean, twice?"

"First the singer, and now you. Quite a contrast in the colour scheme certainly, but you're both beautiful."

She smiled reflectively and flawless teeth gleamed.

"You have good manners and a soft voice, my friend. Far better manners than most of the tramps in this saloon."

Brad's face muscles tightened a little. He couldn't tell why but he suddenly scented danger. His steady blue eyes went over the girl's small, lissom figure, every curve of it revealed in the shirt and riding pants.

"For a hobo," she said at length, glancing over his attire, "you speak well."

"There are ways of educating oneself if one's intelligent," Brad countered.

"Yes, I suppose so, Mr. — er?"

"Brad Morrison."

She mused over the name. "Mmm — I like it. I'm Nariza. All the people around here call me that. I'd like you to do the same."

Brad remained silent. He noticed a brief expression of pique cross the girl's face, then a shoulder rose and fell gracefully.

"Very well, if you don't wish."

"I reckon we should be a-takin' a look at th' cabin, son," Old Timer put in abruptly. "Let's be on our way."

Brad hesitated and glanced at Jeff Willard.

"I'll pick up that stuff of mine some other time, Jeff," he said, referring to his bedroll in the back room; then with the slightest of bows to the girl Brad put on his hat and followed the old prospector from the saloon.

The main street was fairly quiet, the stars motionless in the black sky. Muttering to himself Old Timer went down the steps to his gelding tethered to the hitch-rail.

"Ain't yuh got no cayuse?" he asked, surprised.

"Not yet. I haven't got around to it."

"That's bad." Old Timer frowned in the light streaming out of the saloon. "Yuh can't do without a horse in these parts. It's five mile to th' cabin an' I reckon this gelding o' mine won't hold th' both of us."

"It's simple enough," Brad said calmly. "You ride and I'll walk beside you. Walking never hurt me. As a hobo I'm used to it."

"I can get you a horse, Mr. Morrison, if you really are in need of one."

Brad paused in giving Old Timer a hand into the saddle. Nariza had come gracefully down the steps of the saloon and was now silhouetted against the light. Brad hesitated for a moment and then walked back to her.

"You can get me one, eh? For how much?"

"Oh, not enough to hurt you. I know somebody who'll part with a sorrel. You meet me outside the tabernacle yonder at nine to-morrow morning and it'll be there."

"That's mighty nice of you." Brad contemplated the immobile, reddish-brown face with the dusky eyes. "You're taking a lot of trouble, considering I'm a stranger."

"Perhaps we won't be strangers for long …"

He hesitated. "No. Mebby not. Anyway, thanks. Good night, Nariza."

You speak my name beautifully," she called after him. "That is the first time I ever heard a man pronounce it properly."

With a smile Brad turned away and hurried down the High Street to where Old Timer was neck-reining his horse along at a jog trot.

*

The trail Old Timer took, with Brad walking beside him, led from the ramshackle little town into the great wilderness where the white anemones and primroses to either side of the trail cast back the faint light from the stars. The cool night breeze was full of the smell of the mesa, wine-fresh in its cleanness … Now and again the stillness was disturbed by the weird hoot of an owl and wings flashed softly past the two men and were gone. Ahead of them the mountains were dark, ebony dark, cutting the carpet of stars overhead into jig-sawed patterns,

"Now you know, son, why I jest can't leave these parts," Old Timer said, breaking the quiet. He gave an appreciative sniff. "Smell that air! That smell of th' desert an' mesa! It's sump'n yoh can't never git away frum."

"Makes you feel sort of small just being a man," Brad admitted, with a glance at the sparkling diadems overhead.

"I reckon Thunder Valley is about one o' th' most wonderful spots on God's earth, son," the prospector went on musingly, as the gelding jogged patiently along. "I've a-seen it in all its moods, so I oughta know. I've a-seen it in summer drought an' winter rain. I've a-seen it when thit creek o' mine has been a trickle an' when it's bin a torrent. I've felt it, too, when there's bin snow on th' heights an' the icy wind's blown through these of bones o' mine as it's come down from a-moanin' through the cedars an' pines up in yonder mountains."

"You're gettin' mighty near to poetry," Brad warned him.

"Yeah — s'pose I am. Reckon a man gits to feelin' poetic under these stars, like we are now, an' with th' open space all around … I'll tell yuh somethin' about Thunder Valley, son, somethin' I think yuh oughta know, just in case. It's dangerous. Anywheres in it is dangerous! That's why it's called Thunder Valley."

"Why dangerous?"

"Wil, sometimes there's an avalanche. Nobody don't know how it starts, but sump'n sets one bit o' rock a-movin' an' down comes boulders an' rocks an' half th' mountain-side. I've seen it happen twice while I've bin around these parts. First time I gotten meself nearly buried. I had a pardner then — Jeo Croft. He went under it. Didn't never find his body."

Brad reflected. "There are such valleys, of course," he said finally. "A piercing noise — like a whistle from a railroad engine or something like that — sets up an air vibration and dislodges some rock. That dislodges some more, and the whole thing becomes a cataclysm … So that's what this valley's like, is it?"

"Yeah," Old Timer agreed seriously. "An' my cabin ain't fer away from th' mountain-side, neither. I s'pose it's askin' fer trouble, but somehow it's never happened yet in thit part o' th' range. An' I'm kinda hopin' thit it never will."

"I'm with you in that."

Silence dropped between them again — the great empty silence of the open spaces, only disturbed by the horse's rhythmic feet on the rough stone trail. So, presently, they came to the prospector's cabin. It was dimly visible in the light of the now rising moon, standing square and dark against the implacable grey face of the mountain.

As they finally came right up to it, Brad could see it was made of rough, unpainted boards, but it did have a wide porch and a garden all round it in which was a dimly visible admixture of both vegetables and flowers. Behind the cabin was a low-built structure, a stable or barn of sorts, and a small corral fenced in with mesquite posts and wire.

"I'll be right back," Old Timer murmured, and led his gelding round the side of the cabin to stable it for the night. Then presently he came back and mounted the two steps to the porch and the cabin's screen door. Once inside the little abode, he lighted an oil lamp in the middle of a rough wood table, and the yellow rays cast upon the board walls, their crevices stopped with hardened red clay, upon a small dresser-like piece of furniture, three chairs and an object that had once been a sofa.

"I know it ain't nothin' to go loco about," Old Timer apologized, "but it's th' only sort of wickiup I need. There's a kitchen an' a small range through thit door — an' a bedroom. I reckon thit covers everything." He stopped and grinned with his two top teeth. "This is th' first time in years I've had some company around here, an' I sure appreciate it. Yes, sir! I c'n fix yuh a shakedown fer th' night an' tomorrow we'll sort ourselves out a bit. Right now jest make yuhself at home an' I'll see if I can't rustle up some grub."

Brad nodded, took off his gun belt and hat and then wandered after the old prospector into the adjoining kitchen where he was putting a light to the small range. In time the wood began burning and the coffee-pot was put on to boil.

In half an hour, both men were at the wooden table in the small living-room, eating with a zest begotten of the sharp night air.

Chapter III

"I reckon there's one or two things on which I oughta put yuh wise," Old Timer said presently, his stubbly jaw champing firmly in the lamplight. "Thit Nariza, f'rinstance. She ain't the sorta gal yuh should be a-mixin' up with. I tell yuh she c'n scratch like a wild-cat. I'm thinkin' thit offer of a horse she made yuh's got strings to it, too, but yuh won't find out what they are 'til she's got yuh hooked. Watch out fer her, thit's all."

"I will," Brad promised, putting down his coffee cup. "I got the feeling that she has something on her mind, and that it prompted her to make that offer. In any case I can handle it."

"Yuh hope yuh can," Old Timer said moodily. "She ain't our kind, son. Half wild, I reckon, even if she does seem to be kinda civilized. Yuh'll believe it when some night yuh hear her havin' one of her ceremonials up in th' mountains. I reckon this cabin is th' only place where yuh *will* hear it, too. The town's too far away."

Brad mused for a moment. "What does she *do* exactly? How can you be sure it *is* her?"

"I made sure one night. I couldn't stick thit weird chantin' any longer, so I went up th' mountain trail to take a look around. When I'd gotten near th' sound, I saw Nariza on a rocky ledge, all dressed up in her native robes. She wus wailin' somethin' t' the stars. It wus Nariza all right: no doubt on it."

Brad still reflected, then he changed the subject.

"Know much about that girl singer at the Yellow Nugget?"

"Th' English kid? Nope, I don't know much — 'cept thit she's got class, an' thit she's hooked by Black Joe. Thit sorta puts her outa range of everybody else — 'cept perhaps yuhself," Old Timer added slowly, his eyes bright and hard. "Yuh crossed up Black Joe t'night, didn't yuh?"

"Sure did," Brad grinned. "I told him I didn't like him standing beside a lady with his hat on."

Old Timer sighed. "Thit wus bad business, son. Black Joe ain't the breed to fergit a thing like thit. He's a plain ornery skunk — an' I *mean* skunk. Even Sheriff Grant's leary o' him an' his boys."

"A sheriff who's leary hasn't any right to be one," Brad said grimly.

Old Timer munched for a while and then asked a question.

"So fer I knows precious little about yuh, son — but I like yuh just the same. What's yore record?"

"Not a very good one, I'm afraid. I was brought up in a good family in New Orleans and got all the trimmings of a good education. But I couldn't stick the business my father had ranged up for me, so I — well, I just became a hobo. And I like it. Hearing of gold keep coming from this part of the world to Drew City, I thought I'd try to find some. And maybe we will — between us."

"Mebby," Old Timer muttered. "But it'll have t' be almighty soon, else these ol' bones o' mine won't even let me bend."

*

The following morning after breakfast, shaved and fit after his shakedown for the night, Brad saw the creek for the first time. It started its course somewhere up in the mountains and had become a fastflowing stream by the time it reached ground level a mile from the cabin's front porch.

Brad went far enough to look at it and leave the old prospector panning as usual, then he returned to the cabin, borrowed and saddled the gelding, and rode into Thunder Bend. Outside the tabernacle, on the stroke of nine, the Aztec girl, Nariza, was waiting. She was in the same attire as on the previous evening, mounted on a pinto, and reining a powerful sorrel to the saddle horn.

"Good morning, Mr. Morrison," she greeted politely as he rode up to her — and the brilliant sunshine revealed every detail of her copper-red skin and perfect white teeth. "Here's the horse I promised you. Will he do?"

Brad dismounted and sized the sorrel up. Finally, he gave a satisfied nod.

"He'll do. How much?"

The figure the girl named was absurdly low, and he frowned as he handed her the money from his wallet.

"Look here, this doesn't make sense," he said bluntly.

"You mean that a hobo should have a wallet and pay out a fair sum of money?"

"I mean the price," Brad said grimly. "Why do you want to sell me a horse *that* cheap?"

"I like to think," the girl said, putting the money away in a pocket of her shirt, "that you will be under an obligation to me. Putting one of the ornery fools in this town under an obligation wouldn't mean a thing, but with you it's different. You have the instincts of a gentleman, and because of that you know what it means to be indebted to a woman."

Brad's eyes narrowed at her. "To what extent?"

"I'll have to think that over."

She smiled down at him from the saddle, then she spurred her horse forward and set off down the High Street in a whirl of dust. Brad looked after her in puzzlement, then as he was about to mount the gelding he paused. A graceful blonde-haired girl in a flowery dress was walking along the busy boardwalk towards the Yellow Nugget saloon. Brad smiled to himself, led the two horses on either side of him and presently stopped, raising his hat.

"A very good morning, Miss Tarrant."

The girl stopped in surprise and gazed at him. Devoid of make-up and in the bright eye of the sun she was even more lovely than he had at first imagined. He thought for a moment she was going to ignore him, then evidently changing her mind she stepped down into the street and came towards him.

"I'm taking a risk being seen with you, Mr. Morrison," she said quietly. "And I wouldn't be doing it at all except for one thing. I owe you something in return for last night, when you taught Joe Rutter some good manners."

Brad grinned. "I hope he remembers 'em."

"Because of that," the girl said in a deliberate voice, "you have put yourself right in line for a bullet! You've got to watch every step you take. Joe and his boys are on the prod for you after that affair last night. I'm repaying you by telling you to keep on the alert."

"I'm always that, anyway," Brad said. "What I would like to know, though, is why a girl like you latches on to an ornery cuss like Black Joe. It doesn't make sense to me no matter which way I look at it."

"If you were in my position, Mr. Morrison, you'd know why I'm doing it." The girl gave a brief smile. "Now I must be going — and thanks for letting some of the wind out of Joe."

She turned and went back to the boardwalk. Brad stood musing as he watched her turn into the Yellow Nugget, then he put his hat back on his head and swung into the saddle of the gelding, leading the sorrel beside him. As he rode back along the trail between the carpets of anemone and primroses he had the feeling that things were building up somewhere into explosive force.

Once he had returned to the cabin and turned the two horses into the corral he went in search of Old Timer and found him by the stream as usual.

"Got back, huh?" the old prospector asked, glancing up with eyes slitted in the sunlight. "Git yuhself a horse?"

"Uh-huh. And a woman too, I'm afraid. There's something about the bargain I made with Nariza which I don't like."

"S'pose yuh let me in on it? Mebby I c'n help."

Briefly Brad summed up the details and Old Timer shook his head doubtfully.

"Nope, son, I don't like it! There's claws on thit Nariza an' yuh've kinda let yuhself in fer sump'n. I dunno what, but watch what yore doin'."

Brad reflected for a while, then he pushed up his hat and grinned.

"Come to think of it, all I seem to collect in this place are warnings instead of gold! You warned me against Nariza; then Betty Tarrant, the singer, warns me against Black Joe. Looks like I'll have to keep my eyes skinned plenty."

Old Timer nodded, swinging the pan gently from side to side. Brad squatted beside him and asked a question.

"Think there's any chance of Nariza doing her ceremonial act to-night?"

"I dunno. Mebby so; mebby not. Can't tell, I reckon. Why?"

"I just wondered. I'd like to see what she really does. She's got education and it strikes me as queer that she should adopt ancient ceremonial customs when she's perfectly — civilized."

"Yore sure aimin' t' git yerself all hog-tied, ain't yuh, son?" Old Timer asked, sighing. "Jest keep clear o' thit gurl. *I* know …"

*

After spending part of the morning converting half the bedroom in the cabin to his own uses, Brad turned out to help the old prospector in the creek. Towards mid-afternoon they had become separated, Old Timer working a mile away round the bend of the stream where boulders hid him, and Brad not far from the cabin porch. He worked mechanically, without any real apparent interest in what he was doing. Then he paused in his operations as a graceful silhouette appeared on the baked dust beside him.

He glanced up. It was Nariza in her riding trousers and silk shirt, her pinto nibbling at roots a short distance away.

"Hello," she greeted, smiling.

"Oh — it's you." Brad went on panning for a while. Her boots crunched in the pebbly earth and he watched them move round. After a moment or two she sat down on a low boulder and regarded him with dark, oblique eyes.

"You don't look very convincing, Mr. Morrison," she said finally. "You don't even hold the pan properly for one thing — and that's odd considering you're a prospector."

"Maybe you'd have it more correct if you called me a hobo," he said.

"I doubt it … Just why *are* you in Thunder Valley, Mr. Morrison?"

"To wash dirt," he answered.

"And you expect to find gold in this creek?" The dark head shook. "You'll never find it here — not in any quantity anyway. I know you won't because I understand this part of the world like the back of my hand." Brad put down the pan and eyed her. "That bein' so, Nariza, where do you think I *might* find it?"

"If you'll get on your horse I'll show you."

Like a ghost the warning Old Timer had given him strayed across Brad's mind; then he pushed it on one side. In any case he could take care of himself and Old Timer was out of sight and entirely oblivious to what was going on.

"All right," Brad assented, and went off to the cabin corral with pan in hand. After a few minutes he came cantering back on the sorrel to find the girl in the saddle of her pinto.

She jerked her night-black head briefly and Brad spurred his horse into a gallop until he had caught up with her. Then they proceeded leisurely. She gave him a glance as they followed a foothill trail and the cabin and creek presently became hidden from sight.

"Naturally," Brad said, "you're not doing all this out of kindness of heart, Nariza."

"Why shouldn't I be?" She gave a strange smile, depthless somehow. "I think you should know that of all the men who have come and gone in Thunder Valley you are the only one who looks worth bothering about. You're tall, strong, and good-looking. With gold and wealth you'd really amount to something … You're the kind of man I've dreamed about for years."

"Yeah?" Brad looked straight ahead of him, unsmiling. There was a subtle, deeply female ring in the girl's words.

"I like you a lot, Brad," she said quietly, and he glanced at her at the use of his first name. "I'm hard to please, so you ought to feel flattered."

"Uh-huh," Brad said, and they went on in silence for a while, the horses climbing higher up rocky acclivities, through narrow ravines and shady draws, until finally they arrived at a bare jutting promontory overlooking the foothills and the valley. A vast distance below, as it appeared, was a toy cabin, corral, and horse, and a tiny speck beside a glittering ribbon where Old Timer worked at the creek.

As the girl signalled Brad dismounted and helped her from the saddle. She was slow to alight so that he was forced to support her smooth, clinging body to him for a moment. Then he put her on her feet, eyeing her warily.

"Well, what about this gold?" he asked finally.

She smiled. "You're in a terrible hurry, aren't you? How about giving me a cigarette?"

Controlling his impatience Brad offered her one from the packet and took one himself. When he had lighted them he glanced about him. This promontory seemed to be the termination of the mountain trail. Above it the mountains went up ridge upon ridge, dark in the higher reaches with endless pine, juniper, and cedar. Far down in the valley were the fields of golden brittle-bush and out on the mesa the yuccas in tens of thousands bobbed their creamy blooms in the fashion of an incoming tide.

Nariza followed Brad's roving eyes and laughed softly to herself.

"You'll not find gold by just looking about you, Brad. You have to know where it is."

"Where is it, then?"

She motioned him and he stood beside her. Her dark eyes looked up at him.

"I just don't know," she said simply.

"Then what are we doing here?"

The girl threw down her cigarette and stamped on it. All of a sudden she dropped her gentle pose.

"Are your thoughts so choked up with gold, Brad, that you can't tell when a woman's in love with you? I brought you here because it's the only quiet spot I know, because I wanted you to myself to — to tell you that I love you."

Brad grinned at her round his cigarette.

"A little while back beside the creek you told me I was unconvincing. I reckon I might say the same thing about you at this moment. In other words you're bringing up that obligation I owe you? I'm to fall in love with you and so make up the balance in payment on that sorrel?"

A glitter crept and faded in the dark eyes.

"That's not a very nice way to put it, Brad!"

"Not meant to be." His jaw tightened and then he suddenly caught the girl's slim shoulder. "Suppose you and me get down to facts, Nariza? You've been making a grandstand show for me ever since we met last night in the Yellow Nugget. It may be because you fancy me — I don't know. What I *do* know is that you belong to a breed which is capable of a good deal of cunning. There's something you want from me. Just *what?*"

She seemed momentarily surprised at the steel in his voice, then she relaxed slightly and shook his hand free.

"I can't help it if I've fallen in love with you, can I?"

Brad fished in his shirt pocket and counted out some money. He turned her hand palm upwards and planked the notes in it.

"That's the balance of the price I should have paid for the horse," he said grimly. "I've a pretty good idea why you want me to think you're in love with me, but you got the wrong man. I don't like you, Nariza, or anything about you. Sorry, but that's the way it is. Next time you want to get some information out of me don't try and be subtle. It doesn't become you."

He threw away his cigarette and turned to his horse, When he had vaulted into the saddle he looked down at the girl pensively. He saw her features set in bleak, grim hatred. He nodded briefly, turned the sorrel's head round, and started back down trail. By the time he had reached the creek once more Old Timer had appeared from farther upstream, shaking his grizzled head with the coonskin cap pushed on the back of it.

"I reckon it ain't no different to-day than any other day," he said mournfully, regarding the pan in his hand. "An' if these ol' bones o' mine don't" He stopped and looked puzzled. "Say, hold on a minute, son! Where yuh goin' on yuh horse?"

"I'm not going any place; I'm just coming back. I've been for a ride with Nariza."

"Dog-gone! What fer?"

"To find out why she's so generous towards me." Brad narrowed his blue eyes. "And I think I know why."

Old Timer scratched his cheek. "Look, son, what's all this monkeyin' around fer? I reckon there must be a reason."

Brad hesitated and looked about him. Then he nodded.

"Yes, there's a reason, Old Timer, and I might as well tell you about it. I'm satisfied by now that I can trust you. If you have the facts you'll have a better idea of what I'm up to, otherwise you might gum things up unintentionally. Come over to the cabin and listen … "

When they were back in the cabin's living-room Brad went into his half of the bedroom and came back with some papers and a badge. He laid them on the rough wood table and Old Timer stared at them blankly.

"Sufferin' snakes, a marshal!"

Brad nodded as he sat down. "That's right, Old Timer. I've carried this identification stuff about with me up to now, but I reckoned it would be safe enough in the cabin. What I mean is I didn't leave it lying around in that bedroll which I've still to pick up from Jeff Willard … Anyway, it's about time you knew. Otherwise some of the funny things I might do would take a lot of explaining to you."

"Then — then all thit talk about gold —" Old Timer had consternation on his wizened face. "Yuh mean there jest ain't no gold around here at all? An' yuh got me all worked up fer —"

"Somewhere around here there *is* gold — loads of it!" Brad thumped his fist on the table. "That's why I'm here. I was sent by the Drew City authorities to investigate. Recently gold has been coming into Drew City disguised in an ordinary parcel package, sent by rail. For all I know the parcels may have been coming for years. It was only found out because a baggage-master at Drew City dropped one of the ordinary-looking parcels and found two gold bags inside it. It's illegal to send gold that way without the authorities knowing about it because the gold is really the property of the person owning the land where the gold comes from — and if not that it's the property of the State. There has to be a declaration one way or the other. So the possibility is that it's stolen gold, and the person who really owns it may not know a thing about what's going on."

"So?" Old Timer narrowed his sharp eyes and sat thinking.

"Well, as you know yourself, there are lost mines all over Arizona. Somebody might have land over one — be the real owner — and not know the mine exists. But somebody *else* might know and is taking the gold illegally."

"Yeah — I c'n figger that. But ain't th' packages got an address on 'em?"

"Sure they have — to somebody named J. T. Barryman, to be left at the station depot each time to be called for."

"Well, that's simple enough, isn't it? All yuh've got t' do is wait an' see who collects 'em an' then arrest him."

Brad grinned. " You think we didn't figure that one out? Of course we did! I was the one who waited. Then I discovered that the person who collects them sometimes doesn't come above once in three months and takes all packages away at once. Though we stopped all new packages to Barryman — each one with gold in — we had no luck waiting for him. So, each parcel being franked from Thunder Bend I was detailed to come out to the source and make inquiry. And here I am. I had to get some facts together before I could really start inquiring, of the baggage master here for instance."

"So yuh turned up like a hobo to take 'em off guard?" the old prospector chuckled, lighting his pipe.

"Correct — the best way to get to know the local characters without drawing suspicion to myself. I've talked with the most educated people I can find — Betty Tarrant for one, and I decided she hasn't got anything to do with it. You see, it occurred to me that a scheme like this reveals brains, and that usually matches up with education ... Then I had words with Black Joe, and in spite of his record I don't think he's in on it. Then came that Aztec girl — whom I led on just to see how far she'd go. I'm pretty sure she's the one I'm looking for."

"Y'are, huh? Why?"

"Several reasons. In the first place she's deadly anxious to pretend that she's fallen in love with me. No woman would fall that quick — not even for me." Brad grinned transiently. "What she is really aiming at is to worm the facts out of me as to why I'm in Thunder Valley. She probably suspects what I really am and wants to confirm it. She tried really hard this afternoon but I left her cold ... In the second place you say that she lives the life of a recluse in the mountains somewhere and that she's been here about two years. That seems to suggest that she's here for a purpose, and also you can't live the life of a mysterious recluse without having plenty of money to go on. That, tied up, suggests gold. Last of all, I'll gamble that her ceremonial wailing is so much bunk."

Old Timer made a sour face over his pipe.

"I reckon yuh won't once yuh've heard it, son."

"I don't mean I disbelieve you," Brad said, pondering. "What I'm getting at is this: If she has to go up the mountain for some reason — as she probably might to find her way into a mine — she might also think that she ought to have an excuse if anybody happened to trail her. So, to cover up her activities she pretends she goes up there for a ceremonial."

"Gosh durn me, I never thought of it!" Old Timer ejaculated. " Yuh mean a sort of — cover up?"

"That's just what I mean. And I'm willing to bet that the place she took me to this afternoon, ways up on the mountain-side, isn't so very far from where she gets gold. She went to it straight as an arrow. It's not the first time she's been there by a long sight."

For a while there was silence in the cabin. It was broken by the scraping of the prospector's hand against his stubble.

"Figgerin' it thit way, son, yore probably right. Mebby this gurl Nariza has somethin' at that. Bein' an Aztec she probably knows this country better'n most folk. Wil, what yuh aimin' t' do? Go an' pick her up?"

"I can't without proof. I'm going to watch her closely and see what she does next. The first time I hear any of her ceremonial wailing I'll be after her pronto. The only thing that worries me is that now she suspects I'm a marshal she may stop her ceremony."

"Mebby." Old Timer reflected and then he grinned cunningly. "But I reckon she won't stop a-robbin' thit bonanza. If yuh think it's where yuh both went to-day all we've got to do is jest keep watchin'."

"We?"

"Sure! Yuh don't think yore goin' to tell me this much an' then expect me t' lie down, do yuh? An' if there is a bonanza some place mebby I c'n git somethin' out of it afore these ol' bones o' mine finally crack up. I'm sold on this 'un, marshal, whether yuh like it or not!"

Chapter IV

Brad Morrison Had no objections to Old Timer's assistance; in fact he found it useful. The old prospector knew the ins and outs of the valley which could only come from long association. In particular he knew a short cut to the mountain trail up which Brad had been taken by the Aztec girl, and here the prospector and he took up their stand each evening at dusk, in readiness. For two nights they had no luck- — then on the third night as it was nearing moonrise there was the sound of a horse's feet crunching in the loose stones of the acclivity and coming ever nearer.

Old Timer straightened up from his lounging position amidst the cedar trees. Beside him, Brad was only a dim shadow.

"I reckon this may be it," the prospector whispered. " If not it's sure *sump'n!*"

Their horses being tethered some distance away, there was no fear of them giving things away. Silently Brad wormed his way forward so that between the trees he could just see the starlit trail. He had been in dim light so long he had become accustomed to it. This fact made the single rider on the nimble pinto quite visible to him, but for a moment he didn't recognize who it was. A blanket-like cape seemed to be flowing from the rider's shoulders.

"That's ur," Old Timer breathed, peering. "Them's those ceremonial clothes I told yuh about. I've seen her in 'em afore. Looks like a redskin or sump'n on th' way to a palaver."

"You stay here," Brad instructed. "I've got to move fast — and on my own two feet. You can't do it at your age."

Like a shadow he had gone. Old Timer muttered something and settled himself to wait. Silently, the noise of the pinto drowning his own movements, Brad kept the tough little horse within seeing distance as it went up the remainder of the trail, then he smiled to himself as he realized he was taking the same trip as on the other afternoon. He recognized the surroundings. So finally came the flat promontory and the girl dismounted.

Motionless in the shadows Brad waited. She muttered something to the all-knowing horse and then turned towards the rocks that formed the face of the mountains. She was only visible for a moment and then, to Brad's annoyance, hampered as he was by dim starlight, she disappeared. He hesitated for a while and finally crept forward, but all his searching failed to discover exactly where the girl had gone. It must have been into some concealed crevice which she knew about.

He debated for a while, then, making up his mind, he returned down the trail to where he found Old Timer only eagerly waiting.

"Find anythin'?" he demanded.

"It's no use trying to work in the dark, Old Timer. She's got some secret way of getting in and out of the rocks. I'll look in the daylight — or rather we will. At all costs, I don't want her to know that I'm watching her, or she'll take good care I never get the evidence I want. One thing I do know: she's got to come back down this trail, and when she does, I'm going to follow and see where she goes. Since nobody seems to know where her home is, I mean to find it."

"Okay," the prospector murmured. "Suits me."

"Not you for that," Brad told him. "Just me. It'll take me all my time to keep out of her sight: two of us could never do it. I can't let you in on that, I'm afraid, but we'll certainly work together when we both start exploring around here."

Old Timer grunted and said no more. They were both silent for a considerable while, then Brad gave a start as the night was split by the most unearthly yell he had ever heard. It came from somewhere up the trail and was flung back from the mountain face in a myriad echoes.

"That's it!" Old Timer muttered. "What did I tell yuh? Sounds like Old Nick himself was up there. It fair makes me belly crawl every time I hears it."

"Which may be the effect intended," Brad said, listening as it came again. "Most folks would be leary of finding out what makes a noise like that, and nobody knows it better than Nariza. But it's a woman's voice all right, not an animal's. In fact, it's one of the nicest ways of keepin' folks away that I've yet struck." The cry did not come again, and finally Brad stirred. "All right, let's get back to our horses."

They went over to the spot among the trees where they had left them tethered and mounted swiftly. When they reached the floor of the valley, Brad drew rein.

"You go back to the cabin, Old Timer, and stay there. I'll join you later."

"All right," the prospector growled, "but don't yuh go a-thinkin' I likes it!"

He set his horse cantering off into the starlight, and Brad dismounted, searched round until he found a rock big enough to conceal himself and his horse, and there he waited. He waited nearly thirty minutes before there were sounds on the trail and at length the girl herself, blanket-cape flowing, came speeding past him. He watched her go racing into the night, then, swinging into the saddle, he sped after her, keeping far enough away to be sure that the sound of his own horse would not be heard above hers.

He kept her just in view for nearly five miles, along the trail that led through the carpet of anemones and primroses. Every minute he expected her to detour sharply and head for her mysterious hide-out, but, to his surprise, she kept straight on into Thunder Bend, Puzzled, he still followed.

She went through the main street in a cloud of dust, and outside the lighted windows of the Yellow Nugget saloon, one or two half-drunk saddle tramps turned to stare after her. Then it suddenly dawned on Brad where she was heading. It could hardly be anywhere else from the direction she was taking — the railroad depot.

The moment he realized it, he turned off down a dusty stretch between two wooden-walled stores and out into the baked earth at the back of the main street. In a swift three-minute gallop, he had reached the weather-beaten railroad depot from the end facing the High Street and dismounted. Tethering his snorting horse to the wire enclosure, just beyond the depot, he advanced silently on foot, looking intently about him.

The depot was hardly worthy of the name. It had only two buildings, both wooden, on each side of the railroad. Brad watched them intently from a distance, and, as he had expected, the girl on her pinto suddenly came into view beside the building nearest to him. She dismounted quickly, glanced once about her, and then, to his surprise, she seemed to vanish in the boardwalk in front of the wooden building. Frowning, he waited, and after perhaps five minutes she emerged again.

He took no action there and then. Nariza remounted her horse and sped swiftly away into the darkness. Brad gave her plenty of time to get clear, and then went across to the spot where he had seen her vanish into the boardwalk. It did not take him long to find a couple of loose boards. He raised them and dropped below, feeling his way past the rough wood supports which raised the building a couple of feet from the ground.

Finally he struck a match and looked about him in the yellow flicker. A half-formed thought that there might be hidden gold under here was promptly dashed. There was only the ground, and above his head, boarding.

Then he caught sight of something, just as the match burned his fingers. He muttered to himself, dropped it, and struck another. It confirmed his first look. Two of the boards above his head were not lying dead true. They had been hurriedly put into place. He pressed up on them gently, and they lifted without a sound. He poked his head through the opening, the match still glimmering, and found himself in the midst of boxes, crates, parcels, and the general paraphernalia of the station baggage depot.

The thing was so simple he could hardly credit it for a moment. A strong lock on the door, a barred window — and yet a floor that could be pushed up by an outsider climbing under the boardwalk …

"Like puttin' a horse in the corral and taking the wire enclosure down," he muttered.

He began to prowl, concealing the match flame with his cupped hand. He was not absolutely sure, but it did seem that there ought to be a parcel somewhere here addressed to J. T. Barryman at Drew City — to be called for. And there was. After ten minutes' wandering amongst the packages and parcels he found it — a harmless-looking package wrapped in brown paper, and about a foot square by six inches deep. He lifted it and found it was heavy — remarkably so.

For a moment he stood in the dark, thinking, then, making up his mind, he unfastened the string carefully and pulled away the paper. Inside a strong cardboard box were two bags with string around their necks. The moment he had opened one, he did not need to look at the other. It contained a mass of finely powdered rock, but it was rock dusted with a thick element of gold and only needing an expert to detach it from the useless crust.

"Nice work," Brad murmured, tightening his lips. " And our friend Mr. Barryman is due for a surprise." He stuffed one bag in each pocket, then refastening the parcel he returned it, empty, to its former position. This done, he left the way he had come, restoring both sets of boards as he went. When he had got as far as his tethered horse, light footsteps made him swing round, his hand flying to his holster.

"Lay off, Morrison!" a voice snapped. " Lift that rod of yourn and I'll blow your mit off with it!" Brad relaxed, but his nerves were taut. It was Joe Rutter who had come up silently in the dark. Behind him loomed two shadowy figures — the inevitable gun hawks. Starlight glinted momentarily on their levelled sixes.

"Nice of you to give me a chance to go on living," Brad murmured, as his gun was taken from him, "I'd got the idea you're the sort of man who shoots those you don't like. Or is it that you *do* like me?"

"You talk too much," Black Joe told him sourly. "You're alive for only one reason, Morrison, an' that's because dead men can't speak."

"Sounds logical," Brad agreed dryly.

"An' don't git smart!" Joe breathed. "Now start walkin'. You an' me have got somethin' to talk over, and this place isn't quite as private as I'd like — Lefty," he added, over his shoulder, "fetch the horses, including Morrison's."

Brad began walking, his hands slightly raised, because there was nothing else he could do. After he had gone about half a mile and they were all out of earshot of the station and possible passers-by, Joe called a halt.

"All right, Morrison, turn around."

Brad obeyed. Black Joe's powerful form and big hat were vaguely visible, the horses and gun hawks motionless behind him.

"Now," Joe said, "s'pose you an' me git down to things, Morrison? You're no hobo, and never was. You didn't fool me for a minute."

Brad set his jaw. This could only mean that Black Joe had guessed he was a marshal and in that case —

"You're a city slicker," Joe finished grimly. "You said on the first night you came here — afore you told me to take my hat off, remember — that you'd heard there was gold around these parts. You told that to my girl Betty, remember?"

"I remember, and I don't reckon you've got the exclusive right to hold her, neither."

"Shut up while I'm talkin'! You've more than *heard* about there being gold around these parts. You *know* there is!"

"Oh, I do?"

"Yeah. You don't have hips like them in the ordinary way, do yuh?"

Brad hesitated, but there was still nothing he could do. One of the gun hawks came forward as Joe muttered something to him, and Brad found his trousers pockets relieved of the bulging bags he had thrust into them. He waited while one of them was opened and in a match flame Joe examined them.

"I got you figured right, Mr. Morrison," he said finally. "You've got the lowdown on a bonanza around these parts and these two bags of rock have come from it. These alone are worth plenty but I guess it's the whole bonanza I want … I've had you watched, feller. You an' that Aztec girl, Nariza, are thicker 'n a pair of prairie cubs. I know all about her lettin' yuh have a horse; I've heard how you went up the mountain trail with her. I also know how you chased after her tonight Why, I don't know — Some tiff maybe which wanted clearin' up. But when I got to the depot I was just in time to see yuh go under that boardwalk. What were you aimin' to do? Rob the baggage depot?"

Brad did not answer. It was whirling through his mind at the moment that Black Joe had misconstrued everything from top to bottom.

"Plain as a polecat to me," Joe added. "That Aztec girl knows more about this country than anyone breathin'. An' she's your breed — classy, talks with a polish. Didn't take much figgerin' to see the both of you are thick with each other … So you'd better start talking, feller, and tell me where that bonanza is!"

"It surprises me," Brad said, his fists itching, "that you pick on me instead of Nariza. Since you think she's working with me she must know as much as I do."

"We'll get around to her finally, don't you worry. You happen to be nearest at the moment an' you might know more 'n she does. So — *talk!*" Joe finished savagely, and his free hand came up and struck Brad a stinging blow across the face.

It was precisely the move Brad had been waiting for. Before the hand had finished its course he'd whipped up his own hand and clenched steel-strong fingers round Joe's wrist. A violent wrench jerked him forward to meet a stunning left under the jaw. His gun exploded, sheer blind fire, and dirt snicked up close to Brad's boots. Without giving Joe a chance to recover Brad slammed home a straight right which knocked the powerful rancher into the midst of his two gun hawks as they stood deciding what to do.

Dazed with the blows Joe fell into a sitting position in the dust, gun still in his hand — but it vanished magically as in one dive Brad whipped it from Him and levelled it.

"Get up," he ordered, and added, "If you two owl-hooters let me have it I'll let your boss have it in exchange. Up to you from here on."

Breathing hard, Joe scrambled to his feet, dusted himself down and then felt his jaw.

"All right, boys, take it easy," he cautioned.

Brad edged forward, picked up the gold bags from where Joe had dropped them and stuffed one in each trouser pocket again. Then he recovered his own .45 from Lefty Wilmore's belt. A gun in each hand he considered the trio pensively.

"If it makes you feel any happier, Joe, you're jumping to a whole lot of conclusions," he said finally. "I've no idea where there's a bonanza — and I wouldn't tell you if I had. Now get on your horses and start riding — fast!"

Grimly silent the three men obeyed. "City slicker" or otherwise, Joe Rutter had good reason to know that Brad Morrison could shoot fast and with deadly accuracy.

"Later," Brad added, "I may take a fancy to have a few more words with Miss Tarrant. She'd better not have any complaints against you, Joe, or I'll come looking for you, with my hardware loaded up. Now get out, the perishing bunch of you!"

The three turned and Brad watched the horses go loping away across the starlit expanse. With a grin, he put his own .45 in the holster and Joe's .45 in his belt. Then he turned to his own sorrel and finally, by making a detour of the town and avoiding any stray bullets which Joe's boys might be waiting to aim at him, he regained Old Timer's cabin by the creek.

*

The moment Brad entered the cabin he found Old Timer gripping his arm anxiously. The prospector's wizened face was eager in the lamplight. On the rough table he had set out a meal.

"Don't hold out on me, son — how'd yuh git on?" he demanded. "Did yuh find out where Nariza's a-livin'?"

"Altogether," Brad said with a grim smile, pulling the two gold bags out of his pockets and dropping them with two distinct thuds on the table, "I've had a most interesting time. Pour some coffee while I Wash some of this trail dirt off my face."

Old Timer nodded and Brad went over to the Washbasin. After a few minutes he came back to the table and settled down, started on the meal and hot coffee while he explained. The old prospector listened with an eager intentness, hardly eating for fear the noise of his jaws moving in his ears would drown out the words.

"But what th' blue thunder d'yuh think she was a-doin' at th' baggage room, son? I mean — gittin' under th' boardwalk. What was her idea?"

"Not difficult to guess. So far, as I've told you, I haven't had a chance to question the stationmaster about the disposition of parcels from here to J. T. Barryman — but I'll gamble that when I do ask him he hasn't the remotest idea who sends 'em. Like all these hick towns parcels are just sent and nobody bothers. It's obvious that Nariza has her own way of sending 'em. She puts them in the baggage room to be collected for the train next day and she herself never puts in an appearance. I'll check on it to-morrow but I'll wager that's the answer."

"Yeah … Old Timer filled his pipe and slowly lit it. "Mebby yore right. Then what happens now? Black Joe's on to yuh, ain't he, even if he has gotten the idea th' wrong way round?"

Brad grinned. "As long as Joe continues to think I know the whereabouts of a bonanza he won't put a slug in me, Old Timer. That's my insurance. He'll only do that when he gets to know the whereabouts of the mine from Nariza. *She* knows: there's no longer any doubt."

"An' since he's failed ter git anythin' out o' yuh he'll git it outa her, Brad! Thit's obvious."

"Yes." Brad pondered for a moment, frowning. "That's the bit I don't like thinking about. That girl would be safer in custody — but I can't take her in until I have the proof that she knows the source of the gold, or else with witnesses I catch her planting gold, as she was to-night, for transit to Drew City. Otherwise she could deny everything and I wouldn't have a leg to stand on."

"Yuh could tell th' Sheriff, I reckon."

"I will, at the proper time. He could do no more than me without proof."

Old Timer scratched his grizzled head. "Kinda tough bein' hog-tied with all these laws, son. Black Joe don't bother himself over 'em. He'll find

Nariza somehow, shove a gun in her ribs, and she'll start a-talkin' — but fast."

"She might," Brad said. "That girl doesn't come of the type that breaks down easily. Aztecs are renowned for being passive even under the most brutal treatment. She might never give in. Looking beyond that possibility, there's a point in our favour. Black Joe doesn't know where she lives any more than we do — yet, and another certainty is that he won't find out in the next five minutes. The only time Nariza seems to appear in town is in the evening when she calls in the Nugget for a drink. That's the place I've got to be, if only to protect her from anything Joe might attempt. In other words," Brad finished, "until I can pin something definite on her and wheel her in I've got to be a nursemaid to her. *And* I've got to find out where she lives."

"Yeah, I reckon so. Wil, if yore wantin' any help yuh know where t' come, but I'd take it easy with Black Joe if I was you, son. Y'jest don't know what yore gettin' into."

"Mebby not, but I'm risking it. Next thing I'll do is put all this gold in one bag ready for sending to the authorities."

Chapter V

The following morning Brad Morrison rode out to the railroad depot, taking care not to contact the town itself in case Black Joe or his boys might have some ideas. He found the depot open and one or two people about, none of whom paid any attention to him as he dismounted from his sorrel and went in search of the stationmaster. He found him at length at the back of the baggage office.

"Howdy," the stationmaster greeted, and peered over lop-sided spectacles. "Called to collect sump'n?"

Brad shook his head and looked at him. The station-master waited, noting the twin gun-holsters Brad was now wearing — one borrowed holster from Old Timer containing Joe's .45, and the other his own.

"I'm looking for somebody who keeps sending these parcels," Brad said finally, and picking up the featherweight brown parcel addressed to J. T. Barryman, he handed it across.

"J. T. Barryman, huh?" The stationmaster peered at it. "Yeah — come to think on it I've seen plenty o' these around Who *sends* 'em?" he repeated.

"How'd I be knowing that? Don't expect me to remember everybody around here as sends parcels, do you?"

"You don't take the names and addresses of the senders?" Brad asked.

"No need, I reckon. Just so long as the parcel's got the right number of rail-freight stamps fur the weight that's all I'm bothered about. Looks like this parcel has a durned sight too many stamps on it," the stationmaster finished, weighing it up and down in his palm.

Brad looked at the stamps and mused. It brought up a point which had so far escaped him.

"How does one get these stamps, anyway?"

"How d'you *get* 'em?" The stationmaster handed the parcel back and scratched his ear. "You're kinda new around here, ain't yuh? You get 'em at my ticket office across the track yonder." He nodded through the open doorway. "Yuh stick 'em on the parcel — so many accordin' to weight — and then leave 'em here to be sent by railroad. I do the franking right here with a rubber stamp." The stationmaster paused heavily. "Anythin' else? I'm kinda busy."

"I don't doubt it, but this is important," Brad told him. "Several parcels have been sent from here by somebody — like this one — and all addressed to J. T. Barryman, correctly stamped and' sent by rail. You can't remember who handed them in?"

"I reckon not," the stationmaster said. "If they're in here correctly stamped I frank 'em an' send 'em off. Ain't no more to it."

"You *would* remember somebody distinctive, though," Brad persisted. "Say a small, dark girl with long black hair and a reddish-brown skin?"

The stationmaster reflected. "Can't say I ever remember anybody like that, mister — not recently anyway. Why? What are you gettin' at?"

"Never mind," Brad said quietly, shrugging. "I suppose you close this place up at night?"

"Sure I do. There's only three trains a day and none at all after sundown."

"Uh-huh. Well, let me give you a tip. Nail down those two loose boards in the floor where you're standing — and you'll find two more loose ones in the boardwalk outside. Anybody could get in here and take what they wanted."

The stationmaster stared blankly at the revelation and with a thoughtful smile Brad walked out into the sunlight. Vaulting easily to the saddle of his horse he sat pondering. He sensed there had been strategy — and pretty good strategy too. Obviously Nariza had bought up a quantity of railroad stamps in readiness, had put the correct number of them on each parcel after weighing it, and then had smuggled it into the baggage room by night.

Thuswise she had, in a sense, dissociated herself from the entire business. Alternatively, she could have taken the gold herself to Drew City — but the drawbacks against her doing it were obvious. Drew City was a hundred miles away — an arid, pitiless journey by horse; and if she went by train her constant comings and goings might in time excite suspicion. Further, her visits to Drew City might get her involved in questioning there …

"I guess she chose the best method at that," Brad muttered. "But somehow I've got to pin her down. I'd give a whole month's pay to know who J. T. Barryman is."

For the moment there seemed to be little more he could do. There was no likelihood of Nariza being about the town in the daytime; nor was there any likelihood of Black Joe being about either since it appeared he was fully occupied at his ranch by day. But this didn't include Betty Tarrant. A slow grin came over Brad's face as he thought of her. He made up his mind suddenly and spurred the horse forward, entering the town's dusty High Street a few minutes later.

It was busy mid-morning with teams and buckboards moving up and down, the stage just in, and men and women coming and going out of the stores and into them. Brad drew rein presently, leaned on the saddle horn and looked about him. In all the mass of heads and hats he couldn't see a wealth of blonde hair or a graceful figure anywhere. He nudged his horse onwards again, jog-trotted down the High Street and dismounted outside the Yellow Nugget. Fastening the horse to the hitch-rail he went through the batswings and into the gloomy morning interior of the saloon.

Among the inverted tables and piled-up chairs he caught sight of Jeff Willard dusting busily, one or two other barhands doing likewise in different parts of the expanse.

"Howdy, Brad," Willard said, straightening up. "Come fer that bedroll of yours?"

"Might as well — though it wasn't my reason."

Jeff went and got it. Brad put it over his shoulder and the barkeep looked troubled.

"You got your gall comin' here, ain't yuh?" he asked.

"Why?"

"Don't yuh know that Black Joe an' his boys are out on the prod fer yuh?"

"Oh, that!" Brad grinned and tossed the bedroll towards the batswings where he could pick it up as he went out. "I suppose he's sore because I frisked him of his gun last night?"

"He's more th'n sore, I reckon: he's blazin' mad! Bein' the barkeep I get to know more things around here than most. Last night Joe came in here an' rounded up all the boys he could find. They're aimin' t' get you, Brad. There seems to be a sorta notion flying around that yuh know where there's a bonanza lode."

Brad looked pensively in front of him.

"It's no more than a notion, Jeff, believe me. As for Joe getting his boys together to beat it out of me, that's no surprise. I'm not worrying. I can look after myself, and Joe too if it comes to it."

"To a certain extent, mebby — but I'm worried. You don't know Black Joe."

"Oh, yes, I do," Brad said grimly. "He's a big bag of wind and before I'm through I'll probably let the wind out of him … Anyway, thanks for the warning. What I really came here for was to find Betty Tarrant,"

"With Joe gunnin' fer yuh you're lookin' fer *her? His* girl?" Jeff stared incredulously. "Now I *know* you're loco! An' anyway she ain't here. Not yet, that is. Bit late this mornin' but she'll be in soon to practise her number fer to-night"

Jeff broke off and glanced towards the batswings. They were swinging open and shut as the girl herself came in. She advanced with an easy grace, her blonde hair flowing to her shoulders now instead of being piled up, the breeze she made as she walked moulding the light frock to her slender form … Suddenly she caught sight of Brad in the dim light of the place and stopped.

"Well, Mr. Morrison!" she exclaimed.

"Morning, Miss Tarrant," Brad tugged off his hat and smiled as she came up. "I reckon there's sun inside as well as out now you've come in."

She smiled faintly at his clumsy simile and her blue eyes studied him.

"Just what are you doing here, Mr. Morrison? Or don't you value your life?"

"I value it enough to know how to take care of it, I guess. Meaning, I suppose, that you're warning me that Black Joe is gunning for me?"

"I've warned you once before. It goes double now. I heard all about what you did to him last night."

"How *much* did you hear?" Brad asked quietly.

'That you know where there's a bonanza, and instead of sharing your information with everybody else, as you should to enter into the spirit of the community, you keep it to yourself, and when Joe asked you about it you half killed him and took his gun from him."

Brad grinned widely. "And you believe that?"

She was silent; then she made a little movement. "I've — I've a song to rehearse for to-night. If you'll excuse me? I'm late as it is"

"As far as I'm concerned you're going to be a lot later. I have one or two things to ask you."

Brad put his hat on again, caught her arm, and led her towards the batswings. On the way he hauled his bedroll on to his shoulder by the rope around it. When they had come to the boardwalk outside the saloon the girl hesitated.

"Look, Mr. Morrison, if Joe should see us together —"

"Right now I'm not thinking about Joe, Miss Tarrant." Brad hitched the bedroll farther round his back. "I'm only thinking about you. I'd like to have a talk with you — and this isn't quite the place to do it. None too healthy if you know what I mean." "Where then? I can't ask you to come to my rooms at Mrs. Denning's. Might look bad."

"I thought of the valley trail. And the fact that you haven't got a horse and aren't dressed for riding doesn't make two cents' worth of difference."

Brad released her arm and untied his sorrel. She looked at him in vague wonder as he swung to the saddle — then before she had grasped what had happened he had swept her up side saddle before him, one powerful arm round her waist.

"Comfortable?" he asked, smiling.

"Yes, but — What about my song? How am I going to explain things to Joe if I can't sing it properly tonight?"

"Forget it. Joe's going to learn to put up with quite a lot of things before he's finished. I'll see you're all right."

Brad spurred the horse into a trot, giving him his head once they had left the town's sunbaked reaches behind. The girl did not argue nor attempt to dislodge the arm clasped protectively about her. There was even a half-smile on her pretty face, the warm wind from the mesa blowing the blonde hair from her head.

Brad rode hard until he was within a mile of Old Timer's cabin, then he drew rein amidst the rocks of the down-trail which led to the creek and jumped from the saddle. He fixed his bedroll securely to the pommel then reached up and held the girl as she dropped into his arms. As he released her she smoothed her dress and gave him a glance that was almost shy.

"I hope you know what you're doing, Mr. Morrison."

"My name's Brad," he answered. "I like it a heap better. And I know what I'm doing … Have a seat."

He motioned to the dry, sun-seared grass between the rocks and they sat down side by side in the shadow. Brad cuffed up his hat and considered the girl thoughtfully.

"You're about the only woman in this town I feel I can talk to," he said at length. "And talk safely, I mean, without the fear of it being spread all over the place. You're also one who keeps her eyes open, I imagine, especially when it's your own sex. So, do you know anything about Nariza?"

Betty looked astonished. "About Nariza? The Aztec girl? Do you mean you've brought me right out here just to ask a thing like that?"

"Not *just* for that, but it's partly my reason … Well, do you?"

"Hardly a thing," she answered, shrugging. "Nobody does. She takes care of that. She's secretive, mysterious, even vicious if need be, I'd think. What particularly do you want to know about her?"

"I want to find out where she lives."

"Oh, I see." A chill settled on Betty Tarrant's voice and her blue eyes looked away towards the trail moodily.

"Anything wrong?" Brad asked, puzzled.

"You don't spare my feelings much, do you?" She looked straight at him. "First I hear from Joe about Nariza and you being together on the mountain-side after she had done everything except kiss you in the saloon the other night — and now you have the nerve to ask me if I know where she lives! Even if I did know I wouldn't tell you. Since you're so thick with her why don't you ask *her*? Why do you have to ask *me*?" Betty had got to her feet while she'd been talking. Her mouth was pouting crossly and a frown marred her face. The colour deepened in her cheeks as Brad sat back in the grass and laughed silently.

"I don't think it's so all-fired funny!" she objected — then she gave a gasp as his hand shot up, grabbed her wrist, and pulled her down beside him again.

"I do," he said, his mirth subsiding. "At least it shows that you're jealous, otherwise you wouldn't care what I do when I'm with Nariza."

"Jealous! Of *you*? You flatter yourself!"

"Listen, Betty"

"My name's Miss Tarrant, *if* you please."

"All right, Betty, I'll try and remember. Now listen: let me straighten you out a bit. That little Aztec wild-cat doesn't mean a thing to me, nor do I mean anything to her, except for the fact that she'd like to worm some information out of me. There's only one way a woman can do that, and that's by exerting every feminine charm she's got. That part of the business you'll probably understand."

Betty still looked cross, though not quite so cross.

"Each occasion I've been with her it's been her doing, not mine. I fell in with her suggestions because I want to know all about her — not because she means anything from an emotional standpoint, but because I'm sure she knows where there's a gold mine."

"But ..." Betty gazed at him, obviously puzzled. "I thought it was *you* who knows where there's a gold mine? That's what Joe said, anyway."

"Joe couldn't tell a straight story even if he had his tongue in splints. I *don't* know, but I mean to find out — and Nariza is the key. Don't you understand? Once I know I can see to it that all of us benefit ... That's why I want to find out where she lives."

For a long time Betty sat considering, playing with her fingers in her lap. Then she shook her blonde head slowly.

"Sorry, Brad, but I don't know anything about her — that is, not anything you don't know already. And I'm afraid I jumped to conclusions. I shouldn't have done."

"All forgiven," he smiled. "But look, surely there is *somebody* who ought to know where she hangs out?"

"Why should there be? Until you came into town nobody even had the remotest idea that there might be gold anywhere round here, that is gold worth having. We all know there are lost mines, but finding them is a different matter. And somehow ..."

Betty paused, rubbing a finger in gentle indecision against her mouth.

... somehow," she went on, "I don't feel too sure of your story. Why should you want to go to all that trouble to let everybody know about a gold mine? It doesn't make sense. Why did you half kill Joe last night when he asked you about it? He could probably help you if you'd give him half a chance."

"The only person Joe will ever help is himself," Brad said grimly. It hovered on his tongue to admit his real reason for wanting to know Nariza's whereabouts, but he checked it. Betty was too closely tied to Joe at present for her to be given the chance to let anything slip, no matter how unintentionally.

Brad sighed and became pensive for a while. When he spoke again he had changed the subject.

"Mebby I'd better get around to my other reasons for bringing you out here. They're quite natural ones. I want to know — as I've wanted to know right from the start — what a girl like you is doing wasting herself in

Thunder Bend and letting herself be tied up to Black Joe. You said before that if I were you I'd understand. I'll never be that, so how about explaining?"

"I tied myself up to Black Joe for two reasons — one because he owns the Yellow Nugget and gave me a job — which I sorely needed — and second because he's the most powerful man in Thunder Bend. That satisfy you?"

"And personal inclinations don't enter into it?"

"They hardly can when you've no money to speak of," she answered moodily. Then her expression sharpened. "And while we are about it, how about explaining a few things about yourself? You say you're a prospector — but when I first met you, you looked — from your clothes — just like an hombre. And now — I just don't know what to think. Why did you come to this part of the world, anyway?"

"To look for gold," Brad answered truthfully. "I'm not the first man or woman to do that by any means. What brought you here — the climate?"

She gave a taut, serious little smile.

"No — though it's better than any I've struck yet. I came from my own country because my uncle over here had bequeathed a ranch to me — the Bending S. That's five years ago now. Having no parents to think about and a job that wasn't much good I decided to scrape together what money I could and come to the States. In my imagination I had pictured a prosperous ranch with good cattle and pasture land. All I found was a broken-down wreck, completely derelict, without even a watercourse. Cattle gone — nothing left, and the lawyers couldn't tell me anything about what had occurred to bring it to that state. It's so battered I couldn't even sell it. So, with most of my money gone I was left high and dry. I looked for work in Thunder Bend, and thanks to my voice I found it — with Joe Rutter."

"How has he treated you?" Brad asked quietly.

"Fair enough, so far. He doesn't leave any doubt about the fact that he intends to marry me, though so far I've managed to stall him every time he's wanted to put a diamond ring on my finger."

"Do you know much about him? His record, I mean?"

"That," Betty said soberly, "is the part I'd prefer to forget. It's not a good record: I've found out that much, chiefly from 'Innocent' Jeff, the Nugget's bar-keep. Just the same there is no *proof* of Joe having ever done anything wrong, but he didn't get his prosperous cattle, his Double-G ranch at Arrow Point, and all the money he needs just by being nice to folks. And those two gun hawks of his aren't exactly church ushers either."

"And in spite of all this you intend to marry him?" Betty tightened her mouth and gave a helpless shrug. "Without money, Brad, what else can I do? It's — it's simply bowing to the inevitable, that's all."

Brad thought it out and then glanced up as the girl got to her feet in sudden anxiety.

"I've really got to be getting back! I'm worried over that song I have to sing. If I don't rehearse it, get it right for to-night, there's no knowing what Joe will do. I've never failed him yet and I'm not anxious to find out how he'll behave if I do."

Brad nodded and scrambled up. "Okay. I'll ride you back into town."

He climbed into the saddle again and drew her up before him, his arm once more about her waist. She noticed that on this return trip he didn't set the horse moving at anything more than a jog-trot.

"So you've got a ranch that nobody will buy, eh?" he asked finally. "Whereabouts is it?"

"At the far end of the valley, where the mountains take a sharp curve to Arrow Point. There's a stretch of land there that was once pasture. Now the watercourse has dried up it's shrivelled and useless. If only there were water, some good cattle, an expert foreman, and — oh, what's the use!"

Brad jogged the horse onwards for a while between the carpets of flowers, the sun beating from high overhead and casting back from the golden head in front of him. For these few moments life seemed very quiet and very lovely.

"Back at the saloon there, Betty, when I first met you, you said that if you had money you'd be singing in New York, London, Paris, and sundry other places. Did you really mean that?"

She turned to glance at him. "Yes, I meant it. It would have to be some very big reason that would make me change my mind. When I was in England I paid nearly all the spare money I had into singing lessons. I'm not trying to be conceited or anything but, professionally speaking, I have a very good voice. I can go two notes above high C when I want and that's something! With money I could finish my training and maybe get into the Metropolitan — or something."

"Instead of which you propose to marry a man who has risen to power with guns in his hands? A man who'll take darned good care you never get beyond Thunder Bend, never mind London, Paris, and New York ..."

"Brad!" She shot him an appealing look. "Please!"

"It won't work out, Betty," he said quietly. "I say it won't. It isn't natural."

"Maybe not, but what can *you* do?"

"I dunno yet, but I'll certainly do something. And before very long, too."

She became silent again and remained that way until they had reached Thunder Bend. Brad dismounted, held up his hands and lifted her down to the dusty street.

"I mean it, Betty," he murmured, still holding her.

Her gaze went over his lean, bronzed face, the frank sincerity of his agate-blue eyes. Then under sudden impulse his powerful hands tightened and her lips tingled from his kiss.

"Sorry," he said, releasing her. "Just felt that way. I reckon — and if a man loves a woman, it's only fair he should show it ... I'll be seeing you again, Betty — mebby sooner than you think."

Without another word he leapt into the saddle and sped back through the dust the way he had come.

Chapter VI

That afternoon, at Brad's suggestion, Old Timer abandoned his usual practice of panning at the creek, and instead, saddled his horse and accompanied Brad to the mountain trail he had followed when Nariza had tried to foster her phony romance.

"There's got to be some explanation as to where she vanished last night, Old Timer," Brad said, as their horses carried them along in the afternoon sunlight. "There's some sort of secret entrance, and it's up to us to find it."

"Okay by me," the prospector shrugged. "What *I* want t' be a-knowin' is — who gits anythin' out of it if we *do* find it? Us or.th' State?"

"That depends on who owns the land where it's situated. As I told you."

"Seems t' me it's time we made a deal o' some sort. My ol' bones ain't a-goin' t' keep me movin' much longer, I reckon — not down by th' creek leastways. An' fifteen years of siftin' mud ain't much of a reward come t' think on it."

He said no more, for they had reached the mountain trail — a rough, stony acclivity climbing at a steep angle between towering boulders of rock. They had ascended perhaps fifty feet when Brad halted and pointed. From this position the valley floor was spread out to leftwards, tangled with whispering bells and anemones — but only for a certain distance. Then the beauty stopped and faded into arid sandy waste stretching close beside the foothills. Here in this wilderness was a deserted ranch and an empty corral — extensive, but useless.

"That," Brad said, "belongs to Betty Tarrant. Must be it. She said it was on the bend where the mountains curve to Arrow Point."

"Yeah?" Old Timer was looking puzzled. "How come y'know that, son?"

"She told me. I had a talk with her."

"I often git to a-wonderin' about it. It was pretty thrivin' fer all th' time Old Blake Mascrof owned it. Then after he died th' water seemed t' just dry up. I ain't seen anybody near th' place in years. I figgered it wus just derelict. Betty Tarrant's, huh? Yeah, come t' think on it, I kinda remember she did once say she was tryin' t' sell it."

"Blake Mascrof was her uncle," Brad explained.

"Think o' that!"

Brad did not say any more. He spurred his sorrel forward again and by degrees, Old Timer on his gelding following up behind, they came to the promontory that terminated the ascent.

"Now," Brad said, dismounting and hooking his thumbs in his belt as he looked about him, "let's see what we can find."

He began to examine the sheer face of the rocks, the towering spurs which lined the edge of the promontory, the niches, the crevices, the cracks — but wherever he looked, with Old Timer looking too, there was no apparent explanation as to how the Aztec girl had got this far and then vanished.

From this ledge there seemed to be only two ways of disappearing — either over its edge into the gulf of Thunder Valley with the toy creek and cabin far below, or else along the trail itself. Up above, the grey invincible ramparts flung themselves in defiance to the sky, forming a saw-toothed edge against it.

"Wil," Old Timer said at last, scratching his jaw, "I reckon thit if th' gurl's got some way o' turnin' herself into a shadow, she might manage it — but I'll be dog-goned if there's any other way!"

Brad signed and nodded moodily.

"I guess you're right there. This is a waste of time.

The only person who can explain the mystery is the girl herself, ... I'll get it out of her somehow. Come on — let's get back."

He remounted his horse, and together they returned down the path. When they had reached the valley floor again, Brad turned left instead of right, sent his horse cantering through the flowers until he came to the arid area. He drew rein as he came fully in sight of the ranch Betty Tarrant had said she owned.

"Sure ain't no prize packet to leave th' gurl," Old Timer commented, leaning on his saddle horn and spitting into the dust.

Brad dismounted and walked forward through the stone chippings, sand, and pumice dust to examine the spread more closely. The wire enclosure round the corral was partly broken down; the gate leading into it had gone entirely. The railed veranda of the ranch-house itself was sagging from constant lack of attention and exposure to bleaching heat. There was a dead, funeral aspect about the place, about the dust blown in the hot wind, about the cracked and broken windows. It was a ghost ranch, a derelict without water, which sooner or later would be smothered in the eternally drifting sand.

Brad turned away at last, pondering. Old Timer still sat on his horse, smoking his crackling pipe and considering

"Kinda funny really," he said at length, as Brad rejoined him.

"Funny? You've got a queer sense of humour, Old Timer. On the contrary, I'd say it's tragic!"

"I ain't a-talkin' about th' ranch, son — I mean about th' way th' watercourse has dried up. There wus plenty o' water when Mascrof had th' spread."

"There was?" Brad's blue eyes narrowed for a moment as he looked about him.

"Sure was — an' T know what I'm talkin' about livin' in these parts. All this wus pasture at one time, an' Mascrof had one o' th' best herds o' cattle I ever did see." Old Timer jerked his pipe to indicate the mountain face. "Tik a look there, son. Th' spring came straight down them mountains an' across this land. Kinda queer it should dry up. Springs don't dry up as a rule: I reckon I never heard of one a-doin' it before. There usta be one as big as thit creek o' mine runnin' through here, even in summer."

"Have you any idea where it started?" Brad asked sharply.

"Nope. Never had any reason t' find out, but it musta bin in the mountains somewheres."

"A watercourse like that must have left erosion traces," Brad said, climbing back on his horse. "I'm going to see what I can find out. You know where it used to be."

Old Timer nodded, knocked the ashes out of his pipe and then trotted his horse forward to catch up with Brad. In ten minutes they had come to a shelving fold of the land, half covered with blown sand, but though it was now an arroyo, it showed distinctly the course it had taken as a mountain stream.

To follow it was easy, and when it ceased to appear as a wide gouge in the sun-baked earth, it was in the form of stained, brown rock. So, by degrees, going ever higher, horses and riders followed the course, actually riding along it in places with flat-headed, water-smoothed stones under the horses' feet — until at perhaps two hundred feet above the valley floor, they came within the sound of gurgling water ahead of them.

Brad dismounted and hurried forward over the rocks, pausing as he came unexpectedly upon a wide, welling mountain pool discharging itself in a torrent somewhere on the other side of the basin.

Old Timer came up and stood looking at it, rubbing his jaw pensively.

"Somethin' kinda queer here, son," he said finally. "I never saw Dame Nature chuck down rocks as even as these are — nor did I ever hear o' her puttin' red clay between 'em neither!"

"Dame Nature never did," Brad answered him, his mouth hard. "This watercourse has been dammed up by men, and then diverted. We want to know where to. The thing's becoming obvious. When Mascrof died and nobody immediately took over — because it was some months before Betty Tarrant arrived from England — somebody diverted the watercourse. With there being nobody in control of the Mascrof ranch they got away with it, and that girl was cheated out of her inheritance … We're going to find out where this water goes if it takes us all night. Come on."

They began the difficult journey round the edge of the pool, picking their way on slippery rock along the narrow ledge. Once they had worked their way round it they had to climb to get some idea of where the foaming torrent was pouring.

Fifty feet up they arrived at a massive pinnacle of rock. Two lone figures against the cloudless sky they gazed down into the valley where it curved sharply round the base of the mountains. That moisture was present was obvious. The aridity which existed around the Bending S was not evident here — the whispering bells and anemone had returned. The watercourse itself was plainly visible as a glittering thread in the sunlight, stretching away — and still away — in the direction of an extensive ranch.

"Thit's Arrow Point, and th' spread is Black Joe's Double-G," Old Timer said. "Once y' git past Mascrof's place the valley floor curves around until seven miles further on it meets up with Joe's place … Ain't much surprise t' find he's back o' damming th' watercourse. No wonder he's gotten the best cattle. He oughta with all thit pasture an' water."

"How right you are!" Brad clenched his fists. "And in return the dirty skunk gives the girl a job in his saloon. He knows that'll make an attraction and bring him more custom and more money. Next he aims to marry her. Big of him, isn't it? I'll wager that when Mascrof died Joe made it worth the while of Mascrof's boys to shift the cattle up the valley to his own spread and say no more about it."

"Knowin' Black Joe I wouldn't put it past him," Old Timer agreed.

"When I get the chance," Brad said slowly, "Black Joe and I are going to have words about this … All right — now let's get back."

*

The noise in the Yellow Nugget saloon was at its height when after sundown that evening Brad stepped through the batswing doors and walked across to the counter. He knew perfectly well that a dozen eyes followed him, that the noise seemed to lessen somewhat, but he took no apparent notice. At the bar he glanced at Jeff Willard and received a meaning, half-scared glance.

"Double whisky," Brad said briefly, and as he poured it out the bar-keep murmured:

"Better git out, feller. They're gangin' up on you, like I said."

Brad smiled, took up the drink and looked about him. As usual, the place was crowded with men and women, some of them watching him intently, others going on with their card and pool games or just loafing and drinking.

On the opposite side of the saloon Black Joe was standing in his black suit and hat, shirt front gleaming behind a shoe-string tie. Though he and Brad exchanged looks across the smoky expanse nothing happened. Brad couldn't spot the two lean-faced gun hawks but he had no doubts that they were somewhere handy.

For a moment the lack of action puzzled him — then it explained itself as Betty Tarrant appeared in her low-cut ill-fitting evening gown and walked on to the platform above the piano. Black Joe clapped and so everybody else did also — then there was silence as the girl started singing.

There was no doubt it was a voice in a thousand. For the time being it made Brad forget everything else. Then Betty evidently caught sight of him across the room for she hesitated for a moment, caught the note again and continued. Then again she hesitated and finally stopped.

Black Joe turned deliberately and looked at her.

"What ails yuh, Betty?" he demanded.

"I — I don't seem to remember the song … She twirled a handkerchief in restless fingers. "I suppose I haven't rehearsed it enough."

Black Joe hurried up on to the stage and caught her arm.

"What in blue thunder d'you mean — haven't rehearsed it enough? You rehearsed it this mornin' like I told yuh, didn't yuh?"

Betty was silent, trying ineffectually to dislodge the grip he had upon her wrist. Then the pianist below answered for her.

"I reckon she didn't, Joe. She wasn't here this mornin'. I came but she didn't turn up."

"You didn't, huh?" Joe swung back to her, still gripping her arm. "What d'yuh think I pay you for, Betty? Don't you realize that these folks here expect yuh to sing? An' so do I! Why didn't you turn up, anyway? Why didn't —"

"Take your paw off that girl's arm, Joe!" Unnoticed, Brad had moved silently between the tables and had now come up on to the stage. His thumbs were hooked in his belt, his lean face as immobile as ever.

Black Joe turned, hesitated, and then seemed to think something out. Nevertheless, he released Betty and eyed Brad narrowly.

"You, huh? Now I begin to get it. Y'told me last night that yuh'd have more words with Betty — an' I reckon you did, this mornin' when my back was turned."

"Supposing I did? Any business of yours?"

"This is *my* girl"

"I've told you to stop saying that, Joe."

Normally Joe's hand would have flashed to his gun — a Colt, this time, holstered low down on his right thigh. But for some reason best known to himself he stalled. With a grim face he turned to look at the assembly in the saloon.

"Remember what I told yuh last night, folks, about this jigger? He comes into town, knows where a bonanza is, and don't say a thing about it to nobody. He knows that mine ought to become State property and be shared among us equally. That's the law once the State's apportioned it. But he keeps quiet — keeps it all to himself. I reckon it's about time we had the truth outa him. He knows where that gold is. Last night I found him with two bags of it stuffed in his pants pockets ..."

Joe paused and looked through the haze. A girl's slim figure, black hair flowing about her head and to her shoulders, was just leaving the saloon silently. Joe made a motion to somebody. Brad watched and saw Rod Jenkins, one of the gun hawks, follow the girl out. Evidently she had entered unobserved, heard everything, and then gone out again. Brad wondered why, then Joe's grim voice forced him back to attention again.

"The fact remains, folks, this hombre knows where there's gold. What do we do about it?"

"Git th' truth outa him!"

"Take him to the Sheriff! He'll enforce law soon enough."

Joe shook his head and gave a grim smile. "I reckon the Sheriff we've got ain't worth botherin' about. If we want anythin' we'll have to do it ourselves."

"You're not going to do anything," Betty interrupted, seizing Joe's arm. "Joe, listen to me! You can t

"Aw, get outa my way!"

His powerful arm swung, elbow crooked so that it struck the girl hard in the stomach. She doubled anguishedly and reeled backwards.

Brad gave one glance about him, saw an angry surging below, and then he dived. His left hand clutched Joe's shoulder and whirled him round from looking at the winded girl. He turned to meet smashing knuckles between the eyes.

"When I said lay off the girl I meant it!" Brad snapped.

His left shot up and Joe staggered, recovered himself, and lammed out a short-armed jab. Brad took it on the chest and retaliated with a stinging piston blow that made Joe's head sing. He stumbled and clutched the curtains at the side of the stage, only to be yanked up again and receive a hammer blow on the back of his neck. He gulped, retched inwardly — and fire burst before his eyes from a smashing right-hander to the jaw. Dazed, half-blinded, he toppled over the edge of the stage and into the midst of the men and women moving below.

Brad swung, swept up the still gasping girl in his arms, and leapt. He struck the floor with a resounding jolt, released Betty and yanked up his right-hand .45. He was behind the crowd now, as he had planned he would be.

"Take it easy," he warned. "One shot from any of you before we get to the door and I'll —"

"Look *out!*" Betty screamed, as her eye caught sight of an aimed revolver in the hand of a giant standing on a distant chair.

Even as she screamed the warning there was a shot — but not from the giant. It came from the batswings.

The distant gun hawk dropped his gun and vanished in the crowd. Brad cast a startled sideways glance. Old Timer was standing there, coonskin hat on the back of his head, his smoking gun in his hand. He gave a dry chuckle.

"Glad me ol' fingers ain't lost their trigger-itch," he murmured, his eyes steel-bright in his leathery face. "Okay, kids. Git outside. I'll keep yuh covered."

Brad nodded, put his arm about Betty's waist and hurried her through the batswings. It only took seconds to unfasten his horse, leap into the saddle and sweep the girl up beside him. They had hardly reached the end of the street before Old Timer on his gelding caught up with them.

"Nice work," Brad commented. "You probably saved my life and Betty from plenty of trouble — but it's a pity you had to leave the cabin. I told you to stop there."

"I know y' did, son — but I had t' have a drink. I ain't missed it every night fer fifteen year. Not 'til tonight, an' me throat's like Death Valley right now. Anyway, there wasn't nothin' t' stop fer at th' cabin."

"You're wrong," Brad said seriously. "In that cabin are all the facts about me and who I am. Anybody wanting to know about me could get in the cabin by night if nobody's on guard. Nobody would risk it by day. I'll wager that Nariza is there right now. I saw her leave just after Joe started pitching into Betty here."

"Anyway, I saved yuh a heap o' trouble," Old Timer said obstinately. "An' missed me drink into th' bargain'" he added sourly.

They rode swiftly through the starlit expanse and there was no sign of pursuit. Then at last the girl herself asked a question.

"Where are we going, Brad? What's the idea?"

"For the moment we're going to Old Timer's cabin. Tonight you got a pretty good idea of how Black Joe will treat you if you stay latched on to him, and I don't intend to let that happen. You'll be safe with us — 'Sides, there's something you should know about your ranch."

"What?"

"I'll tell you later … Brad urged his horse to greater speed and the dust rose under the stars as they hurtled on.

Chapter VII

As silently as a phantom the figure moved about the little room in the cabin by the creek. It was Nariza, the wide-open window showing how she had gained entrance. Momentarily a match spluttered in her cupped hands as she peered at a series of papers, a badge, and a single fat bag tied round the neck — all of them lying in the drawer of the rough wooden dresser.

"So, Mr. Morrison, you *are* a marshal after all," she murmured. "Well, what you can't find out one way you can find out another."

Her face taut, she unfastened the bag swiftly and looked inside it. Then she strung it up again.

"So you know it's me ... Black Joe must have been speaking the truth when he said he saw you with two bags of gold in your pockets last night. Only one place where you could have got them from — the baggage station where I left them. And that means you know I'm responsible for those parcels."

The match flickered and expired. Nariza felt for the bag and glided back to the window, slid silently into the night again and drew the sash down behind her. Without a sound she drifted across in the starlight to where she had left her pinto — then suddenly a gun was hard pressed in the small of her back.

"I'll take that bag yore carryin'."

She half turned, aware of a tall, gangling figure. Though she could not see the face she recognized the voice of Rod Jenkins. Suddenly her fingers were relieved of the weight of the gold bag and the gun prodded her again.

"I reckon th' boss'll like a few words with you, Nariza. Get on your horse — an' no fancy business neither! An' keep yuh hands up!"

The girl began to walk, waited while the gun hawk unfastened the reins of her horse, and then she climbed into the saddle — but the instant she was in it she dug her heels into the pinto's sides. The horse swung round, stung, darting off into the night before the gun hawk even realized what had happened. Half in his saddle and half out of it he was beaten. He stared blankly as the night swallowed the girl up.

"Dog-gone!" he muttered, scowling. "Lightnin' ain't got much on that pinto, I reckon ... He looked at the heavy gold bag and reflected, to glance up again as to his ears came the unmistakable sound of approaching horses. He swung, cantered the horse away into the starlight and finally, at a distance far enough to escape detection, he watched two horses, one carrying two riders. Then he turned and spurred his horse back to Thunder Bend.

He covered the distance in twelve minutes flat, jumped from the snorting, sweating horse, tied the reins to the hitch rail and then hurried into the Yellow Nugget. All signs of the recent disorder had disappeared.

"Where's th' boss?" Rod looked at Jeff Willard.

"His office."

The gun hawk hurried to it, tapped on the door and entered. Black Joe and Lefty Wilmore were inside. Joe was seated at his roll top desk, dabbing his jaw with a steaming rag and gazing blue murder.

"Well, what in hell do you want?" he barked.

"How's this, boss?" Rod dropped the gold bag on the desk with a thud and Black Joe stared at it. Then he put the hot rag into a steaming bowl and opened the bag-neck quickly.

"*Another* lot o' gold an' rock!" he ejaculated. "An' all in one bag this time! Where'd yuh get it?"

"I found that dame Nariza sneakin' off with it from Old Timer's cabin. That gold certainly ain't Old Timer's, but since we know Brad Morrison's bunkin' there I reckon it's his."

"Yore durned right, it is. Wonder what he did with th' other two bags he had? He's on to gold all right — an' plenty of it! This proves it! Two bags last night an' one to-night — what about the girl? That's what I sent you after her fer, wasn't it?"

"I guess so," Rod admitted, shifting uncomfortably, "but she wus too quick fer me. That pinto of hers was off like a streak — an' this gold sort of weighted me down, too."

"So does th' water in y' brain," Joe told him sourly; then he thought for a moment. "Perhaps it doesn't matter, though. Look, here's how I figger it: if that Morrison jigger and Nariza was in on this together she wouldn't be stealin' from him, would she? Don't make sense."

"Reckon not," Rod agreed, glad of the more genial mood.

"In that case ..." Joe rubbed his jaw, winced and desisted. "In that case it means my first guess was right. This Morrison feller has access to a gold mine some place. That Aztec girl must have heard me say he had two bags o' gold on him last night and knowin' Brad was in the saloon — an' thinkin' she'd only have that old prospector to deal with — she went to look if there was anythin' she could take. As it happened Old Timer left the way clear fer her and she stole this. Yes, she and Morrison ain't in with each other."

"Then what about that love stuff between them, boss?" Lefty demanded. "We saw it in the saloon the first night the guy breezed into town, an' they sure went up the mountain-side together."

"It may have been genuine, but now they've fallen out — so th' girl has no objections to stealin' stuff from him. That's the angle, I guess. That means it's him we've got to get, not her. For the time bein' we'll leave her out of it and squeeze the truth outa Brad Morrison somehow."

"Why not to-night?" Lefty snapped. "He's as good as frisked the Tarrant girl from under yuh nose an' he beat you up plenty too. I'm all fer goin' to that cabin right now and havin' a showdown."

"You would be." Joe regarded him coldly. "That's just what he'll be expectin' and he'll be on his guard against it. No, let him start gettin' unwary, an' then one night …"

*

In the cabin by the creek Brad Morrison sat at the wooden table, his face grim. A meal was laid and the coffee pot was wisping steam as it stood beside the glowing oil lamp. Old Timer munched slowly, his eyes brightly inquiring. Opposite him Betty Tarrant looked mystified, and it was an expression which gradually deepened.

"There's only one explanation for it," Brad said at length, setting his chin. "While we were away Nariza got into this cabin. That bag of gold's gone from the dresser drawer and my official papers and badge have been disturbed. That means she knows … Couldn't expect much else with Joe shooting his mouth off, I suppose. When he said he'd found me with two gold bags she knew that I must be wise to her little game and so set herself to find out the true facts about me. Thanks to the cabin being left deserted she managed it. This means that she'll be on the defensive all the time from now on."

"That's about the size of it, I reckon," Old Timer agreed.

"But what's it all about?" Betty demanded. "Or have you forgotten that I haven't the vaguest idea what's going on?"

Brad smiled at her apologetically. "Sorry, Bet. There's a lot you don't know — but since I don't intend you getting back into Joe's clutches you might as well have the facts. I'm a marshal, sent here specially to investigate the movement of gold — probably illegal gold, too."

"A — a marshal!" Betty stared in amazement. "So *that's* why you hedged every time I tried to get the facts? Then you're after Nariza. Is that it?"

"That's it. She's gotten hold of a hidden gold mine somewheres and I had hoped to find out where. So far I've been unlucky, and now she knows I'm a marshal I'm afraid I shall be even more unlucky." Brad rubbed his chin in impatient indecision. "Now you know why I wanted to find out where she lives. The trouble is there's no way of discovering that unless I can manage to follow her back home sometime after she's come into town. But now she knows the facts she isn't likely to give me the opportunity. Even if she did I haven't got the proof I need. I've got to get her right in the mine itself — have witnesses to prove it; or else I've got to catch her with the gold on her person."

"What d'yuh s'pose has happened to thit gold bag she's taken?" Old Timer demanded.

"She's got it, of course. What else? From now on I imagine she'll stop sending gold to the mysterious J. T. Barryman — or else she'll ride to Drew City herself and take it to him that way. First thing I must do is let the Drew City authorities know about this and keep them on their toes."

"Joe seems to think that you have the location of the gold mine," Betty put in.

"That's just what he does think, but he's got his facts twisted." Brad held out his cigarette packet and the girl took one. "He's jumped to conclusions because he saw me with Nariza on the mountain trail."

"Maybe so," the girl said, lighting cigarettes for both of them, "but isn't that going to make it tough for you? You don't suppose Black Joe will take that hammering you gave him and do nothing about it, do you? Before you know it, Brad, you're liable to wind up with a bullet between your shoulder blades. In fact" Betty gave an uneasy glance round the shadowy cabin, "I can't understand why he hasn't done something already. Leaving us in peace like this isn't his usual way of doing things — and to add to it you've yanked me away from him, too. He knows you are living here because he told me as much."

"Evidently a direct onslaught doesn't appeal to him." Brad gave a shrug. "Prefers something more snaky, mebby."

Silence fell for a while as each of them formed their own speculations, then the girl seemed to recollect something.

"Didn't you say you had something to tell me about that ranch of mine, Brad?"

"Plenty!" Brad gave a start and aroused himself. For the moment he had forgotten all about the Bending S. "I had a look at your spread this afternoon, and Old Timer here supplied me with plenty of facts. Cutting a long story short, Betty, that ranch would be flourishing right now if it wasn't for the activities of one person … Black Joe."

"Joe?" The girl's pretty face began to harden. It looked as if she were almost glad she had a chance to pin something definite on him. "Joe?" she repeated. "Why, what's he got to do with it?"

"But for him diverting the watercourse — and probably bribing your late uncle's men to the limit — you'd have a flourishing ranch …" Brad went quickly through the details. When he had finished, the girl crushed out her cigarette in the tin lid which was doing service for an ashtray.

"So that's what happened." She fell to musing. "Joe got to work in between uncle dying and me getting here … I know what I'm going to do: tell the Sheriff!"

Brad and Old Timer were silent, but they raised their eyebrows at her.

"It's the logical thing to do, isn't it?" she demanded. "He represents law and order around here."

"Maybe he does, but he's like me, Betty — he can't move without proof."

"But there *is* proof! The watercourse has been diverted and Joe's land is getting the benefit of it. What more proof do we need?"

"The proof that *he* diverted it. Old Timer and I know that it looks as if it has been dammed up and its course altered so that it flows to Joe's spread and pasture, but unless we can prove that he or men employed by him did it, we're stymied. That, more's the pity, is the law."

"But we might never be able to prove that!" Betty protested.

"On the other hand," Brad answered slowly, " a shooting iron is a mighty useful thing sometimes. I'm going to make sure — and you can help me, Old Timer — if any of the men employed now by Black Joe were formerly employed by Blake Mascrof. If so, we'll get one of the men and grind the truth out of him the hard way. I know it's not ethical, but it's effective. Once I get that statement I'll force him to repeat it to the Sheriff, and that'll start things moving."

The girl gave a little smile. "Well, of course, that's one way of doing it — and it's something I can't do ... But it occurs to me I might be able to do something else to help you, Brad."

"Yes?" He tried not to sound uneasy.

"Find out for you where Nariza lives."

Brad exchanged a glance with Old Timer and the prospector shook his grizzled head. "Too dog-goned dangerous, I reckon."

"Not it!" the girl scoffed. "Nariza's a woman and I'm a woman. I'll tackle my own sex anywhere on this earth and give them good measure. I can shoot and I can ride: I've learned those things since I came here. If you'll let me borrow a pair of pants and a shirt, Old Timer — since you're about my size — I'll start off to-morrow and find Nariza's home if I have to go all over Arizona."

"I still don't like it," Brad muttered.

"You can't stop me, Brad." She laid a hand on his arm with quiet firmness. "You are helping me and I'm going to help you. Obviously I'm all washed up with Joe and Thunder Bend. I'll have to shake down here until we see what develops ... You don't suppose I'm the kind of girl who wants to be under a glass case, do you?"

"It's the risk," Brad protested. "Black Joe will do all he can to drag you back"

"Maybe he will, but he won't kill me. He'd rather marry me than that. And if anybody starts shooting at me, I can soon shoot back. And I will! There's one code I've learned since I came to this wild spot: If you find you're being gypped out of something — as I am out of my ranch — the only answer is to hit back in the same coin, and harder. I can't do that, but you are doing it for me — so I'll handle the woman angle. That," Betty finished, setting her firm little chin as Brad half protested again, "is settled, Brad! I mean it!"

*

Brad and Old Timer bunked for the night in the living-room and gave up the bedroom to the girl. She went to bed with Joe's own "frisked" .45 under her pillow and reappeared in the morning in the riding pants, shirt and boots which Old Timer had loaned her. They fitted her passably well and revealed for the first time the lithe strength in her limbs which so far had been hidden by the dresses she had worn. Her face healthily coloured from a wash in fresh water and her blonde hair swept back from her wide forehead she was, Brad silently reflected, as pretty a picture as any man could wish to see.

"Morning, boys," she greeted, and holding up the .45 she added, "I'll stick to this if you don't mind. It's a heavy bit of hardware, but it being Joe's, I sort of feel I'd like to use it — on him if need be. And if you think I can't shoot because I'm a woman, take a look at this."

She went to the open cabin doorway and out on to the sunlit porch. Sighting the gun on a distant mesquite post which helped to support the garden enclosure, she aimed and fired. The gun exploded and a chip flew out of the post at the top.

"Any doubts?" she asked dryly, turning back into an aroma of frying ham and coffee.

"Not anymore," Brad grinned. "Just as long as the cartridge belt doesn't make you one-sided!"

She gave him a hurt glance and settled down at the table. Breakfast was half-way through when she broke into the conversation with a question.

"What do you plan to do next, Brad?"

"Old Timer and I are going through the valley and up the mountains, to get as near as we can to Joe's spread. I've got a pair of field-glasses in my tackle. I'm going to have Old Timer watch the boys through them just to see if he can spot any who used to be with your uncle. If that good luck comes our way, I'll go further. If it doesn't — well, think of some new angle, I suppose. And you, I take it, are going chasing off to nowhere in particular?"

"Don't be too sure of that. You say that Nariza was certainly here last night. All right, then: she must have gone to her home from here. Round this cabin the ground is dusty and sun-baked — but it's not so baked that it won't take the impression of a horse's hoofs. And Nariza rides a pinto, which is distinctive. I'm no Indian tracker, but I'm going to do my best to emulate one."

"Uh-huh," Brad agreed dubiously. "You can do that, of course. You'd better take Old Timer's horse, by the way — it's less cumbersome than mine, and swifter. Besides my sorrel is better able to take a combined weight."

The girl nodded, and immediately breakfast was over she strapped the cartridge belt about her slim waist, thrust the .45 into the holster, and then gathered together a few provisions and a water bottle. Thus equipped, she set off into the bright morning sunshine, waved once, and then bent her attention to the ground.

As she had surmised, there *were* tracks in the banked dust, deeply gouged half-moons which bespoke where a horse had been moving at high speed. She followed them with a rising sense of elation at her own ability — for half a mile, a mile, and the cabin was out of her sight as she followed the tracks close beside the creek. To her satisfaction, they didn't branch off or lose themselves in the scrub; they remained near to the water, following the stream until the mountain foothills had been reached — then she lost them on hard rock.

Annoyed, she drew rein and looked about her. It was sweltering hot here, the massive mountain wall blocking the wind from the mesa. She shaded her eyes and looked in every direction. On her left was the mountain; behind her the more or less open stretch of pasture land and mesa and the trail she had followed so far. To her right was the endless carpet of flowers which terminated on the distant outskirts of Thunder Bend. And ahead? Narrow, frowning rocks, outcroppings of the mountains, leading into parts of Thunder Valley where she had never yet explored.

Finally, she spurred the horse on again and after a quarter of a mile, where the valley narrowed sharply, the creek suddenly took a leftward turn and lost itself in the foothills. Betty gave it a glance, not particularly interested in where it began its course, and then spurred her horse onwards again along a narrow rutted fissure between high rocks. At one time it had probably been the bed of a fast-flowing mountain stream.

Back of her mind a vague doubt was forming. This was, perhaps, not getting her anywhere, only burning the strength out of her and wearying the gelding — but the fact did remain that the traces of Nariza's horse *had* vanished a quarter of a mile further back. That meant, since there had been no return tracks, that Nariza must have come this way, because there was no other possible direction except up the mountains, and one glance at their towering heights decided Betty that that was not the answer.

The bed of the extinct mountain river continued for at least another three miles, then Betty drew rein again at a small spring and watered the horse. She took a drink from her flask and then carried on again — and presently the rocks began to fall away into wider land. Sparse cactus bushes grew here and there and ahead of her was a clear line of cobalt-blue sky which suggested that she was coming to open country again.

She drove the horse beneath two mighty spurs of rock shaped like an inverted U, and found herself facing an expanse of arid land, entirely surrounded by hills, in the centre of which with smoke curling lazily from its chimney was a solitary bungalow.

Betty leaned on the saddle horn, pushing back her hair and considering the view. The place was certainly not a ranch. There was no corral, no sign of cattle. Actually the building was little more than an overgrown cabin with a smaller wooden structure adjoining which could be a stable. And, to judge from the smoke, the place was tenanted … Only by degrees did Betty realize the unique position of the place. It was in truth a lost habitation.

Just at this point the mountain range was hollowed into a gigantic cup, perhaps from some incredibly ancient volcanic upheaval. It had produced the cumulative effect of mountain range all round this one spot. It was the kind of place that could only be spotted from the air, or else by accident. Betty wondered whether beginner's luck had led her right to it. Certainly no ordinary searching and trail following would ever have revealed it: it lay at least ten miles from the nearest known trail.

"Whether it's what we're looking for we don't know," she murmured to the horse, patting its glossy neck, "but it seems reasonable to suppose that it is since Nariza's horse came this way. Have to find out, that's all."

She slipped from the saddle, tied the reins round a rock projection, then began to worm her way quietly in and out of the rocks which surrounded this basin in the mountains. As she moved she kept low. She had left her gelding so it couldn't be seen from below — but it was even more essential that she shouldn't. Gradually, by moving swiftly from the cover of rock to rock, she achieved a nearer vantage point and settled down to watch, peeping over the edge of a lip of rock in front of her. From here the entire front porch of the bungalow was within view. She could see the veranda, the screen door, the windows — but the curtains at them prevented any glimpse of what was going on inside.

After fifteen minutes of fruitless waiting Betty began to wish she had a pair of field-glasses. It was no joke squatting here in the blazing sun waiting for a sign of the bungalow's inmate. Then presently she hit upon an idea. It might work: it might not. It depended upon the power of her arm and the sensitiveness of the horse in the stable — if there was a horse and if it was a stable. She knew that if it was Nariza's pinto it would be sharp, sensitive, easily alarmed.

Turning, she picked up a comfortably heavy stone and threw it with all her strength. It fell short so she tried again, and this time it landed full on the stable roof with a sharp, heavy bang. Instantly there was a startled whinnying upon the silence of the little hollow and Betty crouched down and waited … The ruse worked. The screen door of the bungalow opened suddenly and Nariza herself in her usual attire of shirt and riding trousers came into view. She hurried across to the stable and after a while the whinnying ceased. Nariza reappeared, shading her eyes and looking about her in obvious suspicion. Finally she gave it up as an unexplained problem and returned into the bungalow.

"Thanks, sweetheart — that's all I wanted to know,"

Betty murmured, smiling to herself, and she scrambled to her feet. Then as she turned she stopped dead, rigid with shock.

Beside the next spur of rock a tall, lean man was standing, smoking lazily, his Colt levelled steadily.

"Howdy, Miss Tarrant," he greeted calmly.

Chapter VIII

"Lefty!" Betty gasped, beginning to move again. "How — how did you get here?"

"Followed you. Yore surprised, I reckon?" Lefty grinned cynically. "There ain't no call to be that, Miss Tarrant. Yuh don't s'pose th' boss is goin' to let yuh git away from him *that* easy, do yuh? An' that wus a nice trick y' pulled to get that Nariza dame outa her bungalow. Guess we'd still be waitin' if you hadn't gotten yuhself a smart brain."

"Never mind Nariza," Betty snapped, inwardly furious that her discovery should also be the property of Joe's callous gunman, which would only perhaps complicate things still more. "What d'you mean by following me about? Joe hasn't *bought* me even if he thinks he has. If I choose to leave him I can do so."

"Yeah — sure," Lefty acknowledged. "Only he don't kinda take nicely to thit sort o' treatment. I got my orders to watch yuh — so I did just that. Brad Morrison took yuh to th' cabin by the creek: that we knew. All I had t'do was take it up from there ... Kinda funny that a gal like you should be the one t'find out where this Aztec dame hangs out. We men all tried it an' got no place."

Betty glared at him. "And what do you think you're going to do now?"

"Wal, that's kinda plain, isn't it?" Though Lefty spoke languidly his eyes were watching every move she made. "I'm a-takin' yuh to the Double-G, the boss's spread. I guess he'll want to talk a few things over with yuh."

"If you think you're going to get me to Joe's ranch you're crazy!" Betty snapped.

"Mebby. Mebby not." Lefty considered her and then he stood up straight. "Get movin'!" he ordered, his face ugly under the hat brim. "Git on your horse — quick! No dame's a-goin' to tell me what to do."

Betty hesitated. She had no fear of the gun. She knew perfectly well that Lefty would never dare to use it on her: it would be more than his life was worth at the hands of Joe Rutter. A dim thought began to turn over in her mind. She went past him, then ahead of him, dodging from rock to rock to prevent the possibly watchful Nariza from seeing what was going on. Lefty took the same precautions and so presently they came to where Betty had left her horse, Lefty's own sorrel standing nearby.

Without a word Betty climbed into the saddle but she didn't take the reins into her hands immediately.

Lefty holstered his gun and swung up into his own saddle, jogged the horse forward until he was beside her.

"What's the idea o' waitin'?" he demanded. "Git movin'!"

"All right." Betty shrugged. "But there's no reason why we can't do it as comfortably as possible, is there? I'm about dying for a cigarette. Give me one, will you?"

A grin cracked the gun hawk's leather-hard face.

"Sociable, huh? That's more like it. I like a dame to be sociable ..." He fished in his shirt pocket and brought out a packet of cigarettes, jerked it so that one popped up for her to grasp. He lighted it for her and she nodded briefly and drew in the smoke, then taking the reins of the horse she went ahead of him over the rough, scattered rocks.

There was only room for them to move single file — a fact she had remembered — and as she went she ceased smoking and instead crushed the cigarette in her hand after snicking off the lighted end. Gently she kneaded it back and forth in her palm, taking care that none escaped. After a while she drew her horse almost to a standstill, kicked one foot free of the stirrup and allowed herself to slide sideways. It took all her nerve to do it. She landed in the dust at the side of the trail, flat on her back with arms outflung, one foot still dragged upwards by the remaining stirrup.

She kept her eyes closed, felt the blazing sun on her face and heard the thud of Lefty's boots as he dismounted and came over to her. He released her trapped foot, just as she had guessed he would, then his arm was about her shoulders as he raised her into a sitting position.

"What's gotten into yuh?" he demanded. "Sun get yuh?"

He muttered something and she felt him fumbling with her water bottle about her waist. She stirred slowly, kept her eyes closed, and drew up her right hand languidly.

Lefty desisted in his efforts to free the water bottle and she slitted her eyes very slightly to see him peering into her face. Instantly she opened her right palm and blew with all her power.

"Dog-gone it, you — you *hell-cat*!" Lefty gave a screech and jumped up, clawing his face. "Yuh've blinded me!"

Betty leapt to her feet, swung out her right foot and knocked the gun hawk's legs from under him. He crashed in the dust, clawing at his eyes and swearing volubly. Grim-faced, the girl hurried across to his horse, gave it a resounding slap across the withers and sent it bounding nervously away along the rocky pathway; then she vaulted into her own saddle and prepared to follow.

Lefty had got to his knees, an arm over his face.

"You're not blinded," the girl told him cynically. "It's only tobacco dust. Good trick, isn't it? I read about it once. When the nicotine loses its effect you'll be all right — but you'll have a long walk home! Give my regards to Black Joe and tell him I hope he chokes!"

She tossed the hair from her face, dug her heels in the gelding's sides, and followed in pursuit of Lefty's escaping horse.

*

High up in the rocks overlooking the Double-G ranch Old Timer stood motionless, field-glasses resting on the needle of rock in front of him, his keen eyes gazing with steady intensity. It was nearly mid-morning and Brad and he had been in this lofty vantage point for nearly half an hour, the horses tethered nearby and nodding patiently in the sunshine.

Brad, his face set, waited for the old prospector to make some comment. From this height all Brad could distinguish was the ranch itself, the movement of cattle within the corral and the figures of men moving about on horseback, while others walked about their business on the ranch.

"Yeah, there ain't no doubt about it," Old Timer said finally, and spat in the dust. "There's a lot o' boys down there thit was on Mascrof's spread — but there's one in particklar about who I can't be wrong. Hank Grimshaw — big, hefty feller — he usta be Mascrof's foreman. I c'n spot him easily down there. Looks like he ain't a foreman no more but he's certainly workin' fer Joe Rutter. Look, son, see thit figger beside th' gate?"

Brad pulled down his hat brim and gazed earnestly. He could dimly descry the outline of a man.

"Thit's him," Old Timer said, motioning to the field-glasses. "Yuh jest want to take a look fer yuhself an' then yuh'll know him again."

Brad peered through the lenses, the details of the man now thrown into pin-sharp relief. He gave a little start of surprise and glanced up.

"Say, that's the jigger who was about to take a potshot at me in the saloon last night before you winged him! He's got a bandage round his forehead. I can just see it under his hat."

"Right," the old prospector chuckled. "Reckon I sure parted his hair fer him, huh? Thit's why I singled him out in particklar. I reckon thit if yuh want t'squeeze some information outa him yuh won't be too particklar how yuh do it after him tryin' to blast yuh down last night."

"There," Brad said, slipping the field-glasses back in the case, "you've got something, Old Timer. This is all I need to know. Tonight I'll keep a watch on the Yellow Nugget and when Hank Grimshaw leaves he'll find somebody to welcome him."

"Yeah." Old Timer grinned with his two teeth. "The both of us, huh?"

"No — just me. You're staying behind with a gun on your knee to keep an eye on Betty. I'm not taking the chance of leaving her alone in the cabin."

"Aw, shucks, son, why can't we *all* go anyway?"

"Because it wouldn't be safe. Three people trying to keep out of sight is too tough a proposition. For one it's not difficult. It's got to be that way, and I'm relying on you."

Old Timer grimaced and pulled out his pipe. Then he sighed.

"Okay — it's your party, I reckon. We'd better be gettin' back fer some dinner and see if Betty's come back. If she hasn't I'm fer goin' an' lookin' where she's gotten to."

"If I'd have had my way she'd never have gone on her own in any case," Brad said, jumping into the saddle and giving the prospector a lift up behind him. "But when a determined woman makes up her mind — well, that's one hard nut I can't crack, I'm afraid."

His trepidations were short-lived, however, for when they got back to the cabin they found that the girl had not only returned but had the dinner laid out on the living-room table — and with far more neatness than had ever been noticeable when the men had done the job.

"Bet!" Brad strode across to her the moment he came in at the doorway. He hugged her to him tightly. "Then you got back safely?"

"It's — obvious, isn't it? And stop *squeezing* me —!" she gasped. "I'm — smothering …"

He laughed, kissed her twice and then released her.

"What, no apology for kissing me?" she asked naively.

"None whatever. Only a threat — to do it again on the slightest provocation … Well, how did you get on? What did you find out?"

Brad threw his hat and gun-belt on one side and waited, but womanlike Betty kept him in suspense and finished off the preparations for the meal. Then, when the two men had washed and were seated at the table with her at the head of it helping out the food, she began to explain.

By the time she had finished Old Timer had to be thumped hard on the back to save him from choking as he tried to eat and laugh at the same time.

"I'll — I'll be dog-goned!" he gasped at last, tears running down his leathery cheeks. "I've seen jiggers use their shootin' irons and their fists on Lefty an' never git no place — then this slip of a kid blows a cigarette in his pan an' leaves him hogtied! I tell yuh, yuh can't never figure women."

"It was smart at that," Brad agreed, grinning. "Good job the wind didn't blow the tobacco dust back into your own eyes, Bet."

"It couldn't. I had my eyes shut. That was why I pretended to faint, to make it seem convincing …" The girl became serious. "Anyway, that's where Nariza lives and it completes my share of the business for the time being. Any time you want her you know where she is."

"And so does Black Joe," Brad muttered, thinking. "That's the part I don't like. If he once tumbles to the fact that she is the one who knows about the mine instead of me he'll make things mighty tough for her."

Betty shrugged indifferently. "She deserves it, doesn't she? I certainly shan't weep any tears."

"That's not the point. Eventually she'll be my prisoner. I'll have to find a way to search her place and get what evidence I can against her, then I'll have a legitimate reason for taking her into custody. That will keep her safe from Black Joe. There is no immediate hurry since he still thinks I'm the chief in the woodpile. Come to think of it, I don't think I'll bother to advise Drew City to keep a look out for Nariza. I can't see her going there at present as things are…"

Brad stopped and thought, then he changed the subject.

"There's some other business to attend to first before Nariza. Tonight I'm going to find out what I can about that diverted watercourse — from Hank Grimshaw, who used to be your uncle's ranch foreman. He's working for Joe now."

"Hank used to work for my uncle?" Betty looked surprised. "I didn't know. And by the way, he's the one who tried to fire at you in the Yellow Nugget last night."

"Yes, I know." Brad's voice was grim. "That's what is going to make it tough on him."

Anxiety crossed the girl's face. "Brad, please take care what you're doing! Hank's big, strong, powerful. And he's a crack shot. If you make any mistakes in baiting him you're liable to finish up in the obituary notices."

"I'll get by," Brad told her, smiling. "And I'm not such a poor shot myself. Remember Joe's hat? What's more to the point I understand judo — ju-jitsu. It's part of a marshal's routine. I'll get what I want — and I'll get it to-night. You'll be staying here with Old Timer."

"I'll be — what?" the girl asked slowly.

"And no arguments!" Brad added. "This time I'm determined on it. I've had my heart in my mouth all morning and I don't intend to get that way again."

"Well, maybe you're right," Betty sighed. "Especially after my giving Lefty Wilmore such a long walk home. He — or somebody anyway — will most certainly be watching for a chance to get at me after that, 'specially by night."

"Right," Brad agreed. "But they're not likely to come to the cabin itself. They'll know somebody will be on the watch. They could be picked off as they approached and be called trespassers. You'll be safe enough — just as I will. Black Joe won't attempt to finish me until he's convinced that I don't really know anything about that bonanza."

"That bein' all set there ain't no reason why we can't finish our dinners," Old Timer said. "An' then what happens this afternoon? I'd figgered on doin' some more pannin'."

"This afternoon," Brad said calmly, "you can do what you like, Old Timer. Betty and I are going for a little walk — no further than half a mile radius of the cabin. We're going to sit and talk. And we shan't talk about things that an old leatherneck like you will want to hear, either."

Old Timer winked a bright eye. "Don't yuh fergit it, son! A man's never too old fer that, I reckon."

The sun had set in a sea of amethyst and vermilion when Brad left the cabin by the creek that evening. He waved once to the girl and Old Timer as they stood on the porch to see him off — then he soon vanished in the fast-closing twilight.

He detoured on purpose, keeping his horse on a gentle trot until the magnificent blaze of hues in the western sky dimmed and the stars took command. Only then did he turn his sorrel's head and travel across the deserted expanses to the upflung blaze of white light which marked the presence of Thunder Bend.

Once he had reached it he jogged the horse along the backs of the wooden buildings until he came to the rear of the Yellow Nugget saloon. Dismounting, he tethered the horse to a two-by-four upright at the corner of the boardwalk and settled in the shadows to wait. From this position, sideways, he could see the batswings of the saloon, and he could certainly hear the cacophony coming from it.

Almost everybody in town and out of it was in there, as they usually were at this time of night, and this meant that only now and again did Brad have to remain still and silent as a man or woman passed along the boardwalks or the street close to the side alley where he was standing.

Then gradually there were signs that the night was ending for the saloon. More and more cowpunchers, saddle tramps, men and women, storekeepers and ranch owners came out into the fresh air — some plain cold sober, others roaring drunk, still others in a halfway state which inclined them to argument at the least word.

Brad waited, one hand on the butt of his .45. Black Joe's .45 was in the opposite holster in reserve. There was a wait of perhaps ten minutes and then Hank Grimshaw appeared. Being the sort of man he was — strong as a bull and a hard drinker to boot, it was difficult to tell whether he was drunk or not. He emerged through the batswings and sniffed the air, then he fished a cheroot from somewhere and stuck it in his mouth. The lighted match was half-way to it when he heard Brad's voice.

"Come down here, Hank, and make it quick! You're covered! And I said quick! No words or you'll get it neat."

The big fellow hesitated and the match dropped from his fingers. He ground it under his boot along with the cheroot, glanced back into the saloon, and then evidently decided that the command was not a joke. He stepped off the boardwalk and into the entry. Instantly the muzzle of the .45 bedded snugly in his ribs.

"Walk," Brad murmured.

Without a word Grimshaw did so. As he walked, Brad coming up behind him, Brad noticed how big the man was. All of six feet four, square-shouldered, with a neck like a pillar. Then presently Hank spoke, in a growling mutter.

"What in hell's th' idea o' this set-up, Morrison?"

"You'll find out — and right now. Turn around." Hank obeyed, then when he saw Brad had lowered the .45 his hand flew to his holster. It never got there. His wrist was seized, bent upwards and backwards until it was high between his shoulder-blades. It remained there, a merciless pressure nipping the nerve at the side of his hand. Sweat suddenly wetted his face and trickled from under the bandage round his forehead.

"Lay off me!" he panted. "What's it *fur*, anyway?"

"A little more pressure on this nerve, Hank, and you'll start to vomit," Brad murmured. "That's up to you. Either that or start talking. Why did you start work for Joe Rutter?"

"Why? Becos I had to have a job, of course."

"And he made it worth your while?"

"To do — wh-what?" Hank gasped sharply as the pain in his hand tweaked him for a moment.

"To keep your mouth shut about the Bending S ranch. There was a lot of good cattle there, Hank — and good grazing ground and watercourse. That all faded out for only one reason — because of Black Joe. I'm right, aren't I?"

"No," Hank said hastily — too hastily. "Joe didn't have nothin' t'do with it."

"The cattle were rustled down the valley to Joe's spread — he fixed that neat and tidy, and you and most of Mascrof's boys helped in it. Those who didn' just — disappeared, didn't they? Then the watercourse was diverted to Joe's place. He'd already got water but he could do with more — same as every rancher around here. So he fixed it."

"He didn't! He For God's sake!" Hank writhed and caught his breath at the searing pain in his hand and arm.

"I can get it a lot tighter yet," Brad said implacably. "He *did*, didn't he? You know he did!"

"I — I — Let up, can't yuh? Yore killing me —" Hank actually screamed for a moment as Brad exerted full pressure. It made the sweat roll down the ex-foreman's face in great beads.

"Well?" Brad murmured, relaxing again.

"Yes — yes, he did," Hank gasped chokingly. "But yuh can't blame me fer that! You can't blame me fer takin' a good job an' keepin' me mouth shut!" Suddenly Brad released him and whipped up his gun instead.

"That's all I wanted to know, Hank. You're coming with me to the Sheriff and sign a statement." Hank half turned to obey — then suddenly blind fury exploded. He whirled round with cyclonic violence, slamming up his left with terrific force. It impacted on Brad's jaw and sent him tottering backwards. He had no time to aim his gun and even less time to fire it. As he fell it was wrenched from him.

He realized that in that split second he was in danger of his life. Sprawling, his hand flew to his second gun. He whipped it up and fired. It missed Hank, but at least it deflected his own aim so that the bullet tore up dust not two inches from Brad's ear — then Brad was on his feet again, seizing the big fellow round the waist and thrusting the flat of his palm under the square, whiskery jaw.

This sort of fighting was new to the cowhand. He whirled up his left fist, intending to beat it down with crashing force on the back of Brad's neck, but it never reached there. Instead, something that felt like a knife bit deep into his spine and paralysed his efforts. There was an abominable pain at the root of his skull. He was too dumb to recognize a judo hold otherwise he would have made no attempt to escape from it. His effort sent him flying over Brad's head to crash on his face in the dust.

"Finished playin' games?" inquired a laconic voice, and Brad's hand flashed to his holster.

Chapter IX

"Take it easy, Morrison," Joe Rutter warned. "There's three guns aimed at you — Okay Hank — get up, y' big lug."

Brad breathed hard. He had been so intent on his task he had never noticed that Black Joe and his gun hawks had come up silently out of the darkness. Now he could see the starlight glinting on their revolver barrels.

"What's th' idea, Morrison?" Joe asked grimly, and the red end of a cheroot glowed for a moment as he spoke. "I should ha' thought that after last night yuh'd have more sense 'n come back into town hollerin fer trouble. What d'you want with Hank? We heard your gunplay an' came to take a look."

"He made me tell him about that watercourse yuh switched, boss — an' about the cattle yuh took," Hank panted, getting to his feet.

"Yuh don't have to say it so loud, yuh durned fool!" Black Joe snapped at him; then turning to Brad again, "So that was it, huh? Started rootin' around again, have yuh? Why? What's th' idea of makin' yuhsef so plumb busy in this town?"

Brad didn't reply. He compressed his lips as he found his remaining gun was taken from him. He saw Joe contemplate it in the gloom and then slip it in his belt.

"Thanks. I'm sorta glad to get this bit o' hardware back … An' it seems it's about time you and me straightened a few things out, Morrison. There could only be one reason for yuh nosin' around the Bending S, and that reason's Betty Tarrant, who you took from me last night. Then there's the matter of that bearin' up you handed me — *and* some unfinished business about a gold mine. I'd figgered on gettin' you alone on the trail some night — unless you was smart enough to blow town. Since you're right here I reckon we might as well get down to cases."

Still Brad did not speak. Anything he might say, in fact, would perhaps only make matters worse. Shorn of his guns and surrounded by four enemies, there was no point in making any comment.

"Get the horses," Joe ordered, and Hank went off to do so. There was silence under the stars until he returned, astride his own horse and leading four others.

"Get on your horse, Morrison," Joe instructed, and Brad obeyed. Then his hands were lashed securely to the saddle horn. When the others had climbed into their saddles Brad found his horse jolted forward.

Gradually the party went by way of the backs of the town buildings to the trail which led to the creek. Half-way there Joe called a halt and dismounted. Brad was released from the saddle horn and his hands were fastened behind him instead.

"Now, my obstinate friend …"

Black Joe's feet were a little apart as he lighted a fresh cheroot and for a moment the flicker of the match illuminated his grim, square face.

"Y'seem to be pretty good at diggin' secrets out of a guy," he went on, "so mebby it's about time I tried it myself. I want to know the location of that bonanza — and I reckon there's only you who *does* know it. In case you ain't aware of it, that Aztec girl Nariza lifted another lot o' gold from that cabin of Old Timer's last night. But she didn't get away with it. *I've* got that gold now, an' I'm stickin' to it. Now I want the rest of it… Seems I had you figgered all wrong, Morrison. I thought the Aztec girl was with you in this. I reckon she couldn't be when she starts stealin' from yuh."

Brad said no word, mentally weighing the situation up.

"Blast yuh obstinate hide, I'm talkin' to yuh!" Joe roared, slapping him hard across the face so that he couldn't help but stagger. "Where's that mine, Morrison? And I ain't kiddin', believe me! I've plenty to catch up on as far as yore concerned."

Brad straightened up again.

"You're wasting your time, Joe," he said quietly. "I don't talk easy."

"Yuh don't, huh? Hank, you've reason to feel sore How's about limberin' this jigger up a bit?"

"Yeah, suits me fine," Hank agreed, and since he didn't understand the art of judo and the excruciating torture it could produce he used more straightforward methods and slammed his massive fist into Brad's face.

He fell flat and lay there, unable to shift because of his bound hands. He said nothing, but there was a murderous glint in his eyes if Hank could only have seen it.

Then the massive cowhand hauled Brad up again. He was all set to land another blow when Joe snatched his arm back.

"Stop playin' around with yuh mits, you big ape! That won't get us any place. There's a better way. This time you'll talk, Morrison Yes, you'll talk, an' fast."

Joe blew the end of his cheroot into a brightly glowing circle.

*

There was an intense quietness about the cabin by the creek. The windows of the living room were open and the oil lamp was extinguished. Beside each window, gazing out into the peaceful stillness of the Arizona night, Old Timer and Betty Tarrant sat two yards apart, each of them with a gun handy for untoward happenings.

But there was nothing, save the occasional distant roar of a mountain lion, or the hoot of an owl, and sometimes a sudden unexplained squirming and scratching in a not far distant manzanita thicket.

"Bet, I don't like it," Old Timer said finally, scratching his chin. "It's ways past midnight, an' I reckon th' Yeller Nugget must ha' closed long ago. It shouldn't take Brad all this time t' git back. I'm a-tellin' yuh, the whole thing's plumb wrong. He shoulda lit me go with him — an' you too. All we've done is sit around here like a coupla mules an' wait fer sump'n t' happen, which doesn't."

There was a slight movement from Betty as she put her revolver in the holster, strapped the belt about her waist, and got to her feet.

"I'm going to look for him," she announced briefly.

"Thit's more like it," Old Timer said, pushing back his chair. "An' I'm a-comin' with yuh."

He closed the window, took down his coonskin hat from the door, and then followed the girl outside on to the porch. The moon was rising now, filling the endless expanse of desert and prairie with an uncertain, pallid glow. Quickly, worriedly indeed, Betty hurried round to the small stable to saddle the gelding, then she came back with it to where Old Timer was waiting for her. He swung into the saddle behind her, clung to her slim waist as she spurred the horse to the trail leading to Thunder Bend.

"If anything's happened to Brad, Old Timer, I'm going gunning for Black Joe," Betty said presently, and her voice showed she meant every word she said. "There wouldn't be anybody else but Joe responsible for Brad getting into a whole heap of trouble — and Brad's come to mean a mighty lot to me."

"So I noticed," Old Timer murmured. "Can't say I blame either of yuh, neither. Only thing I'm sorta regrettin' is that I'm old enough to be yuh grandpappy. I reckon I always seem t' miss th' best things outa life."

His suddenly reminiscent mood had no interest for Betty. She was looking about her in sharp anxiety, helped by the strengthening light of the moon. Not only was she looking for Brad: she had the fear that somewhere in this tranquillity Black Joe or one of his gun hawks might be waiting, intent on seizing her on fulfilling the plan in which Lefty Wilmore had so blatantly failed.

As it happened, it was Old Timer who saw something first. His hawk eyes were watching over the girl's shoulder. Pushing a sudden flurrying of her blonde hair out of his eyes, he pointed ahead of them.

"What d'yuh reckon to thit there, Bet? Side o' the trail yonder. Might be an animal, but I reckon it's too big."

Betty saw the object at almost the same moment and spurred the horse into a sudden final burst of speed. Then she drew rein in a cloud of dust and slid from the saddle, hurried across the stubbly grass and hauled up the head and shoulders of Brad in her arms.

"It's — it's Brad," she gasped, horrified, as Old Timer came over to her. "There's — blood on his face and — blisters or something"

"Yeah." Old Timer's voice was bitter with fury. He caught at Brad's wrist and held it for a moment, then he released it again. " Ain't dead, anyway," he said in relief. "But he's sure taken a beatin' from th' looks of him. We'd best git him back to th' cabin."

It took their united strength to haul Brad's weight to the horse and heave him on to it. Then the girl looked at the prospector in the moonlight.

"You ride, Old Timer. I'm young enough to walk. The gelding can't take the three of us."

He nodded, got into the saddle and, supporting Brad at the same time, set the horse going at a jog-trot, the girl keeping up alongside. It seemed to her to take an interminable time before they finally reached the cabin, then again came the struggle with Brad's dead weight as they hauled him into the room the girl had been using and laid him on the bed.

Old Timer turned quickly and lighted the oil lamp.

"I'll stable th' horse," he said, and hurried out.

The girl said nothing. For a second or two she stared in horror at the blood-streaked cuts and burns on Brad's face, then setting her mouth she hurried into the living-room for water, searched round until she found an old, clean neckerchief and tore it into strips. Thus equipped, she came back and when Old Timer came in again, she was busily removing the traces of damage from Brad's face.

"Only one person back o' this, I reckon," he said, frowning at the injuries.

"Yes." The girl's face was pale with anger.

"Black Joe! He must — He moved!" she broke off suddenly. "He's coming to!" She caught Brad's arm and shook it gently. "Brad, wake up. It's Betty! Wake up ..."

Brad opened his eyes lazily and stared at her in the lamplight. A frown crossed his face and he winced painfully.

"Get some water," the girl ordered, and Old Timer went and brought back a drink. Raising Brad's head, Betty gave it to him. It seemed to revive him and he gave a cracked grin.

"Don't look much like a marshal trying to take a criminal in charge, do I?" he sighed.

Relief swept Betty's face at hearing him speak so rationally.

"Who did this, son?" Old Timer snapped, his voice brittle. "I'll bet it were thit stinkin' son of a polecat, Black Joe."

"Sure it was," Brad assented grimly. "Don't you recognize his handiwork?" With an effort he tried to sit up, then sank back again, wincing. "Guess I got kicked around more than I thought," he muttered. "Give me a cigarette, one of you."

Old Timer gave him one, lighted it for him. Brad inhaled deeply.

"Yes, it was Joe," he said. "I'd just managed to get the truth about your ranch out of Hank, Betty, but we had a spot of gunplay which Joe and his boys overheard when they were leaving the Nugget. They took me out on the trail and tried to make me tell 'em where the gold mine is. Naturally, I couldn't, because I don't know. They tried everything, from fists to the hot end of a cheroot. Finally, Lefty took a straight shot at me. I'm sure he thought he'd got me — but he hadn't. He was a bit to one side and the moon wasn't up. Then they left me. I suppose they think I'm bush-whacked, and not likely to give them any more trouble. They probably think that if my body is found there'll be nobody to prove who did it, anyway."

"I'll go an' hot up some coffee," Old Timer said, and muttering dire threats under his breath, he left the room.

The girl settled on the edge of the bed, her blue eyes fixed on Brad in the lamplight. He grinned again and patted her hand.

"Thanks a lot, Bet," he said gently. "You and Old Timer between you, that is. If you hadn't have found me I mightn't have lasted out until morning. Exposure doesn't improve your complexion much."

"You're sure you'll be all right now?" she asked, anxiously.

"Of course I will! I don't break easy."

She nodded her blonde head and went to work with the strips of bandage, tying them round his forehead where the burns from Joe's cheroot stub were the most noticeable. As she finished tying the knot at the back of his head, Brad reached up and caught her arms gently, drew her face down and kissed her.

"That makes me feel loads better," he murmured.

She smiled, kissed him again of her own accord, and then contemplated him seriously.

"And what happens now?" she asked, her voice grim.

"Well, it's pretty clear that Joe doesn't think Nariza has anything to do with the gold mine because he believes she stole from me. I didn't tell Joe that she was merely recovering stuff I had taken from the baggage depot … I just don't know what Joe will do next. Obviously he must know now where Nariza lives, because Lefty will have told him all about it. As far as I can see, he's hamstrung for the moment, and unless I have him figured all wrong, he'll lay low to see what happens if my body is found. Ten to one he's sure I'm dead. I should think his next move will be to try and get at you."

"Just let him try!" Betty breathed, her eyes flaming. "After what's he's done to you, I'll willingly put a forty-five right through him!"

"He won't try it by day — too risky, but he might later on to-night or to-morrow night. If he does, we'll be ready for him."

Old Timer came in with steaming coffee for all of them and handed it round. Then Brad went on talking between sips.

"The moment I'm fit enough to get around again — which should only be a matter of hours with my constitution — I'm going to put the facts before the Sheriff First, concerning the trickery with your ranch, Bet — about which I now have every fact — and second, this beating-up I've had.

That's quite enough to pin Joe in jail, and with him nailed down, the rest of his boys will soon talk, especially those who used to work for your uncle. With their boss behind bars, they'll talk fast if only to save their own skins. That only leaves Nariza, and she certainly is one large-sized problem."

"Why?" Old Timer asked, pulling out his pipe. "She's back of this whole gold racket. Now y'know where she is what's a-stoppin' yuh goin' an' gittin' her?"

"The old trouble — lack of proof. That gold was the only proof I had, but now it's changed hands and Joe's got it, I've lost my evidence. For me to just talk and not produce any gold to back it up would be a waste of time, particularly as I've no proof either as to how *Joe* got it. On the other hand, Nariza realizes that I know what she's up to so I don't think she'll touch any more gold until she knows the coast is clear. The way it looks now," Brad muttered, reflecting, "Nariza is free as the air, and until I have the proof I need she'll remain that way."

There was silence for a while and then Betty gave a little sigh.

"Well, I should think that for one night we can let things stay as they are. You try and get some sleep, Brad, after Old Timer's helped you to undress. He and I will prop up in chairs in the living-room … Old Timer," Betty went on, turning to him, "you take the first watch in case anybody tries anything: wake me up when you've had enough and I'll watch while you sleep. By the time morning comes we'll probably have thought of some new angle."

*

Morning came, in a blaze of liquid gold and crimson, following a night in which nothing untoward had occurred. Old Timer and Betty, not much refreshed after uncomfortable slumber, stirred into the wakefulness of the day. The girl's first thought, while Old Timer prepared for breakfast — was for Brad. He had slept and looked better, but stiffness had him in its grip and pounded limbs almost refused to move.

"Which means you're going to have your breakfast in bed here," Betty decided firmly. "I'll shave and wash you. By that time everything should be ready."

She went out again, got the hot water and razor, and did her best to act as barber. Then by the time she had freshened herself up and combed her thick blonde hair Old Timer had the breakfast ready. Though he grumbled at being treated like a baby Brad was secretly glad of the chance to get his digestion working before he tried moving.

He spent most of the morning getting out of bed by degrees. By noon, thanks to the alternate help of Old Timer and the girl, he had succeeded far enough to sit at the table for dinner … They were in the midst of it when a sudden rushing of horse's feet started Old Timer and the girl up quickly from their chairs. Brad tried also, winced, hesitated, and sat down again. Silently Betty sneaked to the door and opened it ever so slightly. Then she relaxed with a laugh and threw the door wide. Outside, pawing the pebbled pathway, was Brad's sorrel, riderless, the saddle still in position.

"Well, that's a help anyway," he grinned. "I wondered what Joe had done with him. Must have taken him to add to his own stock and he escaped. Better fix him up, Bet."

She nodded, put the gun back in its holster, and caught the horse's reins. After she had fed, watered, and stabled him she came back into the cabin to finish her meal — then again she turned to her self-imposed task of helping Brad.

All afternoon she persisted with him, holding his elbow as he went in and out of the cabin in the bright sunlight, walking as far as the creek, slowly easing himself back into trim and working strained and battered ligatures into their proper position. By the time the evening meal had come round he was infinitely better, and by twilight almost his normal self.

In the setting sun, the warm breeze blowing around them from the mesa, they all three sat on the cabin porch, gazing at the towering grey of the mountains with the sunset behind them, and the bubbling of the creek near to hand.

"Y'know somethin'," Old Timer said, knocking the ashes out of his pipe, "I'm durned near passin' out."

Brad glanced at him in surprise. "But why? What's wrong? As far as I can see you've eaten plenty."

"Yeah, mebby — but eatin' ain't the be-all an' end-all of a man's existence!" Old Timer licked his lips. "Believe it or not, if I don't git a drink soon I'll go put a slug through me head. I haven't had one fer two nights now. First night there wus thit gunplay; last night I was stuck here. If I don't git one to-night I'll …"

He took out his gun and contemplated it seriously.

Betty threw back her head and laughed silently. Brad grinned widely through his bandages and Old Timer looked up with dark suspicion.

"All right fer you two to laugh, I reckon. Fer me it's a pretty serious business. I ain't missed a drink any night fer fifteen year!"

"Then go and get one," Brad told him, shrugging. "What's stopping you?"

Old Timer holstered the gun, strapped the belt about his waist and then got up quickly.

"Y'mean thit, son?"

"Sure I mean it. Only I should think that you'd have more sense than go to the Yellow Nugget. Black Joe won't exactly be waiting to kiss you. He knows you're on our side and partly responsible for our safety. *And* he knows you took a pot-shot at Hank Grimshaw."

Old Timer grinned. "That ain't worryin' me. Th' Nugget's the only place where I can git a drink, an' I've got to have one. Y'don't have t' worry. I can look after meself."

"I guess you can at that," Brad admitted, seeing it was useless to argue. "We'll stay here. In fact I've got to. But the minute you've had your drink come back here and bring the bottle with you. You're taking too big a risk for my liking."

Old Timer grinned and hurried round the back of the cabin for his horse. In a few minutes he reappeared in the saddle, waved his hand, and then cantered off into the gathering twilight amidst a cloud of dust.

The fact that he might be going straight into danger did not seem to have occurred to him — or if it had he felt able to deal with it and therefore was unconcerned. It was a drink he wanted, and old habits die hard.

Chapter X

When Old Timer arrived at the Yellow Nugget it was crowded as usual with men and women. He entered with his shambling walk, coonskin hat on the back of his head, and went across to the bar. Jeff Willard who had been watching his approach gave him a blank look, licked his lips, and then gave him the gin he had ordered.

"Yuh gone loco, Old Timer?" he asked in a hoarse whisper, polishing the counter and looking away as he spoke.

Old Timer swallowed the drink and grinned with his two teeth.

"I reckon I would've but fer this. This ain't no country fer a man to go without his drink … Same again."

Jeff Willard shrugged and took the empty glass. Then he gave a start. A little farther along the counter Joe Rutter was standing smoking a cheroot, his hat pushed on to the back of his head, his eyes fixed on the old prospector.

"Some time since I saw you around here, Old Timer," Joe commented at length.

"I wouldn't be here now, I reckon, 'cept that it's th' only place I c'n oil me throat."

"Sure, sure," Joe agreed calmly. "I don't want t' turn away custom, so don't get me wrong. Have a drink on the house while yuh at it." Joe snapped his fingers at Jeff Willard. "Fix him up with all he wants, Jeff. Sky's th' limit."

Old Timer's keen eyes opened a little wider.

"Y'mean I c'n drink all I want?"

"That," Joe answered, nodding, "is just what I mean And bring it over to our table," Joe added to the barkeep, then he took the old prospector's arm and led him across to a quiet comer.

At the other side of the saloon, lounging near the empty platform — for evidently a substitute for Betty Tarrant had not yet been found — Lefty Wilmore and Rod Jenkins smoked cigarettes lazily and watched. They exchanged glances, and then exchanged them again.

"I don't git the angle on this," Old Timer said presently, when Jeff Willard had brought his gin and beer for Joe. "I sorta thought yuh'd want t' use me as a floor-mop for pokin' my nose in here — if yuh know what I mean?"

Joe grinned amiably. "You mean firin' at Hank Grimshaw the other night?"

"Yeah. I thought y' might be sore at me fer it."

"Forget it," Joe said, shrugging. "Hank's a hothead — an' anyway yuh saved him from committing murder, didn't yuh? Why should I be sore over a thing like that? Now get your drink down and don't worry."

Old Timer swallowed the drink swiftly and mused.

Then he pulled out his pipe and lighted it. Joe considered him in abysmal calm for a moment.

"Have another drink?" he suggested.

"We-ll, I sorta reckon I —"

"On the house, Old Timer. Yore not goin' t' refuse a drink, surely? Another, Jeff!" Joe called. "Make it a double."

Old Timer pushed back his coonskin cap and rubbed his forehead. Though he looked befuddled his bright little eyes gave the lie to it.

"Y'know," Joe said pensively, "I've come around to thinkin' that Betty Tarrant did th' right thing in leaving me — even though I admit I was sore at the time. This isn't no place ter a girl like her. She's got class every time. She'll do better on her own, I reckon."

Old Timer put his pipe down on the table. "Yuh can bet she will! An' since we're on th' subject what about that beatin' up y' gave Brad Morrison?"

Joe drained his glass and set it down. Jeff arrived with a double gin and set it before the prospector.

"Yeah, I heard about that." Joe shook his head. "Pretty bad, I guess. But yuh don't think *I* did it, do yuh? Hank Grimshaw got outa hand after the grief he'd taken from Morrison — so Hank beat him up. Only natural, I guess. He burned him with a cigarette end an' then shot him. I did hear that he'd killed him only I haven't heard yet what happened to th' body."

Old Timer took a long draught from the glass, set it down, and picked up his pipe. He squinted at it pensively and finally put it in his pocket. Joe's only sign of irritation was in the way he crossed his legs.

"Well, he ain't dead — see?" Old Timer banged his fist on the table. "You an' yer boys ain't kiddin' me a bit, Mr. Black — hup! — Joe. Brad

Morrison's as alive as I am at this moment. In fact *more* alive, I reckon. These ol' bones of mine are durned near rattlin' apart."

Joe considered his cheroot pensively.

"So he's alive, is he? Well, that's good hearin'. I thought Hank had killed him"

"Sure it weren't Lefty? That's what Brad himself said."

"I said *Hank!*" Joe's voice was measured. "I've been tryin' to figger a way t' keep him out of a murder rap but now I reckon it won't be necessary. I don't like murder, Old Timer: it gets yuh in bad."

Old Timer finished his drink and held on to the table edge as though to steady himself in his chair.

"Yuh not foolin' me a bit, Joe," he insisted, wagging a finger in front of his wizened face.

"I'm not tryin' to," Joe shrugged. "Where's Brad now, then? Lookin' after Betty?"

"Yuh can — hup! — bet on it! So's yuh'll never git near her."

Joe chewed his cheroot and a hardness shaded his dark eyes. Old Timer flopped back in his chair and fanned himself lazily.

"There's a lot o' things yuh don't know, Joe," he said at length, giving a laugh with a hiccup in it. "'Bout Brad, an' Nariza, an' gold."

"One thing I *do* know," Joe said deliberately, leaning across the table. "Brad Morrison knows where there's a bonanza."

"So *you* think! Thit's why yuh beat him up an' left him fer dead last night, I reckon. Y'don't think I'm so plumb loco that I — hup! — can't see it, do yuh?" Old Timer half closed his eyes. "But yer wrong, feller — quite wrong. Brad Morrison don't know a thing about a gold mine, an' never did. It's thit gurl Nariza who has that secret — an' Brad's as anxious to find it as you are, I reckon."

Joe waited, eyes narrowed, the cheroot smoke hazing his big, square face.

"Keep right on talkin'," he murmured.

Old Timer wagged a finger again. "That gold Nariza stole from my cabin. It wus her *own* gold, see? Brad Morrison took it from the baggage depot where she'd put it, an' she took it back again. Then I reckon one of your boys took it from her, which sorta complicated things … She knows where there's gold all right," Old Timer went on, nodding blearily. "In tryin' to be smart yuh got hold o' the wrong one. Brad couldn't tell yuh nothin' becos he — hup! — don't *know* nothin'! See?"

Joe put his cheroot in the ashtray and crushed it out. "So that's the set-up, is it? What's Brad doing now, then? Tryin' to make Nariza tell him where the gold is?"

"I reckon not. He ain't doin' nothin' until he's got proof. That's his trouble."

"Proof?" Joe frowned and gave a start. "Proof of *what?* What are yer gettin' at?'"

"Proof thit Nariza's shippin' gold outa Thunder Bend. He's got to have it, so he says, afore he c'n arrest her. Thit's one thing yuh didn't know, huh?"

"I know it now," Joe said slowly. "And that means that Brad Morrison must be a —"

He stopped and got to his feet. Leaning over the table he seized the old prospector by the coat collar and whirled him to his feet.

"What's the big idea?" Old Timer demanded, struggling feebly as he cast a squinting look around him. "What yuh figgerin' on doin'?"

"Kickin' you outa my saloon, yuh drunken old has-been — like this!"

There were grins from the men and women at the tables as Old Timer was whirled through the saloon, through the batswings, and then down the steps into the dust.

For a moment or two he lay there and then got to his feet. He dusted his pants and coat, set his hat straight, then with a cracked grin headed for his horse and clambered to the saddle.

"Had t' make it look good, I reckon," he muttered. "Yuh'd think after me drinkin' fer fifteen year every night thit Joe'd know I can take twenty times as much as he give me an' not even feel the stuff. Git on with yuh," he told the horse, and spurred it forward … In fifteen minutes he had arrived back at the cabin and quickly entered the living-room. Brad and the girl were seated at the table, the oil lamp between them and beside it the girl's gun. They had obviously been playing cards.

"Get your drink?" Brad inquired.

"I did more'n that, son. I got meself tight — or leastways Black Joe thought I was. I never got tight in all me life, believe it or not. Don't seem t' be thit way constructed, I reckon … Anyway, I — I started sump'n. Yes, sir."

Brad's expression changed and Betty exchanged a look with him.

"What are you talking about?" Brad snapped.

Old Timer looked uncomfortable as he came into the range of the oil lamp.

"Well, I s'pose yuh c'n think on this how you like, son — but I figgered that since yore sort a hog-tied about Nariza an' waitin' fer somethin' t' happen, it mightn't be such a bad idea if I *made* it happen."

"So?" Brad asked, in ominous calm.

"So I let Joe know that *she's* the only one who knows anythin' about thit bonanza."

"You did *what?*" Betty gasped, jumping up.

"Carry on," Brad ordered, tightening his lips.

Old Timer went quickly through the details and then finished, "Since he knows now where Nariza is he'll go an' try and git th' truth outa her. Thit's the only natural thing to expect, I reckon. Yuh say yuh want the proof of what she's a-doin'? Wil, yuh'll git it if yore at hand while she admits th' truth about it. Black Joe won't spare her none: he'll do th' work for yuh. Once yuh've got them facts yuh can arrest her — an' him too fer ditchin' the Bendin' S ranch."

Brad reflected and looked troubled.

"I can see how you worked it out, Old Timer — but I'm not sure whether you've worked it out right. Anyway," he shrugged, "the thing's done now and we've got to get out to Nariza's place and keep on the watch. Joe will act right away, I expect. You'd better come with me in case he tries anything here — and I mean both of you, of course. Though I shouldn't be surprised if, now he knows I'm alive and a marshal — which he's obviously guessed — he doesn't hold his hand against me. Things are getting mighty warm for him and he must surely be aware of it without tangling himself up with a possible murder of a marshal."

"Are you sure you're fit to ride, Brad?" Betty asked him anxiously.

"I'm going to, anyway. Better saddle my sorrel while I get these confounded bandages off my face."

*

Old Timer's assumptions concerning Joe's reactions were quite correct. The moment he had thrown the old prospector out of the saloon Joe hurried across to his two gun hawks at the other side of the big room.

"We're on to something, boys," he told them briefly. "That Aztec dame Nariza's th' one we want, not Brad Morrison. I just got it outa that old gin-sponge … An' perhaps it's just as well that slug of yours didn't strike home last night, Lefty."

Lefty gave a start. "Yuh mean I missed?"

"Yeah — missed a U.S. marshal! If you'd have gotten him a whole heap o' trouble would ha' been down on top of us — not that it won't be even now mebby — but we're goin' t' risk it. Come on!" Joe jerked his head. "We've got a date with that Aztec dame. You know the way, Lefty."

The two gun hawks followed Joe across the saloon and through the batswing doors. They were mounted in their saddles before Lefty asked a question.

"What happens, boss, if that old fool tells Brad Morrison — as he probably will — what he told you?"

"I'm riskin' that."

"An' it's a big risk," Lefty objected. "Fer one thing, Morrison's not dead — fer another he's a marshal, an' I reckon he's gotten his horse back by now. It escaped from the corral, remember."

Joe swung on him. "Will you shut up? There's no time t' be lost arguin' about what *might* be! We've got to get some action — an' quick! Come on!"

He whipped his horse into action savagely, and because he knew the way Lefty took the lead. They took care to approach the narrow canyon which led to Nariza's bungalow at the farthest point from Old Timer's cabin. The fact that there were no lights showing in the cabin made Lefty frown.

"I don't like it, boss," he said. "If there's some trick in all this an' Brad Morrison's ahead waitin' fer us anythin' c'n happen."

"Stop bellyachin' an' keep goin'," Joe told him.

Lefty said no more and guided the horse up the narrow, rutted, starlit trail at the base of the mountain. Behind him came Joe and then Rod Jenkins. Though each one of them was on the lookout for trouble, none came, and finally they reached the huge inverted U of rock which gave entrance on to the cup in the mountains. In the starlight glow, the shack was visible, but there were no lights in the windows.

"Gettin' some shut-eye, mebby," Lefty hazarded, dismounting.

"Then we'll soon wake her up." Joe alighted and yanked his .45 from its holster. "An' leave th' talkin' to me," he added.

"D'yuh think," Lefty asked, "there might be some use fer this, boss?"

From the saddle pommel he took the vicious stockwhip which he used when working on the ranch.

"Could be," Joe admitted. "Fetch it. Now let's go."

He set the example by scrambling down the rough rock which formed the wall of the mountain cup. It was only about fifty feet to the crater floor and once he had reached it, with Lefty and Rod close behind him, Joe crept forward until the three of them had gained the shack's screen door.

Joe hesitated for a moment, then he smashed the wirework with the butt of his gun, reached inside and unlocked the door. The lock of the second door he shot away with one resounding explosion and then hurried into the darkness. He had reached the shadowy living-room when a figure loomed transiently in a doorway.

"Stay right where you are!" he ordered. "If you move I'll let yuh have it — Light the lamp, Lefty."

The figure remained motionless. Lefty moved and there was the scrape and flicker of a match. Then the kerosene lamp kindled and cast a yellow brilliance over the proceedings. The figure in the adjoining doorway — the bedroom evidently — was revealed as Nariza, her dark hair flowing, a glint of both anger and fear in her oblique eyes.

"Sorry t' burst in on yuh like this," Joe said dryly, going over to her, "but I had to act fast afore you cottoned on to the idea. I want a word with yuh … Step forward!"

He waved his gun menacingly, and the girl advanced into the centre of the room, a silk robe sashed tightly about her slender waist. Below it showed the legs of pyjamas.

"You've got your nerve breaking into my place like this." She clenched her fists and glared. "How did you ever manage to find it, anyway?"

"That's beside th' point," Joe told her. "I've just discovered that yuh know where there's a bonanza, an' that means you're goin' to tell me all about it."

The girl folded her arms and regarded him acidly.

"I always knew you were a fool, Joe Rutter — a big, windy fool, too. This is absolute proof of it. You don't think I'd be such an idiot as to tell you anything, do you?"

"Up to you," Joe shrugged. "It'd be better fer your health, I reckon. I may have t' use persuasion otherwise."

Nariza looked about her.

"Three powerful men, all armed — and one woman, unarmed. I'll bet you feel sure of yourselves!"

"This is a matter o' business,' Joe snapped, an ugly look crossing his face. "Quit stallin', Nariza, and come out with what I wanta know."

"Not on your —"

Nariza broke off with a gasp as Rod Jenkins suddenly moved forward, took her wrists and forced them behind her. With a thin length of cord he had taken from his pocket, he secured the girl's hands immovably — then he gave her a shove so that she stumbled to one of the upright wooden pillars supporting the beamed roof.

This time it was Lefty who acted. Snatching the cord from the window curtains, he wound it twice round the Aztec girl's body and then knotted it behind the pillar. She waited, her dark eyes smouldering.

"Well," Joe asked, sitting on the edge of the table and regarding her, "where is it?"

Nariza made no answer. Her large mouth set in a firm, obstinate line. Joe shrugged and glanced at Lefty. The gun hawk held out the stockwhip so that the short, vicious tail hung down menacingly.

"I'm not anxious t' beat it outa you, Nariza," Joe said, "but if I have to I will — or Lefty will."

"I'm not stopping you," the Aztec girl answered coldly.

Lefty saw the nod he received and grinned. He whirled the stockwhip round and over his head. Had the tail struck home, it would certainly have slashed the girl right across the face — but instead, there was the explosion of a revolver from the living-room window, and Lefty swung with numbed fingers as the stockwhip was blown right out of his hand.

Instantly four faces jerked to the window. Brad's head and shoulders were there, his gun — or rather Old Timer's — cocked.

"Put your hardware on the table, boys," he instructed briefly; then while the order was obeyed, he clambered through the window frame and came slowly into the centre of the room.

Behind him, Old Timer and Betty moved silently. Joe still sat on the edge of the table, fury tightening his jaw.

"Y'know somethin', Morrison," he said finally. "Yuh've got the most unpleasant habit of upsettin' my arrangements every time I get things fixed … an' I don't like it."

"You're not supposed to," Brad told him curtly. "And you disappoint me, Joe. I thought you limited yourself to beating up bound men and then shooting them. When it comes to trying to thrash a defenceless woman tied to a post, it's time you were locked up behind bars."

Brad motioned with his free hand, and Betty, interpreting the move, unfastened the cords with which the Aztec girl was bound. She looked at Betty with smouldering eyes, nodded a slow thanks, then looked again at Brad.

"These men —" she started to say, but Brad interrupted her.

"I know what they did, Nariza — and what they said. I was watching and listening right from the start, outside the window. They came here with only one object — to find out about that gold mine of yours. I'm here for the same reason, but if you won't tell me about it, you needn't fear that I'll beat it out of you." Brad looked at the three men with his cold eyes. "As for you three, there are certain things the Sheriff might like to know concerning you, and the Bending S Ranch is one of those things —"

Like a sudden whirlwind Joe acted. He dived a hand backwards at the guns on the table and at the same time thrust out both his heavy booted feet in front of him. They took Brad in the stomach and doubled him up. Then Joe had a gun in his hand — and lost it again as Old Timer snatched Brad's gun and fired.

But, in the split-second interval, Lefty and Rod had also seized their guns and there was an abrupt exchange of fire across the room. Old Timer, wary as ever, took one dive and used the back of an easy chair for protection. The bullets aimed at him buried themselves in the dense upholstery.

Brad straightened with an effort, but a straight left hit him on the chin and he reeled backwards into the empty fireplace. Betty whipped up her own gun and jumped forward to help him. It was an action which probably saved her life for a bullet whanged into the wall where her head had been.

"Hold it — hold it!" Joe snapped. "I'm takin' no chances on killin' a marshal — not with all these witnesses. And yuh certainly not takin' me to any sheriff, Morrison! Neither now nor at any other time. If you want me, come an' get me But I'm warnin' you. If y' step on my property to get me, I'll invoke the law of trespass an' shoot yuh — or have yuh shot — on sight!"

Brad remained where he had fallen in the fireplace. Betty stayed crouched beside him, and Old Timer behind the easy chair knew better than to fire now with three guns trained on him.

"All right, you —" Joe waved a hand at Nariza.

"Yore comin' with us."

She shook her head stubbornly. "I'm not going anywhere with you, Joe, and you'll never make me!"

"Get her, Lefty," Joe ordered.

"Not me, boss. It's goin' to distract our attention to grab a strugglin' woman, an' I'm not goin' t'risk a slug in me belly."

"Why, yuh yeller" Joe stopped himself and scowled. Then he nodded grimly. "Mebby yore right," he admitted. "Well, there are more nights than tonight, I reckon."

He motioned with his head, and the three of them backed out of the room. Within a few seconds there was the sound of their feet hurrying through the loose gravel outside.

Chapter XI

"Wil," Old Timer commented, emerging from behind the easy chair and holstering his gun, "I reckon yuh've lost them coyotes, son."

"Only for the moment," Brad told him. He helped Betty to her feet, and she handed her gun to him. "I don't think Joe will skip town," he went on. "He's too many interests here. In any case, I'll attend to him later. Right now, Nariza, I'm going to attend to you."

"At least," she said slowly, considering him, "I owe you my thanks for saving me."

"I only saved you so that I can question you, so don't start getting any ideas. You can either answer my questions here, or you can answer them before the authorities in Drew City. It concerns the gold you've been sending to J. T. Barryman."

"Can you prove that I have?" the girl asked calmly.

"Technically, no, but I can take out warrant to have this place searched, and I'm pretty sure it will yield up all I want to know."

The girl smiled faintly. "You're not fooling me a bit, Mr. Morrison. You haven't got the evidence you need to arrest me, and no matter how far you search in this cabin you won't find it. I've taken care to —"

She checked herself, her mouth setting.

"To remove it all?" Brad suggested dryly. "Well, that's as good an admission as any. And that gold you've been taking doesn't belong to you, and you know it!"

It appeared as though Nariza had suddenly decided to throw all pretence on one side.

"Who are you to say it doesn't belong to me?" she demanded. "All Arizona, all America, belongs to me! Don't forget that though the Aztecs originated in Mexico we soon spread all over the continent. Everything in America belongs to us, by right of ancestry."

"The law doesn't agree with you," Brad said calmly. "However, it doesn't appear that you've been taking gold for yourself — so who's J. T. Barryman?"

The girl looked at him sullenly, then she shrugged.

"J. T. Barryman is an alias for my brother. He's a highly educated man. In fact, both of us come from a well-connected family."

"I'd gathered that from your speech and general manner. You've explained half of it: why not all of it?"

A deep thought was apparently going through the girl's mind. It was almost a surprise when she finally nodded assent.

"All right, I will … Some years ago my brother was on a vacation here in Arizona — camp-style, not in Thunder Bend, or anything like that. It was his habit to take a roving vacation from Drew City every year. Quite by accident he came across a lost gold mine, the very walls of which are studded with rich nuggets and veins. He couldn't stop to take advantage of the situation because his business in Drew City — he's a lawyer — demanded his personal attention. So he passed the information on to me. I'd frequently expressed the wish to escape the city and live with Nature, which is to me a natural inherited love. It was decided that I should come to Thunder Valley, find the most inaccessible spot, have a shack built and furnish it — all of which my brother arranged with men he could trust. So I domiciled here and became something of an Aztec recluse. For a year I showed myself intermittently in Thunder Bend — a necessity if I was to have supplies to keep going and also because I wanted to spread so-called legends about myself. As I intended, I became known as a mysterious and dangerous character. I got to know everybody worthwhile — which explains by the way, my ability to get you a horse at short notice, Mr. Morrison."

"We'll skip that," Brad said. "Go on."

"There isn't much more to tell. I sent the gold to my brother in ordinary packages which I smuggled into the depot baggage room. He always sent one of his men to collect the packages and after that he disposed of them in his own way and turned them into money."

"Which means that he — and you too, I suppose — have built up a fortune from stolen gold?" Brad demanded.

"If you wish to call it 'stolen' — yes. But I claim that Arizona gold, or *any* gold in this country, is mine by right of ancestry."

"Then you are going to discover differently, Nariza. I presume that when I came to town you suspected that I was on your track and so started that phony love business?"

"It was not phony," she answered deliberately. "Certainly I wanted to find out all about you — but I could have done that at the point of a gun. It was because I loved you — and still do — that I tried less forceful methods."

"As far as love's concerned you'd better start forgetting all about it," Betty put in curtly. "I'm the only woman Brad thinks about — and he's the only man I think about. You don't think he'd ever fall in love with — with a civilized savage like you, do you?"

The oblique eyes looked at Betty steadily. It was hard to tell the state of mind behind them. Betty had spoken viciously, and had meant to.

"When you knew I was on to you why didn't you get out?" Brad asked.

"I hoped to wear you down. Besides, one doesn't leave the location of a gold mine *that* quickly, my friend. Only a fool would turn her back on untold wealth."

"Look here," Old Timer interrupted. "About them ceremonial noises o' yours, Nariza. I mean when y'go up on th' mountain-side with thit fancy blanket an' start a-wailin'. Is it the real thing, or jest fer effect?"

"For effect, of course," the girl answered him. "You don't suppose that any civilized woman, even if she is Aztec, would make those sort of noises for any other reason, do you? I did it merely to provide a reason for going up the mountain. I reasoned that it would be enough to scare the dumb sort of folk that live around here."

"That," Brad said, "I had guessed ..." He looked at his revolver for a moment, thinking. Then he glanced at Nariza again. "I've been up the trail to the ledge, Nariza, and I've examined every part of it — and though I watched you vanish one night I can't find a single trace of where you went."

"And you expect me to tell you?" she asked cynically.

"No, I don't. But there are ways of finding out, even if it means blasting open the mountain face."

Nariza considered this possibility deeply and then gave a little sigh.

"You saved me tonight, Brad," she said at length, "and since I've told you so much I suppose I may as well finish it. I'm prepared to show you how to get into the gold mine."

Brad glanced at Betty and then Old Timer. They were looking plainly astonished.

"You don't seem enthusiastic," Nariza commented, and anger flashed into her dark eyes.

"Matter of fact I didn't expect it," Brad told her frankly. "I'd have thought it would have been the last thing you'd do."

"I'll do it for you, Brad — but for nobody else." She looked in cold contempt at Betty and Old Timer. "And I wouldn't even do it for you if I didn't feel — as I do towards you."

"Very well," Brad said quietly. "Let's go."

She shook her dark head. "Not at this hour. It's long past midnight. First thing in the morning …"

"All right — but you're coming back to the cabin with us. I'm not taking the risk of you escaping in the interval. You may be in love with me, but I don't trust you, I'm afraid. Betty" — Brad handed her his gun — "go with her while she dresses. While you're doing that we'll get the pinto saddled."

Betty nodded, took the gun and motioned the Aztec girl back into the bedroom. The door closed.

Old Timer scratched his jaw pensively.

"Seems like yuh got all the info'mation yuh needed plumb easy, son. Meself, I don't like it bein' so free. I sorta git th' idea she's up to sump'n."

"If she is," Brad said, "I can cope with it. In any case I can't turn down the offer to see where the gold mine is."

"Nope; I reckon yuh can't An' what about Joe an' his boys? What are yuh aimin' t'do about them?"

"I'll deal with them first thing to-morrow after Nariza's shown me the gold mine. I'll put the facts before the Sheriff and if he doesn't think there's enough evidence to act I'll take a trip to Drew City and see what they have to say there. In fact," Brad added, thinking, "I may do that in any case. Nariza's brother will have to be arrested too … I don't think Joe and his boys will pull anything in the meantime. It's obvious that they're leary of attacking me because they know it'll finish them completely."

Nariza gave no trouble, either on the way back to the cabin or when it was reached. A rough bed was made for her on the floor of the living-room and Brad, Old Timer, and Betty disposed themselves in various parts of the room, one or other keeping guard at intervals. To Brad, still stiff from his experiences, it was a tough assignment, but he made no complaint.

The Aztec girl made no effort to escape, however. She slept peacefully throughout the night and at the arrival of dawn she tidied up the blankets which had been loaned to her, washed herself, and then smoked a cigarette while Betty prepared the breakfast.

Brad, except for remains of stiffness, looked and felt practically his normal self. He found it easier to shave than it had been, too, with the result that when he settled at the breakfast table he was looking smooth-jawed and determined.

"I want it to be clearly understood," Nariza said, when the meal was over, "that the information I'm giving you, Brad, isn't to be given to anybody else — except the authorities, I mean. It mustn't become general knowledge."

Brad looked at her oddly and then shrugged.

"All right …" He got up from the table, strapped on his gun belt and looked at Betty and Old Timer. "You two stay here until we come back. I don't have to warn you to look after yourselves. And it seems to me …"

Brad reached forward and whipped Nariza's gun from the holster at her side. She compressed her lips.

"Seems to me," Brad said, "we're a gun short since Joe took mine. This'll make up for it: Nariza won't be needing it."

Betty took the .38 and lifted it up and down comfortably in her hand. With a nod to Nariza, Brad headed for the door, went out behind the girl, and they got their respective horses from the little stable and saddled them. Then they set off for the mountain trail in the brilliance of morning sunshine.

"Supposing," Nariza said slowly, as they jogged along, "that that girl Betty Tarrant hadn't have come into the picture before me — when you met her at the Yellow Nugget. Would you have felt any differently towards me?"

"Not in the least," Brad replied, giving her a straight look. "And though I don't want to sound ungallant, Nariza, I wish you'd drop the subject. You don't seem to realize the position. I'm a marshal: you are a suspected person. We are virtually captor and captive."

"Are we?" She gave an ambiguous smile. Then she shook her head and sighed. "It's such a pity! In Drew City I never found any man I liked, which was one reason why I longed so much to get away amongst Nature. Then when I saw you for the first time I realized you were the sort of man I'd been looking for all my life … What's wrong with me, Brad? Am I so very unattractive?"

In spite of himself Brad was forced back to the topic.

"Anything but," he answered, shrugging. "And if no man in Drew City felt attracted towards you I just don't understand why. You have breed, youth, figure, looks ... and money," he finished dryly.

"Yet I'm alone." She looked moodily ahead of her down the trail. "I have a brother who uses me for his own ends, my parents are dead, I have only myself — and the man I love is in love with another. I just don't feel that life has been fair to me, somehow."

"On the whole," Brad said, "life isn't fair to anybody. All you can do is squeeze what you can out of it and let it go at that."

"I'm not made like that," she said. "When things don't go as I want them to I feel I have to hit back ... and I do. Maybe it's the savage left in me," she finished pensively.

"Possible," Brad assented, and deliberately forced a silence on the conversation.

Lost in their thoughts they finished the journey along the valley and took to the mountain trail, at length reaching the promontory, where the girl dismounted. She had a rather cynical smile on her lips as Brad tethered the horses to a spur.

"So my disappearance baffled you? Well, it's really quite simple. Look for yourself."

He followed her as she climbed up one of the rocks and dropped on the other side of it. From a crevice she took a powerful electric torch — evidently there for future activities — and then she pressed her slight body against a crack in the cliff face. Brad watched in amazement as a section perhaps thirty feet high and two broad swung gently round without a sound and left a black abyss beyond.

"A naturally balanced rock," she explained. "When my brother came up here he fell off his horse and collided with this rock by accident. He found that it moved, and so he explored. Anyway, I'll show you."

"Go ahead of me," Brad instructed, taking the torch. She stopped and picked up a heavy stone, wedged it against the pivoted rock.

"For safety," she said. "You can only open and shut this swivel-rock from the outside. The balance is different inside. I know because once I nearly -trapped myself with taking the risk."

Brad nodded and she went ahead of him into a long, natural tunnel, a vast volcanic blowhole, so flawlessly bitten out with scalding steam at some unguessable time in the past that the walls were perfectly smooth. In general the tunnel was circular and only just high enough for them to proceed along it in an upright position. It seemed to stretch to infinity in the glow of Brad's torch, and always in a downward direction, bending slightly as it went, leftwards.

"We've quite a distance to go," the girl said, glancing over her shoulder. "It's nearly three miles to the actual position of the mine."

"Uh-huh," Brad acknowledged, and said no more. He was trying mentally to picture whereabouts the mine actually was in relation to the outside world. It wasn't in the mountain range itself, apparently, but somewhat beyond the foothills.

Then at last the long wearying downward journey was over and they entered an immense natural cavern with spurs of rock sticking from the floor like teeth. The girl waved an arm and her voice echoed in the great hollow space.

"Wealth," she said. "Beyond your wildest dreams or mine."

Brad looked about him and wherever he looked the glimmer of the torch flashed on gold veins in the rocks, and in places on protruding nuggets of the stuff. In one corner stood a pickaxe and shovel with which the girl had evidently busied herself on past occasions.

"What surprises me," Brad said at length, "is, seeing the value of this stuff, your brother didn't try to get it legally and do the thing properly."

"He didn't for one very good reason. It would have started a gold rush, and in the effort to retain his own claim he might very easily have lost everything. So he chose the other, more secretive way. In any case we didn't intend that *all* this gold should be taken. That would take several lifetimes. All we are trying to do is to make a fortune and then silently retire."

"You mean you *were* trying to," Brad corrected. "That's all over now, Nariza."

"Is it?" She smiled, and then suddenly her hand came up. Up to this moment both of them had been thrust idly in the pockets of her riding trousers, but now the right one held a .30 automatic.

"Is it?" she repeated, the smile fading from her face. "Rather a pity you didn't look further when you handed my revolver to Betty Tarrant, wasn't it?" Suddenly Brad found the torch snatched from him and the blaze was turned full on him so he could not see a thing beyond it.

"You don't think," Nariza continued, from behind the brilliance, "that I admitted everything and brought you here just because I wanted to make a clean breast of everything and get myself in jail, do you? No, Brad, I'm not quite such a fool as that! I brought you here so that you could see the gold, and stay with it — for what is left of your life. I gave you your chance. If you'd have renounced everything and promised to marry me — the only man in the world I want — I'd never have been forced into this. Now you leave me no choice. If I can't have you, that lily-skinned girl with the yellow hair certainly won't!" Brad was silent, narrowing his eyes in the torchlight. Nariza still talked deliberately.

"I don't want to kill you, Brad — leave you here to die. You've forced it on me!"

"You're talking like an idiot!" Brad snapped.

"Old Timer and Betty both know where I've —"

"Yes, but they don't know how to get into this mine, do they? — any more than you did until I showed you. They'll never find you, Brad, and you can't get out of here from the inside. Nobody can hear you shout, either; the rocks are too thick."

"At least," Brad said, "there are witnesses to the fact that you were the last person seen with me, and that will mean your arrest for murder if I'm not found." The girl laughed softly.

"Old Timer and Betty are the only two I need to worry about: they are the only ones beside you who heard my confession last night. Do you think I intend to leave them free to say whatever they please? No, Brad. That old fool of a prospector is an easy one to deal with, and the girl I'll manage very easily, too. I intend," Nariza finished, her voice hardening to steel sharpness, "to obliterate every trace of the evidence you've got and wipe out the witnesses who heard me speak when I was in the position I couldn't do' anything else. After that, to safeguard myself, maybe I'll do a little deal with Joe Rutter."

"Nariza, you insane little fool!"

Brad ignored the automatic and dived at her. It didn't fire — but in the glare Brad could not see where he was going. He caught the girl's arm, felt the soft flesh compress under his crushing grip, then a brilliant star burst soundlessly in his skull as the automatic struck him across the back of the neck.

He staggered, sighed, then collapsed at her feet. Silent, she flashed the beam over his sprawled figure and then put her automatic back in her pocket. Quickly she hurried through the long tunnel and emerged at length through the opening. Bracing herself against the rock she swung it back into position until only that hair-thin crack was left. Though she knew it could not be budged from the inside she took double precaution by wedging a V-shaped stone under it from the exterior.

Untying the horses she leapt into the saddle of her pinto and trailed Brad's sorrel behind her until she came to a small wood of cedars at the base of the mountain path. In here she fastened Brad's horse. This done she spurred her pinto forward and finally into a gallop which took her in the direction of the cabin by the creek.

As she came within sight of it she deliberately lost her expression of grim satisfaction and instead looked anxious. She still looked this way as she dismounted at the cabin porchway and hurried into the living-room. Old Timer and Betty were on their feet in surprise, having seen her approach through the window.

"What's the matter?" Betty demanded. "Where's Brad?"

"That's just it ..." Nariza breathed hard and pushed the black hair from her face. "Black Joe was there waiting for us!"

"Black *Joe* was?" Betty gasped,

"He's shut Brad in the gold mine. I managed to escape and came back here at top speed for help. We can save him between us — you and me, Betty, I mean. You, Old Timer, had better go and get the Sheriff right away. Black Joe's got to be arrested and locked up before he starts any more trouble. Quickly! Hurry!"

"Guess I'd better," Old Timer assented, and raced to the doorway, snatching his cap as he went.

Nariza jerked her head to Betty. "Come on and help me. You can ride on my horse."

Betty snapped open Nariza's gun as it lay on the table, nodded, then holstered it and followed the Aztec girl outside, vaulting into the pinto's saddle behind her. Nariza spurred the animal's sides and sent it cantering along the valley floor just as Old Timer, his gelding saddled, went careering off in the opposite direction.

"I don't quite get the hang of all this," Betty said, as the horse jolted Nariza and her along the uneven valley floor. "Isn't Joe still there with his boys?"

"Of course he is — in the mine, with Brad at the end of a gun. That's the point. I've shut them all in — all except Lefty. I'll need you to help me deal with him. Then we've only got to get the Sheriff and the game's up for those boys."

"Yes" … Betty made the admission slowly. "Yes, I suppose it is."

She knew, she could feel with everything inside her, that there was something wrong somewhere — but on the other hand, her instincts might be at fault and in that case, it was up to her to give all the assistance she could.

So she said no more and clung tightly to the Aztec girl's waist as the pinto bounded up the mountain trail. On the way up it, Betty gazed at something and frowned.

"There was a horse there," she said. "Amidst the cedars. It looked like Brad's sorrel."

"It was," Nariza said. "That's where his horse and mine were left. Naturally, I took mine when I escaped."

Again a perfectly feasible answer, and again a feeling of something not quite right somewhere. Then, some fifty feet before the trail ended at the promontory — and the mine entrance — Nariza swung the horse's head suddenly leftwards and sent the animal stumbling and bounding along a narrow cleft smouldering in the merciless heat of the sun.

Long familiarity with the mountains kept the girl going along it for half a mile. It finished suddenly in a small crater-like depression, lined on three sides with rock walls twenty feet high, and on the fourth side by the mighty face of the mountain itself.

Here Nariza drew rein and jumped from the saddle. Betty did likewise and looked about her, shading her eyes in the glare.

"This the mine entrance?" she asked at last, turning.

Nariza shook her black head. Betty's eyes lowered from the girl's red-skinned, inexorable face to the automatic glinting in her hand. Reaching forward, she took the gun from Betty's holster in a swift movement.

"The mine entrance is nearly two miles from here," she replied presently, "and it's much further up the mountain. You are here for only one purpose, Miss Tarrant — to die!"

Betty set her mouth. "I expected something like this: I shouldn't have been such a fool as to fall for it. At least tell me what you've done with Brad."

"Brad is where he can't do anybody any harm, or any good, any more. He's sealed in the mine — and he can never get out! The only person outstanding after you is Old Timer. When he comes back with the Sheriff, I'll deny that I ever *sent* him for the Sheriff. Without my verification he won't have a leg to stand on. Later I'll deal with him and silence him for good. I've got everything worked out ... But it is you who interests me now. You who took Brad Morrison away from me with your yellow hair and your singing voice. You can't even begin to realize how much I hate you, Betty Tarrant!"

Chapter XII

Betty looked at the motionless automatic clenched her fists, but made no move. She knew she couldn't act fast enough to save her life if she had wanted. The Aztec girl had completely changed. There was a wildness in her oblique eyes; much of the savage which was her primordial heritage was uppermost.

"Many is the time I've come here," she went on, spitting the words out viciously. "Here I can perform certain rites sacred to my race. Here, at some forgotten time in the past, living sacrifices were offered to the great god Huitzilopochtli, the god of war, and to Quetzalcoatl, the god of light. I know they were. I have learned all the history of this part of Arizona, and my people have travelled far ... Here on this stone the living were offered by fire to propitiate the gods!"

Betty set her mouth and did her utmost to conceal the devouring fear she felt. The pure Aztec blood of Nariza was running high, inflamed by the devouring hate she felt for this girl who had come between her and the only man she claimed she had ever loved.

Betty looked at the broad, flat stone in the centre of the little clearing. The stone was about six feet long and three wide, parts of it blackened with smoke. It was raised on edgewise stones about a foot from the parched ground.

"Yes," Nariza breathed, her wide mouth split into a vicious grin, "the sacrifices died by fire!"

"You're crazy!" Betty whispered, staring at her. "Utterly crazy! You've gone back to the dark ages! Besides ... besides, you might be seen by the Sheriff at any moment when he comes back with Old Timer."

"Not here," Nariza answered curtly. "This spot is hidden round the side of the mountain, and it might take months to find it — even if anybody *wanted* to find it. The smoke from the fire certainly won't be seen because this particular part of the mountain face opens, out on to prairie land. You've no way out, Betty Tarrant, and you may just as well start realizing it."

Betty looked at the gun again and the slender body of the girl holding it. The gun was the biggest danger, otherwise Betty was by far the more powerful girl, some inches taller and far more developed. Finally, desperation acted for her. She flung herself on Nariza with all the speed and strength she could muster.

To her surprise, the gun did not explode at her. Instead, the Aztec girl side-stepped and Betty missed her completely. A hand clamped down on her left wrist and whirled her round. In spite of herself she was forced to her knees, the twist on her arm making it impossible for her to do otherwise.

Nariza laughed softly. "I thought you'd do that, Miss Tarrant! I could have shot you dead, only the noise of the shot might have earned too far to suit me. Besides, to kill you that way would be too quick. I want you to have something to remember. I owe you a good deal, don't forget! You took Brad Morrison away from me!"

Betty struggled helplessly on her knees, but she could not rise. She groped towards a stone with her free right hand, but Nariza snatched the hand away and forced it backwards to join the other one. Futilely Betty struggled, but the grip on her was relentless. Then the neckerchief was suddenly whipped from about her shirt, and she felt it being twisted in and out of her wrists, securing them finally in an immovable knot.

"Get up!" Nariza snapped.

Betty obeyed, tossed the hair out of her defiant face, and made a tremendous and useless effort to free her wrists. Nariza contemplated her for a moment or two, then she took off her own neckerchief, and in a sudden dive, flung it about Betty's ankles and secured them. The speed at which she acted prevented Betty from aiming a well-delivered kick which might have turned the tables.

"That's good enough for a start," Nariza commented, straightening up, and, thrusting out her right hand, she struck Betty savagely on the shoulder.

Unable to keep her balance, Betty toppled backwards and struck the edge of the massive flat sacrificial stone. She winced at the anguish the blow caused her and remained motionless for a moment — but only for a moment.

With surprising strength, considering her smallness, Nariza caught her beneath the arms and dragged her struggling body on to the stone. In swift movements she had unbuckled the cartridge belt from Betty's waist and passed it under the stone, buckling the squirming girl down completely.

Finally, Betty desisted, breathing hard, turning he face away from the blazing sunlight. The heat of the stone was burning through her thin shirt.

"Now I'll show you," Nariza muttered. "A few twigs and brushwood, and then …"

She turned and hurried away. Betty watched her vanish over the rock barrier nearby, in search of wood, then she battled frantically to tear apart the knots holding her wrists. But the Aztec girl had tied knots impossible to move. Betty was limp and exhausted with her efforts when the Aztec girl returned, bearing in her arms a pile of wood and small branches from the bushes growing on the mountain-side. With a crackling rush she bundled them under the flat stone.

"Nariza, for heaven's sake!" Betty jerked up her head and stared at her desperately. "You can't do this!"

Nariza's only response was a stinging slap across the face which flung Betty flat on the stone again …

*

Brad Morrison opened his eyes slowly to the realization of sounds, flashing lights, and an abominable pain in the back of his head. Then it began to decrease as he moved and gazed about him. He was lying on his back in an immense cavern, lights casting round inquisitively on veins of precious yellow metal. Automatically his hand flew to his right holster just as one of the wavering lights fell on him and dazzled him.

"Get up, Morrison!" ordered Joe Rutter's voice.

For answer Brad blurred up his gun and fired — straight into the lamp blazing down at him. It splintered and extinguished. There was an agonized howl. In the split seconds of darkness Brad dived for one of the numberless tooth-like rocks jutting out of the cavern floor and concealed himself.

The lights of two other torches tried in vain to seek him out as they swept away from exploring the gold veins.

"Better come out, Morrison," Joe advised grimly. "Yore cornered, and yuh know it!"

Brad kept quiet, determined not to give away his position by his voice.

"We followed yuh and that Aztec girl," Joe went on. "We figgered she must ha' left yuh in here when she came out alone — so we came t' look. Durned convenient. From th' way she jammed th' door she meant yuh stayin' in here an' dyin', I reckon. That suits me fine. That's just what yore goin' to do, an' nobody'll be able to blame *us* fer it! Yuh'd better come outa hidin', Morrison!"

Brad peered round the corner of the rock. He could hear Lefty muttering to himself. Evidently he had been the one who had been holding the torch and had received a slug right through his hand. It was roughly bandaged now, blood trickling down his fingers.

Brad's eyes narrowed. He could descry three figures — each one of them bent on only one thing — his destruction. Unless he acted first in self-defence. Suddenly, understanding how the position stood, he abandoned his silence.

"When you came in this mine, Joe, did you shut that rock door?"

Joe turned to look towards the source of the voice.

"Of course I shut it. Yuh don't think I'd give things away by leavin' it wide open, do yuh?"

Brad gave a grim chuckle. "For your especial information, Joe, you're as doomed as I am. That door can't be opened from the inside. Nariza told me as much … That's what I call perfect. I can't even die in peace without having you three apes for company!"

"You kiddin' about that door?" Joe asked anxiously.

"Tell one of your boys to try it and see."

"Hop to it, Lefty," Joe ordered, and there was the sound of feet and the bobbing of a torch as the gun hawk hurried back along the tunnel.

Grim-faced, his gun ready, Brad emerged from his hiding-place.

"Not so good, Joe, is it?" he inquired, as the remaining torch swung to illuminate him. "You've broken practically every rule in the book to get at this gold, and now you've found it you can't get out to make use of it! Kind of poetic, to my way of thinking."

Joe hesitated, then he snapped, "Even if it's right that I have t' die down here, I don't need to have a polecat like you fer my last moments!"

Brad dived, guessing a split second ahead what was coming. A bullet whanged past his ear. With his own gun he fired point-blank. Rock chippings splintered beside Joe's head and his torch swung wildly. The instant he'd fired Brad plunged to the shelter of a rock and a rattle of shots followed him, echoing and re-echoing in the cavern. Behind him, it sounded as though one slug actually split rock, which was of course impossible for a .45 slug … Or was it? Brad glanced quickly to the rear.

There was a hair-thin line, jagged and blindingly brilliant, just in his line of vision — sunlight?

Another shot whanged, closer this time. He crept farther behind the rock, waiting. Peeping over it he fired twice in quick succession, taking no particular aim — but it drew fire back, which was what he wanted. Then came the sound he had been waiting for. In firing back both Rod Jenkins and Joe clicked their hammers on empty chambers.

Immediately Brad holstered his gun, jumped to the top of the rock, measured the position of the two men in the torch light — and then jumped.

With arms flung wide he landed, as the two men worked at frantic speed to reload their weapons. Brad's arms locked round both their necks and bore them to the floor. The torch, still lighted, dropped. Brad snatched out his gun and brought the butt down with smashing force on Rod's head. He sagged, collapsed limply.

Joe dived for the torch, but he wasn't quick enough. Brad's well-aimed boot came up and kicked him under the jaw, jerking him backwards with a throaty gasp of pain and fury. His gun still useless he reholstered it and clenched his fists. For a moment both men measured each other in the light of the fallen torch.

"I could shoot you, Joe, and quick," Brad told him slowly. "Only I don't fight that way. For one thing it's against my principles and for another I'm a marshal and can't do tricks like that. Just the same I —"

Brad stopped and levelled his gun as there was the sound of feet in the tunnel. They came nearer and then Lefty burst into view.

"It's right, boss," he gulped. "There ain't no way out" He broke off as he saw the gun aimed at him.

"Toss your gun here, Lefty," Brad told him.

Lefty did so with his uninjured hand. Brad caught it and threw it away into the far reaches of the cavern.

"I reckon there isn't much you can do with that damaged mit," Brad added. "You're welcome to try … It's you I'm going to deal with, Joe. I've an account to settle for the way you beat me up the other night."

Brad holstered his gun and waited. He didn't have to wait long. Joe and Lefty dived for him simultaneously. He sidestepped Joe's bull rush and grabbed hold of Lefty's uninjured hand. A vicious twist, a bewildering judo movement, and Lefty flew over Brad's head and crashed with

114

stunning force into a near-by rock spur. He made one effort to rise, then slumped down with the senses smashed out of him.

Brad had just time to see the effect, then Joe was at him again, his powerful hands tearing at his throat. Brad crooked his right arm, doubled his fist, and cannoned it viciously into the back of Joe's neck — once, twice, three times, until the concussive effect forced him to, release his grip. The instant he did so a sledgehammer swung out of the torchlight, crashed into the right side of his jaw and smashed him flat on the dusty floor. He shook his head dazedly, the salt taste of blood in his mouth.

"I know this isn't ethical for a marshal, Joe," Brad told him, his voice coldly level. "It's just a personal score I'm wiping off, and at the same time I'm softening you up along with these other mugs in case a chance turns up to get out of here. If it doesn't — well, I'll feel better anyway for having paid you back for what you did to me."

"You dirty —"

Joe mumbled something and then struggled to his feet. He whipped off his encumbering jacket and threw it away, then he slammed up a mighty fist with all his strength. Not quite fast enough to miss it Brad took it on the chest and stumbled back. He recovered himself immediately and pistoned a straight left into Joe's mouth. Another blow slashed diagonally across Joe's nose, and yet another smashed into the pit of his stomach.

Wheezing, gulping, he doubled up. For split seconds there was calm, then a blow landed on Joe's ear which made it a hell of blazing pain. Goaded, he lunged, grabbed wildly at Brad's neck and tore at it with all his strength. While he battled to shut off the wind from Brad's lungs Joe was hardly aware of a leg snaking between his knees. It locked suddenly at the back of his calf and jerked, pulling his foot from under him. He crashed on his back with Brad on top of him.

Instantly Brad was free of the strangling grip. Astride Joe he rained blows into his face from right and left without mercy. Until it was no use raining them anymore. With a groaning sigh Joe relaxed, battered into unconsciousness.

Brad got up unsteadily, mopped his streaming face with his shirt sleeve. Deep inside him he felt better. He had been owing that to Joe for some time. Now, if while all three men were in this state it was possible to escape somehow and notify the Sheriff

Brad turned, moving back to the rock where he was sure he had seen a thin, blinding line. He *had* seen it. It was still there. Puzzled, narrowing his eyes at the glare, he moved towards it. As he did so he realized that it was not so much ahead of him as above him. Angles were hard to judge inside this cavern.

Clambering up a rock he finally reached it and discovered it was about an inch wide. Puzzled, he peered through it, then as a lofty, infinitely high fleck of cirrus cloud crossed his vision he realized that he was looking at the sky from the ground up.

The thought animated him. He dug his fingers into the crack and found it was only very thin. Then the truth dawned on him. One of Joe's stray bullets must have split right through a thin layer of hardened pumice rock, perhaps nothing more than a frail crust of volcanic plasma … It was a way out! Brad dragged out his gun, stuck the muzzle in the crack, then worked it back and forth vigorously. Rock dust came powdering down into his face. It was slow, tedious work. Too slow in fact. Finally he levelled the gun and fired three shots at the crack. Bits and pieces flew out amidst deafening noise and more cracks appeared.

Again he went to work with his revolver butt, hammering savagely, until at length a big chunk gave way. He reached up and hauled himself out of the hole and into blazing sunlight.

A deep sighing breath of relief escaped him. Intently, he looked around. He had come up not fifty yards from the front porch of Betty Tarrant's abandoned ranch. This particular stretch of plasma was a little distance from the mountain foothills, buried under a drifting of sand.

Finally Brad turned and looked round for — and found — a flat, heavy stone. He laid it flush across the opening he had made, and with chunks of earth filled up the crack. Down below, when Joe and his boys recovered, they might wonder where Brad had gone, but without a guiding light to reveal a way to the other world they would never find it, could not even guess that there *was* one in fact. And the Sheriff would do the rest.

Brad grinned to himself light-heartedly. Things had worked out better than he had expected. The thing to do now was get the Sheriff, clean up Joe and the boys, and then deal with Nariza — who, he presumed, had gone back to the cabin by the creek. And if she had carried out her threat to deal with Old Timer and Betty?

Brad's face clouded again. He began to move at a half-run along the valley floor towards the mountain trail. There was a hope in his mind that his horse might be somewhere there since it seemed to him unlikely that Nariza would have drawn attention to herself by taking it with her. He came upon it sooner than he had expected, amongst the cedars. Puzzled, he untied the reins, led the horse into the clear, then swung into the saddle.

Looking about him he pondered his next move — then his eyes sharpened towards a cloud of dust approaching along the trail. In time it resolved into four riders — Old Timer and the Sheriff in the forefront and two deputies behind. Spurring his horse Brad rode out to meet them. Old Timer gazed at him blankly.

"Yuh — yuh got free then?" he demanded.

"Free?"

"Yeah. Nariza told us Joe had trapped yuh in th' gold mine. She went with Betty to git yuh out, an' I went fer the Sheriff."

"Nariza went with *Betty*!" Brad couldn't keep the alarm out of his voice. "But I haven't even seen Betty! It was *Nariza* who trapped me in the mine and —"

"Look!" the Sheriff snapped, pointing, "There goes that Aztec girl now!"

They all looked towards the base of the mountain trail. A pinto driven at a furious pace had come into view and in the saddle was the unmistakable form of Nariza.

"She's tryin' to outrun us!" the Sheriff said. "I reckon she won't manage it — She's plenty of explainin' to do!"

He wheeled his horse, motioned his deputies, and they hurtled in a thunder of hoofs after the fleeing pinto and its rider.

"What *about* Joe?" Old Timer asked Brad sharply. "What goes on?"

"He's safe enough, locked up in the mine," Brad answered. "Right now it's Betty I'm worried about. Where she —"

He stopped. Suddenly upon the windless air there had come a cry — a desperate, anguished cry for help. It started low down in the scale and went up into a high, piercing scream.

"That's Bet!" Brad gasped. "I'd know her voice anywhere — an' that high C of hers. Somewhere in the mountains" He twirled about in his saddle, staring at the invincible walls.

"Help! *Help*!" Again it came, ending on that high, quavering note.

"Snakes alive, look!" Old Timer gulped suddenly.

He pointed and Brad gave a start at the sight of a mass of rock crumbling from high up the heights. It came cascading down amidst a rattle of stones. Some more came, and with it dust — and then came a deep growling as of thunder.

"What on earth ... Brad whispered, bewildered.

"I reckon th' valley's goin' t' start a-thunderin'," Old Timer gasped out. "It does at times, like I told yuh. A rock slide It's thit gurl's screamin' thit's done it! Thit high top note o' hers Son, we've got t' move — an' quick!"

Brad ignored him and cupping his hands round his mouth shouted at the top of his voice:

"*Betty! Where are you?*"

"*Brad! Here —! Help!*"

Brad fixed the direction whence the voice came, but the girl's high-pitched scream and the clarity of it consummated the rock unbalance. Supersonics had done their work. The growling and rumbling increased and from the heights stones, boulders, dust and then large rocks began their hurtling descent down the mountain-face.

"I'm going to find her!" Brad snapped. He spurred his horse and forced it up the mountain trail, a hail of stones and chippings descending on him as he did so.

The gathering noise was paralysing. A titanic boulder splintered into bits behind Brad as he forced the unwilling horse forward. He shouted the girl's name with all the force of his lungs as he went, and faintly above the din he heard her respond. When he got nearly to the top of the trail, bits of stone hailing about him, he saw the leftward path and blundered the horse along it.

Suddenly he came upon the little cup in the rocks where Betty lay buckled to the sacrificial stone, smoke gushing round her.

"Brad! Brad, for God's sake!" she screamed, then she broke off in a cry of pain as flame rushed upwards suddenly.

Brad flung himself off his horse and across to her, hewed the belt through with his knife and swept her up in his arms. She sagged fainting in his grasp. Her arms were blistered, half her shirt burned away in smouldering rags, her hair crimped and withered where flame had struck it. It was as he gathered her up that Brad realized no shirt at all remained on her back. The skin was a mass of weals and flaming red patches from the hot stone.

His face white with fury he stumbled back through the smoke and ever-increasing showers of stones towards the horse — but at the very moment he reached it a heavy boulder dropped and smote it across the withers. It shied, whinnied, threw its forelegs in the air, then dashed away down the narrow trail in blind panic. Brad stared after it dazedly, only too well aware that no power on earth would induce it to come back.

He swung. The world was a sudden catastrophic roaring as the real avalanche began from above. Staring upwards he could see vast rocks flying outwards and hurtling and bouncing down the mountain slopes towards him. He flung the unconscious girl over one shoulder and staggered along the pathway with desperate speed. Stones belted him savagely as he went and the din increased a thousand-fold.

He reached the end of the pathway amidst a million thunders and began a stumbling descent of the trail. The only advantage was that it was downhill. Weighted down by the girl's body he slipped, and picked himself up again. The ground gulped and shook as the first rocks of the avalanche struck bottom. Trees splintered, dust gushed upwards and outwards. Brad found himself running blindly through a fog with ever-increasing noise behind him. A bouncing boulder as big as a cabin hurtled past him not three yards away. It slammed straight into a tree and there jammed itself.

Instantly Brad dived towards it. To beat the cataclysm was now impossible — but he might be able to break the worst of it. Once behind the boulder he crouched down, protecting the girl as best he could. With a set and sweating face he waited as the roaring, battering tide of stone hammered and rolled around, as an endless sea of rocks and spurs bumped and shifted and thundered in all directions. Once the huge boulder was struck with a force that shifted it. The tree supporting it creaked and tore up half its roots — but it held … Then gradually the din began to subside and the dust drifted in the scorching air. Things began to take on shape again, but the entire set-up had changed. Practically all the trees at the base of the mountain trail had been destroyed. In their place reposed a wilderness of rocks extending far into the valley.

Brad stirred, lifted the girl up in his arms again, and began to carry her over the tumbled ruin. Presently he realized that Old Timer, the Sheriff, and the deputies were waiting for him. Evidently the avalanche had kept them at a distance. In their midst, her hands tied to the horn of her saddle, was Nariza. As she saw the injured girl in Brad's arms a coldly satisfied smile crossed her face.

"Brad, son!" Old Timer gasped thankfully, leaping off his horse and stumbling forward. "I sure never reckoned t' see yuh alive again. Yuh horse came runnin' without yuh. Got buried under the avalanche, I reckon … I'll take th' gurl," he added, and the Sheriff came up to help him.

The Sheriff's brows lowered as he beheld the mass of burns on the girl's back.

"Nanza's got plenty to answer fer," he said briefly. "All right, I'll take care o' her. We'll rush to my place with her and get a doctor."

"There's the matter of Joe and his boys," Brad said, through dust-caked lips. "They're —"

He stopped. The valley floor had completely changed. The foothills of the mountains extended now right to the door of Betty's Bending S ranch, a wilderness of towering boulders.

"If Joe an' his boys are under that lot they'll be dead afore we c'n get at 'em," the Sheriff said grimly.

"And the other entrance is blocked too," Brad muttered. "I saw the stones do that."

"I reckon," Old Timer said, "we saved th' State some expense, huh?"

*

Brad, with a bunch of vivid flowers in his hand, and Old Timer shined and polished so that his own mother would not have known him, entered the ground floor room of the Sheriff's home quietly. Betty Tarrant, seated in a basket chair by the window, deep in soft cushions, looked up quickly as they came in and her blue eyes brightened.

"Brad! Old Timer!" She held out her hands. "Oh, it's wonderful to see you both again! It's seemed such a long time!"

"It's *been* a long time," Brad assured her, smiling and putting the flowers on the blanket tucked round her knees. "We owe the Sheriff and his wife all our gratitude, letting you stay here and looking after you, and the doctor coming and going … But you're all right now, or will be soon."

"Very soon," she agreed, nodding and then smelling the flowers. "I've been wrapped up in oiled wadding for so long now I'm beginning to feel like a piece of precious machinery."

"Precious anyway," Brad said seriously, pulling up a chair and sitting beside her. "And I've been meaning to ask you, Bet. What happened when Nariza tried to ... to turn you into a sacrifice?"

"She lighted the wood under the stone and then left me, but the wood must have been more sappy than she thought. Anyway, it didn't burst into flame right away. I screamed for help, and thank heaven you came just as it caught fire. Otherwise ..." Betty set her mouth. "I'd rather not talk about it. What's been happening while I've been ill? I hear Nariza's being brought to trial?"

"For theft and attempted murder," Brad acknowledged. "Her brother is being tried too. That story she told about him was true enough. The case comes up next month ... As for Joe and his two gun hawks, they're under thousands of tons of rock."

"That too I know," Betty said.

"What you don't know," Brad murmured, gripping her hand, "is that you are one of the richest women in Arizona!"

She looked at him quickly. "I *am?* But — why?"

"That seam of gold is on your ranch property. I've been checking up on it. All that has to be done is to clear the rubble and start working."

The girl was silent, assimilating the incredible fact.

"It's *my* gold?" she insisted, incredulously.

"Yours." Brad gave a little smile. "It sorts of makes it tough on me in a way, too. I've been meaning to propose to you for long enough but didn't seem to get around to it. Now I *can* propose it looks as though I'm doing it so's I can cut myself in on the gold."

The girl laughed. "I'm only a woman, Brad, and I'll certainly need a man to arrange the details and protect anything so valuable as a gold mine. Besides, only you know the exact location of it. So you've got nothing to worry about. Soon as I'm better we'll get married."

"Yes, but — look, about your singing. You said that if you had money you'd sing in the Metropolitan, in London, in Paris"

"I know — but I also said that any big reason might make me change my mind. Isn't this a big enough reason? I shan't ever leave Arizona now; there's so much to stay for. Besides ..." Betty gave a wistful little smile. "I believe it was my top C which started the avalanche, so perhaps I'd better stick to a lullaby in future!"

Brad grinned and kissed her.

"Just as well you've accepted me," he said. "I've already sent in my resignation to the force. I'm going to turn into a miner."

"An' Old Timer, too," the girl smiled, reaching out her hand to him as he stood grinning with his two teeth.

"You did it at last, Old Timer. You found gold!'

"Yeah, but I reckon I did more'n thit, Betty. I found me some good friends, and dog-gone me if thit doesn't mean more'n gold sometimes!"

Yellow Gulch Law

John Russell Fearn

1. The Square 8 Ranch

"Well, Shorty, there it is, I reckon."

Jess Burton brought his powerful sorrel to a halt, hipped round in the saddle, and surveyed the scenery. It was still early in the morning, only a few hours past dawn, and Arizona was awakening to a new Spring day. The two men high up on the rimrock saw the glorious Mariposa tulips lifting their orange cups and the sweetpea blossoms creeping over a violet carpet of hyptis and verbena. The very perfume in the air was life itself.

But Nature's beauty had nothing in common with the valley into which the two men looked. A ranch sprawled there, with extensive corrals penning some five thousand head. Down there at the Square-8 lived Wilton de Brock, self-styled cattle emperor and overlord of the entire small state of Yellow Gulch. The brutal dominance of Wilton de Brock was something of which most men and women knew, from the lowliest cattle-tenders on the far-flung ranches of these mighty spaces, to the wealthy cattle-owners, themselves. The tales told of him were varied, but they added up to the same thing: he made his own laws and had the power to enforce them. Yellow Gulch was de Brock's property and he ran it in his own way.

There were dozens of such semi-feudal territories scattered throughout the vast American continent, for the great United States of America was as yet only a dream. Men fought and lived and died by their guns — and Wilton de Brock could outshoot the fastest of them.

"Well, what d'you think of it?" Jess Burton asked at length, in his slow but powerful voice.

He was a tall, rangy man in the mid-thirties, his exposed skin a burned-in brown, his eyes deep blue, his cheekbones high. Though he did not smile readily, his face was likeable.

"Good enough, I guess," his short, tubby companion answered, cuffing up his Stetson on to his forehead. "Leastways it should be better'n kickin' around in th' desert an' goin' no place in partic'lar. Ain't much fun in bein' lone rangers … "

Shorty Pearson reflected for a moment, his pale, grey eyes travelling over the scene, then he added: "Jus' th' same, Jess, there is somethin' worth havin' in the open sky an' th' wide spaces. Mebby it's better'n bein'

124

cooped up an' doin' as yore told. I s'pose it all depends if that guy de Brock's willin' t' take us on, doesn't it?"

"Yeah — but there's no reason why he shouldn't. What we don't know 'bout cow-pokin' ain't worth mentionin'.''

"Jus' th' same, frum what I've heard uv de Brock, cow-punchin' mebby ain't th' only thing he wants. He's a tough character, an' afore we're finished, 'specially the way you talk, anythin' might happen.''

Jess grinned. "Anyways, let's be seein' what we can do about it."

He spurred his sorrel and set the animal sweeping down the grassy valley side. Only a few yards behind him came Shorty, presently catching up. As they rode together both men became aware of signs of activity about the Square-8 spread. Men were going back and forth in the huge corrals and across the main yard. A wagon and team was being prepared for a journey, probably into the two mile distant town of Yellow Gulch itself.

When he reached the gateway of the yard he drew his mount to a halt and hailed one of the punchers nearby, who turned and came ambling forward slowly.

"How does a feller get to see de Brock?" Jess enquired.

"Mostly, he doesn't," the cowpoke answered, squinting up into the sunlight. "Depends on what yore hankerin' after."

"Jobs for me an' my pardner here. We heard back along th' desert trail that de Brock was takin' on new hands for his outfit, so we rode over."

"Best thing yuh can do is go up to the ranch-house an' ask if he'll see yuh," the puncher suggested.

Jess nodded, jerked his head to Shorty, and together they rode across the wide yard. Leaving their horses tethered to the tie-rack, they mounted the three steps to the porch and Jess thumped on the screen-door. A square-shouldered hard-faced woman of middle age presently arrived to deal with them. There was a certain suspicion in her expression as she surveyed the two men.

"Well?" she asked briefly.

"Mornin', ma'm." Jess touched his hat brim. "We were wonderin' if Mr de Brock's still takin' on hands for this spread of his. We're both — "

"Saddle tramps, by the looks of you!"

Jess eyed the woman levelly. "I reckon you can't ride the trail for long hours around here, ma'm, without getting' a mite dirty. Still, if there isn't anythin' we can do around here we can ride further, an' thanks for — "

"I'm not turning you away," the woman interrupted. "Just sizin' you up, that's all. You'd best ask my husband for yourselves." She drew the door open wider. "Walk straight across the hall and into th' living room there."

"Thank you kindly, ma'm." Tugging off his hat Jess led the way and entered the room the woman had indicated.

It was comfortably furnished in the log-wall, skin-rug style. At a broad desk near the window an ox-shouldered man with close-cropped grey hair sat writing. He only looked up when Jess and Shorty were facing him across a pile of papers and correspondence.

"Well?" he asked curtly — and sat back in his chair.

Wilton de Brock was probably fifty years of age, as solidly power-packed as one of his own stallions. His head was perfectly round, a fact rendered even more noticeable by his scrub haircut. Square features, verging on the cruel, were deeply sun-tanned. His eyes were glacial blue, so light that with the morning sunshine catching them diagonally they appeared transparent.

Here, Jess decided, was a man who loved power for power's sake, and who was not particularly concerned as to how he gained or maintained it.

"Do you have to stand there all day!" he demanded at length, and it seemed queer in such a man to find his voice smooth and well educated.

"Er — sorry," Jess apologized, holding his hat by the brim in front of him. "I'm Jess Burton and this is my sidekick "Shorty" Pearson. We're looking for jobs. We heard you were extending your outfit."

"Where did you hear it?" de Brock asked curtly. "I'm not in the habit of advertising my activities."

"Ways back on the trail. A guy by the name of Cornish. Said he'd been in your outfit but that you'd fired him. He told us you were taking on hands, so havin' nothing particular in mind we figured we might as well ride in and see if we could do anything. Just being footloose can get tirin'."

Wilton de Brock gave a hard grin. "For your edification, Burton, Cornish was not fired. He ran away! I found it necessary to exercise certain disciplinary measures and — well, he turned yellow and bolted. However, that is neither here nor there. Where are you from? What can you do? Your appearance isn't exactly neat."

"I guess neither of us are from anywheres particular," Jess responded. "We've just bin roaming around for the last three years. Last regular job we had was at the Straight-J back in Kansas. We got sick of livin' to rule, though, and decided to hit leather — but like I said it's a hard life roamin' around with nothin' to fix your mind on but desert — "

"In other words, you're hombres? Saddle tramps?"

A glint came and went in Jess' bright blue eyes but his tone remained respectful. "I guess so," he admitted, "but we can handle steers an' we know all the runs of a layout like yours. Whether the spread's big or little makes no odds to us."

The pale, cruel eyes flashed to Shorty and pinned him. Shorty swallowed to himself and waited.

"What about you, Pearson? Just plain dumb or incapable of speaking for yourself?"

"Course I ain't," Shorty retorted. "Just don't seem no sense in two of us talkin' when Jess can do it for th' both of us. He always did do the talkin' in our team."

"Very logical," the cattle baron agreed, with a dry grin. "I may as well tell you two men that I don't like saddle tramps in my outfit because I don't trust them, but it so happens that I have regulations and laws which prevent any doublecrossing, thieving, or gunplay. In plain words, all my men are equal, that is, amongst those who do the hard work. There are bosses to whom they're answerable; and they in turn are answerable to me. You understand?"

"You mean," Jess said slowly, "that if we are crazy enough to think of gettin' smart ideas you'd bushwhack us afore we could turn round?"

"That's just what I mean, and it's as well for you to grasp the fact from the start. My foreman, Clint Andrews, is well paid to see that my orders are carried out. That being so I'm willing to give you two desert rats a trial. You'll get five dollars a week each and your keep."

Jess and Shorty exchanged glances; de Brock's cold eyes switched from one to the other.

"If you don't like it you can get off this territory," he said briefly. "I didn't ask you to join my outfit, remember. In fact I'm doing you a favour taking you on at all."

"It's a mighty low wage," Jess said bluntly.

"What do you expect for cow-poking? A fortune?"

"No, just enough dollars to make a living, and that isn't my idea of it," Jess' voice slowed and he gave a shrug. "Just the same it's better 'n the desert and wandering, I suppose ... Okay, we'll take it."

"You'll find Clint Andrews somewhere about outside," de Brock said. "If you've any complaints to make see him about them. I haven't the time to deal with them. Just one thing I would add — don't complain unless you have to. Clint doesn't like grousers."

Without further words Jess and Shorty left the ranch-house, glancing at each other significantly as they went. They had gained the yard again and were standing beside their horses before Shorty made a comment.

"I dunno that you'd call me the anti-social type," he said, spitting casually into the dust, "but there's somethin' about that jigger de Brock which I don't like. Seems to me that all th' things that've been sed about him have bin true. The guy's a low-down, an' all th' worse for bein' rich an' powerful into th' bargain."

"Yeah ... " Jess gave a sigh. "However, since we've very little money, Shorty, and even less prospects, I guess we'd better go th' way of the wind, leastways for the time being. Better be finding that foreman, hadn't we?"

They came upon him eventually in the midst of the job of branding yearlings. Their mournful bleatings mixed with the stench of scorching hair and hide. Jess stood watching for a while, his eyes narrowing a little as he saw the unnecessary cruelty with which the young animals were being treated.

Suddenly he started forward with little strides, his fists clenched at his sides.

There ain't no call for tying that steer's back and front legs," he snapped abruptly. It's simpler to — "

"You tellin' me what t' do, stranger?" The foreman stood up, throwing the smoking branding-iron back in the brazier again. He grinned crookedly. If so, I shouldn't. It ain't healthy to do that around here."

Jess hesitated, not because he was afraid of the broad-shouldered, thick-featured giant in front of him but because he wanted a job. It was no use ruining his and Shorty's chances before they had even got started.

"You Clint Andrews?" Jess asked.

"Yeah. What about it?"

"Mr de Brock told us to report to you."

The foreman grinned all the wider and put his hands on his hips.

"He did, huh? Well, ain't that nice! Couldn't suit me better than t' have a wise guy workin' under me."

"I don't work for anybody 'less he plays the game straight," Jess snapped.

The foreman spat and then considered. "I guess I've broken in better men'n you, feller, as you may find out before long. Til lay off yuh this time 'cos yore new, but don't go shootin' your face off too much. I mightn't like it."

Jess hesitated and then slowly he relaxed. Keeping his temper had always been his hardest task.

"Guess I'm a bit edgy," he muttered. "Bin doin' a lot of hard riding lately."

"Okay. Then you can make yourself really tired by clearin' out them sheds over there. I reckon we ain't so partic'lar about stinks around here as a rule, but them sheds is more than even we can stick. Get busy, an' make 'em clean!"

Jess turned, jerked his head, and Shorty followed him in the direction of the outhouses. The odour from within retched their stomachs, but they went to work just the same, their kerchiefs tied about their faces ... And this job was only the first. By the end of a gruelling, sizzling day they had done practically every dirty job which the foreman could rake up. Their tempers were not improved in consequence.

It was after supper in the bunkhouse, with the rest of the outfit gathered around him, that Jess let himself go. Since the foreman was not present it did not seem to him that it mattered if he let off steam.

"How do you fellers stick it!" he demanded, looking about him. "What kind of a spread does this guy de Brock think he's running, anyway? I guess even convicts get better treatment than this. Even the food stinks."

He whipped up the remains of his meal, which he had not been able to tolerate, and flung it on the floor. The oozing mass stuck to the unwashed boards. For a while there was dead silence and the men looked grimly at each other.

"Ain't healthy to argue about it," a cowpoke remarked. "Or don't yuh know, stranger, jus' how much power de Brock's got in these parts?"

"Course I know!" Jess retorted. "His name stinks from one end of the country to the other, and I can plainly see why now. However much power he's got it doesn't entitle him to treat us like pigs!"

"Mebbe not," the cowpoke agreed, "but who's t' stop him gettin' away with it? He's the law throughout this entire territory an' there ain't no other."

"There's a certain amount of State law in being," Jess snapped. "A man can't do just as he likes without gettin' one of the State Governors down on him mighty quick. I guess de Brock's illegal methods must be known to the authorities, but they're hogtied without proof. Just the same, it seems a visit from one of them, say from North Point City, is a long way overdue."

One of the men chuckled, a big, lumbering giant of a man with a plug-ugly face and unruly black hair.

"What's so funny?" Jess demanded, wheeling on him.

"Just one thing, stranger. One or two folks got the same notion as you an' tried to get a Governor down here from North Point. They figgered they could get through as living proof of de Brock's ill treatment, but though that city's only fifty mile away the stunt didn't work. Those who tried it was ambushed afore they could finish. If yuh want t' keep your health, feller, yuh'd best start in realizin' that Wilton de Brock is th' be-all and end-all hereabouts."

Jess was silent for a while, thinking, and looking across to where the big fellow was lounging on a hard chair, its back propped against the wooden wall.

"Ever hear of Joe Cornish?" Jess asked presently.

"Sure," the big fellow assented. "He usta work in this outfit. One uv de Brock's paid spies an' gunmen. One uv the nastiest characters I ever happened on."

Jess gave a start and glanced at Shorty, then back to the big fellow.

"How'd you mean?" Jess questioned. "I used to know Cornish some years ago an' he was a straight-shooter enough then. It was because of that I took his word for it when he told me an' Shorty that de Brock was wantin' men for his spread. If it hadn't have bin for him we wouldn't have come."

The ironic laughter which broke out made Jess frown.

"What gives?" he asked coldly, looking about him. You boys mean that Shorty an' me were tricked into comin' here?"

"Yeah, that's it." The big fellow got to his feet and, his thumbs latched in his pant's belt, came ambling over to where Jess had sat on the long table, "de Brock is such a tyrant that he can't git any labour the straight way, so

130

th' only other method is to hi-jack whoever he can get. Some of th' men who are as ornery as he is rake in workers where they can. An' Cornish is just such a man. In a word, feller, yuh wus sold out to de Brock."

Jess was silent, his lips tight, a glitter in his blue eyes.

The big fellow looked at him for a moment, then added: "Yore here now, an' th' only way yuh'll ever get out of the territory, where you might spread information as to what goes on here, is feet first, with a slug in your heart. Since others have tried it an' gotten themselves bushwhacked there's no reason for supposin' yuh could do any better."

"Mmmm ..." Jess' eyes narrowed. "Which explains what de Brock meant when he talked of discipline an' regulations ... An' you guys here stand for it, do you?" he demanded, looking around him again and frowning.

"Becos we ain't plain crazy, yes," another puncher said. "If we try anythin' we either git flogged or solitary without water fur four days. That ain't worth riskin'. Best do as yore told, collect what bit o' money is comin' to yuh, an' shut your eyes an' ears to everythin' else. Mebby not exactly as we'd like it, but we stay sorta healthy."

"On the kind of muck this heel gives us to eat?" Jess snapped. "I'd sooner starve to death!"

"Guess that's what yuh will do, feller, if yuh don't eat what's set before yuh."

The big fellow gave a grim smile. "Which gives yuh some idea, stranger, uv the kind uv yellow-bellies I haveta mix with! I'd break out tomorrow an' wipe out de Brock, Clint Andrews, an' all th' rest uv the stinkin' bunch, if I could." He looked over the assembly with narrowed eyes, his ugly face set in arrogant contempt. "But I guess I can't do it single-handed."

"Mebby you won't have to," Jess said quietly. "I've seen enough in one day to satisfy me that I don't like this place: it's too much like a penal settlement. An' when I choose to hit th' trail it'll take a stronger man than de Brock to pin me down."

"That's my language too, feller." The big cowpuncher rubbed his massive hands together; then he held one forward impulsively in welcome. "Nixon's th' monicker," he said, his ugly face lighting in a grin, "but most folks call me 'Ox'."

"Okay, Ox it is." Jess shook hands. "I'm Jess Burton. This is Shorty Pearson. Whilst we're about it, Ox, tell me more. What exactly goes on in this territory? What's de Brock driving at? Is he just a plain tyrant or has he some object in his roughshod methods?"

"Bit of each, I reckon." Ox squatted on the table beside Jess and became thoughtful for a moment or two. Then he went on: "All of us boys here have bin more or less roped in to work fur him through hi-jackin', an' so far we ain't done nothing about it. In this region th' sheriff an' mayor is both in de Brock's pay, so they shut their eyes to anythin' that goes on. Anybody sayin' anythin' against the skunk is usually strung up. His aim is to run not only this partic'lar territory of Yellow Gulch, but all Arizona afore he's through."

"When, an' if, a Union comes inter bein' he reckons to be one uv th' most powerful men in it. Becost of that hope he's extendin' his power everywheres. All his cattle deals is illegal an' nobody can stop it. A lot uv his steers have bin rustled from the neighourin' ranches in th' territory. What he really aims at is t' drive every settler outa th' region, either by persuasion or open violence, an' unless I'm plain loco he'll do it afore he's finished."

"Nice feller," Jess commented, sighing. "And what good will that do him? The settlers have bought the land from him, haven't they? They must have some say in the matter, or are they too plumb scared of this skunk to say so?"

"Ain't quite that way," Ox replied. "The settlers bought th' land from Amos Crand, who wus the sort uv boss around here before de Brock blew in with his owl-hooters an' rubbed out Crand an' everybody connected with him. de Brock's idea is to drive th' settlers out, reclaim the land fur himself, an' then sell it at the highest price if a Union comes, as looks mighty likely one day."

Ox spat on the floor and lighted the cigarette he had been rolling whilst talking.

"Now yuh see what we're up against," he said, musing amidst the fumes. "An' believe me, feller, I'd risk most anythin' t' rub out th' dirty skunk, an' as I see it yore uv the same notion."

"As nice a setup as I've struck in some time," Jess said, pondering. "Seems like the stories that have been spread around aren't so exaggerated."

"You sed it," Ox agreed.

"What it amounts to is that the settlers around here are in fear of their lives and against de Brock's hired gunmen they don't stand a chance? Nobody to protect their interests. That the trouble?"

"That's it. Those who've tried t' break away an' get help to this territory have bin wiped out, like I told yuh. Position ain't so much better for us. Yuh notice none uv us is allowed to keep guns, an' there's guards around outside who keep a watch on anybody tryin' t' make a break from this outfit. Once in this area, feller, yore in it fur keeps less you've the brains to get out." Ox gave a wide grin. "I don't reckon t' have any brains meself. My fists have always gotten me through, but you look as if yuh might have a head on yuh."

"Thanks," Jess conceded dryly. "Just the same you've been here longer than I have. You must have made some kind of plan in that time."

"Nope. It weren't any use makin' any with these yellow-bellies refusin' t' back me up if I tried somethin', so I just got around to leavin' things alone 'til somethin' happened I could make use uv."

Ox looked about him sourly and one or two of the men shifted uneasily. Jess looked about him, too: then he said quietly:

"Look, you fellers. If Ox an' me found a way to get clear of here would you support us?"

"Not if they've any blasted sense!" a voice commented.

Every man turned, Jess and Ox included. Clint Andrews was in the doorway of the bunkhouse, a heavy .45 in his hand. With cold menace on his thick features he came forward slowly, the floorboards creaking under his weight. When he arrived at the food Jess had flung down he regarded it ominously, then moved his attention to the set-faced men gathered around him.

"Who around here don't like the menu we serve?" he demanded.

Nobody answered. The men looked at each other and some of them folded their arms. Andrews' left hand rested casually on a leather butt tucked in his belt, then suddenly with a blast of rage he ripped the butt out, a lashing whiptail on the end of it. Its cutting thong belaboured the backs and faces of the nearest men, Ox and Jess included.

"Stand here like a lot of dumb swine, eh?" Clint Andrews screamed. "By hell, we'll see about that! Answer me, damn you!"

Still nobody said anything, but in the eyes of Jess there was bleak murder. Unnoticed, he reached down into the back of his half-boot and gripped the handle of a thin, wickedly sharp dagger. He waited in smouldering calm until the foreman came to the peak of his blind fury, raising his lash again. Then Jess acted.

His knife slashed up and down again, a briefly glinting line in the oil lights. It was so swift an action hardly anybody saw what happened. But Clint Andrews crashed to the floor, blood soddening his shirt across the left breast. His whip fell a few feet away, his gun slid into a corner. Not two yards from his head was the plate of down-flung food.

There was hard breathing, the men looking tensely at one another. Slowly Jess slipped the knife back into his half-boot and drew the back of his hand over his sweating forehead.

"One place they didn't think t' look for a weapon," he said.

"You didn't oughta have done that, feller," a puncher whispered, his eyes popping.

"It'll mean th' rope," another said, staring. "Looks like yuh've killed Clint."

"Yeah," Ox breathed, staring down at the foreman as though hypnotized.

"I reckon one could call it justifiable homicide," Jess said, his voice steel-hard. "A man like Clint Andrews wasn't fit to be in charge of an outfit. In fact he wasn't fit t' live at all. I'm not regrettin' my action one little bit. Pity is somebody didn't do it sooner."

"Git him outa sight, an' fur th' love of God hurry it up!" gasped a puncher near the doorway. "Somebody's a-comin'. Mebby de Brock himself."

It was, and there was no time to shift the dead foreman's sprawled body, or to make a dash for his fallen gun. The cattle baron came into the bunkhouse and looked about him. Such was the iron-hand control of the man over his emotions he did not even blink when he saw the foreman. Instead he halted and stood with his head on one side, considering.

"So," he remarked at length. "In spite of all the warnings you have had, and knowledge of the dire consequences following any infraction of orders, one of you found it necessary to play games!"

There was no response. The men stood looking at him whilst his transparent eyes flashed from one to the other. Then he came forward again, his hand resting on the butt of his gun. He moved with a swagger, but every nerve was obviously taut for action.

"Needless to remark," he resumed, his voice so low and deadly it was hardly audible, "I have no liking for talking to myself. I asked you men a question, and I'll give you five seconds in which to answer. If you prefer not to take advantage of my leniency I will see that each one of you is flogged without mercy until one or other of you breaks and tells me the facts. Believe me, I will get the truth out of you no matter how much you suffer or how long I have to wait."

He removed a costly watch from his fancy vest and contemplated it, withal keeping a wary eye on the men about him.

"One … two … " He began to count relentlessly.

Still nobody spoke. Jess sat on the table edge with his mouth taut. Ox rolled himself a second cigarette and lighted it deliberately. Shorty kept his arms folded, a look of sour disgust on his whiskery visage.

"Very well," de Brock said finally, as the fifth second passed. "You have only yourselves to thank."

He raised his voice in a shout and through the doorway two gunmen came hurrying in. They halted in their sudden forward rush and stared, first at the body on the floor and then at their boss.

"Take this muscle-bound ape and deal with him," de Brock directed them curtly, dashing Ox's cigarette from his mouth to the floor and grinding it under his heel. "He's been trying for long enough to make trouble around here, and this time it seems he's gotten away with it. At the end of thirty lashes he may be inclined to speak. I've been awaiting a chance like this for a long time. Now I may consider it legitimate to hammer some obedience into his thick hide."

"Me?" Ox gasped, staring. "But I never — "

"Shut up and start moving!" de Brock ordered, his gun leaping into his hand. "Outside! Same applies to the rest of you. You can watch what happens and gain some idea of what is coming to each one of you. Maybe you'll learn to have better sense in the future."

Bewildered and swearing, Ox found himself menaced by three guns, two of them belonging to the leather-necked guards. He was bundled out into the big yard, his shirt stripped from him, then he was forced to double over a large horizontal barrel. Ropes were tied round his wrists and were then drawn taut under the barrel to his ankles on the opposite side. Thus-wise his massive naked back was completely exposed.

The assembled men stood watching, their faces grim.

"Before we start," de Brock said levelly, eyeing the gathering in the glow of kerosene light from the ranch-house porch, "you should know that this is justice. Scum like you will never speak through ordinary persuasion. Once I know the guilty man the flogging will cease and the culprit will be dealt with — by hanging."

"By what right do you make laws?" Burton snapped, and the cattle-baron gave him a snakelike stare.

"By the right that in this state I, Wilton de Brock, am the only master. I make the laws and administer them to the full. No more, no less. All right?" he finished, nodding to his gunmen, "get on with the job, and don't spare yourselves, either. He's tough enough to stand it."

The two guards holstered their guns and from their belts took short-tailed whips. Before they could start, however, Jess stepped forward.

"Hold it!" he said briefly. "There's no need for any of this. I'm the man you want, de Brock."

The cattle baron considered him. "You are, are you? A man of unusual violence for a newcomer to our little community, eh? Though from the amount you have had to say I suppose I should not be surprised."

"I wiped out Clint Andrews because he wasn't fit to live. It was as simple as that."

"I see. It so happens, however, that I have a great dislike of having my hired men eliminated so drastically. It upsets all my arrangements."

Jess said nothing. He was preparing for a spring, but the slow tautening of his muscles was not visible in the dim light. Then, as de Brock remained silent Jess resumed talking:

"It seems, de Brock, that so far no man around here — save mebby Ox — has had the guts to stand up to you and your damned sadism. But it's going to change."

"Is it really?"

"Yeah, and right now!"

Jess dived suddenly and with overwhelming force. His right fist came up as he moved, and behind it was all the power of his muscles, de Brock took the blow under the jaw and staggered helplessly backwards into the dust, his gun flying out of his hand. He twisted and made a frantic effort to seize it, but before he could do so he realized that the point of a glinting knife was at his jugular.

2. Breaking Loose

"Take it easy," Jess warned, pinning the cattle baron down. "Since I didn't think twice about blotting out Andrews, there's no reason why I shouldn't do the same with you, is there? In fact you're a bigger plum than he could ever ha' been."

"All right, get on with it!" de Brock muttered, and just for a moment Jess had to admire the man's cynical courage, with death only a hair's breadth from him. "Or perhaps I have the wrong idea and you have some reason for allowing me to live?"

"Yeah, sure I have. I'm not lettin' you have a swift grand exit after the way you've been behavin' in the territory."

"Stop fooling around, man, and come to the point!" de Brock panted.

"I will, in my own time. Y' see, de Brock, you've gotta learn the hard way and see your whole tinhorn empire come crashin' down around your ears, before you finally get yourself blotted out. I sort of figger I'm the man who can deal with that — along with a few others. Yore livin', de Brock, just so's you can die more slowly from here on. That, to me, seems nice an' poetic."

"You don't know the kind of man yore fightin'," de Brock said, his colourless eyes aimed upwards. "But, by God, you will before you're finished! And I mean finished!"

I'm willin' to put that to the test. I may change my mind and slit your throat right now unless you give some orders. First of all get Ox released." de Brock gave the order, his voice hoarse. Ox, the ropes unfastened, stood up from the barrel and dragged on his shirt. Then he looked at the two guards who had released him. He sized them up slowly, his big mouth set in brutal hardness.

"Yuh cheap, low-down ornery skunks," he whispered. "Tickin' on a jigger who's got no guns, huh? Seems like the pair uv yuh is about due fur repayment."

With battering ram impact his left and right fists shot out, knocking each guard backwards one after the other. As they collapsed in the dust Ox whipped up their guns into his own powerful hands.

"Okay!" he shouted. "Since Clint Andrews got what wus comin' to him there ain't no reason why you gorillas shouldn't neither. An' fur that I ..." He got no further. A shot aimed by a guard who had come on the scene unexpectedly struck him across the top of the head. He crashed on his face, completely stunned. For an instant there was a dead silence; then the men began to surge forward angrily. In that split second, however, de Brock also acted.

With a sudden tremendous surge he flung Jess from him and lashed out with his fist. The knife went flying. Another shot exploded and Jess heard the bullet whine past his ear. It was no time to argue, bereft as he was of his only weapon.

He hurled himself on to the high palings surrounding the yard and began to scramble up them. Another shot followed him but in the gloom the aim was poor. He scrambled clear, dropped to the other side of the fence, then began to run under the stars.

For a time he heard the explosion of guns, saw the flash of them in the darkness behind him. But they grew fainter as he went onwards across the pasture land. In every way he had the advantage now, the moonless night sheltering him. Bright though the starlight was it was not sufficient to reveal him against the dark of the greensward.

Once, perhaps an hour after he had escaped, a party of horsemen approached him, but he slipped into a fold of the land and remained until they had gone. Finally, at what he judged must be some time after midnight, he settled himself to sleep in an outcropping of manzanita, satisfied that nobody could approach without awakening him.

Exhausted as he was, sleep came readily, nor was he once disturbed.

In the cold air of the coming dawn he was on his way again, knee-deep in mist wreaths, his joints stiff from the exposure of the night. He hurried to restore his circulation, gradually finding himself becoming warmer and less cramped. At the first golden shafts of sun-up he paused to take his bearings.

He had come a long way during the dark hours. The Square-8 was still visible at the far end of the valley, a good four miles distant perhaps. Nearer to him, in the other direction, nestling at the foot of the mountain range, was another ranch, fairly large, but with none of the prosperous signs of de Brock's spread. Jess contemplated it, fingering his unshaven chin; then at last he made up his mind to risk it and started off through the grass at a loping run. He kept low down on the off chance that one or other of de Brock's gunhawks might be on the lookout for him, but nothing disturbed the mellow peace of the dawn.

As he came nearer the ranch he saw that big though the corrals were there were no more than half a dozen steers in them, and no signs of men working about the place, as there should have been at this hour on any normal spread. There was a forlorn, poverty-stricken look about the place which seemed to suggest that the ruthless hand of Wilton de Brock had already struck here.

Crossing the yard at a run so as not to attract undue attention, Jess came up to the porch and knocked sharply on the inner door, the screen-door being latched back to the wall. There was a long pause; then the door opened perhaps half an inch and a gun barrel projected at him. He gave a start as he saw it and raised his hands slowly.

"Get out of here, and quickly, if you don't want lead!" a girl's voice commanded. It was a voice with the culture of education, at least, sufficient to enable her to place her sentences correctly.

Jess kept his hands raised and tried to see who was back of the voice, but without success. The sun was not yet shining on this side of the ranch-house. There was only a dim, shadowy figure without a sign of outline.

"I'm unarmed," he said. "All I want is a meal, and that I can pay for. If you can provide it, even hand it through the door if you want, I'll be on my way. That's gospel truth, ma'm."

"Stop telling lies! You're one of de Brock's men spying out the place, and it's like your impudence to come right up to the porch to do it. Fortunately I saw you from the window as you crossed the yard. Now go, before I shoot you. I've no time for de Brock or any of the owl-hooters connected with him."

Jess glanced about him and then gave a start. In the far distance a lone rider was approaching, coming towards this very ranch. It could be one of de Brock's gunmen — "Quit fooling around!" Jess implored hoarsely, through the doorcrack. I'm on the level. I'm escaping from de Brock if you must have the truth."

"I don't believe — "

Jess did not waste any further time on words. Suddenly he slammed his foot against the base of the door and then jumped back. The gun exploded harmlessly but the door tore from its chain and swung wide. In one dive he was inside, wrenching the revolver from the girl who held it. Swinging back to the door he closed it and shot the bolts into place.

"All right, then, shoot!" the girl snapped.

Jess turned and looked at her in the dim light of the hall. He could see thick dark hair and the outline of a blue short-sleeved blouse and dark riding skirt. Then without further ceremony he took her shoulder and pushed her into the brighter light of the living room. It was sparsely furnished. Here again was the same air of poverty which had been noticeable outside.

"Shootin' down a woman will be just about your mark, I take it?" the girl asked, flinging back her head in contempt, defiance in her amber-coloured eyes. "You wouldn't be a true disciple of de Brock otherwise. Get on with it! I'm not afraid of you!"

Jess stood looking at her. She was not exactly beautiful, but she had clear, intelligent features, a strong mouth, and the firm lines of a girl accustomed to perpetual open air in these sundrenched wastes. At the moment the icy hatred with which her face was masked made Jess feel profoundly uncomfortable.

"How many times do I have to tell you I'm not a gunman?" he demanded.

"As many times as you like, and I still won't believe you. It's written all over you."

"Listen for a minute, gal, for heaven's sake!"

"Supposing I don't?"

"The name's Jess Burton. I've escaped from de Brock's ranch prison and I need help. Mebby this will convince you that I'm quite harmless."

Jess tossed the gun on the table. Something of the stony contempt left the girl's face at that; then both she and Jess turned sharply at a pounding on the porch door.

"That could be one of de Brock's men," Jess breathed, whipping the gun up again. "And if so it won't take me ten seconds to put him where — "

"No!" The girl shook her dark head quickly. "It'll be my father, I expect. He rode into Yellow Gulch and he's due back around now."

"Sure?"

"Sure as can be, yes."

"Okay, but just the same I'll stand here and watch."

The girl left the room with graceful swiftness and drew back the door bolts. A tall man in riding pants and dark shirt became visible, tugging off his broad-brimmed hat. Immediately he put a protective arm about the girl's shoulders as he saw Jess, stubbled and grim, standing with the gun in the doorway of the living room.

"It's all right, this is my father," the girl said. "You can put that gun down."

"Bolt the door again," Jess instructed. "In case of surprise visits from strangers."

The grey-haired man with the slope shoulders did so; then with a frown he came forward. His features were gaunt and sharply defined, but there was something handsome and distinguished about him.

"What's all this about?" he demanded. "What right have you to come gunnin' on my spread an' scare my gal here?"

Jess tossed the gun back onto the table and shrugged. His eyes met those of the elderly rancher steadily.

"I'm assumin' that you're friendly," he answered. "Automatically you should be if you're opposed to Wilton de Brock. I know your daughter is."

"So that's th' way of things." The tall, gaunt rancher still looked puzzled. "Where are you headed, stranger? Away from de Brock, or towards him?"

"In a sense, both," Jess answered. "I escaped from his ranch at the other end of the valley, but I don't aim to try an' escape any further. It's time somebody stayed put around here and figgered out where de Brock should be made to get off. I'm Jess Burton. I was just a plain hombre until de Brock as good as hijacked me into his outfit. I stayed one day and then quit — in my own way.

Right now I imagine de Brock's men will be out on the prod for me. I haven't seen any of 'em but that isn't any guarantee. Lead might start flyin' at any moment."

"Yore right about de Brock's men," the rancher confirmed. "On my way back from Yellow Gulch I saw quite a few gunnin' parties on the prod, but I didn't know what for. They didn't stop me, an' even if they had I couldn't ha' told 'em anythin', of course."

The rancher studied Jess intently for a while and then seemed to make up his mind.

"All right, Burton, I'll take a chance," he said. "My name is Calvert, Len Calvert. This is my daughter, Fay. We've bin livin' here for 'bout ten years

142

now, ever since my wife died of a chill back in Kansas. Get some breakfast for us, Fay," Calvert added, and with a nod the girl went from the room.

Jess watched her go and then switched back to the rancher.

"Seems to me," Jess said, "that a man's treated like an escaped convict around here if he doesn't do just as de Brock tells him! Or anyways that's bin the set-up so far. I'm minded to make some big changes in the scheme of things."

"Yeah?" The rancher seemed to reflect over this.

"Thanks for trusting me," Jess added quietly, as he and Calvert settled in chairs at the table. "From the look of things around here you've as much grudge against de Brock as I have."

"Meanin'?"

"Your nearly empty corrals and the look of despair about the place. I noticed it straight away. Guess you can pretty well read a man's fortunes from the look of his cattle."

"Yeah, yore pretty well right."

Calvert brooded for a while, watching as his daughter returned and began to set out a breakfast for three.

"Yes, I suppose I do owe most of my troubles to de Brock," Calvert confirmed finally. "But just the same I'm a fatalist. I don't believe in fightin' the inevitable because I guess you get in a far worse mess that way. If a man's got the dice loaded against him he just can't win and it's suicide to try. An' so there it is."

Jess stared. "But, Mr Calvert, you can't mean that you agree with the things de Brock's doin' in this territory. No decent thinkin' man could."

"With most of my cattle stolen and my daughter and I livin' under th' threat of eviction? No! I don't agree with de Brock but I do believe it's safer sometimes to swim with th' current than against it. I'm no longer young enough to fight de Brock. So I leave him be. It's simpler that way, I reckon."

Fay put down the coffee jug irritably and gave Jess a very direct look.

"What my father really means is that he doesn't fight de Brock because he thinks things will be easier if he doesn't ."

"Fay!" her father protested sharply. "The way you put it makes it sound really bad."

143

"It's meant to, dad!" The girl's amber-coloured eyes switched back to Jess. "I've tried to explain to him that that can only lead to disaster in the end, but he doesn't see it. Or else he *won't!*"

"Have it your own way, gal," Calvert said, shrugging, "but we're still here and de Brock's left us alone."

"Now that he's stolen everything we had, yes," the girl retorted, her eyes flaming. "Before de Brock came we had a prosperous spread and a nice cattle business. Now our steers have mysteriously vanished 'til we've only half a dozen left. We know who is to blame, but what's the good of that if we don't act?" Fay sighed and shook her head. "Even the boys have left us because there was no work for them to do. Now we're living on the money we made in the good days, but it can't last for ever. Next thing we know de Brock will swoop and throw us out. I'm expecting it at any moment, which is one reason why I thought you were an advance scout, or something, Mr Burton."

"You mean he'll *buy* us out," Calvert said. "And when he does we'll go."

Fay looked at him helplessly. "But, dad, de Brock doesn't *buy* what he wants: he takes. When he's good and ready we'll be thrown out, same as happened at the Crossed-J, the Leaning-9, and the 5-Circle."

"I'll defy any eviction order de Brock sees fit to issue!" Calvert retorted stubbornly.

"Some good it will do you," Fay snapped. "If we don't go we'll be hanged here on the property as a warning to others who might think of refusing. That's de Brock's technique. I tell you we've only two alternatives — either fight de Brock by gathering together the remaining homesteaders and arming ourselves for attack; or else report the whole business to the nearest State Governor. That's an angle I've been thinking about for some time."

"You'll take too big a risk reporting it to a Governor," Jess said quietly. "I know because I've been on th' inside an' I've heard how de Brock works. But you might stand a chance if you an' the remaining ranchers formed into a body for your own protection. In fact it seems t' me about the only course left open. How many do you think you could count on to lend a hand?"

"About fifty men and women," the girl replied. "And every one of them hating de Brock!"

"Good enough! As I figger it, de Brock has around twenty men who might be called his strong-arm squad. That means that with fifty ranchers on our side we could — "

"I'll have nothin' t' do with it!" Calvert interrupted angrily, banging his fist on the table. "You can do as you like, Burton, once yore on your way, but don't drag us into it. There ain't no call for you to come bustin' in here with a lot of bright ideas!"

"I'm entitled to speak for myself, anyways," Fay said sharply. "What's more, I'm going to!"

"I'm your father, gal, an' as long as I live you'll do as I say. I've got things figgered out to protect th' both of us, and I won't be a party to no range war, for that's what it'd come to. Once the shootin' starts anythin' can happen, and we can't possibly win with the power de Brock's got. I don't aim to take a long chance like that."

"You prefer, then, to sit and take what's coming to you?" Jess asked, tackling his meal.

"I've my own way of runnin' things," Calvert answered. "I've no objections to givin' you a meal an' th' chance to rest up a bit. But that's as far as it goes. An' even that's a risk I don't like takin'. If de Brock's men turn up and find you here I'm liable to get strung up an' you beside me, with mebby Fay thrown in as a makeweight."

"The moment I've finished this meal, for which I'll pay, I'll be on my way," Jess promised. "Forget everything else I said. I'll work things out for myself."

"How?" Fay persisted, ignoring her father's angry glance. "Just how? I really want to know."

"Well, there are about a dozen men back at the Square-8 who are willin' to throw in their lot with me and try and destroy de Brock's stranglehold on this territory. I aim to free them and then we'll work in our own way. Our job is to undo every wrong de Brock has committed and make him suffer into the bargain. When we have finally destroyed his power an' gotten all the evidence we need, we'll bring in a State Governor to look into things. That's the only way ever to get action around here."

"Then you're a danged fool!" Calvert declared, "de Brock'll shoot you outa hand the moment you expose yourself, and you know it!"

"*If* I expose myself," Jess corrected, getting to his feet. "I would have liked you on our side, Mr Calvert, an' your daughter, too. Since that can't be done I'll see how the other ranchers feel about it." He laid a ten dollar on the table. "That should cover the meal an' everythin'," he added. "And thanks again."

The die-hard rancher sat looking at him fixedly. "You're just a sucker for trouble, Burton, ain't you?" he asked. "I've never seen anybody quite like you."

"I know injustice when I see it, an' if it's humanly possible I aim to stop it. Since you won't be joinin' me personally there is one other thing you might do."

"Well?"

Jess nodded to the nickel-plated .45 on the table. "Let me have that to protect myself with. I can't buy it from you 'cos I haven't that much money. You've two guns in your belt there: you can surely spare that one?"

Calvert laid his big hand across it. "Sorry, Burton. If you want to go around killin' folk you must do it with your own hardware. I'm not bein' a party to anything aimed against de Brock."

"But, dad, that's absolutely ridiculous!" Fay protested. "After all that gun — "

"Be quiet, gal, an' let me handle things th' way I see best. This gun stays right where it is. I don't aim to have trouble stirred up in a land that's too full of it already."

Jess hesitated and then hunched a shoulder. "Okay, have it your own way. Thanks again. 'Bye, Miss Fay."

He turned and left, but he had hardly reached the base of the porch steps before the girl came hurrying after him. She caught his arm and stopped him, holding out the .45, butt foremost. He looked at it in surprise.

"Take it," Fay urged. "Heaven knows, you need it."

"I sure do, Miss Fay, but what about your pop? He was mighty positive about me not havin' it."

"It's my gun, not his. I can do what I like with my own property, after all."

Jess studied her, her earnest amber eyes, her wealth of dark hair flowing in the soft breeze. For a moment he compared her to the shadowy creature who had ordered him away not an hour before.

"I can't figure out how a man like your pop comes to have a daughter like you," he said. "You've twice his spirit. Mebby I'd work it out better if I'd known your Ma."

"You don't want to pay too much heed to what dad says," the girl answered. "He's acting as he thinks best, I suppose, trying to protect me in his way by not causing de Brock any trouble. But I don't mind trouble if only we have justice, and that's why I'm with you in your plans even though at this stage I daren't join you personally. My father's religious," she added, as though that explained everything.

"Y'mean that 'turn the other cheek' stuff?"

"You might call it that. Makes him seem cowardly but he isn't really."

Jess smiled. "Thanks for the gun. As for the religious angle, I've nothin' against it. But it doesn't seem such a powerful weapon in a region like this."

Fay changed the subject before he could proceed any further.

"You'll need a horse, won't you?" she questioned.

"It'd help a lot, yes. My own's back at the Square-8 and I ain't sure I'll ever see it again. But yore takin' a big risk lettin' me have a mount, aren't you?"

"Too big a risk!" Calvert himself declared, from the porch. "Come back here, gal, whilst you're safe. You've done enough damage as it is givin' your gun to this hombre."

"He can have my own mare," Fay retorted defiantly. "If you won't help a man to get action, dad, then I will! That, to my way of thinking, is only downright common sense."

Deliberately she turned her back to him and led the way to a stable at the side of the ranch-house. Jess half followed her, then stood waiting, one eye cocked on the silent rancher as he watched stonily. Presently the girl reappeared, leading a frisky and saddled chestnut mare.

"Save you a lot of walking," she said, giving the reins into Jess' hand. "You can return her sometime if you ever get your own horse back."

"I'll come and see you again in any case," Jess promised, vaulting into the saddle after he had shaken the girl's hand firmly. "An' thanks a lot for the help. You'll be hearin' plenty about me before yore much older, I reckon."

Spurring the mare forward he cantered across the yard, waving as he went. The girl responded, but not her father. He remained like a statue on the porch, watching, and Jess could imagine the brooding stare in those eyes.

Then he turned his attention to his own safety. To be on the alert for sudden trouble was essential. At any moment hidden gunmen from the Square-8 might appear, and there was little doubt in Jess' mind but what they'd shoot first and ask questions afterwards. So he turned to the only spot where he could feel reasonably safe. The mountain range.

Here he remained throughout the torrid day, feeding on the few roots and edible berries he found, and slaking his and the mare's thirst from the mountain stream. Then at — nightfall — he prepared for action. He checked over the gun the girl had given him. There were six bullets in it, not many if it came to desperate fighting, but enough to get by perhaps. He decided that the sooner he obtained a gun-belt of .45 cartridges the better he'd feel.

It was completely dark when he left his cave hideout, speeding down the mountain trail which presently became an arroyo stretching away under the stars like a pale grey line amidst the grasslands. With the night wind rushing in his face he rode swiftly along the valley side, his gun ready for instant action, his destination the Square-8.

He reached it in half an hour and then began to ride more warily. A quarter of a mile from it he slipped from the mare, tethered her securely to a thicket, and finished his trip on foot. His eyes were fixed on the lights of the bunkhouse and the glow from the curtained windows of the ranch itself.

When he reached the high paling fence which completely enclosed the ranch yard, he paused and looked about him. There was no sign of any sentries on duty, unless it was that his crouching advance had been stealthy enough to enable him to elude them. With a swift jump he gripped the top of the fence and hauled himself up. On the other side, a few yards away, a gunman lounged. He was in the shadows cast by the kerosene lamps hanging outside the ranch-house. His task, apparently, was not so much to stop anybody coming in as to prevent any of the hijacked outfit getting out.

Jess grinned to himself, poising his lithe body for a moment. Then he leapt. He landed on top of the gunman before he had the least chance to protest or cry out. A violent blow on the back of the neck with the gun butt silenced him completely.

Glancing about him as he worked, Jess took the man's gun and cartridge belt, strapping it about his own waist; then he glided towards the bunkhouse. The doorway was open, pale kerosene glow streaming from within the low-roofed building. There came the low murmuring of men's voices.

Cautiously Jess peered round the door edge into the dreary building. There were perhaps twelve cowpunchers present, and the reason for their quiet behaviour and muttered tones became immediately obvious. Seated facing them, his back to the door, was one of de Brock's guards, a rifle across his knees, a cigarette dangling from the corner of his heavy-lipped mouth.

Jess studied the scene more intently. The men present were chiefly those who had vowed they would not join in any attempted getaway. Those who had been willing to take a chance, including Ox himself, were absent. Jess wondered why, and his lips tightened as he speculated on whether or not they had been shot for their mutinous behaviour.

He came to a snap decision and acted. Leaping forward he had his forearm under the guard's chin and was holding him in an immovable grip before the man could make a move to save himself. He struggled futilely, his hands flailing, but he could not dislodge the grip Jess had on him. The assembly of men watched grim-faced. None made a move to interfere.

"A little information is all I need from you, my friend," Jess breathed, snatching the man's cigarette from his lips. Then to the assembly he added, "And if any of you guys feel like changin' your minds and clearin' out now's your chance! I ain't likely to come again. Or are all of you the yellow-bellies you seem to be?"

The men looked at each other, waverers most of them, but they remained still.

"They got more sense 'n risk floggin', or death — or worse," the guard panted, fighting to free himself. "An' you'll never git outa this alive either, Burton. Yuh must be plain crazy even to think yuh can."

"Yeah? We'll see … Now you can start tellin' me somethin'. Where's Ox an' the rest of the boys who were willin' to back him an' me in a getaway?"

"Why in tarnation should I tell yuh that?"

"Because I want to know — and I can be mighty persuasive when the mood seizes me."

"If yuh think that scares me, Burton, yuh'd best start figgerin' out a new line."

Very deliberately Jess blew the ash from the cigarette he was holding, then he moved it slowly downwards towards the guard's upturned face. As he saw it coming straight for his left eye he thrashed and heaved mightily, but the armlock was too much for him. The glowing point of the weed came at him relentlessly.

"Okay, okay. Wait!" he panted, sweating. "I tell yuh what yuh want to know. They got solitary fur what they did. Ox an' the rest uv them."

"An' where's solitary?" Jess snapped. "Hurry it up! I can't hang around here all night."

"In — in the yard. There's a flagstone in the middle of it, with an iron ring. Ox an' th' others is below. Bin there for some time."

"All right, take me to them." Jess dug his .45 in the man's back as he released his hold on his neck. "If you say one word outa turn, God help you!"

The guard got up slowly, hesitated, and then began to move to the doorway. He had sense enough to realize that he stood no chance and that if need be Jess would shoot to kill. His hands slightly raised he walked out of the bunkhouse and across the yard in the kerosene glow.

Jess followed steadily, his eyes darting about for any fresh guards who might appear. Evidently, though, with the bunkhouse under supervision, the guards were not over-zealous, for nothing was seen of them.

Reaching the flagstone the puncher nodded to it. Through the iron ring in its centre was padlocked an iron bar. Jess stood looking down at it for a moment.

"Get it up!" he ordered.

"It's a two-man job."

"Shut up and get busy. A big lunkhead like you shouldn't need any help."

The man scowled, unfastened the padlock with a key from his pocket, and flung the iron bar aside. Then he heaved the flat stone away. From the pit below there came the sound of voices. Jess stepped to the hole, never once removing his eyes from the guard.

"You fellers down there!" he called, not raising his voice too much in case it carried. "It's safe to come up. Make it quick!"

There was the sound of scrambling and excited conversation from the depths. Then, shoved from beneath, Ox made his appearance over the edge of the cavity, his ugly face emerging into the yellow light.

"Jess!" he gasped, staring. "Say, is this somethin'! We figgered you'd run out on us."

"Then start figgering again, Ox. I was only bidin' my time."

Ox hauled himself out and moved to Jess' side, but when he began talking Jess waved him away.

"Save it, Ox. I've my work cut out watching this guy here. How many are there below?"

"Six — packed tight. They'll be up pronto."

They were, scrambling quickly over the stone rim into the yard. All of them were dirty, unshaven, haggard after their ordeal below.

"This skunk had as much t'do with it as anybody," Ox breathed, clenching his enormous fists and moving towards the guard. "It wus him who kicked us below — an' I mean kicked! de Brock figgered on leavin' us here — 'til we rotted, I guess, which we should ha' done but fur you, Jess. I guess there oughta be some kind uv reply to that sorta thing."

"Mebby there is, but we haven't time for it now," Jess said. "We're leavin' here, all of us. Put that skunk below. Best place for him."

"Pleasure!" Ox grinned, and his big left hand flashed out with the impact of a steam piston.

The guard absorbed the blow across his face and keeled over backwards. A further terrific punch to the base of the skull sent him crashing head first into the cavity. With supreme ease Ox lifted the stone and dropped it back into position, snapping the padlock firmly. A wide grin had spread across his ugly face as he looked at Jess again.

"Now what?" he questioned.

"You okay?" Jess asked him. "Last I saw of you you'd been creased by a bullet."

"That? Huh! Just parted me hair, that's all. I think we oughta go now an' give that mug de Brock what's bin owin' to him fur far too long. He spends too much time talkin' fancy an' doin' as he likes. A mug like that wants payin' back in his own coin."

"Later mebby," Jess said. "Not now."

"Why in hell not! I'm gettin' sick uv takin' on th' lamp fur that guy! He's unprepared an — "

"I said later!" Jess snapped. "Never kill a man whilst you can make use of him. Around here, Ox, I'm runnin' things. An' see that you get it through your thick skull. I've freed you and these other fellers for only one reason, so's you can have a chance to fight back, but under my orders. Any objections?"

The other men were silent as Jess looked at them questioningly.

Ox hesitated, then shook his bullet head. "Okay, Jess, have it your way. But we ain't goin' to get far unarmed. This place is lousy with gunmen, or I don't know de Brock."

"Just what I was thinkin', but it seems to me that a man who does as much shootin' and pillagin' around the territory as de Brock does must have an armoury somewheres from which we can take our pick of weapons. I aim to find it whilst we're here and make a selection."

"That'll take some doin', Jess!" Shorty protested. "Sounds like walkin' right into the enemy camp to me!"

Jess grinned. "Mebby it is. But if de Brock himself tells us where the armoury is we oughta get some place. Let's see what he has to say for himself."

3. Tough Hombres

Inwardly astonished at Jess' audacity, but quite willing to follow his lead, the men trailed behind him up to the ranch-house. He ignored the porch, walking instead to the lighted but curtained floor-to-ceiling window facing the barns and outhouses. Hurling his shoulder against the flimsy frame he tumbled into the living room beyond, bringing up sharp and firing his gun.

He was just in time. In the split second of warning de Brock seated with his wife at a well-laid table, had whipped out his Colt. It spun out of his hand and clattered uselessly into the fire grate. He sat glaring, his fingers tingling, as Jess walked slowly into the room with his grim-faced cohorts behind him.

"Okay, de Brock, so yore surprised," Jess said calmly, a glint in his eyes. "That's how I meant it to be. An' before I'm through mebby you'll be surprised a lot more." "Now you've had your surprise," de Brock grated, "what more do you want?"

"Plenty! But I'll come to it in my own time. Do you good to wait a bit and give somebody else a chance. Okay, boys," Jess added, after an interval which he had made as long as possible. "Help yourselves to food and drink. It's time you had some at de Brock's expense."

The cattle baron remained silent, exchanging glances with his wife as the food and drink on the table was wolfed, Jess too satisfying his gnawing appetite. Then presently he said:

"Remember what I told you last night? That I was goin' to let you live so's you'd take longer to die?"

"You'll never get off this spread alive, any of you!" de Brock vowed breathing hard. "As for you, Burton, and your fool warnings, I don't give a rap if you try to — "

"Shut up an' get on your feet!"

"I'll be — "

Jess fired for the second time and the bullet tore the table-cloth in a smoking line not an inch from the cattle baron's hand. He got up, making a tremendous effort to control his fury. His wife sat on, glancing from one to the other.

"Keep a watch outside, Ox," Jess ordered, without turning. "This gun of mine may bring some of the jackals around to see what gives. Now, de Brock, where do you keep your guns and ammo?"

"That's my business!"

"Mine, too. Start talkin'!"

"To a saddle tramp like you? What the hell do you think I am?"

"Better not be too obstinate, de Brock. I'll give you five seconds to answer my question."

The cattle baron remained silent, his powerful mouth set. Jess eyed him stonily and counted five; then he called Shorty over to him.

"Yeah, Jess?" Shorty asked.

"Put the poker in the fire there an' hot it up with the bellows. When it's good and red see how Mrs de Brock will enjoy havin' her face branded like a steer! Without bein' disrespectful to Mrs de Brock, she ain't exactly beautiful anyways, so mebby a little brandin' will hardly be noticed." Shorty blinked a little. You're kiddin', Jess?" "Do as yore told," Jess ordered implacably, and the little cowpuncher scuttled to obey the instruction even if he could hardly believe his ears.

Mrs de Brock shifted uncomfortably in her chair, emotion showing for the first time in her square features. Her husband looked at her, then his pale, steely eyes fastened sharply on Jess.

"Pretty low down kind of fighter, aren't you?" he asked grimly. "Branding a woman to get information from her husband! I thought of several things you might do, Burton, but never this!"

"Now you know different," Jess said calmly.

"Dragging a woman into it and making her squirm is low tactics, Burton."

"Her husband can prevent it," Jess replied tersely. "And I guess that if you wanted somethin' real badly, de Brock, you wouldn't stop at brandin' a woman either. Yore not the only guy around here who can be tough."

Jess waited, his face murderous in its intentness, his gun rock-steady.

There was a long, grim pause: it was broken by Ox poking his head round the shattered window.

"Two guards so fur, Jess," he announced. "They're out cold. Yore in th' clear fur the moment. If any more come along I'll break their blasted heads ag'inst each other!"

"Okay, Ox, stay on guard. What about that iron, Shorty? Takin' a long time, isn't it?"

"Yeah, Jess, sure is, but I reckon it's good an' red now, like yuh wanted it."

Shorty pulled the iron out of the grate, holding the handle in his folded kerchief. He stopped when he came in front of Mrs de Brock and she shrank back in her chair. Shorty licked his lips, hesitated, then lowered the iron slightly.

"Guess I ain't got th' guts to do this," he muttered. "Durn me, Jess, it's more'n I can take!"

"Gettin' soft, huh?" Jess took the poker in his free hand and stood ready for action. He advanced the poker steadily in an unshaken hand towards the woman's terrified face — then to his infinite relief de Brock stopped him.

"Just a minute, Burton, take it easy. I'll tell you what you want to know. I can see when I'm cornered."

"'bout time," Jess growled, flinging the poker into the grate with a nerve-jarring clatter. "All right, where's the armoury? An' if you play any tricks, de Brock, I'll let you have it here an' now and let the future take care of itself."

The cattle baron jerked his head and led the way into an adjoining room. Jess and the other men followed him — but not Ox. He stayed behind to keep guard over the living room and the rancher's wife. Crossing to a big wall cupboard de Brock unfastened the doors and revealed the rifles, revolvers, and ammunition within.

"Very pretty," Jess commented, giving him a grim look.

"All nicely loaded up to start a range war, huh? Nothin' like bein' prepared in advance."

"I intend finally to rule this territory in its entirety, Burton, and in the process I'll grind you to powder and all these louts who trail around with you. You have me at the pistol point now, but it won't always be so. The moment I'm free to act things will happen such as you'd never thought possible."

"Yeah? Take care it isn't the other way round! You're not idiot enough to think you can cross swords with me and get away with it, are you?"

Jess said nothing further. He helped himself to a .45 complete with loaded gun belt, then motioned to his men to choose their own weapons.

This done he led the way back into the living room and sent Ox to make his selection. He returned with twin .38s strapped to his heavy thighs.

"I guess I feel properly dressed with th' hardware back in place," he commented. "But jus' the same, if things get too awkward I've a pair of mansized fists I can use. All I need is a face 'bout th' size uv de Brock's to plant'em in!"

"Understand this, de Brock," Jess said levelly, his gun still pointed. "We're not thieves."

"You're not? It would be interesting to know what you do call yourselves!"

"We're takin' what is due to us, even though it may not be the original article!" Jess snapped. "From each of us you took guns and cartridges: we're taking 'em back. It will be kinda poetic to hound you down with your own weapons every time you make a move."

de Brock smiled coldly. "You're fool enough to think you can get away with that?"

"You'll see. I'm warnin' you, de Brock. Stay within limits an' run things in a proper way and you'll be okay. I don't consider it my business to worry over things you may have done before I got into this territory. But I shall worry over what you do from now on."

"Oh, you will? Is that supposed to make me quake with terror, or something?"

"Nope. Just plain words, that's all. If you dare to lay a hand on any of the settlers around here you'll pay for it to the limit. That's a promise. In any event, whether you attack any more settlers or not I'm going to ruin your empire for you because it's too dangerous to be left standin'. I'll do it if it takes me the rest of my life!"

"You'll have to act fast then, Burton, because I have the impression your life hasn't much longer to run, at least, not if I have anything to do with it."

Jess ignored the threat. "You also took horses from each of us," he said. "We'll take one each as we leave — and you'll see that we leave safely. Now get moving to the stables. You too, Mrs de Brock. We're not leaving you behind to raise the alarm."

The cattle baron shrugged and led the way outside through the window. Two guards who had just come up immediately trained their guns, then hesitated as de Brock raised his hand. He looked at them grimly, but there was nothing he could do. "Take it easy, boys," he ordered. "No shooting."

They relaxed, compelled to stand watching as all but Jess selected the mounts they fancied, saddled them, and then led them into the yard.

"Which about completes this evening's business," Jess said. "But I don't guarantee but what we'll be back some other evening. I already have a mare so I don't need a mount."

"Where did you get it?" de Brock demanded, frowning. "Stole it, I suppose?"

Jess only grinned enigmatically and motioned his men towards the gates. He kept de Brock covered until he could no longer hold it. Then he leapt on the back of Ox's saddle and the entire party sped off quickly under the stars. Reaching his own tethered mare Jess jumped down, went over to the animal and swung into the saddle, following his comrades as they raced across the starlit pastureland. In a while he caught up with Ox.

"Where are we headin'?" Ox demanded. "You got that figgered out 'mongst other things? Ain't much use in us just goin' any place. These things want organisin'."

You don't have to tell me," Jess retorted. "We're goin' to the mountains. I've a cave up there. But we're not goin' there direct 'cos we need food, and that includes fodder for th' animals if we're to survive. That bein' so we're goin' to town and the general stores."

"Raid the joint, y'mean?" Ox grinned. "That suits me fine! For the fust time, Jess, yuh's started talkin' in my language. Take what we like an — "

"We'll pay for what we get," Jess interrupted. "Get it straight, Ox, that we're not outlaws pilfering as we choose. We'd be no better'n de Brock if we behaved like that. We're goin' to see that there's justice in this valley until we've swept it clean of the stink of that polecat, an' ranchers can breathe free an' easy an' know they're safe. Got that?"

Ox rode on in silence for a while before he answered. His slow-moving brain took a long time to work things out.

"Yeah, I get it," he assented finally. "But I don't see how this small lot uv us is goin' to defeat de Brock. Seems t'me it's a short life an' a merry one 'til we're beaten. Why not make it good an excitin' an' do what we want where we want? I never could see any sense in pullin' yuh punches when there ain't any real need."

"Step out of line, Ox, and I'll finish you," Jess warned him. "That's a threat, an' I mean it. I want you for a trusted henchman, but if you go against th' stream don't be surprised if you drown in it."

"Okay, okay, yuh don't have ta get tough about it. But tell me one thing, where's th' money comin' from to pay fur th' food an' stuff we'll need? Or mebby yore so busy bein' a saint yuh haven't given it a thought!"

"I can tell you right now who's payin' for things," Jess answered dryly. "Shorty."

"Huh?" Shorty squeaked, a little way ahead, hipping round in his saddle. "Why me?"

"Better hand it over, Shorty," Jess advised. "If you thought I didn't see you pick up that roll of notes lyin' on th' mantelshelf in de Brock's livin' room, yore crazy! I've told you before about bein' too light-fingered, but this time it's a help. No reason why de Brock shouldn't finance his enemies. God knows, he's stolen enough stuff himself. I s'pose you thought you'd keep that wad to yourself, huh? Sorry, but it doesn't work that way when we're desperate."

"But Jess, look-ee here — "

Shorty's protest was cut short. "Give, feller, all of it! Y'know better'n to argue when my mind's made up."

Shorty felt in his hip pocket and handed over a wad of notes as Jess came riding up beside him. With one hand he flipped the corners and peered at the bundle in the starlight.

"Hundred-dollar bills!" he commented. "Must be pretty nearly forty of 'em here. Four thousand dollars'll finance the campaign very nicely."

"Are yuh aimin' to tell us that we don't share an' share alike?" Ox asked grimly.

"Not while I'm in charge. But I don't see that a hundred apiece should hurt you," Jess added. "Sort of initiation fee."

He pulled out the necessary separate $100 bills as he rode and handed them over. All the men appeared satisfied, except Ox. He muttered a surly thanks and said no more. Jess passed no remark either but he did wonder what was going on in the big cowpuncher's brutish, slow-witted brain.

The General Stores was closed when they hit town, but under Jess' imperious hammering on the double doors it did not stay closed for long. The little, bald-headed storekeeper was all set to protest vehemently at this sudden invasion after business hours, but he changed his mind as Jess' gun prodded him in the stomach.

"What is this?" the storekeeper demanded, pop-eyed. A hold up or sump'n?"

"Nope, official business. Say nothin' an' you won't get hurt. And you'll get paid, Baldy. The gun's to make sure you open the shop specially for us, see?"

The little man backed into the dim expanse of the store, then at Jess' instructions he lighted the oil lamps. Jess cuffed up his hat on to his forehead and looked about him.

"Yeah, everythin' we need," he decided. "Bedrolls, food, razors, horse fodder, the works." Then he went into an itemised list of requirements, insisting on each man paying for his own necessities out of his hundred-dollar bill.

"Which I don't call fair!" Ox objected, as the storekeeper began to parcel up the provisions in cardboard containers. "Yuh know how much I got left outa that hundred smackers? Twenty! Twenty! What kind uv checken feed is that fur a man?"

"All you'll need," Jess told him. "The kind of life we're goin' to lead you won't need any more money than that."

"If it's all th' same to you, feller, I likes a drink now an ag'in!" Ox snapped. "Twenty dollars sure won't get me much firewater."

Jess looked at him steadily. "Whilst you work with me, Ox, you'll keep a clear head. The drinking's out. You seem to forget that de Brock will leave nothing unturned to get us. We can't afford to be pickled when that happens."

"I'm willin' t' risk it," Ox growled.

"What yore willin' t' do doesn't count. I'm thinkin' for the good uv the lot of us. An' don't try my patience too much, damn you!"

Ox gave a suspicious leer and licked his heavy lips.

"What about th' rest uv that cash you've stored away? Figgerin' on runnin' out with it?"

Jess tightened his lips and said nothing. Ox, too, seemed to realize he was saying too much in front of the storekeeper so he kept quiet thereafter until everything had been transported outside. Then when the men were all astride their mounts he began again:

"I don't reckon that it's right to ask a man t' follow yuh into heck knows what without even a drink!" he protested. "My throat's burnin' fit to crack it wide open."

"Mebbe yore right," Jess grinned. "I'm pretty caked up with dust in the throat myself. 'Sides, I've somethin' to say to the folks of this town, and there's no better place than th' Trail's End Saloon. Let's go."

"Now yore talkin'!" Ox cried, and spurred his horse forward. "Guess I had yuh figgered wrong, Jess."

Outside the saloon they dropped from their mounts and hitched the reins on the tie-rack.

"Not you," Jess said, pulling Shorty back as he waddled towards the boardwalk steps. "Watch these cayuses. There's plenty of stuff on them we can't afford to lose. You can go in when we come out."

Though grumbling, Shorty nevertheless obeyed, returning mournfully to his horse where he sat surveying the practically empty high street in the glow of kerosene light. The Trail's End, however, was anything but deserted. It was jammed full of cowpokes, cattle traders, half-breeds, Mexicans, and saddle-tramps, most of them keeping company with women. The air was thick with tobacco fumes and the gambling tables were busy. In a group Jess and his boys moved languidly across to the bar counter.

"Whisky," Jess told the barkeep, and then looked about him, his right hand resting lightly on his gun.

"I reckon this drink's necessary," Ox murmured to him, his eyes darting about the smoky expanse. "But I guess we're also stickin' our chins out, somethin' I never thought of. That's th' wust of me, I guess. I can never seem t' plan anything properly. Only knows what I want an' does it. But you've got a head on yuh an' should ha' thought uv it. If any uv de Brock's boys are around here they'll recognize us an' then there'll be trouble."

"There'll be trouble in any case," Jess told him. "Might as well be in here as any place else. From now on de Brock's got to realize that he's up against men as tough as himself. If he doesn't it'll be up to us to prove it to him."

Ox nodded and turned to his drink. He tossed it off and ordered another. Jess had just finished and started on the second when he found himself looking at a big man with a star badge on his shirt.

"I'd like a word with you guys," he said briefly "An' I mean all of you."

"Say on," Jess invited, "though I don't get the impression it'll be of any partic'lar interest to us."

"How do you know when I haven't told yuh anythin' yet?"

160

"I know that you only act under the orders of de Brock. That's sufficient, isn't it?"

Sheriff Hardacre's face became a deeper colour. "Mebby I do take orders from de Brock, but since he's the nateral boss around this region that's only sensible, ain't it?"

"I don't think so," Jess told him. "A sheriff's job is to dispense justice, not to be a hired stooge. It's a pity a few of the honest men around here don't shoot the tar outa you!"

"Why, you — "

"Hold it, sheriff!" Jess' gun leapt into his hand. "If you pull a rod on me I'll let you have it. Make no mistake about that. In the ordinary way I can be as kid-gloved as anybody, but around this territory things just ain't ordinary. You can only live if yore faster on the draw than the next guy. If yore minded to see if I'm faster than you with this hair-trigger, I'm ready an' waitin'."

The sheriff hesitated but he did not draw his gun. Jess gave a grim smile.

"Okay," he said briefly. "Now say what you've got t'say."

"I was goin' to tell you that the sooner you get outa here the better." Hardacre snapped. "There's trouble enough in this region without a bunch of hoodlums like you an' yore owl-hooters makin' things worse by crossin' de Brock."

"Thanks for the compliment," Jess said sourly. "How come you've sized us up as a bunch of hoodlums? Looks ain't everythin', y'know."

"I said hoodlums, an' I mean it! I know each one of you by sight 'cos I saw you at work on de Brock's spread when I called on him. It ain't healthy to do things around here which de Brock doesn't order."

Jess grinned, his revolver motionless.

"Speak your piece like a blasted parrot, don't you?" he asked. "My boys an' me are leavin' here when we get good and ready, but not 'til then. What d'you think you can do about it?"

"There's plenty of men in here who feel as I do; they'll shift you quick enough."

"Yeah?"

The sheriff looked about him upon the now silent, smoke-filled room. The men and women were watching, even if they were not taking decisive action. Jess waited, then he relaxed a little more comfortably, one elbow on the counter.

"We're ready for anythin' anybody likes to try," he said. "Don't forget what I told you about anybody who can shoot faster than I can. Come to think of it, I'm glad I met up with you, sheriff, because it decides me that yore another who'll have to be put out of office. A man like you who obeys another man instead of ordinary law ain't fit to be a sheriff. Am I right, folks?"

At the question flung at them, the men and women exchanged looks with each other, hesitating. Then one man rose, a bearded, bronzed fellow, well past middle age and plainly one of the valley settlers.

"Since th' rest uv you is scared t' talk while one man fights for the rest with his gun, I'll speak for you," he said.

"Good!" Jess approved, nodding. "Speak on, old timer, an' don't be scared of these lily-whites. I've got a bead on 'em an' they know it!"

"Yes, stranger, yore right," the rancher asserted. "There's never been any justice in this territory since de Brock took over. How can yuh get it with a crooked mayor an' sheriff? Yuh just can't —"

Sheriff Hardacre wheeled, his face bleak with murderous rage. In a split second he had his gun from its holster and fired point blank. The rancher hesitated, felt at his chest, and looked bewildered. Then he crashed heavily forward across the table in front of him.

"Reach!" Jess ordered, his gun jabbing in the sheriff's back.

The sheriff swung, ignoring the command, his gun flashing round. Jess fired remorselessly. The sheriff dropped his weapon, doubled up, then his knees buckled beneath him. He flattened on the floor, his flailing arm striking a cuspidor. It rolled away drunkenly and came to rest with a clang. There was silence and the stench of cordite fumes.

"I reckon he asked for that," Jess said grimly, looking about him. "In plain sight of all of you he shot down that rancher 'cos he dared raise his voice against de Brock. The sheriff got paid back and no misses. Okay?" he continued, his jaw tightening, "mebby it'll serve as an example far more than any words of mine could do. I came in here to tell you that from now on de Brock is going to find his control over this territory breakin' down. Those of you who believe in him will go with him to disaster: those of you who don't will find friends in me an' my boys. Reckon that puts the case clearly, doesn't it?"

The direct, ruthless methods of this young, unsmiling man with the power-packed body were something the assembled men and women hadn't seen in Yellow Gulch for many a long day. They looked first at Jess, then at the bodies of the rancher and the sheriff. Nobody said anything: the shadowy menace of Wilton de Brock's vengeance still made them consider it safer to keep quiet. Yet there was a murmuring amongst themselves as they exchanged opinions without openly declaring them.

"You'll be needin' a new sheriff," Jess said, stooping and whipping the sheriff's star from his shirt. "I might even take it on myself when I've finished cleanin' up. I'll keep this badge against the day that happens."

"Which is going to be a long time coming, Burton," a well educated voice commented from the batwings. "I think your trouble is that you are a little too impetuous."

Jess pivoted, his gun ready. At the same instant a revolver spat from the doorway, whipping the gun from his fingers. Wilton de Brock, impeccably dressed in a lounge suit, no hat on his shaven head, grinned round the smoke of his pearl-handled. 45.

4. Fire and Murder

"Just a little return for your visit to me at my ranch," he explained, coming forward. "Did it make your fingers sting, my friend? If so, my apologies. I suppose I might call it a little preliminary unpleasantness towards you before the big event, eh?"

Jess waited, his eyes narrowed, Ox and his men behind him. de Brock advanced with easy movements, stopping when he was within a yard of Jess.

"In regard to you, Burton, let me remind you of the old saying, 'a short life and a merry one'," he commented. "I'll be sorry to kill you, of course, because up to now I have quite enjoyed your fire and spirit. Were you to go on living you might become an enemy really worthy of watching, which is one obligation I do not intend to assume."

"Make sure you're not talkin' outa turn, de Brock," Jess breathed. "We've all got to die some day, an' some of us quicker than others, 'specially in this region."

"I always make sure, Burton; that is why I have so much power around here."

"You'd be more to the point if you said you couldn't help but be sure with nobody havin' th' guts to stand up to you. I've caught you out before today, de Brock, an' I aim to do it plenty more times yet."

"I notice," the cattle baron commented, "that you have already started your campaign of terror."

He considered the dead sheriff and the more distant figure of the sprawled rancher.

"Your hired jackal of a sheriff shot that rancher dead. So I shot the sheriff," Jess explained. "Seemed quite logical t' my way of thinkin'. When a man shoots another because he speaks the truth it's time he had some overdue lead comin' to him. I call that justice."

"From your way of thinking I suppose it was," de Brock agreed calmly, motioning the pop-eyed barkeep to hand him a drink. "But, of course, Burton, it just can't go on."

"No?" Jess eyed him narrowly.

"No!" de Brock swallowed some of his drink and continued, "Fortunately you are as big a fool as the rest of those who have tried to cross me. Instead of making good your escape with these assassins of yours you had to come right here into the very heart of the town and brag about your exploits. I hardly thought you'd be such a damned fool.

However, when my look-outs reported that that was what you had done I decided I'd better come over. And here you all are, in a bunch." Cold lights glimmered in de Brock's pale eyes. "Makes it simple, does it not?"

"Mebby ... " Without any show of emotion Jess swallowed down the dregs of his second drink and put the glass back on the counter. He could hear Ox breathing heavily behind him and needed no imagination to guess that those massive fists were clenched.

"In regard to the murder of Sheriff Hardacre," the cattle baron continued, "I have since equalled the score."

Jess' eyes sharpened. "How?"

"You left that idiot Shorty Pearson on guard outside. I slugged him from behind with my Colt. Unfortunately, he had a thin skull ... You'll find his body lying under the porch. I had my men put it there to save making the main street untidy."

"Yuh killed him?" Ox demanded fiercely. "Just like that? Fur nothin' at all?"

De Brock nodded looking surprised. "Why not? One less hoodlum to bother about. Now I shall have to take care of you gentlemen and with you out of my way I can move a little more freely But first, Burton, I'll trouble you for that sheriff's badge. You will never need it, whereas I shall have the mayor put it on a new law officer, one, I trust, with less inclination to open his mouth too wide. You see, I do agree with you in one respect, that Hardacre talked a lot more than was necessary. Discretion, I suppose, should be a sheriff's chief virtue."

Jess did not respond. He turned to the bar, facing it so that he could see everything in the back-bar mirrors. It gave him a chance to sum things up without the movement of his eyes being obvious.

"Hurry it up!" de Brock snapped. "I'm not going to stand here indefinitely waiting for that badge."

Jess still looked into the mirrors, satisfying himself that directly overhead there hung one of the kerosene lamps. The rest of his plan would depend on split-second timing.

"Okay," he said casually, feeling in his shirt with his left hand. Then with his right he suddenly whirled up the whisky bottle standing near de Brock's elbow and flung it unerringly at the lamp overhead. It went out in a splintering of glass and gushing of blazing oil.

Unprepared, de Brock dodged as glass pelted on him, then a ramrod fist struck him on the mouth with crashing force. He jolted backwards, his head and shoulders falling into piled-up bottles at the end of the counter. Helpless, he sagged to his knees. The entire sequence took perhaps five seconds and in that time Jess leapt from his position, dodging the bullets which exploded at him. His own guns in his hands, again he fired savagely, fighting his way to the nearest table. Upending it he jumped behind it for protection, Ox following immediately after him.

Pandemonium struck the saloon as the shots were exchanged. The men and women whirled and scuttled and fled through the bat-wings. The barkeep dodged behind his counter and stayed there. The big mirror splintered in the hail of lead which de Brock's trigger-men let loose.

De Brock himself, his upper lip bleeding profusely, remained crouched by the counter for a moment. Then he worked his way to the end of it and remained there, sniping at intervals, ducking back as woodwork splintered close to his face.

"Kill those other lamps, Ox," Jess murmured. Tut the place in darkness an' then we'll beat it. We can't get away with it otherwise."

"Okay, but it seems a pity t'go just when we wus gettin' warmed up."

Ox twisted round and sighted on the nearest lamp. It exploded in a clink of glass as he fired and the ignited oil spattered on the floor. The remaining and final lamp followed it and more blazing oil dropped. Jess watched it for a moment.

"Quick!" he breathed. "Let's get outa here before the place catches fire!"

To give the order was one thing, to put it into force another. The flames of the shattered lamps were already taking a firm hold on the dry wooden flooring. Apart from the danger of a conflagration the light was a give-away and made Jess, Ox, and those who crept with them, a constant target for the bullets ripping across the saloon.

But finally they reached the bat-wings and so as not to make themselves too noticeable they slid underneath them to prevent them swinging. Outside, three of de Brock's men were waiting on horseback. Taking no chances Jess and Ox fired at them simultaneously. Given no time to take aim the three men reeled from their saddles into the dust of the high street.

"Guess de Brock was right about Shorty," Jess said grimly, looking about him. "No sign of him anywhere but his horse is still there and ours are still loaded up. That's luck. Evidently de Brock didn't take up time relieving us. All right, let's hit leather."

None of the men needed telling twice. They leapt to their saddles, dug in their spurs, and rode like the devil, Jess bringing along Shorty's horse behind him so that its useful bedroll and other necessities would not be lost. From the saloon, as they travelled, there came only a few shots. The probable explanation was that de Brock and his men were too busy trying to stop the fire gaining a hold.

When they were a couple of miles from town, riding the trail which led directly to the mountains, Jess slowed the pace somewhat, Ox riding up beside him in the starlight.

"Seems we got outa that okay, Jess," he remarked. "An' if there's anythin' left of the Trail's End by mornin' I'll be surprised. Mebby we started a fire that'll burn all Yellow Gulch to th' ground afore it's through. That wouldn't be a bad idea, either. Make our job of wipin' out de Brock a whole lot easier."

Jess looked behind him into the violet sky with its brazenly winking stars.

"Yore too optimistic, Ox," he replied. "No sign of fire glow over there. De Brock and his boys musta got the blaze under control. Just as well they have 'cos I don't want the populace to be burned outa house an' home. It wouldn't help our cause a bit. At root we'd be considered responsible."

"Yeah, mebby yore right." Ox rubbed his head impatiently. "Dang me, there I go ag'in! Can't seem to figger things out. I thought it'd help: you say it wouldn't an' now I see yore right. Mebby I'm just plain dumb."

"Could be," Jess agreed, grinning. "But that doesn't mean yore not mighty useful, feller."

"Seems t'me, Jess, that we got precious little outa that saloon dust-up except the pleasure of pumping lead into some uv de Brock's boys. While it lasted it was the nicest thing I've done fur many a long month."

"We got more'n that," Jess rode on steadily. "For one thing we eliminated an unwanted sheriff, an' for another we found that most of the people are behind us but afraid to say so. I aim to start discoverin' next how many ranchers back us up. That'll be a solo job for me alone. There's also a mayor we've gotta take care of."

"Yeah! Sooner th' better fur as I'm concerned."

"From what I hear he's as much a mouthpiece for de Brock as the sheriff was. Those sort aren't wanted, an' when a man out here ain't wanted there's only one thing t' do with him."

"Yeah." Ox grinned widely in the starlight. "I guess yuh don't have ta tell me."

It was some time after midnight when at length Jess, Ox, and the boys were domiciled in the cave in the foothills which Jess himself had been using during the day-time. Having everything they needed for their immediate comfort they all had a meal, attended to the horses, and then sat in the starlight at the cave entrance, talking among themselves. They would have liked to smoke too but Jess forbade it, unless they concealed themselves in the cave. Even the glowing end of a cigarette would be visible for miles in the clear, sharp air of the Arizona night.

"Well, Jess, we've gotten this fur," Ox's voice remarked out of the gloom. "What happens next? Apart from yuh seein' how many ranchers is back uv us. I'm not one who likes loungin' around with nothin' t'deal with."

"As far as we're concerned nothing happens 'til de Brock starts something," Jess answered. "An we can't very well know if he starts something without working out a signal system with the ranchers. That's why I intend to take a ride around 'em tomorrow an' see if they're willin' to co-operate in bringing down de Brock."

"Mebby they'll be too leary t' give you any backing," Ox commented. "From what I've seen uv 'em around here de Brock's got th' livin' daylights scared outa them."

"Mebby. On the other hand, for their own good, they might be glad to be helpful. Then at some other time we're goin' to take care of the mayor. My aim is to eliminante everybody who supports de Brock and so gradually destroy his influence." "Yuh could leave the mayor t'me, Jess," Ox said, brooding. "I'd rub him out quicker'n a bug."

"I'll do it my own way, Ox, thanks."

"Lookee here, Jess, fast as you eliminate folks de Brock'll put somebody else in their places," one of the men objected. "That way we get no place."

"Don't be too sure of that," Jess told him. "Would you be willin' to take on the job of sheriff knowin' it would probably mean you'd die before long? Would you take on the job of mayor if you knew your predecessor had died 'cos he was a mayor? An' don't try an' give a snap answer: think it out first."

"I mightn't have no chance if a gun were fixed on me."

"Yes you would. The instinct of self-preservation is far stronger even than de Brock. I don't believe any man would take on an official job because of de Brock's say-so, not if it meant askin' for lead any time, anywheres. There are some things which even de Brock can't control, human nature f'r instance."

There was silence for a time, the men gazing out over the overlying waste of mist which blanketed the valley. In the direction of Yellow Gulch there was a faint amber glow from the kerosene lights in the main street, and that was all. The fire that had started had evidently been extinguished.

"D'yuh think de Brock's ever likely t'get this fur?" Ox asked at length.

"Mebby, but he'll have a hard job finding us. An' in any case with one or other of us always on th' lookout we'll see him first. One man alone up here can take care of an army, and I guess de Brock knows it. You'd best get some shut-eye, boys, includin' you, Ox," Jess said. "In 'bout two hours I'll wake some of you and hit the hay myself. So we'll work in shifts with somebody always on the alert."

"Okay." The big cowpuncher got lazily to his feet and vanished inside the cave.

The other men followed him, and presently all sound of movement ceased and Jess was left on his lonely vigil, his revolver at his side, his back against the rocks of the cave entrance. He smiled a little tautly to himself as he slowly began to realize what kind of a maelstrom he had precipitated. With nothing but a few hombres, he had launched himself into a win-or-die fight with one of the toughest cattlemen in the region.

He asked himself why he had done so. Where was the point in risking his neck to such an extent? And what did he get out of it when he finished? He decided that the answer lay in a slender girl with black hair and trusting, amber-coloured eyes. He could see her again now as he had seen her in the morning, the sunlight on her wealth of hair as she gave him the gun with which to protect himself.

"A girl doesn't give a strange man a gun unless she likes an' trusts him," Jess breathed, staring into the starlit distances where he knew the Calvert ranch to be. "Guess it'll be worth cleaning up this valley if only so's she can live in peace an' I can convince her old man that it pays to stand on your own two feet sometimes an' not go grovellin' on your knees to a tinhorn like de Brock."

Another thought also occurred to him as he sat pondering. He had promised to return the mare the girl had loaned him if he ever had the opportunity. Now that chance had arisen, even if tragically. He could use the horse which the unfortunate Shorty had had and return the mare, with thanks. It would be as good an excuse as any for visiting the Calvert spread again.

So, after breakfast the following morning, Jess was on his way, riding Shorty's mount and trailing the mare behind him. With Ox left as deputy in case of emergency, he had given orders for none of the men to move from the rendezvous until he returned, and to shoot any interlopers on sight. Ox had not seemed particularly taken with the idea, but by this time he had learned the necessity of obeying orders.

Indeed, with the thought of Fay Calvert on his mind, Jess was not particularly concerned with the machinations of de Brock for the time being. He believed, as any healthy man should, that business must be mixed with pleasure. None the less he was not so absorbed that he did not stay on the alert all the time he rode to the Calvert spread. Nobody interfered with him, however, and without his having seen a soul in the vast, sundrenched spaces he finally reached the forlorn-looking ranch towards ten o'clock.

It was the girl herself who opened the ranch-house door, and there was no mistaking the welcome which leapt into her eyes as she saw Jess standing outside.

"Mr Burton!" she ejaculated. "Back again so soon? This is better than I'd hoped for."

"Mornin', Miss Fay." Jess took off his hat and smiled at her. He knew that this time he was worth looking at. He was closely shaved and wearing a new shirt and kerchief, a very different man from the evil-smelling, dirt-caked figure who had sought shelter when escaping from the Square-8."

Abruptly the door opened wider, so suddenly that Fay, leaning on it, staggered back a little. Her father stood there, his gaunt face hard and friendless.

"Don't you think yore causin' enough trouble around here, Burton, without bringin' it right to our door?" he demanded. "Th' very fact that yore here leaves my gal an' me open to attack by de Brock's men if they're around."

"They're not," Jess told him quietly "An' even if they were I'm takin' the liberty of thinkin' you'd be man enough to fight it out against them."

Calvert glared. "I thought I'd made it clear to you that I don't intend to fight anybody, you or them. Now git off my spread, Burton, an' don't come back any more neither. I reckon I'm gettin' mighty tired of telling you."

Jess hesitated then he said, "I didn't come here just for the ride, Mr Calvert. I've brought back the mare your daughter loaned me. There she is, at the tie-rail. I've grabbed another horse, thanks to de Brock."

"Yuh nean you stole it?"

"I took it in return for my own. That's fair exchange, not stealin'."

"Have it your own way," Calvert said. "Now get goin'. An' I don't reckon it was so much honesty as led you to bring back th' mare. You thought you'd see my gal here ag'in. Mebby figgered I'd be out. Yore wrong on both counts so you'd best be on the move."

"Before I go," Jess persisted, "you may as well know that I have other reasons too for being around here."

"I ain't interested!"

"Hear me out, Mr Calvert. I'm contacting the rest of the ranchers in this neighbourhood to see how many of 'em would be willin' to back me in a fight against de Brock. I have in mind a system of signals. You might like to hear more about a method for helpin' yourself."

"I danged well would not! If I leave de Brock alone I'm satisfied that he won't bother me neither."

"Dad, why do you keep on living in a fools' paradise?" the girl demanded angrily. "This passive attitude of yours won't get you anywhere if there is an attack. What sort of signalling have you in mind, Mr Burton?" she asked turning to Jess quickly.

"It's simple enough. All you have to do is build a heap of brushwood somewheres near here. Since it isn't the rainy season it should stay dry for several months. If yore attacked any time find some excuse to get out and light the stack. We'll see the smoke an' come an' help you out."

"An' where'll you be so's you can see the smoke?" Calvert snapped. "Haveta be somewheres pretty close, won't it?"

"We'll be in the — " Jess paused, studying the rancher's grim face then he shrugged. "In the mountains, Mr Calvert. We've a hide out there, an' I'm not sure that I'm not a durned fool for sayin' as much, not knowin' just where you stand. However, I'm bein' frank with you in the hope your attitude towards me will change in time."

"My attitude towards you won't ever change, Burton, so you can stop expectin' miracles. You know where I stand, neither for nor against. I shan't tell anybody where yore hidin', an' I shan't start buildin' beacon fires neither. De Brock won't bother me if I don't bother him. It's opposition that turns him sour, an' I don't aim to make any."

Jess grinned cynically. "You don't suppose he's taken all your cattle, bar these few you have left, without intendin' to finish the job, d'you? He'll take you for everythin' you've got before yore finished, includin' your daughter mebby. I can't see him passin' up the chance to make use of a girl as attractive as her; an' if only for her sake you should take steps to get protection."

"I reckon I can handle things in my own way, Burton, without your crazy notions."

As if to put an end to argument Calvert turned back into the ranch-house without adding further words. Jess looked after him, then to the girl again. She looked even more attractive this time than when he had first seen her. Her blouse and riding skirt had been abandoned for a simple cotton dress which gave her the true lines of a young woman.

"Well-er — " Jess looked awkward, his blue eyes upon her. "I-I guess that covers everythin', though I'd have bin a darned sight happier if I could have made your pop see reason. Still, there it is. All I can do now is be on my way and see the other ranchers around here."

"How will you know where to find them?" Fay asked simply. "They're pretty scattered."

"I know. But the territory isn't so huge. I'll find 'em all in due time."

"There are sixteen ranches around here over which de Brock is casting his shadow," the girl said. "Some are bunched together; others are widely separated. I know them all, and the best thing would be for me to act as

172

your guide. I'm as interested as you are in seeing that you achieve success. If anything, more so."

Jess looked troubled. "That's mighty kind of you, Miss Calvert, but it'll be a dangerous job. I'm number one target for any gunman, remember, and if that gunman turns up he ain't likely to think twice 'bout puttin' lead between your shoulder-blades either. Should anythin' happen to you just because you stringed along with me I"d never forgive myself."

"I'll risk it. You have my mare waiting, so all I need do is change. Wait for me."

"An' how's about your pop?"

"I can deal with him." The girl smiled, and turned back into the ranch-house.

Evidently she could, for despite angry words which came from within the ranch, and then presently died away, Fay reappeared in a while in riding kit, a gun at her hip, and her mass of dark hair held back from her sunny face by a single childish blue ribbon.

Jess looked at her questioningly and she gave a shrug.

"Pa's not particularly pleased with my behaviour," she said, "but he knows he can't hold me when my mind's made up. I don't altogether like defying his wishes, but in this case his outlook is so utterly absurd."

Jess followed her down the steps and helped her into the mare's saddle. Then he vaulted to his own horse and side by side he and the girl rode through the drenching sunlight, presently coming to the rimrock which gave a vast, unhampered view of the territory immediately beyond the valley.

It had a breathtaking loveliness all its own. The very ground itself was pink and white with anemone blooms, outcroppings of yellow primrose and whispering bells peeping here and there. Further distant, upon the endless spaces of the distant mesa from which came the smell of the torrid desert, were the fields of golden brittle-bush and stately eight-foot high clusters of the Lord's Candles.

Even the looming mountain range nearby was in its finest garb, splashed with the silver-white of Apache plumes and the scarlet of the mallow. It was the season of the year when the rain gods of the Indians had been kind and Arizona had burst forth in its most voluptuous offerings. Here was a beauty in its wildest and sweetest sense, rioting in a world utterly alien to Wilton de Brock.

"I've lived around here since being twelve years of age and in ten years I've never tired of looking at this beauty in the spring," Fay said, as she and Jess rode along. "It's beautiful, too, by night, and in the winter when the rains and snows take their turn on the stage. But at this time of the year I know of nothing in the whole wide world to touch it!"

Jess glanced at her, smiling a little to himself.

"You must find it kinda lonely back there at the spread," he said. "I mean, yore young and you want life to keep you company. Yore too nice a girl to find it in a dump like Yellow Gulch. Far too good an education. An' livin' with your pop and his grouses must be as much as you can stand."

"It is a bit difficult sometimes," she admitted, sighing. "And dad's always so morose. The more he studies religion the more unhappy he seems to become. Not that there's anything wrong in religion," she added. "It's the way he interprets it. He's too literal in thinking one should forgive one's enemies. I'm not that way. I believe in fighting for what is right, no matter what the cost to myself. The pioneers of this land have always looked at things that way, so I suppose it's the common-sense view."

"In this part of the world, and with men like de Brock around, one has to," Jess said quietly. "He's the kind of man who is dying out from this country, ruthless, cold-blooded, intent on nothing but his own advancement no matter who is trampled down in the process. Somebody's got to stop him, an' somebody's going to! An' whilst I'm about it, Miss Calvert, I — "

"Please drop the prefix and the surname," she broke in, with a shy little smile. "I'd much rather have 'Fay'. It's so formal the other way and despite our rather ... er ... uneasy introduction we have become such firm friends."

Jess laughed. "I'm glad we have, Fay. That was what I was going to say, that I'm glad to find you trust me. It's a big thing which I've taken on, cleaning up the tyrannical gunplay in this territory, I was only thinking last night when I was perched on the watch in the mountains. You get to meditatin' on lots of things when everybody is asleep but yourself and there's nothin' but the loneliness of great spaces. Yeah, I guess I need all the friends I can get. An' don't forget to call me Jess."

The girl laughed, throwing back her head. Jess noticed how white and firm her teeth were. She breathed the atmosphere of the West. It was in the manner in which she handled her horse, the erectness of her figure, the tone of her voice, in her very attitude to life itself.

"That where we're headin'?" Jess asked presently, nodding to a distant ranch.

"Yes. That's the first of the sixteen — the Lucky-F. Mr Gorton and his wife and two young daughters live there, and all of them seem to have plenty of sense. They'll give you all the support you need, I'm sure."

Jess nodded and glanced about him as he rode. This was one of the most pleasurable journeys he had ever known: his only fear was that a gunman would suddenly appear and bring death or injury into the scene. But the landscape still remained deserted and he and the girl reached the Lucky-F without mishap some ten minutes later.

The moment they arrived at the gates of the yard, however, they could sense that there was something wrong. There was nobody in sight: the corrals and stables were empty; and in the centre of the yard itself was a monstrous circle of burned grass and debris where apparently a considerable amount of wooden material had been destroyed.

"I don't like this," Fay said, frowning as she dismounted. "It begins to look as though de Brock's been here already."

"Oh?" Jess glanced about him. "How can you tell?"

"His pet method is to burn up all the furniture and belongings when he drives out the ranchers. If they won't be driven out they get hanged. We wouldn't see this fire from our place: the height of the rimrock would hide it. The sooner we find out what has been happening the better."

Jess at her side, Fay headed for the ranch-house porch, to find the doors swinging wide and aimlessly in the strong, warm wind. Their guns at the ready they entered the shady hall, noting that it was bereft of furniture, and so entered the living room. Here they stopped, appalled for a moment by the shock they received.

The room had been completely stripped of furniture but in it were four people. A man and a woman, their hands secured behind them, swung from the central beam across the ceiling, ropes above their necks. Near to them, fastened back-to-back, and with one rope serving for both necks, were the two young daughters, aged perhaps eight and twelve. The bodies swung slightly in the wind through the smashed windows.

"It's ghastly!" Fay whispered, turning away for a moment but withal keeping a grip on herself. "It was right in my guess, it seems. De Brock's been here all right, or else his men have. Ranchers who won't quit are left like this as a warning to others to get out. And helpless children, too!"

"Yeah!" Jess' face was merciless. "Do your pop good to see this. Perhaps change his mind about bein' pleasant to the enemy. We'd best get outa here, Fay: there's nothing we can do."

Sobered by what they had seen they departed, riding to the next ranch some two miles distant. Here everything was in order, and thanks to Fay's help in backing him up Jess secured his much needed cooperation and a promise to light a beacon if an attack were made at any time.

By noon, when the sun was at its fiercest, they had made six calls and received full promise of cooperation in each case. At the Double Y they stayed for lunch and then rode quickly on again until by early evening every ranch had been visited. Of the fifteen ranchers interviewed twelve had agreed to the signal system: the others had hung back, clearly afraid to commit themselves to crossing de Brock, although there was little doubt they would come into line once they had seen somebody take the first plunge.

"I reckon twelve outa fifteens a high enough number to count on," Jess commented in satisfaction, as he and the girl ambled their horses back along the trail towards her own ranch. "An' many thanks for th' help you've bin. I certainly couldn't have gotten so much co-operation without you."

"Why shouldn't I help? I'm in this even more than you are. I know what you're driving at and it is as much in my interests as anybody's to see that you succeed. In fact there's only one thing lacking to my mind. I only wish I were a man and could ride beside you in every move you make against de Brock."

"I'm mighty glad yore not," Jess grinned.

"Wouldn't be half as nice to ride with you."

She smiled back at him and then demurely dropped the subject. Fifteen more minutes brought them back to her ranch and Jess lifted her down from the saddle.

"I don't know when I'll be back this way again," he said gently, his big hands holding her shoulders. "Just depends on how soon I get a free moment and how clear the trail is. But if I see a bonfire go up I'll be here pronto. Later, mebby, when all this trouble has been cleared up we may see quite a lot of each other."

"I'm counting on it," Fay said. "And it's going to seem an awful long time until it happens."

Jess hesitated, her slim, inviting form pressed close against him. One instinct prompted him to kiss her upturned face: another told him that he had not known her long enough. So he dropped his hands from her shoulders and turned to his horse, swinging into the saddle and then raising his hat.

"Bye, Fay," he smiled. "An' don't forget to tell your pop what we saw at the Lucky-F. It may change his mind. If it doesn't he should ride over and take a look-see for himself."

"I'll tell him," she promised. "Oh — there's something else, Jess — "

"Yeah?"

She motioned for him to stoop from the saddle so she could whisper in his ear — or so he expected. Instead he found his cheek brushed lightly with her lips.

"Just for luck, Jess," she murmured, and then she turned away quickly.

He grinned and straightened up again. "God help de Brock after that!" he thought, and with a dig of his spurs sent his horse ripping away across the grasslands. He looked back in the long, golden bars of the sunset until the girl had vanished in the distance.

5. Bushwacked

It was almost dark when Jess reached the mountain hide-out again. The men were squatting or lounging outside the cave entrance, the tethered horses some little distance away, their heads nodding sleepily. Ox, a cigarette clinging to his lower lip watched Jess through his eyelashes as he approached. There was a certain indefinable unfriendliness in his attitude.

"Enjoy yuhself with the girl friend?" he asked dryly "Or is that a needless question?"

Jess came to a halt, his gaze hard. "Meanin' what?"

"Just wonderin', that's all. From here we c'n see a bit uv the trail near th' rimrock. We saw you an' the gal headed that way this mornin'. Saw yuh comin' back too 'bout an hour ago. In th' meantime we've bin stuck here, waitin' fur anythin' that might happen, and in case yuh don't know it, Jess, it gets mighty monotonous."

"So?" Jess snapped.

"So it seems like yore gettin' most uv th' gravy!" Jess looked about him.

"Th' rest of you men feel that way?" he demanded.

None of the men answered. They either looked at each other or on the ground. Jess tightened his lips.

"For your information," he added, "the gal is Fay Calvert. Some of you may know her. She acted as my guide 'cos I didn't know where all the spreads were. And if I hadn't have had her with me I'd have bin several weeks gettin' myself initiated. What's more, I can't see what damned business it is of yours whether she rode with me or not."

"It's our business 'cos we can't afford t'have anybody else in on our plans," Ox retorted. "An' a woman least of all! I reckon that all the troubles that happen to a man are 'cos of a woman. As I figure it, she'll shoot off'n her face th' minnit it suits her. Then where'll we be?"

Jess hesitated for a moment, then suddenly he lashed out a right-hander with all his strength. Ox absorbed the blow and jolted back against the rocks, his cigarette dashed from his lips.

"That's just a reminder that I do as I like — within limits," Jess explained coldly. "An' if you've anything more t'say 'bout Fay Calvert keep it outa my hearing if yore wise. I don't aim to stand for it."

178

Ox heaved back into position, his eyes glinting. "Yuh don't suppose I'm takin' that frum you, do yuh?" he snapped. "I still say a woman's a danger if she knows too much. An' it bein' Fay Calvert makes it worse."

"What gave you that idea, y' big lug?" Jess demanded.

"I knows her well enough, an' her old man a durned sight better. He's loco on religion an' if the mood seized him he'd spit in our faces an' tell de Brock everythin' he knows 'bout us. I never did trust a guy who goes around smitin' a prayer book. Ain't nateral, t'my way uv thinkin'. Blasted cover-up fur sump'n else, most likely."

"I agree that old man Calvert's an awkward customer," Jess replied quietly, "but the girl isn't. She won't betray us. She's for us, one hundred per cent. I've ridden around with her long enough to be sure o' that."

"An' she knows where we are?" Ox asked.

"She knows we're in th' mountains, but that might mean just any place." Ox spat contemptuously.

"Not to a gal who knows th' district like she does!" he retorted. "She knows that the only hideouts in this range are in these foothill caves. What's t'stop her sayin' as much? Not to de Brock, mebby, but to her old man."

"She isn't that sort," Jess answered, keeping tight rein on his temper. "Better realize that, Ox, an' save yourself a lot of grief."

"If that old has-been wanted t'know where we wus, yuh don't suppose he'd let a kid like his daughter keep her mouth shut, do yuh?"

"You're lookin' for trouble before it's here, Ox." Jess said. "Skip it. We'll start worryin' fast enough if anything happens. Don't forget that you never did have the gift of seein' ahead."

Ox said nothing. He lit up a fresh cigarette and scowled. Jess waited a moment and then went into the cave to rustle some food together for himself. Whilst he ate he explained in detail how he had spent the day and how many ranchers were willing to co-operate in the matter of signalling. There was no comment from amongst the men as he gave the facts.

"Which means that we'll have ta be constantly on our toes," he finished. "A smoke-signal by day; a fire-signal by night. Either, will mean that we're wanted pronto. You, Joe, had better take first look-out on that high rock yonder where you can see any smoke or fire there might be. You'll follow him, Jed, two hours later, then will come you, Ox. Then me. That duty has never t'be relaxed."

Ox and the rest of the men nodded assent and Joe, with first watch, went off to the rock in question and settled down on its blunt peak, a solitary figure against the glitering stars. Ox spat out his cigarette and slouched forward to where Jess was squatted in front of his meal.

"Sump'n I want to ask yuh, Jess ..."

"Okay, shoot, but take care what it is. If it's anythin' more to do with Fay Calvert I'm not in the mood to listen."

"Nope, nothin' t'do with her. I'm just wonderin' what about that mayor we wus goin' to take care of?"

"No hurry, is there?"

"Mebby not to your way uv thinkin', but I want some action!"

"Mebby you do, but to go lookin' for it is just stickin' your neck out!"

"It's my neck and I'm willing to risk it."

"Well, I'm not willin' that you should," Jess retorted. "If anything happens to you it can happen to all of us. Quit thinkin' of yourself for once and give the rest of us a chance."

Ox rubbed the back of his neck uncertainly. "Well-okay," he agreed grudgingly. "But I still say that if de Brock doesn't start somethin' fur sometime we'll just sit here on our backsides an' do nothin', which ain't my idea of fun. I say, let us begin trouble, startin' with th' mayor."

"What you say doesn't matter," Jess told him. "Yore not the boss of this outfit, Ox."

"Mebby we"d get on better if I wus! At least I wouldn"t be aimin' to mix wimmin in my plans!"

"Why, you big, overgrown gorilla, I'll — " Jess leapt to his feet, his fist retracted to deal the massive cowpuncher a haymaker, then he stopped and glanced round as Joe came suddenly into the cave.

"A fire!" he gasped. "Be 'bout six miles away. Must be somethin' doin', Jess."

"Let's go," Jess said brusquely. "I can tell which ranch it is as we ride. You, Joe, stay behind and keep guard over everything. The rest of you come with me."

The abrupt call to action killed all private squabbling for the moment. In five minutes each man, except Joe, was riding at full speed down the mountain trail, watching the small and wavering red spot in the distance which beckoned them.

"Looks like the Double-Y where Miss Calvert and I had lunch today," Jess said presently. "An' that's a tidy ride! Let's speed things up a bit."

He goaded his horse to the limit, and not to be outdone the men with him did likewise. In a thunder of hoofs they swept across the pasture-lands which rolled away from the foothills, presently hitting the roughly defined trail which led out to the mesa. From here they had the distant visions of the beacon fire clearly before them.

And now they beheld something else. Not only the beacon was burning but towering piles of wood as well. Dim figures were visibly going back and forth to the ranch-house, carrying material out and dumping it in the blaze.

"Same old technique!" Jess commented grimly. "Burnin' up th' furniture, an' unless old man Glenthorpe an' his wife have gotten away they'll be strung up. Take it easy from here on," he added. "Anythin' can happen. One mistake on our part and this is th' last fire-raisin' party we'll attend." A hundred yards from the blaze he jumped down from the saddle and drew his guns. Detailing one of the men to watch the horses, he, Ox, and the others went swiftly forward, not towards the fire but round the back of the ranch-house.

"What's th' big idea?" Ox demanded. "We came here t'blast hell outa these jiggers, didn't we? Not creeep round corners. You lost yore nerve, Jess?"

"Use your head!" Jess told him. "We don't want that fire glare showin' where we are, do we? Besides, it's probable that Glenthorpe an' his wife have bin hung in the livin' room: we've them to free first of all."

"Yeah!" Ox agreed blankly. "Dang me, I never thought uv that!"

"You wouldn't. Come on!"

They entered the ranch-house through the open back door and, uninterrupted at this point, went quickly through to the living room. An old lamp was burning on the table and as yet the old rancher and his wife were still alive. They lay on the floor, tightly bound, but otherwise apparently unhurt, struggling on savagely to release themselves.

"Thank God that yuh came, Jess!" Glenthorpe panted, relief on his weather-beaten face. "I risked lightin' th' beacon. These hoodlums don't know why I did it; they said it wus nice o' me to prepare a fire for burnin' up my possessions. They've 'bout taken everything," he added bitterly. "Furniture, private papers, beddin' — all the lot."

"Okay, okay, take it easy," Jess murmured. "Jed, untie 'em. Th' rest of you get ready."

He had hardly finished his sentence before two of the gunmen came back and headed for the table, one of the last articles of furniture remaining in the room. They had just about reached it when they realized that things were not as they had left them.

"What the — " One of the men stopped and stared at Jed as he busily untied the rancher. "Where in blue tarnation did you come from?"

"Hold it!" Jess ordered, stepping out of the shadows. "Drop that gun! You too!" he barked to the second man. "Ox, take their weapons."

Ox did so, grinning at the thought of what was to come.

"Get out on the porch and call your pals here," Jess instructed. "I'll be right behind you. One wrong word an' yore finished. Go ahead!"

Unable to do anything else the sullen gunmen did as ordered. It brought the four remaining men from the blazing bonfire of furniture. Only when they got into the dim living room to behold guns relentlessly fixed on them did they realize what had happened.

Jess considered them, thinking, as Glenthorpe and his wife got slowly on their feet.

"Unfortunately," Jess said, "I can't make you return the furniture you've destroyed, but I can an' will extract payment for it." He looked across at the rancher. "What do y' reckon was the value of the stuff burned, Mr Glenthorpe?"

"'Bout five hundred dollars" worth, I'd say. The private papers had no value, 'cept personal. Nothin' we can do 'bout them, I guess."

"We can take it in kind," Jess decided. "How many papers were taken?"

"Five. Private deeds an' such."

"Okay." Jess meditated for a moment or two and then nodded to himself. "Right! Five lashes for the papers taken. That's five lashes for each of these hoodlums."

"Yuh think yuh can do that?" one of the men roared. "We'll durned well show yuh whether — "

"Yeah, we can do it all right," Ox interrupted, his jaw jutting. "I took many a heatin' back at the Square-8 so it'll be a real pleasure t'hand some uv it back." He put down his gun and very deliberately rolled his sleeves back along his heavily muscled arms.

"Gunmen like these are usually well supplied with greenbacks," Jess added. "Frisk 'em, Ox, and see if y' can find five hundred. If there happens t'be more we'll take it just th' same."

Ox grinned, seized the nearest man by the shirt collar, and then went through his pockets by the simple expedience of ripping away each one. With each man he did the same, administering a killing blow in the face wherever he met resistance. The sum total of the money he collected was four hundred and eighty dollars. He held the money up in the air in his massive hands.

"Okay, that's near enough," Jess said. "Now we want a whip. Get one, Mr Glenthorpe. A stockwhip for preference: one that'll sting like hell."

"There's a whip in one of the stables," the rancher replied. "But do you think   you —"

"Yeah, I do!" Jess snapped. "Havin' it taken outa their hides every time they strike will make these owl-hooters think twice. Hop to it, Ox."

"You betcha, Jess."

Ox hurried from the living room through the open window. In a few minutes he returned, the stockwhip in his powerful hand. Obviously enjoying himself, he tied the first man across the table, ripped off his shirt, and then swung the lash with all the power of his iron muscles.

At the end of delivering the punishment upon each man he was winded and sweating but grinning sadistically. Jess nodded as the groaning gunmen staggered by the wall, trying to struggle back into their shirts. Finally they gave it up, their flayed backs too tender to bear the friction of the cloth. Jess studied them silently, no hint of compassion in his coldly glinting eyes.

"That will teach you, my friends, that to go around pillaging and murdering doesn't pay," he said presently. "It's a small punishment for the things you've done. I'd have killed you all only I don't know which of you are really responsible for murder: so this will have to suffice for the present. I'm referring to the hangin' of Gorton an' his wife an' two daughters at the Lucky-F. What they went through at your filthy hands Gods knows, an' I'm only too sorry I'm forced by a sense of justice to leave you in one piece, so's you can recover an' I suppose be as vile again. But I'm warnin' you, if yore caught molesting any of the ranchers again you'll hang on the spot! Okay, boys, put 'em on their horses and tie their hands to the saddle backs."

183

Knowing he could safely leave Ox to finish the job, Jess relaxed as the whipped men were bundled out of the room. He patted Glenthorpe on the shoulder.

"That finishes tonight's work, Mr Glenthorpe," he said. "An' this money should help you out. Here's a few hundreds of mine too which originally belonged to de Brock. I reckon it oughta set you on your feet again. The signal system remains in case anythin' more happens, though I don't think it will for a long time. Those hoodlums have had the biggest beatin' of their lives and they know what they'll get if they try ag'in."

"We can never be grateful enough to yuh, Jess," the rancher whispered, and his wife nodded urgent confirmation.

"That's okay," Jess smiled. "It was about time somebody hit back around here anyway. Think nothin' of it."

*

Wilton de Brock, however, thought a good deal when towards the early hours of the morning his bruised and bloodstained minions tottered into his living room in the Square-8 ranch-house. He said nothing for a moment, so astounded was he; then gradually rage began to darken his colour.

He got slowly to his feet, the deadly gleam in his eyes betraying his fury.

"And what the devil happened to you?" he demanded. "What the devil happened?"

"Burton uv course!" the leader of the men snarled, too hurt to be civil.

"Burton, eh?" de Brock's eyes narrowed. "What did he do?"

"He breezed in out of nowheres with some uv his boys an' that tough gorilla Ox set about us with a stockwhip. They took all our money an' then Ox set us off on our cayuses like this, our hands tied. We got 'em free after a while. Next time Burton sez he'll hang us on the spot. That's what he calls bein' lenient."

"And you mean that you failed to get rid of Glenthorpe and his wife?"

"Course we failed! They're sittin' as pretty as they ever wus. Burton took care uv that."

The gunmen waited, breathing hard and wincing as de Brock paced slowly up and down, tireless despite the lateness of the hour. His mouth was set in a thin, hard line. Presently he seemed to make up his mind.

"Burton couldn't just have dropped out of the sky," he said finally. "Some kind of signal must have attracted him."

"Yeah — a beacon," one of the men said. "We didn't git the idea at first, but we have since."

"In other words, if you'd have used your brains, granting you have any, the whole debacle could have been sidestepped? At least you have confirmed my inner opinion that all of you are as senseless as animals. A beacon, eh?" de Brock mused. "Flames by night and smoke by day, like the Indians. Not very original, perhaps, but most effective."

He came to a halt, fingering his chin. He spoke again abruptly:

"Very well, this must be taken care of. Tomorrow, in daylight, I'll take personal charge of a raid. We'll reinforce our numbers with every man we can. I'll even bring in the mayor to ride with us. The more the better. We'll ride to the Crooked-K, which has been standing in my way for longer than I like. And we'll see that the beacon is lighted. Then when Jess Burton and his men come riding in we'll ambush 'em and give them the lesson of their lives. Certainly that low-down cowpoke isn't going to upset my plans in this fashion. Now get out, the lot of you, and clean up. You're making my home filthy, and besides, you have got to be ready for morning."

"I've the feelin', boss, that I'll not be able t'do anythin' tough for weeks," one of the men groaned.

"Then get rid of that feeling," de Brock suggested curtly. "I've no room for lily-whites in my outfit. If you feel unable to join us," he grinned sardonically, "you may prefer a long rest from which you'll never be disturbed."

*

At breakfast in the hide-out the following morning Jess and his boys were in a happy mood.

They had had plenty of action; they had beaten the pants off de Brock's gunmen, and not one of them had been hurt. In fact, in retrospect, the adventure of the night seemed as if it had been too good to be true.

"If it's all goin' t'be as simple as that it's not goin' t'be much fun," Ox complained, helping himself to beans. "Just thrashin' them hombres last night an' takin' their money wus too Sunday-school fur me. I'd sooner have stretched their blasted necks, which wus what they deserved. I still say yuh was too kind to 'em, Jess. Pity I wasn't in charge uv that lot."

Jess grinned. "Nice, gentle guy, ain't you? Be satisfied for th' moment, with what's happened, Ox, an don't think we've a bed of roses ahead of us, either! You don't suppose de Brock'll sit down to what we did, do you?"

"I guess not. I'm expectin' him t'come gunnin' fur us at any moment, an' I kinda wish he would. I'd like nothin' better'n to flatten him."

"He has more sense than you think, Ox," Jess answered, shaking his head. "Comin' up here is the last thing he'd risk. If he can he'll try an' trap us. Tonight I figger he might try another raid, just for the sake of drawin' us into it. If he does we'll be ready for him. Won't be the first time we've anticipated an ambush an' given our enemies a thrashin'."

"It's a long ways to tonight," Ox sighed, chewing as he contemplated the sunny morning landscape.

"I like action all th' time else I get sorta quarrelsome. Which reminds me, Jess, I said things last night I didn't mean. I was gettin' edgy, I reckon. Y' know by now the kind uv guy I am. Sez what I thinks an' can't plan t'save me life."

"Okay, it's forgotten," Jess responded, shrugging. "Unless y'feel like rakin' it up again when I tell you I'm goin' this mornin' to see Miss Calvert."

"What fur?" Ox's eyes narrowed in sudden suspicion and the men around him paused in their eating for a moment to hear what was coming next.

Jess got to his feet and looked round on the assembly.

"To pay my respects, for one thing, an' to warn old man Calvert that he'll have t'be on the watch against attack from now on. If de Brock finds out I'm pretty thick with Fay Calvert he'll give her ranch special attention, perhaps try an' strike at me through her. I'm expectin' it, an' for that reason Calvert's got t'be convinced of his danger an' converted to a beacon warnin' if at all possible."

Ox shrugged, but if he disliked the idea of a further visit to Fay he did not say so.

"I'll keep watch whilst yuh go," he volunteered, "but for Pete's sake, Jess, don't stay away 'til evenin'."

"I aim to stay away as long as I see fit."

"Yeah, I know, but it'll have me on the jumps wonderin' how much that gal's learnin' from yuh."

"She won't learn any more than I choose to tell her," Jess said simply, putting on his hat. "Suppose you let me worry about that, huh? Be seein' you later?"

He turned and left the cave, heading for his tethered horse a few yards down the narrow trail. He kept on the alert all the time he rode through the foothills but he gained the Calvert spread without any trouble.

Apparently Fay had seen him coming for she opened the door as he was mounting the steps of the porch.

"Jess!" She took his big hand as he extended it towards her, and smiled a greeting. "I wondered how long it would be before you came again?"

"And your father?" Jess enquired. "That's what I came about, partly, to know what reaction he showed when y' told him what we discovered at the Lucky-F yesterday?

"No reaction at all," she responded, sighing.

"What! You mean that even that kind of butchery doesn't stir him?"

"Apparently not. Anyways, his views have not changed in the slightest. He's out at the moment," Fay added. "Gone into town for provisions."

"An' leave you here to take whatever may come? That it? It sure wouldn't do if you were my daughter. You'd ride with me, where I'd know you were safe."

"I can look after myself," she responded. "Dad and I don't hit it off so well together these days, remember. He knows I think he's cowardly for not standing up to de Brock, and it's sort of strained our relationship."

"Yeah," Jess murmured. "A pity, of course, but I guess that's the way things are. Not that I'm taking the blame for it, even though he'd like me to."

"You've nothing to blame yourself for, Jess. You've done all you can." Fay suddenly changed the subject. "I believe you were busy giving de Brock a welcome at the Double-Y last night? I heard all about it this morning. Mr Glenthorpe's telling every rancher within reach what happened, how you saved him and his wife and thrashed those gunmen."

"Yeah, de Brock's men certainly got more'n they expected," Jess grinned. "Just as they will next time 'til finally they lose their appetite for murder and pillage. Once that happens de Brock's power'll be broken." He thought for a moment and then continued, "I guess I had another reason too for coming here. I thought that what happened last night when we saved Glenthorpe might have given your old man the notion that it mightn't be such a bad idea after all t'have a beacon ready."

"I asked him about that only this morning, when Mr Glenthorpe brought the news, but dad won't hear of it. No use trying, Jess. You'd waste your time."

"Too bad," he muttered. "Going to make it tough for you as well as me. I'll never have an easy moment with no means of knowin' if yore being attacked or not."

The girl smiled. "If we're attacked you'll see a signal all right," she promised. "I'll set fire to that manzanita thicket over yonder" — she nodded to it — "and it being dry it'll be every bit as good as a beacon. There's no need to build wood up in readiness whilst that's there."

Jess glanced at it and nodded. "Good enough." He fidgeted with his hat in his hands and smiled awkwardly. "Which seems to about cover everythin', Fay, more's the pity."

"What do you intend to do now?" she enquired. "Go back to your mountain retreat?"

"Oh, just be a matter of killin' time 'til somethin' happens, an' I don't expect that to be before night." Fay contemplated the sunny glory of the morning for a moment; then she asked:

"Think we might go for a ride together? Plenty I'd like to talk about, Jess. We've a lot in common."

"So I noticed yesterday when you kissed me goodbye. I haven't forgotten the feel of that!"

Fay gave her shy smile and looked away.

"I'll change," she said, and returned to the ranch-house.

And at the moment she did so, Ox, back at the mountain retreat, looked up suddenly from his half dozing attitude inside the cave as Jed, on look-out, came bounding in.

"A smoke signal!" he said breathlessly. "Ways across th' valley! Can't exactly see where it's a-comin' frum, otherwise I'd know if it were genooine. Mebby a nateral fire, but mebby it also means trouble."

"Whichever it is we've gotta find out," Ox responded, surging to his feet. "Jess would haveta be away! I told him wimmin ain't no use in this racket! When yuh want him he ain't t'be found! Okay, I'll do th' job myself. Git on your hosses, boys, 'cept you, Jed. Stay here on guard."

Within a few minutes they were on their way. It was as they came within full sight of the pasture lands from where the smoke was issuing that they could see it belonged to the Crooked-K ranch; and to judge from the noise of gunshots and vision of milling men on horseback, a good deal was going on.

Ox, his right-hand gun ready, surveyed the scene as he rode. Then he glanced at the men with him.

"I ain't one fur fancy business an' goin' through back doors, like Jess," he said. "We'll ride straight into it an' shoot th' jiggers down. Let's go."

He dug his spurs deeply into his horse's flanks, hurtling across the remaining stretch of grassland separating him from the Crooked-K. He did not even have the chance to fire his gun, however. A rifle exploded from nowhere and he went crashing down into darkness with an intolerable pain searing his arm.

When the mists cleared again he was lying on his back on a wooden floor, his wrists and feet secured, dried blood clotting his arm. He moved it stiffly, winced and then gazed about him. In a row, securely trussed, were the men with whom he had been riding. Nearby, his chair on its hind legs, sat a guardian cowpoke, rifle across his knees, a wisp of straw working up and down in his ceaselessly moving jaws.

"Some guy plugged me!" Ox breathed, scowling.

"I did," the guard told him. "Good shot, huh? Only sorry I couldn't finish yuh but th' boss said not t' scramble any of yuh up too much. He's got his own plans."

"If I've a bullet lodgin' in me arm it's only common humanity that I should have a sawbones fix me up," Ox said bitterly. "Or mebby yuh don't know what common humanity is?"

"What's the use when yore goin' t'die anyway?" The guard grinned. "An' yuh ain't got no bullet in yuh. It scored yuh hide, that's all. A tough guy like you ought't even ter feel it. If yuh do, then it's just too bad!"

Ox tightened his lips and said no more. He had gathered by now that he was seated in the empty living room of the Crooked-K. Of the normal occupants there was no sign.

"Looks like we'd ha' done better after all t'get in the back way," growled the man seated next to Ox. "We ran us smack into an ambuscade and got ourselves hogtied afore we could turn around. We've bungled this properly, Ox. Th' guy who owned this spread, an' his wife, have bin hanged in th' stable. We saw it happen. Right now the furniture's burnin' up outside. An' I guess it won't be long afore plenty happens to us too."

"Jess wouldn't ha' messed it up like this," growled the man at the end of the row. "I reckon he had th' right idea creepin' in the back way. That's yur trouble, Ox, no sense uv plannin'!"

"Aw, quit beefin'!" Ox spat back at him. "I did me best, didn't I? Anyways, I came here, which is more'n Jess has done, spendin' his time neckin' with that Calvert gal when he oughta be attendin' to business!"

"So that's where Burton is, huh?" the guard asked. "Th' boss wus quite disappointed not ter find him here."

He broke off and turned as the living room door opened and de Brock himself came in. He advanced until he was within a few feet of the bound men; then he stood surveying them.

"Not quite as cocksure this time, my friends, eh?" he asked dryly. "Only pity is that I have you scum and not Burton, the man I really want. Where is he?"

"Out with Fay Calvert, boss, neckin' some place," the guard replied.

"Oh!" de Brock raised his eyebrows. "And leaving you men to take the responsibility, eh? Not very good leadership on his part, is it?"

"You shut up!" Ox retorted, struggling fiercely with his ropes. "What Jess does is no business of yours, or mine either, even if I did open me mouth too wide. An' I'll get you, too, yuh ornery skunk, for blabbin' about it!" He added, glaring at the guard. "Yuh've got the finger on me right now, I admit, but it won't always be so. God help yuh when I get my hands on yuh filthy neck!"

"The Calvert girl, eh?" de Brock mused for a while. "Mmm, I quite admire Burton's choice. Fine girl! Quite surprising, too, considering her psalm-smitin' hypocrite of a father." He looked at Ox and smiled coldly. Thank you for the information, Ox. I'll see that Burton is picked up, and the girl too if need be. First, though, I have you and your friends to deal with. I could shoot you, of course, but that would soon be over, and I am bearing in mind that you have given me a tremendous amount of trouble. I also recall that you gave several of my men a most uncomfortable time at the business end of a stockwhip. Oh, Mr Mayor, what do you think should be done with these cutthroats?"

De Brock turned as the tubby, baby-faced Mayor Anderson came into the room, followed by several of the gunmen who had completed their furniture-burning activities.

"Done with them?" Anderson looked uneasily at the cold, murderous stares of the bound men. He was safe enough at the moment, but if to please de Brock he opened his mouth too wide, and if there was any slip-up later, his life wouldn"t be worth a plug nickel.

"The mayor, huh?" Ox breathed venomously, glaring at him. "I always knew yuh wus on de Brock's side, Mayor. So does Jess; but I never figgered yuh'd ride with one uv these necktie parties."

"I … er … am Mr de Brock's servant," the mayor explained nervously.

"Course yuh are, yuh fat-bellied traitor," Ox sneered. "There ain't hardly a guy in this blasted territory that ain't!"

"Speak up, Mr Mayor," de Brock invited, smiling amiably. "With absolute certainty of security you can say what shall be done with these hoodlums. They murdered the sheriff, don't forget, or at least Burton did, but these men were party to it. They also shot that rancher in the Trail's End. Above all, they are upsetting our plans for justifiable expansion. So, what shall it be?"

"Per-perhaps shooting would be quickest, an' safest," the mayor suggested, with a sidelong look at Ox's ugly, menacing face. "There isn't any real cause for a great deal of ceremony, is there?"

"And leave bullets around for any possible Governor to trace if the bodies should ever be found, and if a Governor ever gets this far?" de Brock shook his head. "Oh, no, Mr Mayor! We have been so careful to avoid the use of bullets, hence the hangings. But we need something even more lasting than that, this time. Something total!"

The mayor said nothing. He was perspiring with uncertainty, licking his lips.

"I had thought of the bonfire outside here," de Brock finished, contemplating it through the window. "Yes, that would do excellently. I shall leave it entirely in your care, Mr Mayor, much though I would have liked to stay and watch the fun."

"My care!" the fat mayor ejaculated, starting. "But-but I thought it was you who always gave the orders around here, Mr de Brock?"

"Indeed I do, and am doing. It will be your task to carry them out to the letter. You see, I have Burton to think of, and the sooner I get to the Calvert ranch and welcome him home again with Miss Calvert the better I'll like it."

"Mind the step!" Ox suggested, as de Brock turned away.

The cattle baron hesitated, half raised his fist, and then dropped it again. Time was too pressing for him to delay.

6. Retribution

To Jess, lounging in the long grass about a mile from the Calvert ranch with Fay beside him, trouble and gunplay might have been at the other end of the earth. At first he and the girl had set out to take a rambling ride together, but two considerations had made them change their minds.

The heat of the sun was overpowering for one thing; and for another they would have made themselves targets. So now they lay side by side, contemplating drifting cumuli far overhead in the cobalt-blue sky, their horses nodding sleepily nearby.

"If all life were as pleasant as this I reckon I'd be satisfied," Jess grinned, stretching out his long legs and putting his hands behind his head.

"No you wouldn't."

"Huh?" Jess looked at the girl. Her face was close to his, her amber-coloured eyes mischievous. The mass of dark hair had half blown over her face in the gentle wind. "You wouldn't," she repeated. "You're a man of action, Jess, not an idler. Lying in the grass looking at me would very soon get tedious."

His grin broadened. "I can think of lots of unpleasanter ways of spendin' a spring morning. For instance, fancy lyin' lookin' at de Brock."

The girl looked up into the sky again, her features slowly becoming thoughtful.

"Jess, supposing you do wipe out de Brock — "

"Supposin'! There's no supposin' about it, Fay. One of us is goin' to die with his boots on before this little joyride is over, an' it ain't goin' to be me. I made up my mind on that long ago."

"All right then, when you have cleaned up de Brock, what do you propose to do? Run the valley yourself?"

"It doesn't need runnin', Fay. It would run itself if the settlers in it are given a chance to rear their cattle an' walk around with their wives an' kids in the sunlight an' starlight without the fear of a rope around their necks, or that their cattle disappear. That is all I'm aimin' for, peace in Yellow Gulch. If I do anythin' official at all it'll be to get myself sworn in as sheriff, not by a phoney mayor like we've got now, but one appointed by the nearest State Governor. Then later mebby Yellow Gulch an' the State it's in will be incorporated into a big Federal Union. It's comin', y'know, when all the States'll be united under one legislation."

"In a valley as quiet as you'll want it, Jess, your job as sheriff would be a mighty easy one. You'd get bored, and once that happened you'd be unbearable with an impetuous nature like yours."

"Oh, I dunno. I'd have other interests, too," Jess sat up and squinted into the blazing sunlight. "A ranch, cattle, good markets, things expandin' … " He paused and then grinned with the awkwardness which showed he was embarrassed. "An' a decent woman t'look after the home side," he added. "I reckon that's an essential thing. Or mebby I'm talking outa turn?"

"You've done nothing else but talk out of turn ever since you laid eyes on my gal!"

Jess looked behind him in surprise; as he did so the lash of a whip struck him savagely across the face. It whirled again, but this time he ducked and jumped up. Old man Calvert came down the bank quickly, caught Fay by one arm and dragged her to her feet. Holding her tightly he glared at Jess, the riding-whip in his free hand.

"I thought I told yuh to keep away frum my gal!" he panted in fury. "The moment I turn my back I find her gone. I start a-looking for her an' after trampin' round the countryside fur God knows how long I see the hosses. Then you an' her stuck here in th' grass."

"We were just talkin', that's all." Jess kept his voice under control, a red weal rising across his cheek.

"Sure that was all?" Calvert sneered. "I reckon a hombre like you mightn't be content with just talkin'!"

Jess' mouth set hard but he did not say anything. Not that he had any particular respect for old man Calvert, but he had a great deal for Fay.

Fay tore herself free of her father's clutch. "Dad, how can you say such things?" she cried angrily. "There is nothing wrong with Jess an' me sitting in the shade here talking and if you think there is — "

"I think what I please, gal!" her father told her, with a stony glance. "I've asked y' to behave like a decent woman, an' live with me, your father, in a right an' proper way. It's your duty t'me with your mother gone, rest her soul. Instead you go around with this gunman! This hombre! It don't take much imagination t' guess what he — "

"Take it easy, Mr Calvert," Jess warned. "The last thing I want to do is hit you. Yore a much older man than me for one thing, an' yore Fay's father for another. If those two factors weren't in th' way I might do plenty. Don't go too far, that's all. I guess you gotten your thinkin' all tangled up. Fay an I have a likin' for each other, sure, an' that's the top an' bottom of it. The sooner you realize a man an' woman get that way sometimes, like you and your wife must have done once, I guess, the better for everybody."

Calvert ignored him. He turned to his daughter in a fury.

"D'you mean, gal, you've sold your soul to this tramp?" he asked, staring at her fixedly.

"You don't have to be Biblical about it, dad," she replied with some spirit. You make the mistake of basing everybody's actions on those of Scriptural characters   and — "

"All right!" Calvert interrupted, raising a hand. "All right! I've nothin' more t'say. You've chosen this man instead of doin' your duty to me, so you can stay with him! He'll only drag yuh down into sin an' perdition, an' when that happens I don't want it t'be said that yore any flesh an' blood of mine! Don't come back home again ever!"

Calvert turned and stalked away over the grass bank, leaving Fay staring after him, tears suddenly brimming in her eyes.

"Dad! Dad, for heaven's sake — "

She half moved to follow him, hesitated, then turned back to where Jess stood in silence. She looked at him dumbly and shrugged her slender shoulders.

"Jess, what do I do?" she asked helplessly. "I've done nothing wrong. Neither of us have. He behaves so — so crazily." Her voice broke as she tried to control her emotions. "I've never told you quite how crazily. This is only one sample of it. I'm sure Mother dying did something to him. He's got the idea that I should take her place, never have any fun, never look at any man, behave like I was old and withered. Just look after him — him — him." She caught up her last words in a shivering little gasp and then stood biting her lower lip.

Jess moved over to her and put an arm about her shoulders. He hugged her gently to him. "If he wants it that way, Fay, leave him be," he advised, with a shrug. "I'm well able to take care of you, even though I don't know what the boys back at the hideout will say. Later, when all this business is cleared up 'til either become sheriff and get regular money that way or else I'll work in some rancherls outfit."

There was silence for a moment, Fay doing her best to smile through her tears. Then Jess spoke again.

"Say, look, I'm forgettin'. You can't just walk out. You've no spare clothes or anythin', have you?"

"Nothing but what I'm wearing," she answered miserably. "I suppose I could buy some more in the town, only I haven't any money with me."

"Then we'll go back to your spread and get whatever belongs to you. Yore entitled to that — "

Jess stopped suddenly, his grip tightening on the girl's shoulder. In surprise she glanced at him and saw him staring as rigidly as an image into the distance. She gave a start at the vision of a towering column of black smoke belching into the hot morning sky from beyond a distant rimrock of mountain.

"Something wrong!" he said abruptly, releasing her. "A ranch afire. Either accidental or else de Brock's pulled a fast one, which is the very thing I've bin expecting would happen. In any case I've got t'look."

He stood hesitating, divided in his allegiance.

The girl made up his mind for him.

"I'll come with you," she said, hurrying towards her horse. "Only I've no gun."

Jess handed her one of his own. "You have now," he told her, lifting her to the saddle. "One will do for me. I don't like doing a job like this with you in th' thick of it, but mebby it's safer than leavin' you stranded."

He said no more, dug in his spurs, and darted his mount forward. The girl kept up with him, and at a spanking pace they hit the ill-defined trail which led out to the mesa. Within ten minutes they had come within sight of the fire itself.

"It's the Crooked-K!" the girl exclaimed. "And that's not just a beacon fire, either! Look at the size of it! Probably it's burning furniture."

"De Brock!" Jess muttered. His eyes narrowed. "An' for some reason he's struck in daylight. For some good reason, mebby." He was silent for a moment or two gazing intently into the distance. "I don't see any sign of Ox or th' boys but I'll gamble they've ridden in to see what it's all about. Best go carefully, Fay; anythin' can happen."

"I can see men moving about near the fire," she said, straining her eyes.

"Yeah. Quite a lot of 'em. Don't know whether they're friends or enemies, an' we daren't go near enough to make sure. Here, quick! In this hollow!" he broke of sharply. "A lone rider's coming!"

He wheeled his horse round, the girl doing likewise. Only just in time they ducked out of sight behind the high ridge of a grass bank, and dismounted. Watching intently they saw the rider pass at a considerable distance, flogging his horse at a furious pace.

"It's de Brock," Jess muttered. "An' too far away for me to take one shot at him, worse luck. Somethin' queer goin' on," he added, reflecting for a moment or two. "de Brock isn't hurt an' nobody's followin' him, which seems to show he's gotten the upper hand. Looks t'me like that big lunkhead Ox has gummed himself up somehow. He's one of those kind of mugs who can never plan things out properly. Bet he's cursin' me too for not bein' around when the signal went up."

"Well, we did see it finally," the girl replied, "so we've nothing to blame ourselves for."

"This," Jess muttered, "takes thinking about. We've got to ride straight into the danger and still win somehow. Must be a way."

"One thing we could do," the girl said, after a while. "I could ride up to the ranch in the ordinary way and so take their attention."

"Dangerous!" Jess decided, pondering.

"No doubt of that, but I'm pretty sure they wouldn't shoot me, not without express orders from de Brock himself, and we know he won't be there. Whilst I'm holding their attention you could creep in round the back way or something."

"Far too big a risk for my likin'," Jess said, gazing at the girl. "If anything should happen to you — "

"It's my risk, not yours, and I'm prepared to take it."

"Mebby, but for all we know de Brock has probably given orders to shoot any strangers on sight. An' that'll include you."

"I don't think so," Fay answered, shaking her head. "He's careful whom he shoots: that's why there are so many hangings. My guess is that he doesn't want to leave tell-tale bullets lying all around. Anyway, Jess, my mind's made up," she decided, and gettng to her feet she moved to her horse. Before Jess could stop her she had swung into the saddle and spurred the beast out of the depression and up to the pastureland.

"Durned crazy," he breathed, "but the gal's got nerve, an' that's what I like."

He mounted his own horse and watched the girl's distant, retreating figure in the sunlight. Whatever might happen now he could not alter it, so he began to put his own plan into action. He rode hard, circuiting the ranch in a detour which kept him a mile away from it, cutting through every low-lying fold of ground he could find, until he had come to a point where he was at the rear of the spread. Only then did he start to hurtle his mount towards it, his approach concealed by the bulk of the ranch-house building and stables.

He rode his horse straight toward the fence surrounding the rear of the yard, dismounted, and then went across the yard with his gun at the ready. As he had hoped, all attention was concentrated at the front of the building, where the furniture bonfire was still burning.

Moving in swift silence he crept round the side of the ranch-house until he had reached a point where, from an angle, he could see the front of the spread. Amidst the smoke-wreaths, which obscured the view at times, he could descry Ox and his men, firmly bound about the arms, held by six of de Brock's owl-hooters and to judge from the expression on Ox's ugly face things had certainly not gone according to plan.

This in itself Jess considered satisfactory for it meant that every available man was being used to keep Ox and his henchmen under surveillance. Further away, apparently engaged in an argument, was Fay. Before her, a smirk on his round, greasy visage, was tubby Mayor Anderson. On the porch, leaning against the rail and keeping things covered with a rifle, stood the guard who had watched over Ox and his boys in the living room. Nor did he seem particularly alert: he had the attitude of a man completely sure of himself.

Jess grinned. The situation was not so difficult as it had at first appeared. Turning, he raced back to his horse, took his lariat from the saddle-horn, and then returned to his vantage point. In the interval of his absence things had become more grim. Ox and his cohorts were being shoved in the direction of the blazing fire. They were struggling violently, trying in vain to protect themselves from its fierce heat as they came near to it.

Jess holstered his gun, poised himself, and then swung his rope carefully, his eyes fixed on the highest branch of the giant cedar tree in the yard. His ropework was good and the noose locked itself securely over the high branch. Whipping his gun back into his hand he twined the rope about his wrist and then leapt into the air.

Pendulum-wise, carried by the rope's swing, he hurtled across the yard. His legs tautly extended in front of him he crashed his heavy riding boots into the backs of the two men driving Ox and his boys towards the fire. Completely unable to save themselves they stumbled blindly forward, tripping and sprawling in the midst of the flames and searing wood, and dragging themselves up again with shrieks of pain.

Clean over the fire Jess travelled, released himself, and dropped. He twirled and fired twice with bewildering speed. The two remaining guards holding Ox and his boys crumpled, their guns flying out of their hands. The two other guards near the ranch-house fired blindly, once only. Then Jess' relentless gun got them one after the other.

A shot came from the rifle of the man on the porch. Jess saw the bullet hit the tree behind him. He grasped the rope again, hurtled himself back over the fire and crashed straight towards the porch. The guard saw the flying body coming and tried desperately to take aim. Instead iron-shod boots struck him a blinding blow in the face and sent him toppling from the porch into the dust below it. Jess dropped, grabbed the rifle and levelled it.

"Okay, take it easy!" he panted, as the two guards near the porch got up and the burned ones struggled into some kind of action.

"Get these blasted ropes of'n me!" Ox roared. Til durned soon wipe up this bunch, Jess! Hurry up, somebody, an' cut th' blasted things."

"Cut them free, Fay," Jess called to the girl, tossing over his penknife.

She nodded, caught the knife deftly, and in a few moments had released each man. Ox swung round, then without speaking any word or asking any questions he strode to where the guard had fallen. He was just getting to his feet, his face gashed and bleeding from where Jess' boot had struck him.

"What's th' idea, Ox?" Jess snapped, giving him a hard look. "There are more things t'do right now than bother with this critter."

"Not to me there ain't, Jess." Ox clenched his massive fists and glared. "He's a blabber-mouth! I happened t'say that yuh was with th' Calvert gal here an' this guy had ter repeat it to de Brock. I warned him what I'd do fur him fur openin' his trap too wide, an' now I aim t'do it!"

"Wait!" Fay cried, hurrying over. "Just a minute, Ox!" She caught his huge, blood-smeared arm as he retracted it to deliver a killing blow on the dazed puncher.

"Well?" Ox growled, obviously still disgruntled at the thought of a woman being mixed up in things.

"As we came here we saw de Brock heading away. D' you suppose he was going to my ranch?"

"He said he wus," Ox retorted. "To give you an' Jess a welcome home. Frum th' way things are I reckon he'll be mighty disappointed," he grinned.

"But my father's at home!" Fay exclaimed, horrified. "Heaven knows what de Brock may do to him!"

"That's right!" Jess gave a start. "We've got to get over to th' Calvert spread right away."

"An' leave these guys t'do as they like!" Ox gasped. "You gone nuts, Jess? Don't yuh know they've hanged the guy who ran this spread? An' his wife, too. In the stables back there. That's murder, an' it makes these skunks ripe fur a hangin', jus' like yuh said yuhself."

"We'll rope 'em up an' take 'em back to th' hideout with us. Later we'll hand 'em over to the authorities."

"Well, okay," Ox growled, unsatisfied, "but I'll be durned if I'm goin' t'be gypped outa payin' this guy a compliment. I've bin promisin' it to myself too long fur that!"

He considered the still semi-conscious guard. Then he spat on his right hand, doubled his fist, and landed the most frightful punch either Jess or the girl had ever seen. It sent the hapless man flying backwards. He hit the woodwork at the base of the porch and half fell through it, to lie motionless. Ox grinned and hitched his slipping pants.

"Okay, I'm satisfied," he said, shrugging. "Least, almost." With narrowed eyes he looked about him. "Where's the pot-bellied runt of a mayor gotten to? I've a bit uv a score t' settle with him, too."

"Yeah," Jess said, gazing around. "I'd like to say somethin' to that critter myself."

"There!" Fay cried, pointing. "Getting onto his horse."

Ox leapt forward, hurtled across the yard as fast as he could move, and flung himself at the mayor just as he was preparing to ride off. The grip on his collar dragged him out of the saddle and he crashed heavily to the earth. In a moment he was on his feet, hauled up by Ox's massive arm.

"Jess wants yuh," Ox explained sweetly. "When he's through with yuh then mebby I'll give your features a lift. Seems t'me they're a mite too flabby."

"I haven't done anythin'," the mayor panted, perspiring and wringing his hands. "Only as I was told. I didn't agree with it, though. It was de Brock's idea to drive you and your boys into the fire."

Ox spat. "Yeah. As I remember it it wus you who suggested shootin' us, wustn't it? Yuh big barrel uv eagle fat, I've a mind ter — "

"Take it easy, Ox," Jess ordered, curtly, coming up. "Take his rifle and keep these cut-throats covered. Get the rest of the boys to help you and tie these guys up good an' proper. I want a word with th' mayor here."

"A word? Nice an' pretty like? How's 'bout cigars an' a few drinks fur th' both uv yuh?"

"Shut up an' do as yore told!"

"Okay," Ox growled, and turned away. He aimed a sour look at Fay as she came running up. She caught Jess' arm.

"How about dad, Jess? We've got to be moving."

"We will, Fay, just as soon as these polecats are roped up. Now, Anderson, yore a pal of de Brock's, ain't you?"

"No!" the mayor retorted. "I do as he tells me, sure, even though I don't like it. I haveta, or take a slug where it'd hurt most. Not bein' crazy, I follows out orders. I guess any man who wants t'go on livin' would do just that."

Jess studied him. "Yeah, I can believe that. Yore not quite such scum as the sheriff was, or this bunch of cut-throats here. But as long as you take orders from de Brock yore not goin' to be mayor around here, see?"

"An' how d'you figger I can stop takin' orders from de Brock!"

"That's simple: you take 'em from me instead. If you don't I aim to blot you out. Plain enough, isn't it?"

"It isn't givin' a man a fair chance," Anderson complained. "If de Brock doesn't plug me, you will. That's what it comes to. I'm hog-tied either way."

"Yeah," Jess agreed calmly. "But with one difference. de Brock won't give you the ghost of a chance if he finds you've ratted on him. I'm prepared to let you keep alive and stay as mayor. But on one condition."

Anderson's flabby face lighted in sudden relief. "Okay. What's the condition?"

"That you hit the trail right now and fetch the State Governor from North Point City, an' take him to de Brock's spread as fast as y'can. You can make it all right, de Brock's used all the men he can spare to make the raid on this spread and guard his own place. So you shouldn't get plugged on th' way. If you come back with the Governor, okay. If you don't — " Jess gave a shrug. "Well, I reckon it'll be just too bad, that's all."

Anderson hesitated for a moment; then he nodded. "I'll try it, anyways. At least I stand a chance with things that way: I don't stand any with de Brock."

"There's one other thing," Jess added, catching the mayor's arm as he turned to go.

"Yeah?"

"As mayor of Yellow Gulch you have access to plenty of legal documents an' information which th' rest of us don't know about. How much can you provide t'prove that de Brock runs things his own way around here?"

"I-I guess I don't know," Anderson replied uneasily. "I ain't had much to do with —"

"Get wise to yourself, Anderson. Your life depends on proving what kind of a no-account murderer de Brock is. Once you've started off to find the Governor you've burned your bridges. So you might as well fix things as well as you can to make yourself safe on return."

The mayor considered this a few moments. "Well," he said, at last, "I might have quite a few documents which wouldn't improve things for de Brock if they became open knowledge. There are land deeds f'r example, showing the prices paid for some of the stuff de Brock's bought; copy wage-bills for his hired gunmen; lots of things like that … "

"They'll help," Jess said. "The rest of the stuff, the really vital stuff, will no doubt be in de Brock's own ranch, I suppose. Okay, give me your office key."

"Huh? Now just a minute, Burton — "

"Stop arguin' an' hand it over! Come on quick! You'll find it healthier."

Reluctantly the mayor did as ordered. Jess nodded and put the key in his shirt pocket.

"All right, Anderson, get on your way, and if you think of detourin' to warn de Brock, or escaping altogether to some place else, forget it! I'll find you if you hand me a double-cross, and when I do, heaven help you!"

"I'm not so crazy I don't know when a guy holds all the aces," Anderson retorted, turning away. He went across to his horse, scrambled up into the saddle, and spurred the beast away rapidly. Jess stood watching him go.

"How much more time are you going to waste, Jess?" Fay pleaded.

"Sorry, Fay. This had to be got going. I'm all set now, though. Got those boys nicely trussed up, Ox?"

"Sure have."

"Okay. Dump 'em on their horses an' let's get movin'."

7. The End of the Trail

Len Calvert was in the midst of sorting out the provisions he had brought back from town when the door of the ranch flew open and de Brock came striding through the narrow hall, his gun levelled. He gave a grim smile as he beheld Calvert standing looking at him in surprise.

"de Brock!" Calvert ejaculated, staring at him in surprise. "This is unnecessary violent intrusion."

"Save it, Calvert," the cattle baron interrupted, glancing about him. "Where's your daughter and Jess Burton?"

"I guess I ain't got a daughter any more," Calvert answered grimly.

"What the hell do you mean? You've had a daughter as long as I've known you. She isn't dead, is she?"

"Far as I'm concerned she might as well be." The rancher shook his head bitterly. "She's sold herself to the devil, and that's th' top an' bottom of it. The shame of it! That a daughter o' mine should go straight down to perdition an' — "

de Brock strode forward and seized Calvert by the lapel of his jacket, shaking him roughly.

"Stop spoutin' that psalmist drivel to me, Calvert, and come to the point. I want Burton, and I hear he's with your daughter. Now, where are they?"

Calvert set his mouth and hesitated before he answered.

"Last I saw of 'em they were in the grass, down the trail apiece. Jus' talkin', so they said, but I got my own notions about that. I warned my gal what she'd get if she ever came back here ag'in. She's dead, de Brock, far as I'm concerned. I never want t'set eyes on her again."

de Brock raised his eyebrows.

"Just because she's fallen for Jess Burton, and he for her?" Iron-hard, ruthless man though he was, de Brock at least had plenty of common-sense. "I always thought you were crazy, Calvert, and now I'm sure of it. Men and women have been falling in love since the world began, or didn't you get to hear of it in this neck of the woods? And a nice, blasted mess you've made of my plans, too, with your cockeyed notions on a girl's purity! I was expecting Burton to come back here with her, then I could have given them both a welcome."

"Why a welcome?" Calvert asked in perplexity. "What good has Burton ever done you?"

"None, and that's just the point. I've roped in all the rest of his boys, and now I want him — the biggest blackguard of them all. My welcome would have been at the business end of this." de Brock raised his gun, but the rancher looked at it unmoved.

"My gal knew I meant what I said," he stated, "and that bein' so she won't come back here, nor will Burton. So I reckon you've had a trip in vain, de Brock."

"Not necessarily." de Brock seated himself at the table and grinned ambiguously. "In fact, now I am here I might as well take care of some unfinished business. Come to think of it, though, it can wait 'til later. Right now my main interest is in Burton. Your girl being so thick with him she must know whereabout he's hiding out, eh?"

"Y' say you've captured Burton's men?" Calvert asked. "Well, what makes you think Burton'll ever go back to his hide-out with all his men gone? Wouldn't be sense, would it? The man's a saddle-tramp, sure, but he isn't plain crazy."

"It makes sense because as yet he doesn't know that I've captured his men. Since he won't be returning here with your daughter the only other place he can go is the hideout. So, where is it located?"

"My gal said somethin' about it bein' in the mountain foothills, but I don't know where exactly. I don't think she did either."

"That'll cover it nicely," de Brock said, his icy smile still there. Then he added, "For a self-professed religious man you haven't much idea of loyalty, Calvert, have you? Not even to your own flesh and blood? I'm no lily-white saint myself and never pretended to be, but I never give away my own folk."

Calvert's lean and colourless cheeks flushed. "Meanin' what exactly?"

"Meaning that you don't think twice about telling me where I can find the man your daughter loves and blot him out. Making sure you keep your own halo fixed straight, aren't you?"

"He took my gal away from me and he's against you," Calvert answered stubbornly "That means I don't care how soon you find him, or what y'do with him."

"Mmmm … Apparently your daughter loves him quite a lot. How would you react, I wonder, if she remained so staunchly loyal to him that she died too? It could happen, you know, quite accidentally, of course."

"She sold her soul to him," Calvert banged the table. "So she must take what goes with it! I told her that straight!"

"You damned, lily-livered humbug!" de Brock said in contempt. "Burton's my enemy, sure, and I'm out to destroy him, but at least I've got a sense of values. I've always had a contempt for religion, and now I look at you, who've studied it all your life, I'm mighty glad of it. Just to satisfy your own vanity you tell me all I want to know and sell out your own daughter and the man she loves. To put it bluntly, Calvert, you stink!"

"What d'you expect me to do?" Calvert demanded. "Fight you when all the power's on your side?"

"Yes, certainly I do!" It was de Brock's turn to thump the table to emphasize his words. "Fight me the same as any real men would, the same as Burton's doing, blast him! He's clever, and he's got courage, and unless I'm mighty quick he'll do what he's set out to do and break my hold over this territory. If he does … "

de Brock mused over this for a moment and then shrugged.

"Well, if he does, okay. But at least he's worth fighting. Not like you." de Brock studied the rancher's cadaverous face. "That leaves only you on this ranch, Calvert, an' I've no time for a sniveller. You can pack your traps and quit by sundown. I'll have my boys see to it that you do. If you don't they'll have orders to blast hell out of you. Pray to your Maker, get on your knees, do what the blazes you like but be out by sundown, that's all!"

de Brock turned to the door, then as a further thought struck him he swung round. Only just in time he saw Calvert level a heavy .45 at him. de Brock fired instantly. The gun clattered out of Calvert's hand to the table. He swayed forward, clutching the table edge for support.

"Serves me right, mebby," he muttered. "I shouldn't ha' done that. Those who live by th' sword … perish by th' sword."

His hold gave way and he crashed to the wooden floor, de Brock stood looking, slowly holstering his gun.

"Misguided dimwit," he growled. "Guess I'll have to get th' boys over here to take the remainder of the cattle. What other stuff there is can be burned and a fresh start made. Nothing else for it."

He departed, descending the steps to his horse. Digging in the spurs he sent the animal swiftly along the trail which led to the looming mountain range nearby.

*

Perhaps half an hour later Jess, Fay, Ox, and their followers came riding into view, whilst behind them, their wrists roped to their saddles, came the hoodlums who had been so hopelessly beaten for the second time.

"Things look quiet enough," Fay said, contemplating the ranch as she slid from the saddle. "In fact, rather too quiet! I distrust it."

Jess jumped to the ground and joined her, leaving Ox in charge of the prisoners. The girl beside him, Jess mounted to the porch, frowned as he saw the door open, and then walked into the living room. There was nobody present. On the table was a big brown bag full of groceries.

"Dad!" Fay called, going back into the hall. "Dad, are you about anywheres?"

There was no response.

The girl looked into the bedrooms and then came back into the living room to find Jess staring thoughtfully at the wooden floor. In a moment she saw what had attracted his attention. There was a trail of crimson spots leading to the doorway. And, as he went further they led out across the hall and then lost themselves on the darker, sun-blistered wood of the porch.

"Do you think — " Fay stopped, mounting anxiety in her eyes as she looked at Jess.

"I dunno, Fay." He cuffed up his hat and gazed about the sun-drenched landscape. "Pretty plain that somebody got hurt, and very recently, too, since the blood's fresh. Whether it was your dad or old man Brock who got the works I can't say." He cupped his hands and shouted. "Hey there, Mr Calvert! You there? Mr Calvert!'

There was no answer from the silent wastes. Only the soft, hot wind and the stir of grass. Ox glanced over inquiringly from his horse.

"What gives, Jess?" he enquired. Jess told him, adding: "We"d better look around and see ii we c'n find Mr Calvert any place. Jim, Harry, you c'n help us. The rest of you stay where you are."

The search began immediately, but though they looked for a full hour, no sign of old man Calvert was found. Fay, sick with worry, at last came drifting back to her horse with Jess walking beside her in silence.

"There's one possibility," he said, after a spell of thought, "de Brock may have taken your father on his horse, since your dad's horse is in the stable, perhaps to hold him as a hostage or somethin'. Mebby he plans somethin' like your father's safe return for you handing me over, de Brock's up to any move on the board, remember. Anyways, there's nothing more we can do here. Our next job is to find out what happened to de Brock, an' also call in at the mayor's office and dig out what information we can which may be useful evidence for the Governor when, and if, he turns up."

"All right," Fay sighed. "Just as you say."

"At the moment," Jess added, when he had lifted her into the saddle, "we have one supreme advantage, Fay. de Brock doesn't know that his little ambush has come unstuck. That may give us just the final opportunity we need."

*

Whilst the search to find Calvert was proceeding, de Brock was riding cautiously up the narrow trail which led from the valley to the mountain foothills. He kept his gun constantly in his hand, his pale eyes darting about him quickly as he travelled.

For over two hours he wandered his horse in and out of the tortuous trails and arroyos and failed to find anything interesting. Then he stopped for a while in the shadow of a rock and lunched off the emergency ration in his saddlebag, also feeding his horse and watering him at a nearby stream. He had just come to the end of his meal when, in happening to glance upwards, he caught sight of a solitary figure on a rock far overhead.

The figure turned slowly, surveying the scenery, de Brock kept well hidden, watching. Then drawing carefully into the shadows he settled his revolver in a niche of the rocks and took careful aim. The report of the gun echoed and re-echoed and the solitary figure fell flat on the spur and remained motionless.

"If Burton's somewheres up there he'll certainly come and see what happened to his look-out," de Brock murmured to himself, staring intently upwards. "If he doesn't I'll go an' get him in any case."

For over ten minutes he waited, but nothing happened; so he decided to take a chance. Leading his horse he went slowly up the trail, revolver in hand, prepared for any sudden attack from a hidden watcher above.

Entirely unmolested he reached the top of the acclivity and stood looking about him. The man he had shot down, Jed, who had been left on look-out by Ox, lay where he had fallen. A brief examination satisfied the cattle baron that the puncher was dead.

Returning to the trail he peered inside the cave, summing up the evidence it afforded. That it was a hide-out was beyond question: so there remained nothing but to conceal his horse and wait for Jess, perhaps with Fay Calvert, to put in an appearance.

At first de Brock squatted on the rock just inside the cave, eagerly expectant, his gun ready.

Then he relaxed somewhat as nothing happened. By the end of the afternoon he was yawning with boredom; and by late evening he could stand it no longer.

Impatiently he strode out on to the mountain trail and gazed about him. There was nothing but silence and the incredibly beautiful colours in the western sky. Slowly it was forced upon him that for some reason Jess was not returning to the rendezvous.

"I don't see how he could have known I'd be here," he mused. "Unless he did go back to the Calvert ranch after all and old man Calvert had enough life left in him to tell him what I'm aiming to do. Don't think he would though; not in the mood he was in. No purpose in sticking here. Have to get the boys together an' find Burton, wherever he is. The victory isn't complete without him corralled."

He turned to his horse, swung into the saddle, and rode quickly down the trail to the pasture-lands, striking out southwards when he gained the valley side, heading in the direction of his own Square-8. The sun had completely set when he arrived, and, with the swiftness common to the region, the evanescent twilight turned into starry night as he descended from his horse in the yard.

He paused for a moment, looking about him. There was a peculiar quietness about his spread which he could not understand, an intense, heavy silence. What noise there was came from the cattle in the corrals.

"Digby," he shouted, raising his voice. "Hey, Digby! You around?"

Digby, his new foreman, and one of those who had been raiding in the morning, failed to appear from the nearby bunkhouse. That building, too, was unusually dark and silent.

Puzzled, his gun in his hand as a precaution, de Brock took his horse with him to the stable, unsaddled it, and frowned still more as he saw that all the horses which had been used in the morning were in their stalls, nodding sleepily. The men had evidently returned all right, then.

Scenting danger, yet failing to see it, de Brock went over to the bunkhouse and peered inside. All was in darkness, something which had never happened before. He struck a match and ignited the nearest lamp. It cast a pale radiance over a deserted scene.

de Brock departed again, looked at the dark ranch-house, and then he settled his gun more firmly in his hand. He had never been a man who lacked courage, and it did not desert him now. Without any attempt at being quiet he strode up the steps, across the porch, wrenched open the screen-door and hammered on the inner frame. To his surprise the door opened immediately, the catch being broken.

"Elsie!" he called, peering into the dark hall and wondering if his wife were present. "Elsie, you there?"

There was no reply. Not a sound in the blackness.

De Brock muttered something to himself, felt for and lighted the oil lamp on the hall table; then carrying it at shoulder level he entered the living room and looked about him. He had just time to notice that his wife was seated near the table, staring at him fixedly. Then she gave a sudden hoarse shout.

"Look out, Wil — !"

De Brock swung, but not quickly enough. A rope whirled out of the dark and settled over his shoulders, pinning his arms. A hand reached out and took the lamp. Another hand whipped the gun from his fingers.

A shadowy figure leapt up and lighted the oil lamp hanging from the ceiling joist; then the lamp de Brock himself had been holding was carried to the table and set down. Jess turned the light full on the side of his face, throwing his high cheekbones and powerful jaw into a relentless profile.

"Why the hell could't you have shouted sooner?" de Brock demanded of his wife.

"Because she had a gun trained on her," Jess answered. "An' even if it was she took her life in her hands yellin' a warnin' to you like she did. She's more loyal to you than you deserve, de Brock!"

The cattle baron relaxed, his arms still pinned. A glance to the rear assured him that Ox was looming there, grim-faced, ready for any action that might be needed. In other parts of the room figures which had been in the shadows were now revealed, every one of them Jess' own men, and Fay Calvert.

"Pretty!" de Brock commented dryly. "Very pretty! So you all hid until I came in; then you sprang this on me. About what I might have expected from you, Burton!"

"Since you might ha' expected it it's a pity you weren't better prepared," Jess answered. "I haven't the least doubt but what, had you bin given the same chance, you'd have prepared a similar welcome for me an Miss Calvert. I happened to think the faster, that's all. You might like to know that your raid on the Crooked-Y was interrupted. Two of your men were shot dead; two others were badly burned. You'll find every one of your men in the room yonder, roped, and those that were burned have bin bandaged up. As for your beloved mayor he's gone to North Point City for the State Governor, and when he comes back my job's done far as yore concerned. You've come to th' end of th' trail, de Brock. I've got you licked!"

"Like hell you have! You don't suppose a few ropes an' a bunch of your damned gunmen can hold me, do you?"

"They help, but they're not everything," Jess agreed. "What really nails you is the evidence I've piled up. There was quite a lot of it in the mayor's office, to which he gave me th' key, and there was even more in your safe there."

De Brock twirled in sudden anger and stared towards the heavy safe standing on ornamental legs in a corner. Its door was swinging wide.

"Save your breath," Jess suggested cynically. "We opened the safe, or at least Ox did, and took out your personal papers. They lay everythin' bare, your whole rotten scheme for drivin' th' settlers outa this valley. Since yore not averse to takin' things yourself you can't blame us for doin' likewise. In fact, de Brock, you've hog-tied yourself completely. While you were so busy lookin' for me I came here with my boys, took care of those you'd left around on guard, and now yore where I want you. There's enough dope piled against you to hang you a dozen times over."

De Brock said nothing. Then he looked at Fay as she snapped a vicious question at him.

"What did you do to my father?"

"I shot him before he could shoot me. An' I reckon the world is well rid of a hypocrite like him."

"Yore trouble is that yore a bit too free in decidin' who's not wanted in this world," Jess snapped. Then glancing about him he added, "Pull that lariat off him, boys, and tie him up properly. After that dump him in the other room with the rest of the stiffs."

He stood watching intently as Ox and the boys went to work to remove the ropes from the cattle baron's arms. Mrs de Brock, however, edged her hand a little nearer to the lamp on the table. It was at the moment that the lariat was freed from her husband's shoulders that she acted. Whirling the lamp up she flung it at Jess as he stood not two yards away.

He gasped, dropping his gun as searing glass and burning oil exploded over him. Though he was not hurt, his upflung arm having protected him, he had completely lost the initiative, de Brock hurtled forward, snatched up the fallen gun and levelled it. He spent a moment or two trampling over the flames on the floor; then he looked about him through the smoke haze.

"Come over here," he instructed his wife; and when she had moved to his side he added, "Go and untie those boys of ours in the next room. Mebby this game isn't quite so played out as our cocksure friend seems to think!"

Smiling to herself, Mrs de Brock crossed the room and opened the nearby door. Jess watched her movements with grim eyes, his hands raised in common with the rest of the men and Fay. The cattle baron considered them, keeping well away to avoid any chance of a sudden spring. Then he looked up expectantly as his released men came trooping out one by one from the adjoining room.

"Take the guns from these men," de Brock ordered. "Use them yourselves since you're unarmed."

This was done, the men grinning at the complete turning of the tables.

"Now, Burton, I'll trouble you for that evidence you've collected concerning me," de Brock said, coming forward.

Jess only tightened his mouth in response.

"All right, if you wish to be obstinate," de Brock shrugged. He turned to one of his gunmen. "You," he ordered, "take a look around. These hoodlums have their horses concealed somewheres about the spread. Ten to one the papers I want are in one of the saddle-bags."

The man nodded and headed for the door. Just as he reached it Ox lunged suddenly and landed a smashing uppercut. It sent the gunman crashing back against the table, his head spinning, de Brock fired. There was a grim silence as Ox's giant figure dropped heavily to the floor and lay motionless.

"I never did like that overgrown ape," the cattle baron commented, blowing a wisp of smoke from his revolver muzzle. The half-stunned gunman picked himself up. de Brock watched him grimly. "You okay again?" he said. "All right, carry on. We'll wait."

He moved to the centre of the room and stood lounging against the table, his wife next to him. Then he said:

"Come to think of it, boys, you'd better get these tramps roped up. I've got plans for them, and we'll have to work fast in case that mayor returns with the Governor after all. When he does he and the Governor are in for a surprise."

His men turned back into the bedroom to get the ropes with which they themselves had been bound. In a moment or two they had returned. Jess was debating whether or not to risk the guns and make a fight for it when something happened. Wilton de Brock abruptly turned an almost complete somersault and landed on his back with teeth jarring-impact.

Simultaneously Ox leapt upwards, holding the carpet strip in his hands which he had jerked from under the cattle baron. Now he flung it over de Brock's head, smothering him with it.

"Grab your chance, Jess!" he yelled. "We've got 'em!" and regardless of guns or anything else he slammed out with his mighty fists.

Two of the gunmen went spinning into the bedroom, hurled into the dresser and toppled over on the floor with the dresser on top of them. The remaining men, slow-witted at the best of times, waved their guns uncertainly, afraid to shoot for fear they hit the struggling, swearing de Brock. Against the window his wife watched helplessly.

Jess swung, his fists ready, and lunged with all his power. In a matter of seconds he and the rest of the boys were slamming hammer-and-tongs, taking and receiving killing punishment as they reeled and swerved about the big room, the single oil lamp in the ceiling casting a yellow glimmer over the violence.

Ox, the most powerful member in the outfit, went down for the count as a chair was broken in pieces over his bullet head. Jess, turning to look at him, stopped a blow under the jaw which knocked him off his feet and dropped him half senseless on the floor. By the time he was able to see properly again he realized that the battle was lost. Panting but triumphant, de Brock's men were grouped around their boss as he stood by the door with twin guns levelled.

"You seem to like making things tough for yourself, Burton," he said bitterly. "This time I shan't give you the chance. I didn't think Ox had enough brains to play dead and pull the carpet from under me." He looked at the giant puncher as he got dizzily to his feet, holding his head. "Anyway, it's my trump this time. I don't see why I should waste time trussing you up before finishing you off. I'd planned to do that and dump the lot of you in the desert where you could never be found. As it is shooting you may be safer."

He paused as the gunman he had sent out to look for the papers came in, his arms full of documents neatly bound in tape.

"Good!" de Brock murmured. "Put them on the table. As I was saying, Burton, shooting's the only safe way, and that includes you, Miss Calvert. I don't say that I particularly like the idea of wiping out a good-looking girl like you, but you know too much, so I can't let you go free."

"If you lay a finger on her, de Brock, I'll come back from the grave an' get you!" Jess breathed, scrambling to his feet.

"Stop talking like an idiot, Burton!" de Brock snapped; and in the brief ensuing silence there was the faint sound of the gun-hammers coming up. The muzzles of his guns swung round directly at the girl and Jess.

But the shots were not fired. Instead there came the explosion of a gun from the hall, de Brock remained like a statue for perhaps three seconds, a faraway look in his pale eyes. Then his knees gave way and he dropped flat on his face.

Immediately two of his men rushed towards him, but they fell back as a tall figure came into view, a gaunt, dust-streaked figure of a man, blood dried on the front of his shirt.

"Dad!" Fay cried hoarsely. "Dad, it's you! Oh, thank God!"

She raced across the room and caught at his arms.

"Don't pull me, gal," he said briefly. "Liable to deflect my aim. Jess, you'd best get these critters roped up good an' pretty, hadn't you!"

"Yeah." Jess gave a surprised glance at the use of his first name. "Let's get busy, boys."

He turned to the task, Ox helping him. Then suddenly Calvert's gun swung round to Mrs de Brock as she sidled towards the door.

"Better hold it, ma'm," he said curtly. "We're not decided yet on what we're goin' to do with you."

"Dad, you're talking as though you really mean it!" Fay said tensely. "You're holding guns and fighting. Like I've always wanted you to."

"Yeah." He grinned a little. "I reckon Scriptures ain't much use to a man out here when a guy plugs you like this guy de Brock did. He got me in the shoulder, nothin' much, even though it looks bad. I decided I'd best get him in return. So I came, keeping outa sight when you searched for me so's I could spring a nice surprise when I wanted. I didn't use a horse, neither, 'case it was seen."

"From the sound of things," Jess said, "you've different views now in regards to Fay and me."

Calvert nodded. "I sure have, son. Besides, I've bin thinking. I'm going to need a strong man an' a lot of his pardners to build up my outfit now de Brock's bin taken care of. I guess you, and Ox, and the rest of 'em can help me plenty, an' all th' other ranchers who need it."

"In between my duties as sheriff, yes," Jess agreed, with a broad smile. "If I'm elected — "

"If!" Ox bellowed. "Huh! We'll pin back the ears uv every critter in town 'til you are! An' say," he added, "I just had a look at de Brock here, he's cashed in his chips, I reckon. Yuh got him clean, Calvert."

For a moment nobody spoke, then Jess looked up sharply.

"That sounds like two horsemen comin'. Must be the mayor an' Governor, I expect. An' the way things are it looks like we finished th' job ourselves."

"You mean you did," Calvert said quietly. "I'd never have tried it without somebody blazin' th' trail first." He looked at Fay earnestly. "I take back what I said, gal. This is one hundred per cent man yore gettin'."

"An' one hundred per cent gal," Jess responded, putting an arm about her shoulders.

Town Without Law

John Russell Fearn

One

Before the final union of the United States of America there existed dozens of small tracts of land, in themselves 'Little States' — most of them created by sudden gold strikes and populated thereafter by prospectors and their families, successful miners or otherwise. Such a State was Mirando, a circular territory which took in what were later to become the corners of Colorado, Utah, New Mexico, and Arizona.

Here the law existed as man made it. No high Governmental authority could issue a command — and likewise no authority could give protection. The law of the gun was the only law, and in Mirando that meant the law of Sherman Hall, the ruthless mayor-cum-sheriff of Gold Point, the sprawling — and the only — town in the State, built in the hey-day of a gold rush and standing on its foundations now only because one inhabitant robbed the other. In Gold Point the lawless West was epitomised in all its starkness. Its villainy, its black-heartedness, its barefaced dishonesty, was a blot on what was otherwise rapidly becoming a fair land under the spreading tide of decency created by men and women of good will fighting to put their country on a decent footing.

Rex M'Clyde was a man who believed in decency. The son of an honest prospector and his wife, long since murdered by claim-jumpers, he had grown up in Gold Point, watching at the same time the rise to two-gun power of Sherman Hall. To Hall, Rex M'Clyde constituted a serious menace. He was honest, a deadly marksman, and completely unafraid. Therefore it was necessary to be rid of him — not with an assassin's bullet, for M'Clyde had many friends who would avenge him — but legally. Completely. In a word, banishment.

Inevitably therefore M'Clyde found himself nailed on a charge of murder, which he had never committed. The evidence, however, was against him at every turn. Sherman Hall had thought out every detail in advance, knowing that no lawyer could possibly win his case with the facts as they were. So, one brilliant morning, with the blazing sunlight streaming through the windows of Gold Point's little court-room, Rex M'Clyde stood in the dock and listened to his innocence being lied away.

The court was crowded. There were punchers, half-breeds, cattlemen drifting through to other towns, women idling away an hour before continuing with their shopping — and of course Sherman Hall himself and the little clique of yes-men with whom he invariably went around. He sat the back of the court, a big-shouldered, long-legged man, high-cheekboned, with sloe-black eyes. He was still only thirty, and proud of his murderous rise to power. While not wealthy in the financial sense he had none the less enough influence to make or break the town by merely opening his mouth. For him this was a red-letter day. His most dangerous and detested enemy was listening in silence to facts which he could not deny.

'Rex M'Clyde,' Judge Barrow said presently, gazing through his steel-rimmed spectacles towards the stand, 'you've heard what the jury has had t'say. They've brought in a verdict of guilty on all counts ... Have y'anything t'say afore I pass sentence on you?'

'Only that you've listened to a pack of lies from start to finish,' Rex responded, shrugging. 'I'm not blamin' Your Honour for that: just the way this setup's been fixed, I reckon.' Rex's cold blue eyes stared across the court-room to where Sherman Hall and his colleagues sat. 'Just that I don't happen to fit in with th' plans of our illustrious mayor and sheriff,' he finished.

Judge Barrow was silent for a moment. Within limits he was an honest man: he really tried to be fair with the sentences he imposed, even though most of them, as in this case, were dictated by Hall. He sat thinking, looking at the young man on the stand. He was tall, clean limbed, more interesting-looking than handsome, with a wide mouth which under different circumstances probably smiled quite a deal. Now it was taut, balanced by a cleanly cut chin.

'Ordinarily,' Judge Barrow resumed, 'the penalty for murder is death — but I'm satisfied that there are some bits in th' evidence we've heard that are open t'doubt.' He gave a defiant glance towards Sherman Hall as he spoke. 'That bein' so I'm not goin' to impose the extreme penalty.'

Rex M'Clyde smiled then, and it transformed his bronzed face. Only there was cynicism in the way the lips parted.

'I know just what you're plannin' on doin', Judge,' he said quietly. 'An' that's the very thing Hall has been aimin' at ever since we were kids together — to get me thrown out of town in disgrace so's I c'n never come back.'

'That's it,' Barrow agreed, looking a trifle uncomfortable. 'In our law there —'

'Y'mean Hall's law,' Rex corrected.

'In *our* law,' the judge repeated, 'there are two alternatives when murder's bin committed. When there's no doubt about it it means the rope; but when there's a shade of doubt the answer is banishment, an' that's your sentence. At sundown to-night, M'Clyde, you'll get outa this town and never return.'

Rex reflected for a moment and then said: 'You asked me if I'd anythin' to say, Judge. Well, I have — an' now's as good a time as any to say it. You know, and all of us know deep down, that this town's rotten to th' foundations. It stinks of graft an' corruption and th' smell of guns. There are a few in it who've tried to put it on even keel and make honesty be the only law — but as long as men like Sherman Hall live, an' those like him, Gold Point will remain one of th' biggest fester spots in th' West.'

Sherman Hall coloured slightly under his tan and his big hand strayed to his right-hand gun. Then he thought again and re-folded his arms.

'Let the jigger go on talkin',' he murmured sourly, as his chief henchman gave him an enquiring glance.

'I've tried, most of th' time single-handed, to make this town fit for decent people t'live in,' Rex went on bitterly. 'I've had good reason to, 'cos my folks died before a murderer's guns, an' the Uncle who brought me up also got a bullet for no partic'lar reason just when I'd reached manhood. I've never run down those assassins, even though I know who they are. It isn't easy to bring a man to justice when he is justice — so called.'

Sherman Hall stood up suddenly, his powerful face set in ugly lines.

'I reckon that's about enough outa this guy, Judge,' he snapped. 'You supposed t'be runnin' this court or ain't yuh? Get the guy outa here into jail an' see he gits outa town at sundown.'

'You never did have much brains, Hall,' Rex told him, 'otherwise you'd know you stand accused right now!'

'I had enough brains to master this town and rule it!'

'Y'mean you had enough ammunition.'

There was something suspiciously like laughter rippling round the court until Judge Barrow's gavel descended and silenced it. Sherman Hall sat down again, glaring. Rex looked again at the judge.

'Not much more I've got t'say, Your Honour,' he said, ''cept to remark that before I'm through I'll find a way to make this town decent, even if I am banished from it.'

'Which sounds kind of contradictory to me,' Barrow said, rubbing his chin dubiously. 'Y'know what the law sez, M'Clyde. Come back into this town after bein' thrown out of it and you'll be shot on sight.'

Rex only smiled; and it was the kind of smile which could have signified just anything as far as his thoughts were concerned. Then when the judge motioned two guards came up from the back and took Rex by either arm. He looked directly across the court at Sherman Hall for a moment, then turned in the grip of his jailers.

*

Rex was standing gazing at the molten glory of the sunset over the distant Calabasa Mountains when there came the rattle of the key in the door of his cell. With a sigh he turned, fully expecting to see the deputy sheriff and a couple of armed men ready for him to march outside, mount his horse, and leave town. Instead he found himself confronted by the big figure of Sherman Hall, his thumbs latched on to his gun belts, a sneering grin on his bronzed face.

'Yuh should feel honoured,' he remarked dryly. 'The sheriff and mayor in person has arrived to see yuh off.'

'Not without some unpleasant reason either, I'll wager,' Rex responded.

'Depends what's called unpleasant. Fur me it'll be one of the nicest sights ever t'see yuh leavin' town bound an' gagged on a cayuse, with no bedroll, no provisions, no arms — no anythin'. Mebbe yuh won't be of the same frame uf mind, though, huh?'

'That sort of treatment isn't legal,' Rex snapped. 'Even a man who's banished is entitled to protect himself. That's in the constitution book of this cockeyed State.'

'Yeah, sure — but some rules are made t'be broken, specially since I'm th' guy who thought uf most of 'em. Fer you, M'Clyde, I'm plannin' a really good send off — partic'larly after all yuh had t'say in court this mornin'.' Hall's expression changed to one of cold menace. 'Yuh shot your face off a bit too free fur my likin'.'

220

'Truth does hurt sometimes, doesn't it?' Rex asked dryly.

'Never mind the smart cracks, M'Clyde. Git outa here quick. There's a horse waitin' fur yuh outside.'

Hall whipped out his right hand gun and held it steadily. Since Rex was completely unarmed it was a somewhat pointless action — but if it did nothing else it showed how afraid he really was of the man he was kicking out of town.

At the cell door Rex paused for a moment. 'Don't forget what I said about makin' this into a worthwhile town one day, Hall. It'll take more than you, an' your trigger men, and your two six-guns to stop me.'

'Shut up!'

Rex shrugged, went out into the passage way, then through the little sheriff's office and so to the boardwalk outside. Here he paused, grimly surprised at beholding a goodly proportion of the town's population gathered in the late evening light, evidently waiting to give him a send-off. The form it would take was more or less evident from the expressions on the men and women's faces.

'There's yuh horse,' Hall said, coming up in the rear and jerking his gun towards a chestnut roan fastened to the boardwalk tie-rail. 'Git on it — an' quick!'

Rex went slowly down the three steps to the dust on the main street and surveyed the animal critically as he walked towards it. It was old and certainly not cut out for a long journey. Also the saddle was absolutely bare. No arms, no bedroll, no anything — just as Sherman Hall had said.

'Whadda yuh waitin' fur?' Hall roared. 'Git up in that saddle, blast yuh!'

Rex obeyed, but before he could take hold of the reins two of Hall's yes-men rushed forward — evidently at a prearranged signal from their leader — and seizing Rex's hands tightly forced them behind him, securing them to the rear of the saddle. His feet they then bound to the stirrups, taking rope under the horse's belly for extra protection. Finally his kerchief was loosened from his neck and drawn taut across his mouth instead.

'Pretty, ain't he?' Hall asked, holstering his gun and surveying Rex in the dying light.

There was a responsive roar of laughter from the lookers-on, then it faded out abruptly as the tubby figure of Judge Barrow became visible marching up the High Street, his broad-brimmed Stetson thrust on the back of his grey head. When he reached Rex he stared up at him, then to Hall.

'This isn't constitutional, Hall, an' you know it!' he snapped.

'T'hell with that,' Hall retorted.

'Not on your life!' Barrow shook his head stubbornly. 'I don't like any of th' laws that apply to this State an' town, but I do try an' keep to 'em. Dang it, we've got to if we're to stop chaos in our midst — There's nothin' that sez a man can't have protection an' ride free even if he *is* banished. This sorta thing's sheer spite — an' as judge, an' here to see justice done, I'm not standin' for it.'

'Don't yuh think yuh'd have a darned sight more sense if yuh shut up?' Hall asked coldly.

Barrow looked at him for a moment, then setting his chubby little mouth he strode over to Rex and began to go to work on the cords holding his wrists. Then he paused again as Hall put the muzzle of his gun in his back.

'Git away from those cords, Judge — or yore a dead 'un. I'm not kiddin' neither. This guy needs special treatment. An' start rememberin' that *I'm* th' mayor an' sheriff around here, which gives me an almighty lot more authority'n yuhself!'

'I believe injustice —' Barrow started to argue, but that was as far as he got. There was the sudden explosion of Hall's gun and the judge sagged, clutching at the roan for support. His nerveless fingers gave way and he fell on his face in the dust.

'Takes his job too seriously,' Hall said, and went down on his knees to make a brief examination of the fallen man. Then he stood up and added, 'I mean he did take his job too seriously. Reckon he won't bother us much more.'

Rex, tugging futilely at his cords, wanted nothing more at that moment than to free himself and then sink his powerful fingers into Hall's throat and crush ... and crush. Instead he could only relax, convinced of his helplessness.

'Okay, folks, yuh know what to do,' Hall shouted, reholstering his gun and motioning for the judge's body to be dragged away. 'Give this guy with th' halo a really good send-off — G'on, move!' he finished, and delivered a terrific blow across the roan's withers.

The startled animal bucked wildly and, the reins released, hurtled forward. Already frightened, he became even more panic-stricken at the hail of shots which followed him. Not one of them actually hit — Hall was insistent on that — but completely terrified the animal took the bit between his teeth and ran with shattering speed down the lamp-lighted street.

The populace, primed beforehand as to what to do, let fly with less dangerous but much more hurtful contributions. From the crowd left behind, and from roofs lining the main street, Rex had to run the gauntlet of rotten tomatoes, eggs, stones, paper bags full of molasses, and 'bombs' which burst in a cascade of flour and soot.

Cut about the face and head, sticky with egg and tomato juice, he was borne helplessly out of town on the back of the fleeing horse. Behind him the roars of laughter became fainter and fainter, until at last he was a target no more and the cold night wind of the desert was blowing in his face, sideways to the trail along which the horse was carrying him ... In no way could he control it, or even speak a word of command. He would just have to sit until the animal exhausted himself — unless he could somehow break free of the tough cords which held him.

To commence with there was just nothing he could do except go where the panic stricken animal took him — and this was away from the trail and across the pasture lands; then, at a slowing pace, away from these lush green areas to ever increasing aridity as the fringes of the desert were reached.

Tired now, his feet slipping and sliding in the loose sand, the horse jogged onwards under the stars. Rex, cramped and bruised with the jolting he had received, pulled mightily on the cords holding him and bit savagely into the kerchief between his teeth, but on the one hand the cords only tightened the more he pulled on them, and on the other the kerchief was made of silk and refused to be torn or bitten through.

At the moment Rex realized that he was in no immediate danger. The air was cold and stimulating: it was not more than three hours since he had had a meal — but with the coming of the day it would be different. He had no hat and, if he still remained bound, he would be at the mercy of the horse's wanderings under the relentless sub-tropical sun, without food or water and no method of guiding the horse except by the pressure of his legs against its sides, which was by no means sufficient. Also, once in the midst of the desert there was nothing easier than to lose all sense of direction, and then —

These thoughts were sufficient to set Rex battling again to free himself, without avail. The night wore on; the horse loped wearily, deeper and deeper into the desert, until at last there came the intense darkness and cold which preceded the dawn. Motionless on the horse, feeling almost as though he were frozen into position, Rex gazed dully at the stars. They paled swiftly before the onrush of day. The mist across the desert stirred and drifted. Distant cacti bushes loomed like crouching men amidst the uncertain shadows and then stood out stark against the vermilion and gold in the east. Like a plate of burnished copper the sun rose and transformed the darkness into dawn.

Rex looked about him stiffly in the newborn light. During the night the horse had travelled so far from Gold Point and the pasture lands surrounding it they were no longer within sight. There was nothing but desert — desert — desert. Not a trace of a township, a living habitation, and certainly not a human being. Nor did there seem to be any sign of a waterhole either.

That the roan was becoming parched with thirst was evident from the way he kept his nose to the ground. Unless he found water there was the chance that before the torrid day was out he would collapse from exhaustion, dragging Rex down with him. Bound as he was there was every chance he would lie pinned, until death came to bring him relief.

He shut his eyes for a moment at the thought and yet again began a struggle to free himself, and yet again he failed. Numbed in mind and body from so long maintaining one rigid position he began after a while to feel himself floating away into brief spells of unconsciousness. The rising warmth of the day after the biting cold of the night, to say nothing of his immovable posture, made him intolerably sleepy. Yet he dared not give way to it for it might mean that he would fall sideways, the sudden pull on the saddle swinging it round so that he would be dragged, bound, through the sand — or else be relentlessly kicked by the horse's feet.

Somehow he had to stay awake, but Nature was a far stronger force than his will. The beating of the sun on his unprotected head was soothing. He did not feel cramped or sense the imminence of death any more. His eyes were slitted against the shimmering wilderness, in all of which he could see no trace of a living thing. Sand, everywhere — pitiless, sun drenched, sucked dry.

Then things seemed to be going dark again. The landscape was swirling and patterned with meaningless shapes ... Rex had a conviction that he was wandering over endless miles of sand, searching in vain for water he could never find. His throat, his head, his whole body was on fire. There was an intolerable ache in his shoulders and legs.

Then, in how long a time he did not know, the heat and the pain seemed to subside and he felt delightfully cool. With a studied effort he opened his eyes — and looked straight into the face of a man.

It was a face prematurely aged, burned deep brown, with a multitude of fine lines etched about the mouth and eyes. Very steady eyes of a deep grey. The chin was weak, and what hair showed under the edges of a battered sombrero was iron-grey with patches of white. Rex looked further — above him at a tattered square of canvas doing duty as tent roof, then out to the endless desert, tiny whirls of sand rising in the scorching wind. Cobalt blue heaven, a distant range of mountains, and outside the tent's thin canvas walls were the shadows of three trees and, beside him, the black outlines of two motionless horses.

'What — goes on?' Rex was surprised to find his voice did not sound like his own. It was cracked and broken. Even more surprising, as he raised a hand to his face, was the discovery that he had quite a goodly beard and moustache.

'Feelin' better, pardner?' the man asked gruffly.

'Yeah — a heap better. I'd probably feel even better'n that if I could figger out what's happened.'

'You've had fever — pretty bad too, but I guess you'll be okay from here on. I've kept an eye t'you.'

'Fever?' Rex repeated. 'For how long?'

'A week mebbe, on an' off ... I'm Pardoe,' the man added. 'Seth Pardoe, I ... ur ... live around here.' And he grinned for a moment which gave him a curiously wild expression.

'The name's Rex M'Clyde,' Rex held out his hand. 'Many thanks for what you've bin doin' for me.'

'Ain't nothin'. I could see you wus in a spot — probably the victim of a bunch of bushwhackers, huh?'

'Yeah.' Cold lights settled in Rex's eyes. 'Yeah, you guessed it, Seth ... But look, what *did* happen?'

'I wus sittin' here in my tent, mindin' my own business as usual, when I saw somethin' movin' in the desert mebbe ten miles away. I got keen eyes, see? I'm usta seein' a thing move far off because usually nothin' does. So, I hit the leather and rode out t'take a look-see. I found you, half fallen off'n

225

your horse, bound to it, and you wus jabberin' like a crazy man 'bout water an' sunlight ... So I cut yuh loose, brought yuh here, and put yuh straight. Your cayuse is okay too now.'

Seth Pardoe was silent for a moment, staring into the sun-drenched distances. Then he added,

'This is about the only water hole there is around these parts, an' it's plumb in the middle of the desert, 'bout a hundred miles to Gold Point an' twenty-five to Satan's Gap. That's where I git my supplies from, and foodstuffs for my horse, which I bought there.'

'What are you doing here?' Rex asked, astonished.

'Just sittin' — glad t'be alone.'

'How long have you been here?' Rex persisted.

'Oh ...' Pardoe squinted up towards the sun. 'Five years mebbe. Ten years p'raps. No tellin'.'

Silence. Pardoe picked up a handful of sand and let it sift down between his knobbly fingers.

'Ever stop t'think that life's a bit like this?' he asked. 'Gone before y'know it — slips through your fingers an' there ain't nothin' y'can do to stop it.'

Such queer philosophy from a desert outcast made Rex feel oddly uncomfortable. He struggled up on to one elbow and looked about him with more interest. As he had already thought, he was in a tent of sorts. There was a small collapsible table with various foodstuffs and a few bottles standing upon it; there was also the camp bed upon which he was lying. Pardoe himself was squatting on a rather insecure canvas stool, his bony legs, draped in tattered riding trousers, drawn awkwardly backwards to aid him in maintaining his balance. Pardoe was probably tall when he stood up.

'Would it be a fair question t'ask what you're doing way out here?' Red asked.

'Yeah — s'pose it would.' Pardoe spat leisurely into the sand. 'Seein' as yuh in pretty much th' same position as I was myself once. I'm here becos a buncha no account jackals figgered I rubbed a guy out ... but I didn't. I was framed — an' run outa town.'

'Which town?'

'Gold Point.'

Silence again. A merciless hardness set about Rex's lips. Seth Pardoe noticed it and gave a wry grin.

'You run outa town too, feller?'

'Yeah. Same town as you. Gold Point. Only —' Rex frowned. 'I don't ever remember you bein' run out, an' I've lived in Gold Point all my life till now.'

'Well, let's see now …' Pardoe narrowed his grey eyes and inspected his horny hands. 'I said I'd bin here five or ten year. Come t'think on it it must be nearer ten than anythin' — And afore I settled here I roamed about plenty, mebbe for another five year or so — I guess you won't be much more'n thirty, huh?'

'Round about that,' Rex agreed. 'And you're thinking that I must have been about fifteen when you got thrown out — Well, could be, and may account for me not rememberin'. Who did it, anyways? Couldn't ha' been Sherman Hall 'cos he's only about my age.'

'It was Calvin Hall,' Pardoe answered. 'As dirty a liar as any I've ever come across — an' a born gunman. Father of the guy who's driven you out, I s'pose.'

Rex nodded slowly, his face still grim. 'An' you just sat down and took it — finally settling here and watching the world go by?'

'I guess so. I couldn't go back t'Gold Point an' stay healthy, an' I didn't seem t'settle down any place else — so when I came on this spot I decided there weren't nothin' more I needed than food an' a roof. An' here I stopped. I kinda like it … The boys back in Satan's Gap where I get my supplies think I'm a bit crazy. But I ain't.' Pardoe gave again that peculiar grin. 'Not Seth Pardoe.'

Rex did not argue the point. Back of his mind he had the impression that whilst not actually insane, Pardoe was certainly a little sun-kissed. Alone for so long, in this empty wilderness, with only bitter memories of injustice done, could hardly have failed to make some kind of impression.

'I'm different to you, Seth,' he said, slowly sitting up on the camp bed and putting his feet on the sand which formed the 'floor' of the dwelling. 'I don't aim to sit around and get my brains fried. I only want one thing … revenge! Gold Point is the biggest hoodlums' town that ever was an' I figger it's a sort of sacred duty to blast it wide open, one day.'

'Fifteen years ago I mighta thought the same,' Pardoe responded. 'Now it don't seem to matter no more.'

'That's because the passage of time has dulled the blow you got. With me it's still fresh — an' it hurts.' Rex removed a hand from his still somewhat spinning head and stood up. 'I don't rightly know what I'm goin' to'do, but certainly something. I'll never rest until Gold Point can be a town fit for decent people to live in.'

'That'll take more than courage, feller. It needs money to fight a town full o' bush-whackers.'

'Mebbe I can find money somewheres. Work for it, p'haps —' Rex stared out across the motionless, shimmering desert; then he glanced round as Pardoe got to his feet. As he had suspected, he was tall, possibly six foot three, with narrow shoulders and curiously jerky movements. Without saying anything he went to the rear of the tent and began fishing inside a heavy tin box.

'What would yuh say that was?' he asked finally, and coming over to Rex with palm extended he revealed an object about the size of a .45 calibre bullet. It glowed dull yellow in the pitiless sunlight.

'I'd say gold,' Rex decided, weighing it in his hand.

Pardoe grinned, 'Yuh'd say right. It is.'

Two

It was a moment or two before the significance of Seth Pardoe's statement sank into Rex's mind. He looked again at the ingot, frowned, then stared at the still grinning hermit.

'Y'mean to tell me you've gold like this and yet y'stick around here doin' just nothin'?' Rex demanded.

''Til now, sure. What'd be the use uf gold t'me? I've only myself — no family, no woman, no anythin'. If I had millions o' dollars it wouldn't make th' least bit difference.'

'I know what I could do with gold.' Rex gazed at it broodingly as it lay in his palm.

'Yeah … an' I know what *I* could do with it — now. Makes a difference, feller, meetin' up with you. We've the same thing in common. I'm not hankerin' after bein' alone any more.'

Rex frowned at him. 'Meanin' what?'

'Listen, feller.' Pardoe came closer to him with a sense of definite urgency. 'I know where there's gold just fur the pickin' up — an' that's a sample of it. Back in that tin box o' mine, which I had one helluva job bringin' here across the desert, there is twenty more nuggets like that. I could fill a thousand boxes with the stuff if I wanted. So far I never have — but I do now. Yuh want t'get even with Sherman Hall and clean up Gold Point, yuh say? Okay — so do I. Whether I deal with the son or his pa makes no odds with me. Same stinkin' family, anyways.'

'Power …' Rex clenched his hand over the ingot, his mouth setting into a hard line. 'That's what this means, Seth. We might be able to really do somethin' with gold at our back. We could buy labour, helpers, lots of things.'

'We could build a town mebbe,' Pardoe said, musing.

'A town?'

'Sure. Why not? A *decent* town — one that decent men and women could be proud to own. Pioneers before us have built towns, an' they just grown and grown. Most of 'em did it because they had th' gold — an' the money — to do it. We could do th' same.'

'A rival town to Gold Point, y'mean?' Rex exclaimed, his imagination leaping.

'Why not? Right here where we stand. There's underground water a-plenty an' its still in the State of Mirando. Yuh don't leave the State 'til yuh touch Satan's Gap. That lies just over the border …' Pardoe chuckled in his leathery way and then added, 'Ysee, feller, I've had years t'think about this, only I never got me the urge t'go on alone. Now I've found you it's different. Both uv us with common cause, as y'might say.'

'Yeah, that's right — Look,' Rex said quietly, 'are you *sure* about the gold?'

'Huh? 'Course I am! The mine's not three miles frum this spot — but there's only me that knows how to get at it.'

'An' you found it by accident?'

'I fell in the durned place dodgin' a sandstorm one day. An' believe me it's a bonanza! Only wants workin' properly.'

'Would you show me where it is?'

Pardoe hesitated, rubbing his sloping chin slowly. He squinted out across the desert.

'Mebbe — when yore rested up a bit.'

'I'm rested right now — thanks to you. Exercise would probably do me good.'

Pardoe was silent, then with a smile Rex patted his arm.

'Don't take it to heart, Seth. Mebbe I asked too much, on such short acquaintance —'

'That's just it,' Pardoe said quickly. 'Not that I don't trust yuh or anythin'; don't think that — but just supposin' it wus all a put up job to make me show where the mine is? Could be, yuh know. Men'll do anythin' fur gold.'

'Right enough,' Rex agreed. 'That being so, what would you like me to do to prove I'm in earnest?'

Pardoe gave a peculiar smile and walked across to his tin box once more. From it, to Rex's amazement, he brought forth about twenty of the ingots, put them in a sack along with the ingot Rex had been holding, and then he handed the sack over, roughly tied about the neck.

'There's enough gold there, feller, to net somethin' like a hundred thousand dollars,' he said. 'In Satan's Gap there's an assayer by the name of Tadworth. Take the gold to him an' get it valued. Then come back here and tell me what he sez ... Savvy?'

'Uh-huh; I'll do it willingly.'

Pardoe nodded. 'Okay. If yore an honest man yuh'll come back all right, with every ingot intact. If yore not yuh'll hit th' trail as fast as yuh can, knowin' that yuh've a hundred thousand dollars in gold, which is a mighty nice pile t'sit on fur the rest of yuh life.'

'I'll come back,' Rex smiled. 'I'm in earnest.'

'Deep down, feller, I believe that — but yuh can't blame me fur wantin' t'make sure ... I'll give yuh a hand to put this stuff on that horse uv yorn.'

Pardoe led the way out of the tent to the cluster of shady trees where the horses were tethered. The roan flicked his tail and showed the whites of his eyes in greeting as he realized Rex was beside him. Pardoe transferred the saddle bag from his own horse and into it thrust the heavy sack of ingots.

'Sure yuh feel fit to make the trip?' he enquired. 'Yuh've bin a mighty sick man.' He handed up a Stetson for Rex to wear.

'I'm all right,' Rex assured him. 'But you'd better loan me a gun. No tellin' what I might run into.' Pardoe nodded, returned into the tent, and reappeared in a moment or two with a loaded belt and a .38 in the holster. Rex took it and strapped it on.

'Yuh can keep that,' Pardoe said. 'Save yuh the trouble of buyin' one — not that yuh've any money on yuh, far as I could see.'

'I was stripped of everythin',' Rex told him, climbing into the saddle. 'But mebbe we'll even that up a bit later on. Be seein' you.'

'Make sure yuh head due south for Satan's Gap — an' due north comin' back,' Pardoe called after him. 'It's th' only way yuh'll ever find me again.'

Rex nodded and started off. Hot though the sun was, it did not worry him. With every minute his normal strength was returning to him — and the roan too seemed glad to be on the move after enforced rest.

As he rode, Rex found himself wondering whether he had by sheer chance fallen in with a genuine discoverer of gold — or whether Seth Pardoe was crazy and had only handed over some worthless chunks of yellow mineral. Out here, as Rex well knew, there were many ores which approached the precious metal in appearance — so much so that only an expert could detect the difference. But there was also the fact that gold mines, both untapped and abandoned, lay in many parts of the State, some of them buried completely, others unworkable.

There was also another point which made Rex ponder a deal. If the assayer, Tadworth, was crooked — and very few men who dealt in gold in this region were not — there would be nothing to prevent him saying the stuff was worthless and then watching what Rex did next. Have to watch him carefully, that was all. The things that had happened to him had made Rex determined to throw his usually quiet tactics overboard. The only law that seemed to be understood was that of the gun …

In a little over an hour and a half he had covered the distance to Satan's Gap — a town cut on much the same pattern as Gold Point, though from the appearance of things conforming placidly to law and order. The men and women in view in the main street were of a far more docile breed than the tough denizens of the outlaws' town.

Reaching the assayer's office Rex slipped from the saddle, tied the roan to the boardwalk rail, and then carried his sack of ingots into the office and dumped it on the counter. After a moment the assayer himself came from behind a wood partition, taking a lens out of his eye. He was small, thin featured, with the kind of eyes that made him look as though he had just awakened from deep sleep.

Rex motioned with his thumb. 'Take a look at this lot,' he said, and the assayer unfastened the sack and heaved the contents in a yellow heap in front of him. His expression altered for a moment and plain greed leapt into his wide eyes — and as quickly vanished.

'More rock, huh?' he asked briefly, glancing up.

Rex considered him. 'You're the assayer. What do *you* say? What have I got here and how much is it worth?'

The assayer put his lens back in his eye and squinted at one of the ingots carefully. Then his uncovered eye angled round and contemplated Rex in something like cynical humour.

'Looks t'me like you've had a lot of trouble for nothin', feller,' he said, shrugging. 'This stuff ain't gold, if that's what yore thinkin'.'

'That's what I *am* thinking. If it isn't gold, what is it?'

'Iron ore, with a mineral cross. That's where it gets its yellow colour.'

'Yeah?'

'Yeah. Yore not the first guy to walk in here an' think he's dug up a bonanza.'

Rex reflected briefly, then suddenly his right hand shot out, gripped the astonished assayer by the front of his shirt, and dragged him bodily over the counter. With a shove Rex landed him on his feet, then pinned him hard against the wood partition.

'Now,' Rex said, his gun poking in the man's midriff. 'I want the truth!'

'That *is* th' truth, blast it! I —'

'No, it isn't. If ever a man had greed in his eyes, you had when you saw those ingots in front of you. I know men: I can read 'em like books. You can either tell me the truth or I'll rub you out and go to somebody who will — Come on!'

The gun jabbed keenly and the assayer swallowed hard, fear in his half-awake eyes.

'Okay, okay,' he panted, struggling vainly in the relentless grip. 'I was kiddin' —'

'Why?'

'Just — just a way I have sometimes —'

'It's a way I don't like. Start talkin'.'

'Yeah — okay. It's gold. Pure gold. Musta come out of a bonanza some place.'

'Never mind 'bout that. How much is it worth?'

'Can't say exactly. At a rough guess mebbe a hundred thousand dollars.'

'So old Pardoe reckoned it up dead right,' Rex murmured; then he suddenly released the assayer and returned his gun to its holster. 'Okay, so it's worth a hundred thousand dollars. That's all I wanted t'know. An' if you've any sense,' Rex added, returning the ingots to the sack and picking it up, 'you'll tell the truth in future. Other men mightn't be as lenient as I've been.'

He turned and went out, walking further down the street until he came to the general stores. Before entering he removed the smallest ingot from the sack, roughly estimated its worth, then went inside the store and dropped the yellow metal on the counter. The store-keeper gave a startled look.

'Yumpin' yimminy, what's this?' he gasped.

'Gold,' Rex answered briefly. 'Load me up provisions into a case to th' amount of that nugget, leavin' enough over for me to have a meal right here — an' now. I also want a bedroll, a saddle-bag, and a couple of forty-fives — good ones.'

The storekeeper picked up the nugget and peered at it.

''Scuse *me*!' he exclaimed, and dashed off into a corner for a private inspection of the metal. When he came back he was grinning genially. 'Yes, *sir* — anythin' y'want. You hit a bonanza or somethin'?'

'You're paid, feller,' Rex answered quietly. 'That's all that matters. How's about that meal first? I'm kinda tired. Not bin so well recently.'

The store-keeper hailed his bosomy wife, and whilst she fixed up a meal in the spotless back parlour, her husband went to work in the store following out Rex's orders. Half an hour later Rex left the store, brought his roan along to be loaded, and then he hit the desert trail again for 'home'. With the excellent meal he had had the last traces of exhaustion had vanished and he felt ready for any kind of action.

Once or twice on the return journey he thought he had missed his direction — but eventually, towards midafternoon, he caught sight of a lone tent in the far distance and within ten minutes was dismounting from his horse whilst Seth Pardoe sat on his camp stool, smoking and squinting upwards.

'Okay — so yore an honest man,' he said. 'I never doubted it, but I'm kinda cautious where a bonanza's concerned.'

'Don't blame you.' Rex dismounted, unfastened the two large boxes that had been roped like pommels across the saddle, and carried them into the tent. Then he unfastened the bedroll and laid it on top of them.

'Off hand,' Pardoe said, coming over and inspecting the stuff, 'I'd say yore figgerin' on movin' in.'

'Right. And here's your gun back.' Rex handed it over in the belt and slapped the new cross-overs about his waist. 'I've got forty-fives back again. Don't feel dressed somehow without 'em.'

'Good enough ... An' the gold? I wasn't kiddin', was I?'

'Nope. You guessed just right.' Rex went out to the horse and took the sack of ingots from the saddle bag. 'Hundred thousand dollars, just like you reckoned.'

'Mmmm. Wus Tadworth free with his information, or did yuh haveta coax him?'

Rex grinned. 'I coaxed him. He told me first I'd got useless metal; then my gun in his belly made his tongue loosen up a bit.'

'An' y'can bet everythin' yuh've got that Tadworth kept his eye on you from the minnit yuh left his office. He's scented a bonanza, don't fergit, an' there ain't a man livin' round these parts who wouldn't think it worth his while t'find out where that bonanza is. So,' Pardoe finished, 'we'll leave it 'til night afore we go an' take a look at th' mine. Mebbe that'll help to stop anybody watchin' what we do.'

Rex nodded. 'Suits me … Now, if you'll give me a hand to open these cases you'll see I've got enough stuff to withstand months out here … 'Cos I'm figgerin' we're goin' t'be here quite a time if we're goin' t'start building a town.'

*

Towards sundown Jed Tadworth, the assayer, rode into Gold Point's main street, dismounted outside the Double Nickel saloon and tied his sorrel to the hitch rail. Inside the gin palace things were fairly quiet. Not for another hour would the habitues start coming in.

Tadworth's half-awake eyes glanced round the place and then settled in satisfaction upon Sherman Hall's big figure as he lounged at the bar-counter, a glass of whisky at his elbow and a cheroot jutting from his powerful mouth. Tadworth went straight across the saloon and Hall gave him a look of surprise.

'Well, if it ain't Taddy!' he ejaculated. 'Haven't seen yuh around in some time.'

'Nope — an' when *y'do* see me it's usually 'cos I've got somethin' worthwhile tellin', huh?'

Hall shrugged, studying the crafty expression on the assayer's thin features.

'Have a drink, Taddy. Name it.'

'Double whisky.'

Hall nodded to the barkeeper, took his cheroot from his teeth and twirled it in his fingers.

'Meanin',' he said, 'that yuh've gotten hold of somethin' I might like ter hear? That it?'

The assayer gulped down his whisky. 'Can't think why you shouldn't. I've just met up with a guy who's struck a bonanza some place — probably the desert.'

'Yeah …? Have another drink.' The second double-whiskey appeared at Tadworth's elbow.

'He came t'me to-day with a sack full o' yellow rock,' Tadworth resumed. 'I knew they was gold ingots, but I tried to tell him they weren't. Wasn't no use, tho'. He stuck a rod in my belly an' I had t'tell him the truth. He'd got a hundred thousand dollars in gold in that sack, and I've more than an idea he could produce plenty more sacks like that.'

'Yeah?' Hall returned his cheroot to his teeth. 'That's mighty interestin' news. So what happens?'

'I followed the guy, an' he took the desert trail. I don't think he saw me on his track, either. Ain't the first time I've tailed somebody. He finished up in the desert at some kind of a tent. I didn't dare go further … What I'm thinkin' is this: there *are* bonanzas buried in the desert. Only thing is, not one person in a thousand knows *where*, but it looks like this guy does. He's onto somethin', Mr Hall — an' I thought you'd like t'know about it.'

Hall became thoughtful, fingering his sheriff's badge absently. Tadworth gave him an anxious look and then swallowed down some more whisky.

'What'd he look like, this jigger?' Hall asked presently.

'Pretty tall and dark-haired. Thirtyish, I'd say.'

'He didn't give a name?'

'Nope.'

Hall finished his drink. Facts were tying up in his mind. Rex M'Clyde had been sent into the desert. A man of his description had apparently found gold.

'Think yore interested?' Tadworth asked.

'Ain't no doubt o' that. Whereabouts in the desert do I find this guy?'

The assayer grinned. 'That'd be tellin' — an' the desert's a mighty big place, Mr Hall, if y'don't know exactly where to look. Last time I gave you some information you paid me a thousand dollars for it. I reckon this is worth five thousand, seein' as it might lead to a gold mine. Ain't anybody else I've tried t'hand this news on to but you.'

'Five thousand?' Hall repeated, his sloe-black eyes glinting. 'Yore crazy, feller!'

'Y'think so? I could follow the guy up myself if it came to it and mebbe make a lot more'n five thousand — only I ain't greedy.'

Hall guffawed. 'Listen, feller, that ain't the reason yuh've come to me. It's because you haven't got the stuff to open up a bonanza even if yuh found one. And the news ain't worth five thousand dollars, either. There's no guarantee there's any more gold than those few nuggets that guy had with him.'

'All right — have it your own way. Mebbe I can find somebody in my own town who's interested. I came t'you first because we've done business before. For five thousand I can show you where the guy's hidin' out — an' I don't think you'd ever find him otherwise. Even if you did mebbe he'd shoot first. He's a tough character.'

For a moment a shade of doubt crossed Hall's mind. The idea of Rex M'Clyde being a tough character was something new to him. Yet for all that it did not seem it could be coincidence that a man of his description was living in the desert.

'All right,' Hall said abruptly. 'Two thousand five hundred now, and the other half when you've shown me the spot — an' that'll be to-night.'

'Suits me.' Tadworth was glowing with satisfaction.

Hall raised a hand and signalled to the man in charge of the distant gaming tables. He came over immediately.

'Got twenty-five hundred in the pool, Charlie?' Hall asked him.

'Uh-huh.'

'Okay — let me have it.'

The man turned away again, knowing better than to ask questions. Technically, Sherman Hall never had any money: he could get all he wanted at the gunpoint, but there were exceptions when actual cash was necessary, in which case he took it from the easiest source. The man returned in a few moments and handed over a wad of bills.

'There y'are,' Hall said, as Tadworth took them. 'That's half. Now let's get goin' and see what yore talkin' about ... An' you'd better be right or there'll be somebody else in the desert too — dead.'

Hall led the way across the saloon and through the bat-wings, Tadworth trailing behind him. In a matter of minutes Hall had got his horse from the stable at the rear of the saloon and joined the assayer as he rode slowly down the high street. Then, side by side, they forced their mounts to a gallop and set out for the trail, bounded on one side by the desert.

'He's not likely t'see us,' Tadworth said presently, as they rode along. 'No moon for three hours or more yet, an' the sand drowns any noise the hoofs might make.'

'Uh-huh,' Hall growled; then he swung his horse's head round and branched off the trail across the pasture lands which led eventually to the desert.

Neither man spoke as they pounded along side by side. The one was thinking of the possibility of hounding Rex M'Clyde still further, and maybe discovering the whereabouts of a lost gold mine into the bargain;

and the other was dwelling on what he would do with his five thousand dollars once he had it.

Half an hour brought them to the edges of the desert. The trackless sandy waste stretched out eternally under the stars to the remote dark of the horizon.

'Findin' the way in this isn't goin' t'be easy,' Tadworth said, urging his horse forward into the sand.

'Just as long as yuh *do* find the way,' Hall murmured. 'If yuh don't after all this trouble you an' me are goin' to pick a quarrel — an' you'll get the worst of it.'

So Tadworth said no more. He kept on riding steadily, his mount slipping occasionally in the sand. Hall came up in the rear, glancing about him, his doubts constantly increasing. He was already making plans for getting his own back on Tadworth when the assayer drew to a halt and pointed into the starlit distances.

'There!' he breathed. 'A camp fire. See it?'

Hall looked. There was a flickering perhaps two miles away, like a brightly glowing star, vanishing now and again as somebody or something passed in front of it.

'That's it all right,' Tadworth said. 'I thought my direction was right. Shows how little they expect anybody to see 'em with their fire burnin' like that.'

'Yeah ...' Hall leaned on the saddle horn and contemplated the distant scene. After a moment or two Tadworth's voice broke in on his thoughts again.

'I guess you won't want me to go any further than this, Mr Hall. I've shown you where the hide-out is, so I might as well ride back into town and wait for y'comin' back. When you do I'll collect that twenty-five hundred you owe me.'

'Yuh'll come with me first to that camp,' Hall said. 'I want t'be sure that you got it right. Might be just anybody. Let's go.'

Tadworth, who had no liking for danger, reluctantly urged his horse forward again, Hall keeping close behind him. When they were within fifty yards of the camp they dismounted, tied their horses to the coarse bushes flourishing on the edge of this solitary water hole, and finished their journey to the camp on foot. By working their way round it at some considerable distance they were able to peer above a sand dune straight into the camp.

'Satisfied?' Tadworth asked, at the vision of the two men talking at the camp fire.

'Partly. I want t'see who they are. I'm goin' closer.' And, risk though it was, Hall did exactly that. He got near enough to become convinced that one of the men was definitely Rex M'Clyde — he having shaved in the interval, which had restored his normal features — then he had to back out quick as the nodding horses were disturbed and whinneyed at the presence of strangers. Within the tent the two men raised their heads and gazed into the starlit night; then resumed their confab.

'All right, I've seen all I need,' Hall murmured, as he returned to Tadworth's side.

'Then I get my twenty-five hundred?'

'Later, mebbe. We haven't finished here yet.'

'But what's that t'do with me? I don't want to be mixed up in this any more than I haveta.'

'Yuh'll stay right beside me, Taddy, an' like it,' Hall told him. 'Those two guys are plannin' to take a jaunt: I caught a bit of their conversation before I had t'move. I want to see where they go. If it's to the mine that'll suit me fine.'

'An' — an' you want me to know where the mine is, too?' Tadworth's surprise was genuine. 'I'd ha' thought you'd have wanted t'keep that to yuhself.'

'Mebbe I will,' Hall said ambiguously; then he settled in the sand to wait and, having no alternative, Tadworth did likewise.

Altogether they had an hour's vigil before Rex and Pardoe killed their camp fire, came out into the night, and mounted their horses. Hall watched them go.

'Okay, we follow,' he said briefly. 'Let's get back to those cayuses of ours.'

They reached them in a few minutes, mounted, and then sped silently across the endless sand in the wake of the far distant Rex and Pardoe. They were only just visible in the starlight, and at that distance Hall kept them, until the fact that they were moving no longer made him draw to a halt, Tadworth beside him. Once again they deserted their mounts, fastening them together to prevent them wandering, and then they stole silently through the sand to where Rex and Pardoe were faintly visible.

Abruptly they vanished, and only their horses remained, tied to a solitary cactus bush. When he reached it Hall drew his gun and looked about him in wonder.

'Where in tarnation did they go?' he demanded, puzzled.

'Sand looks a bit different there,' Tadworth said, pointing. 'Lighter — or somethin'.'

He pointed to an oblong area not ten feet away. He and Hall silently approached it, kneeled beside it, and rubbed their hands in the sand. It moved easily, only consisting of a fine deposit of grains with a metallic area underneath.

'Sort of iron door,' Tadworth said. 'Not that that's anythin' new. Lot of these ancient mines have iron doors on 'em — left from th' days of th' Indians.'

Hall said nothing. He stood up again and Tadworth slowly did likewise, looking about him so that he could memorize the spot. The cactus bush nearby was an excellent landmark. Going back to it through the sand he made a notch in the bush with his jack-knife before Hall caught up with him. He would know that bush again any time he wanted it.

'Might as well ride back into town,' Hall said. 'We can't investigate with those two below ground — an' I don't intend t'let 'em know at this stage that I've any idea what they're up to.'

'An' I get my money when I get back into town?' Tadworth demanded.

'Sure — sure.' Hall sounded unusually pleasant.

Tadworth leapt into the saddle of his horse and Hall did likewise. Together they rode until they had reached the deserted camp. Here Hall paused for a moment, considering something.

'Thinkin' there might be somethin' worth takin'?' Tadworth enquired.

'Yeah — but it mightn't be such good policy to do it. I don't want those two t'have the least inklin' that I'm on to their game. Nope — I'll leave things just as they are. Let's be on our way.'

At what was about the half-way point into town, Hall stopped again. Tadworth also drew rein and glanced round in surprise.

'Get off your horse,' Hall ordered. His voice was cold and uncompromising, and to further emphasise his words he tugged out his gun and levelled it in the starlight.

'What's the idea?' Tadworth demanded, obeying the order none the less. 'What'm I supposed t'have done?'

'Two things.' Hall jumped down into the sand and walked over to him. 'Yuh've taken twenty-five hundred of my dough fur one thing, an' fur another yuh've seen where that mine is. Right now yore figgerin' just how quickly y'can do somethin' about that mine before I make a move myself.'

'Now wait a minute!' Tadworth protested. 'Y'don't s'pose I'd go behind your back an' do somethin' about th' mine when I've as good as handed it over t'you to do what you want?'

'I think yuh'd do just that,' Hall retorted. 'An in any case I mean to make sure yuh don't.'

'Fire that gun at me an' it'll be heard fur miles!' Tadworth shouted hoarsely, groping swiftly for his own weapon. 'Give me a chance, Mr Hall — I ain't aiming t'do anythin' —'

'Y'bet yore not!' Hall suddenly leapt, but he did not fire his gun. He brought it down butt foremost behind the assayer's ear and crumpled him in the sand. The rest Hall accomplished with his powerful fingers about Tadworth's throat. Not until he was satisfied that life was extinct did he remove the twenty-five hundred dollars from the assayer's pocket and then start to scoop a grave in the loose sand.

Perhaps thirty minutes later Hall rode back into town, leading a riderless horse. Somewhere back in the desert, buried deep so none could ever find him, was the only man who could have upset the plans he was laying.

Three

In the week which followed both Rex M'Clyde and Sherman Hall were busy. Rex, quite unaware that tabs were being kept on his movements by one of Hall's most trusted gun-hawks, made several trips to Satan's Gap, and to small towns adjoining. Satisfied with what he had seen of Seth Pardoe's gold mine, and knowing that, properly worked, it could produce a fortune in the yellow metal, he contracted trustworthy mining engineers, bought equipment with the hundred thousand dollars in gold he and Pardoe possessed, and also hired gangs of men to come out into the desert and lay the foundations of a new 'gold' town. Inevitably men and women were attracted by Rex's scheme, for he made no secret of the fact that he intended his town to stand for law and order and invited all those, no matter what their trade, who had a love of justice to come and settle and help build up the population.

So, under the ministrations of engineers and builders the desert around Pardoe's solitary base camp began to come to life and the beginnings of a town sprang up.

These beginnings showed themselves at the end of the first week. By the time a month had gone by the mine was at work and a fair-sized wooden town with a main street and rough-and-ready dwellings and stores had appeared. Day by day Sherman Hall kept in touch with progress, his own trigger-men being among the settlers since, as yet, Rex had no way of discriminating. That Hall must by now know of his activities he had not the least doubt and he hoped he and Pardoe would be ready for whatever emergency might turn up.

But Hall bided his time, paying not the slightest heed to his immediate satellites who insisted he should raid the neighbour town, destroy it, and take over the gold mine and its yields for himself.

'It's crazy not to!' Red Tompkins, his right-hand man, declared one morning, as he and Hall sat together in the sheriff's office. 'I can't figure out what yore waitin' fur. Hank and Curly've both told yuh what kind of a set-up there is in M'Clyde's town. They're pantie-waists, all of 'em. If we was t'make a full scale attack on 'em and —'

'Shut up!' Hall interrupted calmly, and put his feet up on the desk.

'But fer why?' Red demanded. 'My trigger finger's getting itchy. I don't like th' thought uv all that gold bein' dug out an' we do nothin' about it. Or don't yuh realize that with gold unlimited we could buy up every town in the State an' run it just our way? Properly handled we could roll in wealth.'

'Whadda ya mean? Properly handled?' Hall demanded, chewing his cheroot.

Red covered his mistake quickly. 'I mean th' way you handle it, boss — naturally.'

'Listen, Red — yuh don't use your brains; that's your trouble. If we swept down on M'Clyde's town right now we could wipe it out easy — sure, and mebbe him an' that loco prospector, Seth Pardoe, with him. But what good would it do us? There's several hundred people in that town now, an' though yuh call 'em pantie-waists, I'm willing t'bet they'd put up a good show if it came to it. Fact remains we couldn't kill *all* of 'em.'

'No, s'pose not,' Red agreed regretfully. 'Okay then — so those who are left start rebuildin', an' becos the town's only half built that wouldn't take 'em so long. But think how much longer it'd take 'em if everythin' wus destroyed just when they'd gotten everythin' t'perfection.'

Red rubbed the end of his cut-short nose. 'Yeah — I get you, boss. Never thought of it that way. Y'mean let 'em go on buildin' an' minin', getting' everythin' shipshape — then wipe 'em out, which'll make it all the harder and costlier for 'em to start over again?'

'Right. An' it'll also make 'em unwary. They'll think with nobody interferin' with 'em that nobody's goin' to. That's called psychology, feller, case y'don't know it.'

To a man so coarsely hewn as Red Tompkins the reference to psychology did not mean a thing. He lounged back in his chair, his big hands playing with the walnut butts of his Colts.

'There's also somethin' else that needs thinkin' about,' Hall continued. 'When we make the attack on M'Clyde's town — an' believe me we will afore we're through — what d'yuh suppose'll be the first thing those folks'll do? The survivors, I mean?'

'Start rebuildin', won't they? Yuh just said so.'

'They'll do plenty else before that. They'll try and take reprisals — mebbe come and invade Gold Point here, and try an' shoot us up.'

'That,' Red grinned, 'I'd like ter see.'

'An' mebbe yuh will,' Hall told him grimly. 'Don't make th' mistake of underestimatin' the enemy, Red: it's fatal. Those folks in M'Clyde's town are proud of that place they're buildin'. They believe that their psalm-smitin' honesty is absolutely right, an' fer that reason they'll defend it to th' death, I reckon. Fer that reason there is th' chance that they might hit back at us ... unless we stop 'em dead.'

'Yeah. Kill 'em all, y'mean, even if it takes weeks.'

'Stop bein' a damned gun-happy idiot!' Hall roared, putting his feet on the floor with an emphatic bang. 'Yuh don't get *everythin'* around these parts at the business end of a gun. There is lots of other ways. Legal ones. An' M'Clyde and his followers are mighty keen on legal things. Justice an' all that moonshine.'

'Yeah?' Red scratched his bull neck. 'Guess I don't know much about th' legal side — an' I ain't so sure I wanta either.'

'The thing's simple. This town hasn't got the protection of any Government: th' whole State's outside the Union.'

'I know that — otherwise I guess we couldn't get away with what we do. We'd have Rangers an' guys like 'em down on our necks every time we drew a rod.'

'As mayor an' sheriff of this town,' Hall said, thinking, 'I'm puttin' in an application for this town to be incorporated in the Union.'

'Huh?' Red stared blankly. 'Yuh — yuh mean hand everythin' over to them guys in Washington who run the country the way *they* see fit? After all the trouble we had makin' the lame brains around here come to our way of thinkin'? Honest, boss that's plain loco!'

'Hold your horses a minnit, Red, an' let me finish. We've gotten this town pretty well as we want it now: sometimes we go a month an' never draw a gun, so well trained are th' folks around us. If we make the town legal — which simply means it'll be put on the Government map and incorporated with a lot of deeds an' what-have-yuh — it means that anybody who attacks it attacks *Government property*! An' that'll bring the authorities over quick to protect us and drag the attackers off to jail. Get it?'

'Ur — sort of,' Red muttered, his pendulous lips hanging stupidly.

'On the other hand,' Hall continued, 'if we attack M'Clyde's town we're quite safe, 'cos his town ain't legalized. I've told the boys t'watch for

M'Clyde doin' that, but so far he hasn't, nor will he I don't s'pose 'til he's finished buildin'.'

'Yore sort of figgerin' on a kind of insurance, huh?' Red asked at last.

'Uh-huh; y'might call it that, sure.'

'Then it's too deep for me,' Red decided. 'Gimme a gun an' a guy at th' business end of it an' yuh can keep your deeds an' Government. I think the idea stinks.'

In disgust he got to his feet and turned to leave the office. Hall smiled coldly, then snapped:

'Better keep your opinion's to yourself, Red! *I'm* in charge around here, an'd don't yuh forget it! Hop over to Jim Cawley's place. He's the only lawyer round here now Judge Barrow's been taken care of. Tell him to get over here, an' quick. There's some important business I want him t'fix.'

Red hesitated, then nodded sullenly. 'OK, boss.'

Hall grinned as the door slammed, then lighted a cheroot, and sat back in his swivel chair to wait. After perhaps ten minutes Jim Cawley arrived, dressed as usual in his shiny black suit, his smooth, unwrinkled face giving no hint of the untrustworthiness of his nature.

'Howdy,' he greeted, sitting down in the chair Red Tompkins had vacated. 'What's on your mind, Sheriff?' Or did you call me as mayor this time?'

'Stop tryin' t'be funny an' listen,' Hall told him sourly. 'I've decided to put this town on th' map — but I don't know a thing about legal stuff. I want yuh to contact the Government and tell 'em to incorporate — that's the word, ain't it? — Gold Point.'

Jim Cawley rubbed his shiny chin and considered the litter of unattended papers inside the roll top.

'Gone deaf?' Hall asked after a while.

'No ... But you don't realize what you're asking.'

'Who don't? Plain an' simple, ain't it?'

'Like hell. You can't incorporate a *town*. Isn't done. It has to be a State, an' even then there's no guarantee the Government will bite. They'll send representatives down to take a look, and if they don't like the set up they'll do nothing more about it.'

'So that's th' way it is, huh? Well, if they come here to take a look-see I don't think they'll find anythin' to belly-ache about. We'll all be on our best behaviour — or else.'

245

'We could do that, I suppose,' Cawley admitted, 'but it still wouldn't work. As I tell you, it has to be a State — a complete piece of land, not just a town.'

Hall scowled, took his cheroot out of his mouth, and then jammed it back between his jaws.

'Dammit, man, I can't ask 'em to take over the whole State!' Hall protested. 'Fur one thing, Rex M'Clyde an' Seth Pardoe, who're buildin' that town o' theirs twenty-five miles south, would raise objections — an' they'd be listened to since they're *in* the State. Must be some other way.'

Cawley thought for a long time, then a gleam came into his friendly brown eyes.

'There's one thing you could do — offer territory along *with* this town, and call it Gold Point State. One way and another you've pretty well got the mastery of all the land around here — the town and the ranches immediately near to it. For about ten square miles you're the undisputed boss. Right?'

'Right enough,' Hall assented proudly.

'Okay, then. Who's to know how big Gold Point State is when it's never been mentioned to the Union before? I can ask the Government to incorporate this town and a ten square mile area around it. That'd mean the Government would own everything in that area — technically, but you'd go on just as before. With a darned sight less emphasis on the lead,' Cawley added dryly.

'Yeah — but would I get protection? That's what I want t'be knowin' about.'

'Protection from what?' the lawyer asked mildly.

'Rex M'Clyde chiefly. I'm planning to go over t'his town when he's finished it an' dust th' place over. I wanta be sure if he comes ridin' straight back at me here that I c'n call on the law to help me against his attack.'

'Yes, you can call on the law,' Cawley assented. Then he fell to musing for a moment or two. 'So that's the idea, is it? You want to wipe out Rex M'Clyde an' his town if you can and stop him doing the same thing to you?'

'That's it,' Hall grinned. 'Pretty smart, huh?'

'If M'Clyde hasn't legalized *his* town an' some of the land around it it's smart enough, sure — but if he's done the same thing as you're aiming to do you'll run your head straight into a brick wall.'

'As yet he hasn't done anything,' Hall said. 'I've had the boys keeping tabs on him.'

'That's okay then.' The lawyer got to his feet. 'Leave this to me, Hall; I think I can swing it. Providing you're prepared to pay the duty necessary to become incorporated into the Union.'

'I'll find it, whatever's necessary — an' if any of those guys want t'come an' look things over that's okay too. I'll see to it that everybody behaves like sellers of prayer books.'

Cawley nodded and went from the office. Hall rubbed his big hands gently together and smiled.

'Reckon that'll show yuh, Mr M'Clyde!' he murmured.

*

With no conception of the intrigue being planned against them, Rex M'Clyde and Pardoe went straight ahead with their plans to create a town out of the wilderness — and indeed, with the passing of the weeks and no sign of any interference, they both began to believe that Sherman Hall had either turned over a new leaf, or else he was not willing to take the risk of tackling an entire town.

Whatever the causes of Hall's inaction, Rex had little time to think about him. He and Pardoe, their tent headquarters now transformed into a comfortable wooden building in the town's new main street, had their hands full directing operations. Acting as partners, all the plans for the town had to pass through them, as well as the handling of the gold mine two miles distant.

'The sooner we get a railroad station around these parts the better,' Rex decided one morning, as he and Pardoe discussed matters in general. 'It's the gold I'm thinking about chiefly. We're digging it out of the earth at top speed, piling up a fortune which can one day turn this collection of wooden shacks into a city — but we're hampered without a railroad. Sending the gold by the desert and overland trail to Denver means a helluva risk every time we do it.'

'We've gotten through all right so far,' Pardoe said, staring out of the window on to the men and women working in the main street. 'An' th' men who take the wagon are straight-shooters, every one of 'em.'

'I know it — but sooner or later I have the feelin' somebody may take the notion t'start robbin' that wagon, and when that happens we can look out for trouble ...' Rex shrugged. 'Not that there's any other way right now. Just have t'hope for the best until the time comes when the railroad company sees fit to bring a track across the desert.'

Pardoe nodded, then he paused in the act of speaking at a sudden urgent knocking on the outer door of the living-room-cum-office. He walked across and opened it. A girl stood on the wooden threshold, a slender blonde in the late twenties, wearing overalls. Both Pardoe and M'Clyde had seen her once or twice before, usually helping her tinsmith father in the construction of the town.

'Can I see Mr M'Clyde?' she asked, urgently.

Pardoe motioned inside. 'I guess so ... Come in, miss.'

She nodded and then catching sight of Rex as he turned from the window she hurried over to him.

'I'm Louise Atkinson,' she explained. 'My dad's Clem Atkinson who runs the —'

'I know, the tinsmith — and a mighty useful trade,' Rex smiled. 'Have a seat ... What can I do for you?'

The girl sat down and from the long ruler-pocket at the back of her overalls dragged forth a sheet of newspaper. She looked up at Rex with earnest, widely spaced grey eyes.

'There's something in this paper here, Mr M'Clyde, which I think you ought to know about. It's part of the *Denver Clarion*. One of the men who guards the gold wagon lives with us and he brought this paper back with him. There's an article here about Gold Point State being incorporated into the Union.'

Rex gave a start and glanced across in wonder at Pardoe — then back to the girl. He took the paper from her and read the column swiftly. Pardoe came over to him and looked over his shoulder.

'What sort of game does Hall think he's got on, I wonder?' Rex breathed, his eyes glinting. 'He's got no authority to ask the Government to incorporate the entire State —'

'He hasn't,' Pardoe interrupted. 'It sez there *Gold Point* State. This is the State of Mirando. Only the town's known as Gold Point ...'

'Ten-mile-square State of Gold Point ...' Rex began reading again, half to himself; then abruptly he snapped his fingers. 'I get it. He runs most of the territory for ten miles around Gold Point town, so he's called the territory a State and gotten away with it too from the look of things. The incorporation took place three days ago.'

'Does it mean that this town we're building is also in the Union?' Louise Atkinson asked, anxiously.

'No.' Rex shook his head. 'We're just as we were, but once we get within ten miles of Gold Point town we've crossed well into territory over which the Government has jurisdiction, and it'll be mainly subject to their law. Here we make our own laws and are answerable to nobody but ourselves.'

'I don't get it,' Pardoe said, frowning. 'Gold Point is a cut-throats' town. What in heck do they gain by makin' themselves subject to Government law? I would have sed it's about th' last thing they'd want.'

'Probably is — but they get protection.' Rex's eyes narrowed as he pondered. 'Yeah, that's it, Seth. Anybody attacking Gold Point from here on can have the law wrapped around their necks afore they know it.'

'Seems to me that all the shootin' goes on *inside* that town, not from people outside it,' Pardoe said.

'At present. But suppose *we* felt like attacking it?'

'Why should we? Hall an' his boys ain't done nothin' to us, so far.'

'I think we can take this announcement as reasonable warning that they will one day.' Rex folded the paper slowly and handed it back. 'If they do our reaction will be to hit back — an' but for this announcement we'd never have known that we were attacking Government-incorporated property.'

'In other words,' the girl said, 'it's a double-cross by Sherman Hall to try and make us run into a trap one day?'

'That's the way I figger it,' Rex acknowledged. 'An' we're mighty grateful t'you, Miss Atkinson, for the information. You have probably saved us hog-tying ourselves completely.'

The girl was silent for a moment or two, thinking. Then she glanced up again.

'This means that Hall can attack us and we can't call on the law to throw him out or arrest him for trespass. That it?'

'That's it.'

'Then surely the answer to that one is to incorporate *our* town in the Union too, and advertise the fact largely so that Hall will know what he's up against if he tries anything?'

'There are two things against that, Miss Atkinson,' Rex told her. 'One is that this town is not yet completed — and our claim would not be considered until it is; and the other is the much more important reason that if we were incorporated we'd have to turn over our gold mine. We would only get a percentage of the yieldings, not all of it. There would be Governmental tax upon it and on gold it rates mighty high because it's the most valuable form of revenue and the basis of currency throughout the Union.'

The girl gave a rueful little smile. 'That makes it very different, doesn't it? But surely, one day, we'll *have* to incorporate? When all the country is in the Union it wouldn't pay us to stand outside it, would it?'

'By the time that day comes, Miss Atkinson, we'll have gotten all we want out of the mine and our town will be sufficiently developed to be of interest to th' authorities. In the meantime we shall all have to stand prepared for whatever dirty work Hall may pull. I've always thought he'd try somethin' one day because he'll never rest until he runs all Mirando State: that's his sole object, an' he doesn't care who gets shot or tramped on in the doin'. By this time he must know that I'm in partnership with Seth Pardoe here, founding this town an' workin' the mine — an' he has an especial grudge against both of us seein' as we both belonged originally to Gold Point.'

'You did?' the girl asked interestedly. 'I didn't know that. What happened exactly?'

Rex gave her the details without any embellishments or deletions. When he had finished she gave a little sigh.

'As long as men like Hall exist there'll never be peace in this part of the country,' she decided. 'And the only language he understands is that of the gun.'

'I know,' Rex said quietly. 'One day I aim to teach him the language in full. I'm just waiting for the chance to do it legally. Killing a man like him wouldn't be a crime: it'd be a service to th' State. But he's wary — up t'every trick.'

'You're doing a fine job here, Mr M'Clyde,' the girl said, getting to her feet. 'I want you to know that — and I'm not just speaking for myself but for every one of the people who form the population of this town. Maybe you don't realize just *how* fine a job?'

Rex grinned good humouredly. 'I'm always willin' to listen to th' details. Tell me more.'

'Well, take my dad and me, for instance. We had a ranch out in the mid-West to start with. I was born and brought up there — then when I was about fifteen outlaws attacked us one night, stole all our cattle, shot my mother and father, and —' The girl checked herself, biting her lower lip as the memory became bitter. 'Anyway, dad recovered from his wounds, but mother died. We hadn't anything left. We became roamers, looking for a place to settle, but with most towns being like Gold Point and having nothing but gun law, it just wasn't safe. Finally we stayed a few years in Denver, where I managed to get an education of sorts and dad took a job: then we went on the move again. I think we'd have become desert wanderers if we hadn't heard of your grand scheme to build a town fit for decent people to live in. We came along to help. I don't think we've ever been so happy in our lives,' the girl finished, her lashes lowering shyly for a moment.

'That's fine,' Rex said, patting her shoulder. 'Glad to hear it. With so many gun-crazy towns it seemed to me it was time somebody started a town where guns are outlawed 'cept in self-defence.'

'Lots of families who've settled here owe their present peace to you,' the girl added. 'You're a wonderful man, Mr M'Clyde: you had a vision an' made it come true.'

Rex rubbed his ear uncomfortably. 'Matter o' fact, Miss Atkinson, it wasn't me who thought of it at all. I was all blisterin' for revenge. It was Seth Pardoe here who got the idea of a town.'

'Yeah — an' it took me ten years to think it up,' Pardoe grinned. 'Don't pay much attention to this guy, miss: I had the idea, but I guess it was his guts that made th' town come into being.'

'Fifty-fifty, eh?' the girl smiled. 'Well, either way it's a wonderful notion — but if Sherman Hall sets out to destroy it, what do we do then?'

'Fight,' Rex answered briefly. 'There'll be no two ways about it. We're prepared to defend our way of life against all-comers. Our law, mutually agreed, says we shall not use guns. That applies to ourselves, of course — not to sworn enemies. The best thing I can do is let the people know what might happen and we can all be prepared.'

'I'd like to help,' Louise said, her eyes bright. 'I could tell everybody I meet. It'd save your important time.'

Rex smiled. 'Okay, you do that — an' thanks a lot.'

'And if there's anything else you ever want done, don't think twice about sending for me,' the girl added, backing towards the door. 'I — I think of you as I do of other pioneers who've come out West and made something of their work; men like — like Brigham Young.'

She coloured a little, hesitated over something which she did not utter; and then she departed. Seth Pardoe looked at the closed door and rubbed his sloping chin.

'Mighty nice gal,' he commented. 'Or mebbe you noticed it fur yourself?'

Rex cleared his throat and turned from the window where he had been watching the girl, in her clumsy figure-destroying overalls walking down the half-made high street.

'Yeah — yeah, very nice,' he agreed indifferently. 'Now to get down to cases, Seth. I think we should pick out the most reliable men we've got amongst us and plant 'em, ready armed, at strategic points of the town to watch for any sudden raid on us. We'll also double the guard around the mine. Thanks to Miss Atkinson we're forewarned what to expect.'

'I'll see to it,' Pardoe said. 'In fact, I'll do it right now.'

He left the office and Rex returned to his normal day's task of sorting out the hundred and one executive duties attendant on the building of the town. Pardoe returned after about an hour and helped him — then just as they were both thinking about stopping for a meal the door opened suddenly and Louise Atkinson re-appeared, walking backwards.

'What the —' Rex began, jumping to his feet in astonishment; then he saw the reason for her unusual mode of entry. In each hand she held a .38, and they were trained steadily on two cow-punchers who came in from the narrow corridor at her order.

'Over there, by the desk,' she snapped. 'And be quick about it!'

Their swarthy faces sullen the two men obeyed. Rex and Pardoe stared at them, then at the girl.

'What gives?' Rex demanded.

'These two men are spies, Mr M'Clyde,' the girl responded. 'So I thought I'd better bring them to you for questioning.'

'You thought — I'll be doggoned!' Pardoe exclaimed. 'On your own, y'mean?'

'Why not? I can handle guns. They were talking at the rear of the tinsmith's shop dad and I are erecting and I overheard them — quite enough to satisfy me that they're certainly not one of us. Matter of fact they were arguing which one of them should go and give Sherman Hall the latest report on our progress.'

'Oh they were, were they?' Rex moved forward.

'So I borrowed dad's guns and ran them in,' the girl explained casually.

'The gal's lyin'!' one of the men snapped. 'Yuh know what wimmin are sometimes, M'Clyde — git strange ideas.'

'Miss Atkinson's not the type to get strange ideas,' Rex replied, hands on his hips as he faced the two men. 'You'd better start talkin', hadn't you? Are you in Hall's pay or not?'

'Course we're not!' the second man retorted. 'Why should we have any truck with that jigger? All we want t'do is help in buildin' this town o' yourn.'

Rex gave the girl a glance. Her face was grim.

'He's lyin', Mr M'Clyde,' she insisted.

Rex nodded; then suddenly reaching out both his big hands he slammed them together in front of him — with the men's heads between them. They yelped at the impact on their skulls.

'Now-start explainin',' Rex invited. 'Otherwise I'll take th' pair of you apart right now.'

Neither man spoke. One rubbed his head and the other glared at the girl. Rex waited for a moment; then seizing the man nearest him by the front of his shirt he jerked him to him and hit him hard back and forth across the face until tears started into his eyes. The other man watched, clenched his fists, and suddenly whirled up an uppercut. Rex saw it coming, ducked, and delivered a piston rod blow to the man's chin. It hurtled him backwards against the wall. He groped at it helplessly, dropped to his knees, and there remained.

'Get this, you two,' Rex said briefly. 'Either I get the truth outa you or I'll hand you over to the populace in general. I don't have t'tell you how they'll treat traitors, do I? You'll get strung up — an' mighty quick. It's up t'you.'

'Supposin' we *are* workin' fur Hall?' demanded the puncher who had had his face slapped. 'Can't blame us makin' money the easiest way, can yuh? We don't care what happens t'you *or* Hall, just so long as we get some greenbacks.'

'Shut up, you blamed fool!' howled the man on the floor. 'Yuh don't haveta tell this critter anythin'.'

'He does if he wants to stay in one piece,' Rex replied. 'Go on, feller — keep talkin'.'

'S'posin' I do? It'll only mean we'll get thrown to the people in the finish anyways. Might as well keep yuh guessin'.'

'I'll not see either of you two hang if y'give me the facts,' Rex said. 'I'm not even blamin' you two men, because I don't expect much else from some members of our community. I'm just glad you've bin caught, that's all. Tell me what goes on an' y'can leave this town safely — providin' y'never come back.'

The man on his knees still shouted his protests, but his colleague, scenting an easy way out of a difficult spot, let go all reservations.

'We've bin here ever since yuh started buildin' this town. Hall is on t'everythin' yore doin'.'

'That's not news t'me, feller. What I want to know is: when does he aim t'do somethin' to upset our plans?'

'Soon as yuh've built up this town he's figgerin' on knockin' it down.'

'Yeah?' Rex gave a grim smile. 'That's all I wanted t'know.'

'There's somethin' more I want t'be knowin',' Pardoe put in. 'How many more of Hall's spies are planted around here 'sides you two?'

'There's four more,' snapped the man who had been knocked to his knees. 'No reason why we shouldn't say so seein' as we've bin caught out.'

'Names?' Pardoe demanded, and the man gave them.

'Okay, I'll go get 'em right now,' Pardoe decided. 'An' I'll see you guys on your way outa town, too. Let me have them guns, Miss Atkinson: I ain't got mine handy.'

The girl handed them across and Pardoe levelled them, jerking his head at the same time.

'Outside, you mugs — an' be quick about it. An' don't think yore getting' horses t'ride on, either. Y'can walk t'wherever yore goin'.'

Scowling, the men left the office with Pardoe right behind them. Rex turned to the girl and she gave a serious little smile.

'I suppose I did the right thing, Mr M'Clyde?' she asked.

'Couldn't have done better myself. In fact it seems to me yore a mighty useful gal to have around. I sure do appreciate it.'

'You can't build a town without finding rotten elements in it which need weeding out,' the girl said seriously. 'I'm so definitely on your side I don't mind what lengths I go to to help the cause.'

'Thanks.' Rex shook her hand and gave her a direct look. 'I hope most of the other folks are so minded.'

'I think they are. I told them what to expect — that Hall might be attacking — and it seems to me everybody's solidly at your back. With Mr Pardoe rooting out the unwanted ones we ought to be unanimous.'

'Yeah.'

The girl hesitated, then smiled again. 'Maybe we'll talk again later,' she said. 'I've a job I must do for dad ...'

With that she left the office. Rex turned to the window and watched her departure until she was out of sight. At the moment all thoughts of building a town and defeating a ruthless cut-throat had gone from his mind. He was thinking of elemental things — of how gracefully Louise Atkinson walked in spite of her clumsy overalls; of her resourcefulness and courage; of her ready smile ...

'Yeah — mighty fine gal,' he muttered, and rolled himself a cigarette absently.

Four

During the quiet weeks in which the town in the desert progressed to completion, Rex and Pardoe both laid their plans to withstand Sherman Hall's attack when it should come. They deployed their forces to all parts of the town, set up hidden arms dumps, and made arrangements with every man and woman as to their exact 'action stations' in case of trouble ... nor was it by coincidence that Rex arranged his own defensive position to be at Atkinson's tin-smithy. In the thick of trouble he could think of nobody better for his companions than the forthright Louise and her tough, straight-shooting father. Pardoe for his part made his own arrangements, selecting the Honest Dollar saloon as his base of operations, where he could be within reach of gin whilst he fought.

There was, of course, the possibility that Sherman Hall had altered his plans. The outcast spies who had been sent into the desert would certainly work their way back to him and inform him of what had happened — yet he had to attack sometime or else remain content to see a prosperous town growing up only twenty-five miles away from him, and one which in time would certainly over-shadow his own because it had the twin attractions of wealth and honesty ...

Then one night, moonless and misty, Sherman Hall struck. The first signs of the impending attack became evident to the lookouts whom Rex had posted on the edge of the desert at four compass points to watch continuously for any sign of trouble. All four men saw the trouble coming at the same time — line after line of swift moving, hardly visible, horsemen, plainly distinguishable in the starlight at times, then foundering again in the mist — but coming ever nearer to the town.

Four horsemen rode instantly to give the warning. Rex received his at the home of the Atkinsons, where of late he had been spending most of his evenings. Immediately he jumped to his feet.

'Okay, spread the warning,' he ordered. 'Every man and woman knows what to do. We fight from right here. Get goin'.'

The lookout nodded and raced away. Atkinson got to his feet, a big raw-boned man with a hatchet face and determined jaw, and went over to the rack on the wall. From it he took down three rifles, all of them greased and loaded ready for immediate action.

'Reckon this is it,' he said briefly. 'Let's set the furniture to rights.'

Knowing exactly what they had to do from previous rehearsals he, Rex, and the girl, moved the rough-and-ready furniture to the big single window overlooking the high street and banked it up as a barrier for bullets. Outside, again to orders, all the oil lamps were extinguished and the main street lay ghostly and empty in the starlight, no sign of the hidden gunmen and women on roofs and behind windows being visible.

'Guess we'll give these critters a lesson they'll never fergit,' old man Atkinson breathed, raising the window sash and fixing his rifle in position. 'You all set, Loo?'

'All set, dad,' she agreed, crouched and ready.

Rex took up a position between them, sighted along the rifle barrel, and then waited for the storm to break.

It was not long in coming. There was the mounting thunder of horses' hoofs on the night air — then they came in a swarm from both ends of the high street simultaneously, converging in the centre in a solid, jostling phalanx.

'Wait — wait!' Rex shouted, before the girl or her father could fire. 'Somethin' screwy here! Those horses haven't any riders!'

There was just time for Louise and her father to verify the astonishing fact before a hail of bullets burst forth from the windows, roofs, and doors of the high street. The din was appalling, and added to it were the screams and whinneyings of the stricken beasts outside.

'What goes on?' Rex demanded savagely. 'What kind of a fight does Hall call this? He —'

He could not speak any further, for suddenly hell itself broke loose. In the high street there came a terrific explosion. It was followed by another — then several more in quick succession. They were not gun or rifle reports, but the concussions of exploding dynamite. Buildings, made only of wood and not particularly well pinned down as yet, slewed and crumpled before the terrific blast. From one direction sparks shot out, spread quickly and linked up with nearby tinder-dry wood.

'It's T.N.T. or somethin'!' old man Atkinson yelled above the din, then he ducked as the window shattered inwards in a mass of gleaming javelins.

'Only one explanation,' the girl shouted, her startled face visible in the glare of fire outside. 'Hall must have had explosive tied to a herd of horses and sent them into the main street knowing we'd fire. Our bullets exploded the stuff and this is the result. I suppose he thought it was worth losing about two hundred horses to achieve his object and escape unhurt.'

'Yeah — that's it.' Rex set his jaw. 'Those guys we turned outa here must ha' tipped him off an' he thought up this brutally clever strategy. I've got to stop our folks firin' somehow.'

He jumped to his feet, but Atkinson pulled him down again fiercely.

'Don't be danged fool, boy — yuh can't do anythin' in *this*! The whole town's afire an' —'

A whelming concussion drowned the rest of his words. The wooden structure rocked, swayed, and cracked alarmingly along several of its timbers. Then part of the wooden roof fell in, the main beam dropping endwise and crashing through the flimsy floor a foot from where Louise was crouched.

'We've got t'get outa this,' Rex shouted. 'Come on — before the whole lot comes down.'

Clutching their rifles, their eyes and ears filled with dust, they struggled across the shattered flooring to the remains of the door. Tugging it to one side they blundered out into the street and stared around them, their eyes smarting with smoke.

The scene was nerve-shattering. The entire town was ablaze now, the flames having leapt from one building to the other with staggering rapidity. In the main street horses and men and women were inextricably mixed — then both would vanish here and there as more explosive detonated, destroying or mortally wounding the horses and human beings nearest to it.

'Look!' the girl cried abruptly, pointing across the flame-painted darkness. 'The mine's on fire too.'

Too numbed by the savagery and ingenuity of the attack to say anything, Rex and old man Atkinson could only stare at two mighty pillars of flame beyond the town, out in the desert wastes, where the huge wooden towers and shaft gear of the mine were drawn in flaming silhouette against the stars. From that direction too there came explosion after explosion, setting the ground trembling.

Then came a change. Into the high street, shooting their way amidst the struggling explosive-carrying horses, came horde after horde of gunmen, their revolvers blazing and the bullets whanging across the struggling animals and town inhabitants.

'Them yeller bellies 'd never have the nerve to run into the midst o' more explosions,' Atkinson breathed, levelling his rifle and sighting. 'More than likely they've counted how many explosions have gone off an' know they're safe —'

His rifle cracked and one of the yelling gunmen changed his note to a scream as he swept by and plunged from his saddle.

Aware now that they had flesh and blood to deal with, the demoralized inhabitants of the town, their vantage points burned away, scattered quickly and sought every possible refuge they could from which to fire. The best positions were behind the remains of decimated horses and from here there blazed a ceaseless rain of bullets, cross-firing on the gunmen as they pounded through the high street to finish the job the explosives had started.

Squatting on their knees, Atkinson, Rex, and the girl steadied their guns on the shattered end of the porch rail and fired continuously. Some of the whirling, firing horsemen fell; others swept through unharmed — but even they began to realize at last that the inhabitants were well armed and fighting mad — so with a final volley they at last hit the trail and left behind them the blazing buildings and smell of burning horse and human flesh.

Sweating, breathing hard, the three on the porch stood up — and then leapt simultaneously into the dust of the street as the roof above them cracked and crumpled inwards in a cloud of sparks. Clinging together they moved to the centre of the vista of fire and looked around them on their rapidly vanishing handiwork. The work of months and the planning of endless hours was crumbling into flame and ruin ... Driven out by the heat and flames, others of the populace began to drift to their side. In a grim, relentless silence the men and women watched, through minutes which spread into an hour — then two hours, until, at last, the fire had spent itself and nothing remained on the face of the starlit desert but stirring white hot ashes and the half consumed bodies of men and beasts.

A man's voice broke the grim silence.

'You ain't goin' t'let Sherman Hall get away with this, Mister M'Clyde, are you?' he demanded. 'He's blasted us wide open an' it ain't nateral t'expect us to just take it.'

259

'You don't think I *enjoy* lookin' on all this, do you?' Rex asked bitterly. 'I'm hurt as much as the rest of you — mebbe more, since I did most of the plannin', along with Seth Pardoe. Incidentally,' Rex broke off, looking about him, 'where *is* Pardoe?'

Nobody answered, bill several pairs of eyes turned and looked towards the ruin of the Honest Dollar saloon where Pardoe had said he would take up his headquarters.

'Best thing we c'n do is take a roll call,' Atkinson decided. 'Until we've got that squared off we don't know who's left an' who isn't. Let's get it started.'

He took the job unto himself and it occupied half an hour. At the end of it there was the grim realization that nearly thirty of the men and women of the town were missing.

'An' missing means dead, Pardoe among them,' Rex said, clenching his fists. 'This fire's bin complete, wiped out everybody who got mixed up in it.'

'I'm all fur goin' and handin' it back t'Hall in the same coin!' a man shouted, and several other smoke-blackened men and women took up his cry.

'No — wait a minute!' Rex raised his hand and silenced them. 'There's two reasons why we can't do that — one's because Hall will have everythin' ready to meet us, and our numbers are only a quarter of his; and the other is that we'd be committin' trespass if we attacked his town —'

'T'hell with that! The only thing he understands is —'

'Let me finish!' Rex insisted. 'We all want revenge — sure; we wouldn't be human if we didn't, but what we have t'consider is: is it worth stickin' our chins out and mebbe getting the rest of our numbers wiped out, or even carted off to jail since Hall has the law on his side — or do we sit pretty, rebuild, bide our time, and then one day take reprisal in full measure? Right now Hall is itchin' for us to go and attack him. When we don't we'll knock the props from under him. With the passing of time he'll get more and more careless — then one day we'll hit back with such violence he won't know what pole-axed him.'

There was silence for a moment as the men and women looked at one another; then Louise spoke up.

'That's the best idea, folks, and you know it. Why should we play straight into Hall's hands?'

'Yeah, but even if we rebuild he'll only knock us down again,' somebody complained.

'That's a chance we have to take,' Rex responded. 'Though for myself I don't think he will try the same trick twice, because he knows we'll be wary ... we've got to clear up the mess and start over, but one day we'll take care of Hall for this night's work, and that's a promise.'

Again the silence and the doubting glances at one another.

'That agreed?' Rex asked. 'Let's have it unanimous if we can. Show your hands if yore in favour.'

There was a long pause and then hands began to rise slowly, more joining them until at last there was hardly a dissenter.

'Okay,' Rex said. 'That bein' so let's set about the job of clearing up this mess, then by the time dawn comes we can fix up a temporary camp and decide on our next moves to rebuild the town and see what we can do to save the mine.'

*

On this same night, even as Rex had guessed, Sherman Hall was on the alert for trouble, and he was an extremely disappointed person when nothing happened. During the next day and night he and his picked gunmen kept up the same vigil, and yet again all was quiet.

A week passed — a fortnight, and the utter lack of reprisal for his ruthless onslaught had Hall stymied completely. It upset his plans and made an unholy mess of his intentions to tip off the authorities that outlaws were pillaging his town.

'It's just like I told yuh, boss,' Red Tompkins insisted, when the third week of quiet had started. 'Them folks over in M'Clyde's town — what's left of it anyways — is just pantie-waists. They ain't got th' guts t'come out an' fight.'

Hall sat in his swivel chair and chewed his cheroot savagely. Being ignored was, to him, something infinitely more hurtful than open attack.

'That guy M'Clyde is cookin' somethin' up!' he declared, clenching his fist. 'He must be, else he'd ha' come an' tried to get his own back ... I've had one or two boys over near his place — near as they dared get anyways — an' it seems the town's bein' rebuilt an' the mine's workin' again. They've even gotten that blasted mine back into action.'

'Not surprisin', is it?' Red asked, shrugging. 'All we did was blow up parts uv th' shaft. I guess they could clear that rubble in a coupla days. We should ha' done it properly and sealed the mine up.'

'Can't do that,' Hall snapped. 'One o' these days we're taking that mine over ourselves. No use givin' ourselves all that trouble later. All we aim t'do is clear M'Clyde an' his babyfaced followers outa the desert — then we're free to act. At least we got Pardoe,' he added in satisfaction. 'That sort of cuts off M'Clyde's right hand.'

'Look, boss,' Red said, sitting back in his chair and fingering the walnut butts of his Colts. 'I've been thinkin' … Since M'Clyde won't come out inter the open, mebbe we should *make* him.'

Hall gave him a questioning look from his sloe-black eyes.

'Now he's gotten that mine o' his workin' again he must also have that gold-wagon makin' its three times a week trip over the desert an' overland trail to Denver City.'

'He has: I checked up on it. What about it?'

'We might do worse'n rob it an' bump off th' guys who drive an' guard it. That way we'd do three things. We'd git the gold fer our own use; we'd scare M'Clyde plenty — an' he'd *haveta* come into th' open and challenge us if he wants to git any more of his precious gold through t'Denver City.'

Hall toyed with the notion, his cheroot jutting and his eyes considering the desk. He knew perfectly well that the idea was an excellent one. What he could not understand was why a lunkhead like Red had ever come to conceive it.

'Sorta blockade,' Red added, rubbing the end of his upturned nose.

'Yeah — I get it. An' mebbe you've got something at that. Y' mean stop him sending gold — not just this time, but *every* time, 'til he has t'see what he can do to straighten the thing out?'

'That's it,' Red agreed. 'An' in case he's in any doubt as ter who's done it — which he won't be! — we'll leave a note on the wagon, stuck on the body uv one o' the men, sending him love an' kisses. If that don't fetch him I dunno what will.'

Hall slapped his thigh decisively. 'That's a swell idea — an' I'm leavin' you t'take care of it.'

'Sure thing, boss. Nothin' I'd like better.'

'Where d'you aim to make the attack? Better be some place where you've plenty of cover an', if it's possible, where the guys on th' wagon won't be expectin' anythin'.'

Red reflected for a while, his piggy eyes fixed on the smoky ceiling of the office. Then presently he snapped his fingers.

'I got it! How's about Indian's Head Pass? That's where th' desert trail ends an' the main overland route t'Denver begins. Not a chance in a million of bein' interrupted.'

'Good enough,' Hall agreed. 'They'll be sendin' that wagon off again tomorrow, so it's up t'you to get the boys together and make yuh plans. I'll stay here and be ready for anythin' that might happen.'

'Same as yuh did when we attacked M'Clyde's town?' Red suggested cynically, getting to his feet.

Hall flushed a darker colour. 'The leader never puts himself in th' front line,' he retorted. 'He's too valuable — an' sides, he's got all th' thinkin' to do.'

'Okay, okay, just remarkin',' Red growled, and he went lumbering out of the office, intent on gathering together his fellow owl-hooters for the hold-up on the morrow.

It was a job he soon accomplished. In Gold Point he had nearly as much authority as Hall himself, and in any case the five men he picked to help him were more than willing to give their trigger fingers some exercise in order to bring Red M'Clyde into the open. His diffidence at retaliating was causing most of the men in Gold Point to get hot under the collar.

So at sun-up next day, Red and his colleagues rode out of town and hit the desert trail. They were well on their way by the time the sun was climbing; and when it had reached the zenith they had left the desert trail behind them and reached Indian's Head Pass, a distinctive rock formation towering up three hundred feet and forming a natural gateway to the overland trail which led to the north.

'Okay, this is it,' Red called, jumping down from the saddle. 'We've time t'get a bite to eat an' feed an' water the hosses — then that wagon should be about due. You, Jed, start climbin' up them rocks and stay on look-out. Yuh'll have a clear view of th' trail from up there.'

'Helluva climb,' Jed objected, staring upwards and pushing his hat up on his forehead.

'Shut up an' git busy!'

So Jed started climbing, watched by the rest of the men as they had their meal. Then Red went into action again. The horses were drawn carefully out of sight behind rock cover and along with his four companions he settled himself to wait, one gun drawn in readiness and the other waiting in the holster until actual action should be needed.

It was perhaps an hour later before Jed, high up the rocks, gave a cry.

'They're comin', Red! There's a whiff o' dust way out on the desert trail. Too fur away to see what it is, but I guess it's th' wagon.'

'All right,' Red yelled back. 'Come down here an' do yuh stuff with th' rest uv us. Put your masks up,' he added to his comrades, and all of them drew their kerchiefs into position. Then one by one they crept out of their hide-outs and stood waiting at the side of the trail, their guns ready. After a while Jed came and joined them.

'An' remember,' Red said, glancing about him; 'shoot t'kill. This ain't no time to argue.'

After a while the noise of the approaching wagon and the reverberating thunder of horses' hoofs became evident — growing ever louder — until the wagon itself became visible round the bend in the trail, moving at high speed. Upon it were the driver and another man beside him, a rifle across his knees; whilst in the rear of the wagon, standing guard over the gold, were three more men. They caught sight of the masked outlaws at the side of the trail and made to level their weapons — only they were not quick enough.

Deliberately Red and his boys levelled and fired. Against the rain of bullets which struck them the men in the wagon stood no chance. They dropped, or fell over the side of the vehicle into the dust, the horses plunging wildly in panic at the din let loose around them.

'Grab 'em!' Red ordered. 'Stop those blamed hosses frum boltin'.'

Two of the men beside him dashed forward, clutched the horses' reins, and dragged them to a standstill. Red pulled his kerchief back in position, holstered his guns, and then began an examination of the men who had been in the wagon.

'Very nice fur one day's work,' he commented, grinning. 'Not one of 'em left alive. Guess this'll give yeller belly M'Clyde somethin' t'think about, huh? Okay — dump these stiffs in the wagon, but take the gold out first.'

His order was obeyed, and within fifteen minutes the five dead men were in the rear of the wagon, one of them with a note pinned on his shirt. At the side of the trail lay the wooden cases containing the gold shipment.

'Unhitch them cayuses and bring 'em along with us,' Red ordered. 'I reckon it's time we wus getting back t'town. Th' boss oughta be pleased with this day's work.'

Five

Rex M'Clyde, working with Atkinson — who seemed to have taken the place of Pardoe — and Louise, on the rebuilding of the town, gave little heed at first to the non-return of the wagon men at their scheduled time the following day. He had a great deal to do, many matters to supervise in the rebuilding of the town and the renewed mining of the gold ... but gradually he began to wonder. Then wonder changed to anxiety — and finally alarm.

'I don't get it,' he said, frowning. 'Joe, an' Bill, an' the rest of 'em should have been back by eleven this morning. Now it's nearly six an' not a sign of 'em.'

Atkinson and the girl looked at him from the other side of the makeshift office-cum-living room.

'You think mebbe — Hall?' Atkinson asked, grimly.

'It wouldn't surprise me. In fact the surprise to me has been that he hasn't attacked our gold wagon before now. The best thing I c'n do is follow the trail and see if there's anythin' to be learned.'

'I'll come with you,' Atkinson said. 'You stay right here, Loo. Y'can attend t'whatever's wanted while we're gone.'

'Sure can,' she agreed, and moved the .38 on the desk beside her to a more convenient position. 'And you two take care of yourselves.'

'Do our best,' Rex said — and led the way out of the office.

The girl saw them off, prepared for the vigil which was ahead of her since it would probably be early dawn before her father and Rex returned. As events transpired it was longer than that. It was noon next day when they came back, their two horses in the shafts of the wagon and their grim cargo in the back. Hard-faced, dirty and tired from long hours of riding, they drove down the partly re-made high street and stopped outside their own particular domain.

But others of the populace had seen the dead men they were carrying and the news spread swiftly. By the time they had been in their shack to reassure Louise, half the town's inhabitants had gathered, staring at the five corpses and then waiting for Rex to reappear. When he did so he raised his hand at the angry chorus which greeted him.

266

'All right, I know what you're all thinkin',' he exclaimed. 'There are five dead men in that wagon — five men who were friends of all of us an' related to one or other of you here. On top o' that the gold was stolen, an' the horses. We found the wagon abandoned on the overland trail with the bodies in it. One of the bodies had a note pinned on it, an' I've got it right here.' Rex took it from his shirt pocket and read aloud:

This State's not big enough for two towns to be in it — so you'd best get out of your town — what's left of it — mighty quick, and take your bunch of heels with you. If you don't plenty worse things than this will happen.

'And the note's signed Sherman Hall,' Rex added, looking up

'That does it,' one of the men in the forefront of the assembly said grimly. 'You can weigh this up how you like, M'Clyde, but things have gone too far this time. Five more of our folks killed an' the gold stolen into the bargain —'

'Yeah — an' it won't be the first to go either. More we send the more we'll lose. Hall's bent on that, that's plain.'

'Look here, Mr M'Clyde, I think we should —'

'Just a minute!' Rex protested, raising his hand. 'Let me finish talkin'! Naturally things *have* gone too far, an' I'm the first to agree with you —'

'All right, then, what are we a-waiting for?' a woman demanded. 'Joe there was my husband an' I'm all for shooting it out with this skunk Hall, and that bunch of coyotes he has a-yappin' round his heels.'

'Yore dead right, ma',' a man shouted at her. 'If M'Clyde here's goin' to spout a lot more about legal stuff I reckon we should act without him. Hall ain't actin' legal: why should we?'

'There's somethin' t'be said for acting sensibly, isn't there?' Rex demanded, clenching his fists. 'You don't think I mean to take this lot lying down, do you? No — I've got a plan. I think it'll satisfy you, *an'* what's more, it might get us our gold back too. Right now, I'm going to get a meal and a rest. Mr Atkinson an' I have been riding solid most of the night an' we owe ourselves that. I'll talk t'you here in the main street in an hour. Okay?'

The men and women nodded, satisfied that M'Clyde would keep his word. Wearily he turned into the little dwelling and sank down heavily at the table. Atkinson sat down too and gave him a grim look. Without a word Louise busied herself in preparing a meal for them. Presently she set it on the rough table, together with coffee.

'Get something inside you,' she said, sitting down too. 'I guess you'll feel better and think straighten'

They both nodded and ate the food she had set down for them. She poured out coffee and pushed it over to them, then prepared a cup for herself.

'What are yuh aimin' t'do, Rex?' Atkinson asked at length.

'May sound queer, concernin' a cut-throat like Hall, but I'm thinking of trying some psychology,' Rex answered, musing as he ate.

'And what in heck's that?'

'Mental approach, dad,' Louise said. 'I learned about that when I went to school.'

'Yeah?' The tinsmith stared at her, then back at Rex. 'Y'sure get some queer ideas, son — an' I don't think they're the kind of ideas that are goin' to appeal much to our folks who are waitin' t'see definite action.'

'They'll get action aplenty,' Rex retorted. Then he went on urgently, 'Look, both of you — can't y'see what Hall's drivin' at?'

'Yeah — extermination!' Atkinson set his mouth. 'In fact he's hell bent on it, and only we can stop him.'

'That's his ultimate aim, sure — but right now he's got a different notion. As I figger it this attack on our wagon is to make us do somethin' to him, and so step over the boundary into his territory where he can call in the law t'help him.'

'Don't rightly see how he could,' the tinsmith mused, staring at his coffee. 'He murdered those five men in the wagon — an' even admits it on that note he left behind. If he called on the law to nail us we wouldn't exactly keep the wagon holdup a secret.'

'No — but could we prove Hall had done everythin'?' Rex demanded. 'We just couldn't — an' that note wouldn't count for anythin' as evidence. Hall's been careful too to keep himself outa sight. He wasn't on that big raid when we got burned out — an' ten to one he wasn't mixed up in the hold-up either. He's got men who work for him so that if anybody takes the rap *they* do ... He could call in the law all right, Mr Atkinson; don't you forget it.'

'You beatin' up for stayin' put again?' Atkinson asked suspiciously. 'If so, son, yore not the man I figgered you were.'

Rex shook his head. 'I'm not stayin' put — but neither am I sticking my neck out so Hall can do as he likes with us. We'll hit him mighty hard — but he won't see us do it.

'Come outside — you too, Loo — and hear what I have to say.'

Rex got to his feet and led the way to the door. From the higher standpoint of the small porch he gazed on the men and women who were hanging about waiting for his statement. His reappearance was the signal for the more distant inhabitants to drop their work and come hurrying over.

'Folks,' Rex said quietly, 'every one of us here believes it's time Sherman Hall was given somethin' back for his trouble recently — so here's what I've doped out … The two things that rankle most are that he set Fire to an' destroyed our town; and the other is that he had five men shot dead as they were goin' about their lawful business of gold transport. Right?'

'That's right, Mr Clyde.'

'Sure is.'

'Very well then. In return we'll set fire to Gold Point town to-night — *and* we'll get our gold back; and mebbe if things work out that way we'll kill five men in reprisal for our own lost ones. But we won't seek 'em deliberately. They'll only eat lead if they get in th' way.'

There was silence — that of disappointment, it seemed.

'I figgered,' one man said, coming forward, 'that all of us ought to go in an army and shoot the foundations out of Gold Point, and take care of those skunks inside it.'

'Which would suit Hall perfectly — therefore we're not goin' t'do it,' Rex replied. 'Look, you folks … If this town were to catch fire again what would be the first thing you'd do?'

'Try an' put it out,' a cowpuncher said, with somewhat earthy logic.

'You'd do somethin' else first, Len,' Rex told him. 'You'd try and save your most valuable possession. That's the first human instinct. A mother would think first of her child or children, an' the fire afterwards. A man, mebbe, would think of his money or his guns, and get 'em to safety quickly. So, workin' on that principle, I reckon that the first thing Hall'll do when he finds his town's afire will be to move the gold he stole to a place where the flames can't reach it.'

'Say, I guess you've got somethin' there,' Atkinson mused.

'It's psychology, dad,' Louise explained, with a little smile. 'Now you see how it works. It's a good idea, Rex,' she added earnestly, and glanced at the people below the porch. 'If you folks have the brains I think you have there's no better way of taking revenge and getting our gold back at the same time.'

'We don't get t'do any shootin', though,' one man objected.

'Just straight shootin' is something any lunkhead can do,' Rex retorted. 'Look what Hall accomplished by bein' a bit ingenious in sending those horses loaded with dynamite into our town. Well, we c'n be just as ingenious. An' there may be some shootin', Sam — depends how things make out. There may even be quite a lot of it if that gold's brought into view and we start to take it away.'

'What exactly do we do then?' a woman enquired. 'You've only got t'say the word, Mr M'Clyde, an' I'll ride as hard an' shoot as fast as any of you men.'

Rex smiled a little. 'I don't doubt it, Ma — but you won't be needed. In fact the less there are of us the better, for two reasons. A lot of us would make a noise and attract attention; and if we all left this town we're rebuilding it would give Hall a chance to send some of his boys to wipe the place out again. So we're not taking that risk. I aim to go myself, with Mr Atkinson … Nobody else.'

That most of the men were disappointed was clearly evident, but they were loyal enough to Rex not to question his decision. Then Louise spoke.

'You don't suppose *I'm* going to be kept out of this, Rex, do you?'

Rex turned to her. 'You'd be a mighty sight safer if you were, Loo.'

'What good would safety be to me if I lost dad and you? You're the only two people in the world I've any connection with. Without you there wouldn't be any point in living. I'd sooner take my chance and come with you … After all, I *did* root out those two spies. That entitles me to a reward, doesn't it?'

Rex rubbed his chin doubtfully and Atkinson grinned.

'Don't waste your time thinkin' up an argument, son,' he said. 'I've known Loo since she wus a baby, remember — an' I reckon she's the breed who'll die with, her boots on an' a shootin' iron in her hand.'

'Right!' Louise agreed promptly, with a proud toss of her blonde head.

'Okay then,' Rex agreed. 'We three'll do the dirty work — to-night after sundown, and the rest of you keep your eyes peeled and your guns ready for anything Hall might try to pull. We'll either come back with gold and Hall's town in flames — or else we'll not come back at all ... You folks agree?'

The assent was general, though not immediate. Most of the men seemed to consider they had been shoe-horned out of a shooting match — but Rex was their leader and, for the time being anyway, they were prepared to follow his orders. Nobody knew better than Rex himself that if any further disaster hit the slowly rebuilding town his grip over the populace might slip.

'Let's get inside,' he said briefly, glancing at the girl and then her father. 'We've plans to make ...'

They returned into the living room and settled down again at the table.

'Fortunately,' Rex said, 'I know Gold Point inside out, since I was born and raised there — an' that bein' so I know the best way to approach it without attracting attention. Far as that goes all you'll have t'do will be to follow me ... At present the wind's south, so we have to start the fire at the south end of the town and leave the wind to carry it.'

'Yeah — but s'pose the gold's hidden in the south end?' Atkinson asked. 'Won't give Hall a chance to make a dash t'save it, will it?'

'The gold won't be there,' Rex assured him. 'At that end of the town there's only stores and livery stables: the last place he'd put gold. The more likely spots — the Double Nickel saloon an' the sheriff-mayor's office — are at the other end of the main street, which is what I'm bankin' on. As for us: our best point of vantage is between MacArdle's drug store and the offices of the *Gold Point Echo*. There's a narrow alleyway between th' buildings from which we can see all the high street — but unless yore dead opposite it nobody can see you. Get it?'

'Sure,' Atkinson agreed. 'Is it easy to get to?'

'Nothin' simpler. We can ride into it from the back of th' town without attractin' anybody's attention — and that's what we will do. Now, Loo —' Rex turned to her. 'Since you insist on coming with us your job will be to set the town on fire.'

'After what happened here I'll enjoy every minute of it,' she said, her grey eyes gleaming.

'Good! We've six tins of kerosene we can take with us. I'll fix an oil fuse to them before we go, then all you'll have to do, Loo, is light the fuse and vamoose quick — but in doin' so you must go up the high street fast as you can and shout 'Fire! Fire!' at the top of your voice.'

'Won't that make her a sittin' target?' Atkinson asked anxiously.

'I don't think so: the very surprise of th' thing'll do it. Nobody'll be expectin' it and she'll be outa range before anythin' can happen. Naturally, Loo,' Rex added, 'you'll double back around the rear of th' town to join us — and you'll also wear a hat and tuck your hair up in it. With only the street lamps nobody'll recognize you.'

Louise nodded eagerly. 'You can rely on me for that, Rex. During which time you and dad just wait and see what happens?'

'That's the general idea, yes. We'll be nearly facin' the saloon where we're goin', and that's the one place Hall is likely to be. The minute he comes out we watch him carefully.'

There was silence. Then Atkinson gave a heavy yawn.

'Which seems to cover everythin',' he said. 'I reckon we'd best set about the disposal of those five bodies we brought back and then hit the hay for a few hours. We're both in need of sleep, an' considerin' what's likely to happen to-night, it's time we had some.'

*

An hour after sundown, waved an encouraging goodbye by their fellow townsfolk, Rex, Atkinson, and the girl set off on their mission, each horse carrying two kerosene cans apiece over the back of the saddle, whilst in his own saddle bag Rex had put the carefully prepared oil wick which was to act as the fuse.

'T'be hoped they don't have too many lookouts waitin' for us,' Atkinson commented, as they rode hard under the looming stars.

'That's one of the risks,' Rex said. 'If there are any we'll deal with 'em as we come to them.'

There, for the time being, the matter stood and the journey continued along the desert trail. In time they left the arid regions behind and sped like three avenging ghosts through the soft starlight, the horses making little noise now in the grass of the rich pasturelands surrounding the central focus of Gold Point itself.

Five miles more of grass riding brought them within seeing distance of their goal. It lay as a fan of light immediately ahead of them, ranged on one side by the utter black of the mountains.

'Start taking it easy from here on,' Rex said. 'We're over the border now an' in Government-owned territory. Anythin' can happen, an' there might be lookouts.'

They slowed their speed accordingly and drew their guns in readiness. They had little fear of being seen, riding as they did from the shadowy shelter of tree out-croppings, then speeding across grassy areas where only the starlight alleviated the intense dark of the night … But suddenly, as they came to the hard-worn trail which led directly to Gold Point they became aware of a solitary figure perched high on a rock overlooking the single rubble path. Rex saw him first and drew to a halt.

'Get down,' he breathed. 'I don't think he's seen us yet or he'd have fired.'

The girl and her father slid from their saddles and with a few murmured words into the ears of the horses they made them lie down also.

'Stay here,' Rex breathed. 'I'll take care of that guy without any firin' if I can: last thing we want t'do is attract attention.'

He moved away silently in the starlight and, keeping low, headed for the spur on which the lookout stood. When he came to the base of it he paused for a moment, measuring his distance — then with toe and finger hold he clambered swiftly up the projections in the stone.

The lookout caught sight of him at the same moment and his hand was dimly visible dropping to his gun holster — but Rex was upon him before he could manage it. A violent blow in the middle put an end to the man's efforts to whip out his weapons; a second uppercut under the jaw hurtled him backwards over the rock to the ground below — then Rex jumped down on top of him, delivering two more smashing blows which left the man completely knocked out. In a few moments Rex had completed his job. He threw the man's guns away, tied his hands and feet together with his pants' belt, and gagged him with his kerchief.

'For the time being, my friend, that should take care of you,' Rex breathed, and hurried back through the gloom to where he had left the girl and her father.

'Settle him?' Atkinson enquired.

'Sure did — an' I don't think there'll be any more look-outs to worry about, unless they're in the town itself — but since we'll be enterin' it from the rear that shouldn't bother us.'

Rex brought his horse to its feet and re-mounted it, waited for the girl and Atkinson to do likewise — then they resumed their journey along the trail, alert all the time for any signs of a second look-out; but, as Rex had guessed, there were no other men posted. The one who had been taken care of had evidently carried the onus of giving warning in case of need.

So, finally, the south end of Gold Point was reached. Its main street, dim and shadowy in the kerosene lights, was empty. The only building with any sign of activity was the saloon at the further end of the vista, though here and there lights gleamed at the curtained windows of one or two of the shack-like dwellings.

'Couldn't be better,' Rex murmured. 'Now, Loo — you see that alley-way up there? — midway along the street on the left?'

'Uh-huh,' the girl assented.

'That's where your dad an' I will be. We'll give you a hand to set these cans in place then we'll be goin'. Your job after is to dash through this street shouting 'Fire!' — then work your way back to us in the alley-way.'

Louise nodded and dismounted from the saddle. Rex and Atkinson jumped down too and swiftly unfastened the kerosene cans from the three saddles.

'That's the place we want,' Rex said, nodding to the nearest building. 'It's a store-house so nobody's liable to get hurt without warning — an' it's propped up on pillars like the rest of the buildings around here. Come on.'

Hugging a couple of cans to him he hurried across to the building and wormed his way into the narrow space between the floor and the ground. Atkinson followed him, and then the girl came. In the darkness they crouched, arranging the tins according to Rex's directions and unscrewing the caps.

'Set them in a row,' Rex said. 'I forgot the fuse from my saddle bag. Be back in a moment.'

He squirmed out into the open again, then as he stood up he looked sharply down the high street. A solitary cowpuncher was slinking along it in the direction of the saloon, giving a sideways glance as he went.

'So there *was* another look-out,' Rex muttered — and dived for his horse. In one bound he vaulted into the saddle, spurred the startled animal forward, then swept down the high street with devastating speed.

The puncher glanced behind him, realized what was coming, and tried to swing to one side, but he was a second or so too slow. Down came Rex's revolver, butt-end, on the back of the man's neck, crashing him over into the dirt. If, as seemed likely, he had been on his way to give warning that strangers were in town, his message was likely to be considerably delayed.

Rex drew to a halt, glanced around him, and then finding things quiet he went back to where the other two horses stood. Taking the wick from the saddle bag he dismounted and returned to the girl and her father under the store-building floor.

'Somethin' happen?' Atkinson asked. 'We were wonderin'.'

'Just had t'take care of a guy who'd seen too much,' Rex explained, setting the fuse so that it snaked along from one tin to the other, its oil-soaked mass dropping into each open hole. Finally, he tugged a box of matches from his pocket and gave them to the girl.

'All yours, Loo,' he said. 'And for God's sake don't forget to get moving the instant you've set fire to the end of this fuse. It'll move fast an' if you delay the whole lot will blow up on your face.'

'I can look after myself,' the girl said calmly. 'You two get moving; I'll join you.'

Rex patted her on the shoulder, then he and Atkinson scrambled clear and hurried over to their horses. Leaping into the saddle they whipped the animals round and darted for the shadows cast by the rear of the buildings. In five minutes they had reached the alley-way between the drug store and the newspaper offices and leaned on their saddle horns to watch events. Straight across the toad from them were the big windows of the Double Nickel saloon, with a dim vision of smoky haze away beyond the bat-wings. Diagonally, to the right, was the southward end of the street from which at any moment things should start happening.

They did. Abruptly there came a belching, soft explosion of flame, followed by the instant crepitation of burning wood — then only a few minutes later, following out her orders to the letter, Louise came flying by on her horse, her hat jammed down on her head to hide her masses of blonde hair.

'*Fire!*' she bawled, making a megaphone of her right hand. '*Fire!* FIRE!'

She particularly increased her shouting as she swept by the saloon, and added emphasis by hurling a stone through the main window. Her cries, though, had been heard further down the street, for out of the buildings where the windows showed there were people at home there came men and women to see what the trouble was about.

Then from the saloon more men and women came tumbling, the bat-wings swinging wildly before them. There was a rush to the boardwalk rail, but of Louise the only sign was of a dim figure rapidly foundering into darkness. In any case the blaze roaring into the sky from the further end of the town was the instant focus of attention. From all directions the men and women came surging into the street, moving in tide towards the swiftly devouring flames.

'So far so good,' Atkinson murmured, grinning. 'I reckon Loo couldn't ha' done it better if she —'

'There's Hall!' Rex interrupted sharply, his eyes narrowed. 'Just come outa the saloon.'

Hall moved slowly at first, until he reached the street and saw what was going on — then he let out a yell.

'Hey — Red! Charley! Hank!' he bellowed. 'Take a look at this! The whole dad-blamed outfit's goin' t'go up in smoke if we don't act quick —'

'Who done it?' demanded Red, staring.

'Ain't much mystery about it, is there?' Hall snarled at him. 'It's M'Clyde's crowd! They've hit back — jus' when we wasn't ready for 'em. They musta taken care of the men we had posted. Come on — we'd best see what we c'n do.'

Just the same, Hall made no move to advance to the raging inferno which, driven by the southerly wind, was eating the core out of the buildings in its track.

'Whadda ya waitin' fur?' Hall demanded, when his men remained with him.

'Jus' don't see what we c'n do with that,' Red retorted. 'An' anyway those folks down there are doin' what they can. I'm all fur leavin' it to 'em an' lookin' after ourselves ...'

Hall hesitated, trying to make up his mind about something. The glare illuminated his features clearly, revealing every expression. Rex, his eyes smouldering, watched intently — then he glanced round at the sudden commotion of a horse's hoofs and Louise appeared, smoke-dirty and smiling triumphantly.

'How'm I doin'?' she asked brightly.

'Swell,' Atkinson said. 'Ain't no gal around these parts t'touch you, Loo —'

'Hey, boss!' It was one of the men grouped around Hall who shouted suddenly. 'What about that gold we got? It won't catch fire, but if th' building's goin' t'be burned down *anybody* can get the stuff afterwards.'

'This,' Rex breathed, 'is *it*, I think.'

'Gold?' Hall twirled round with a start from watching the advancing fire. 'Hell, I'd furgotten it … Okay, you boys see what y'can do t'shift it. Take it any place where the fire can't get at it. I'm going t'direct these mugs who are tryin' to stop these flames. They act like they've no blamed sense.'

He turned and hurried away up the street. Red watched him go and then spat expressively.

'Reckon he would pick th' easiest job,' he growled, almost inaudibly; then swinging round, 'All right, you mugs — let's be shiftin' the stuff.'

He and the three men with him turned and hurried away in the opposite direction to Hall, and the eyes of the three in the alley-way never left them.

'Where'd y'suppose they're goin'?' Atkinson asked, puzzled.

Rex did not answer — until he saw Red go bounding up the three steps outside the sheriff's office whilst the three other men hurried across to the livery stable.

'I get it!' Louise said suddenly. 'Probably the gold's in the jail! Since they're all outlaws in this town anyway they won't have much use for the jail — but it's a grand place to put gold so nobody can get at it.'

'Yeah — reckon that's 'bout the size of it,' her father agreed. 'What do we do, Rex?'

'See what they do next,' he answered. 'No point in us interruptin' 'em until they've actually gotten the gold in view — then we'll act plenty fast. With all the rest of the folks busy at the other end of the street we've only those four to deal with — an' that should be a pushover.'

He ceased talking and watched again earnestly as from the livery stable a buckboard and two horses were driven — across the street to the sheriff's office. One man remained holding the horses; the other two went quickly into the office and there remained for a while. When they came out again Red was with them and between them they were carrying heavy cases.

'That's the gold!' Atkinson breathed. 'Our cases, too!'

'Yeah.' Rex watched tensely. 'Two more cases yet — when they've brought those we go into action — an' remember, we don't pull any punches either.'

He glanced quickly southwards. The men and women fighting the flames were still far too busy on that job to pay heed to anything else, and the fire too was spreading at tremendous speed on the sun blistered woodwork. It had crossed the street now, doubling the work of the firefighters.

'Two more cases!' Louise said, abruptly. 'That's the lot, isn't it?'

'Uh-huh — Just let's see what they do next.' Rex drew his gun and watched.

Red and his men were not slow to move. Red himself took the driving seat and his three cohorts bundled on to the wagon as best they could. Flogging the horses unmercifully, Red drove the wagon out of the high street towards the north at a furious pace.

'After 'em!' Rex snapped, and hurtled out of the alley-way with Louise and her father not a yard or two behind him.

At top speed, forcing their horses to expend every scrap of energy they possessed, they tore out of the main street and onwards to the dark trail which led northwards. In a matter of minutes they were within seeing distance of the speeding wagon in the starshine — and at the same moment the men on the bouncing, bumping vehicle became aware of the pursuit.

They fired, but the frantic pace at which they were moving made it impossible for them to achieve steadiness of aim. Their bullets went completely wide.

Rex, ahead of Atkinson and the girl, stood up in his stirrups, his knees pressed hard into his horse's sides, and carefully took aim, allowing his body to give with the horse's movement so that he kept his gun trained on his objective. His first bullet landed, and one of the men fell off the wagon. So swiftly did Rex catch up that the man had no time to get up even had he been able. Hoofs pounded and battered into his face and body, and he went rolling away into the ditch.

Atkinson ducked; a bullet tore dangerously close to his ear.

'Dirty critters,' he breathed, and fired twice. A second man dropped helplessly to the wagon's floor. Red kept on driving savagely, having enough to do with the horses without drawing his guns. His one remaining colleague kept down low, sniping at intervals, but failing to reach his mark.

Then, in a sudden tremendous spurt, Rex flung his horse forward, dived, and plunged from his saddle into the wagon. He stumbled and fell on his face.

Six

Realizing he had at least a temporary advantage, the man jerked his gun round — and fired, but at the identical moment the wagon hit a sun-baked chunk of earth in the trail and bounced wildly, flinging the gunman off his feet and pitching Rex over as he staggered up — but this time he was the first to recover his balance. His right hand clamped down on the man's wrist, twisted it violently, and the gun went flying over the wagon side.

A terrific right to the jaw hurled the gunman against the side of the wagon; then Rex dived for his feet and heaved. With a yell the man overbalanced and vanished in the ditch bordering the trail.

By this time Atkinson and Louise had caught up. They did not attempt to vault into the wagon but kept within a few feet of it, their guns ready for action.

'Okay, feller, stop the wagon!' Rex ordered, jamming his gun in Red's back.

Red tugged on the reins savagely and drew the wagon to a standstill, but in swinging round in the driving seat he brought his right fist up with terrific force. Unprepared for the man taking such a risk, Rex absorbed the blow to his face and staggered backwards. It gave Red the opportunity he was waiting for and he snatched out his gun and levelled it.

Atkinson fired at the same moment — dead true. A dark stain appeared on the gunman's shirt in the moonlight; the revolver dropped from his slack fingers. Then he heeled over from the driving seat and dropped inertly into the dirt of the trail.

Slowly Rex got up again and glanced at the side of the wagon as Atkinson and the girl came alongside it.

'Well, I guess that takes care of all three of 'em,' Atkinson said. 'Sooner we get on our way with this gold the better. It may dawn on Hall t'come an' look for us.'

'You take my horse along with you,' Rex said. 'I'll drive the wagon back home …' And he scrambled quickly to the driving seat, cracked the whip, and started the team off into the starlight.

And whilst he rode, Sherman Hall was about at the end of his efforts to direct the populace of his town in fire-fighting. The blaze had been brought under control, thanks to an endless chain of helpers, an unlimited supply of buckets from the general stores, and a fairly efficient spring-water supply. For all that, half the town had been gutted and Hall's face was grim as he began to return slowly up the high street, surveying the smoking, steaming ruins as he went.

'I'll get M'Clyde for this if it's the last thing I do,' he breathed. 'I'll give Red a free hand — an' unless I'm dead wrong he'll kill everybody in sight once he knows he doesn't haveta pull his punches.'

'Y'speakin' t'me, boss?' one of his henchmen asked, catching up with him.

'No, Lefty; I was just thinkin' somethin' out t'my-self. Since yore here, though, you might as well come with me to th' jail. I want t'see what happened to that gold we had there. I told Red t'take it to a place of safety. I reckon he'll have done that an' be back by now.'

The bull-necked Lefty nodded, but said nothing. He followed his chief into the dark regions of the sheriff's office and they worked their way to the jail at the back. The barred door was swinging wide and that was all.

'Looks like he ain't gotten back yet,' Lefty commented.

'I c'n see that, y'damned fool — but why *hasn't* he? He's had time enough …' Hall stood in the gloom, a match expiring in his hand.

'Y'don't suppose he took the gold an' didn't intend t'come back, do yuh?' Lefty suggested.

'Red ain't that kind.'

'They're all that kind, boss. I know what *I'd* do with a pile uv gold in me charge — an' I reckon Red's no better a man'n I am.'

'You an' Red never got on,' Hall said. 'That's all that's eatin' yuh …'

Nevertheless doubt had been sown in his mind. Muttering something inaudible he left the dark regions near the cell door, strode through the sheriff's office and to the boardwalk again. Hands on hips he stood looking up and down the street in the dawning moonrise.

'I don't like it,' he said abruptly. 'Sooner we see where Red's gotten to, the better. Git your horse an' mine from the stable yonder.'

'Okay.'

Lefty hurried off across the street and Hall stood waiting, gazing at the distant smouldering ruins of the half-destroyed town. His mouth set hard — then a new line of thought took hold of him as he caught sight of

Cawley, the lawyer — who had been amongst the firefighters — heading homewards.

'Hey, Cawley! Come here a minnit.'

Smoke-dirtied, but otherwise as imperturbable as usual, Cawley changed direction and came across to where Hall was standing.

'Well?' he enquired. 'Didn't do so good when M'Clyde decided to pay back, did you?'

'Shut up an' lissen! I'm goin' t'get him fur this — or at least the authorities are. I want yuh to contact 'em quick as y'can and tell 'em outlaws from M'Clyde's town have burned half my place down.'

Cawley wiped his face on his kerchief and did not say anything. Hall stared at him for a moment.

'Gone deaf?' he demanded, angrily.

'No — though it's a wonder I haven't, the way you shout. No use me telling the authorities anything, Hall. It couldn't be proved.'

'*What* couldn't?'

'That M'Clyde was back of this fire-raising. You may *think* he was, but where's your evidence?'

'The evidence is that just after th' fire started a girl rode through town here sayin' th' place wus afire. That girl wus Loo Atkinson; I'll swear to it, and so will plenty uv other folk I talked to while we dealt with that fire.'

'Hearsay,' the lawyer said, shrugging. 'No use whatever.'

'Listen, Cawley —' Hall reached out his hand and grabbed the lawyer by the front of his jacket. 'I've gotten th' idea that yuh more on th' side uv M'Clyde than me. Better not be: mightn't be too healthy fur yuh.'

Cawley pushed the hands away. 'You can't do without me, Hall, and you know it. One day you may get into a spot from which only a smart lawyer can get you out: and I'm the smartest lawyer hereabouts. That's my insurance ticket. Understand? And I'm not kidding when I say you've no evidence concerning this fire. You *haven't*. Without concrete proof the authorities wouldn't listen for five minutes. Just that a girl was seen in uncertain street light, a girl who *might* have been Louise Atkinson, doesn't mean a thing. Was she seen to start the fire? Were M'Clyde or any of his men visible? No ... You've got to swallow this one, Hall, whether you like it or not — and M'Clyde knows it. He's been just as smart as you were when you sent those loaded horses into his main street.'

The lawyer turned away. Lefty, who had been standing nearby with two saddles horses, looked after him — then back at Hall.

'I don't like that guy, boss. Too smooth an' too eddicated, if you ask me. He oughta be taken care of.'

Hall shook his head and scowled. 'Ferget it, Lefty. Trouble is, he's right. I might need him some day, an' I guess he'll stick on our side, 'cos Gold Point's the only home he's got … Okay, let's be seein' if we can find out what happened t'Red.'

He swung into the saddle of his horse and dug his spurs into the beast's sides. Lefty caught up with him as they headed northwards out of the high street.

'Sure Red went this way?' Lefty enquired, when they had reached the northward trail.

'He musta done. He didn't pass us when we wus fightin' the fire, so this is the only other way fur it.' Lefty asked no more questions and side by side he and Hall continued on their way, the risen waning moon casting a leprous glow on the white dust of the trail. Then after a while Hall, who was slightly in the forefront, drew to a halt. Lefty pulled up his horse sharp and waited.

'That's queer,' Hall muttered. 'I think we passed somethin' about quarter of a mile back. Looked like a twisted tree branch in the moonlight, stickin' outa the ditch. Now I come t'think on it it *could* ha' bin a hand!'

'Yeah?' Lefty asked in astonishment.

Hall swung his horse round and rode back to the spot. Jumping down from the saddle he hurried over to the side of the trail and stooped. Lefty slid down to join him and stood watching as Hall dragged forth the limp body of a man.

'It's Curly!' Lefty gasped. 'Looks like he's bin plenty trampled on, too. Is he dead?'

'Yeah.' Hall stood up, hands on hips, then with a shrug he reached out his boot and rolled the body back into the ditch. 'Somethin' screwy around here, Lefty. Better see if there's anythin' else lyin' around that shouldn't be.'

They moved on again, leading their horses beside them, keeping a sharp watch-out for the unusual. At the close of an hour they had come to the end of their search and Hall could hardly control his voice amidst the anger devouring him.

'Rubbed out — every one of 'em!' he breathed, clenching his fists. 'My best men — an' Red among them. Whatever else he wus, he could shoot faster an' straighter than any other guy I know. An' the gold an' wagon gone too!'

'Yeah ...' Lefty looked about him in the moonlight. 'Jus' th' same, boss, it *were* M'Clyde's gold, not yourn. I guess he only took back what belonged t'him.'

'Shut up!' Hall blazed at him. 'When I want yuh opinions I'll tell yuh ... Let's get back t'town. I'm goin' t'call a meetin' and decide what's goin' t'be done with this jigger M'Clyde. If he thinks he c'n git away with this he sure is crazy!'

*

Rex, Atkinson, Louise, and the population in general of M'Clyde's Town — by which name it now seemed to have become known — were fully prepared for anything Sherman Hall might attempt to even up the score ... but nothing happened. A week went by, during which time Rex and Atkinson between them supervised a great deal of reconstruction and saw further consignments of gold sent by wagon to Denver. The wagon, its guard doubled, was not attacked; nor was there any sign of Hall operating in other directions.

'Mebbe he's learned his lesson?' Atkinson suggested, when the week had become a fortnight. 'Not a thing's happened since the night we set fire to his lay-out. Or else mebbe he was killed in th' fire.'

Rex shook his head. 'Hall's not th' kind of man t'get himself killed in a fire, Mr Atkinson. He's lying low for some reason — an' I'll bet it isn't a good one. I distrust him far more when he's quiet than when he's active. Nothing we can do about it right now, though. At the moment it's honours — or *dis*honours — even. We shan't attack him again if he leaves us alone. If he *does* have a go at us — well, we'll tackle that when we get to it.'

And there the matter rested; but not trusting the situation for one moment, Rex took good care to keep guards at all points of the town, and two of his best men guarding the entrance to the gold mine workings. Formerly there had only been one watchman, and not a particularly young one at that.

Sherman Hall certainly had a plan, and he was about ready to carry it out. He had prepared his scheme when the first flush of his rage had abated and he was able to view the situation a little more dispassionately. Much of the plan had been conceived by the unemotional lawyer, Cawley, but not for one moment would Hall admit that he was beholden to another man for ideas.

Lefty, who had automatically taken the place of the extinguished Red Tompkins, heard the outlines of the scheme one morning, three weeks after Gold Point had been set ablaze.

'I think we got everythin' figgered this time, Lefty,' Hall told him, sitting complacently in his swivel-chair. 'An' this time I'll take care of things myself, since it seems I can't rely on any other guys.'

'Yuh can rely on me not t'let you down, boss,' Lefty said. 'Red mighta done — but I won't.'

'I'll darned well see you don't,' Hall assured him grimly. 'Now listen — this struggle between M'Clyde an' me has gotten into a range war, an' nothin' can settle it but the rubbin' out of either me or M'Clyde. That's th' issue. With one leader or th' other killed the rest of the folks don't matter. They won't have th' heart t'carry on alone. Since *I* don't mean t'be rubbed out that means M'Clyde's *got* t'be. Only M'Clyde alone wouldn't be enough. Atkinson an' his daughter might step into his shoes an' keep things goin' if they went free. So we've got t'take care of all three of 'em.'

'Okay. How?' Lefty asked.

'You an' me are ridin' t'M'Clyde's town to-night — an' afore we do anythin' we're goin' t'make sure that M'Clyde, Atkinson, and that gal are all nicely bedded down fur the night. See?'

'Sure I see — but I don't get the angle.'

'You will in a minnit. Once we've made sure they *are* bedded down we go along to th' mine an' take care uv the guards. I don't know how many of 'em there'll be, but we'll take care of 'em anyways. Then we go down the mine an' with us we take two cases of gelignite, which in the first place we'll carry on pack hosses. To them we'll fix a long-term fuse — a candle stuck in a trail of gunpowder so's we can reckon how long it'll take fur th' fuse to get lit. An' we bury that soup so's it'll be right under M'Clyde's town,' Hall finished emphatically. 'When it goes off the whole town'll go with it — blown off the face of th' map. See?'

'Yore aimin' to seal up the mine? That's it? Thought that wus one thing you didn't want t'do becos of th' trouble it'll make fur us to open it up again.'

'I'm chancin' that. We'll find a way to open that mine when we want, believe you me. The point we've got t'make sure of is that we wreck M'Clyde's town completely. Most of the people will be abed when it happens, so it oughta take care uv them too. What survivors there are should realize by then they can't fight us any longer ... an' there'll be no proof that we did it.'

'How does all this tie up with M'Clyde, Atkinson, an' th' girl being abed?' Lefty asked, frowning.

'I'm goin' t'write a note, wrap it round a stone, an' throw it through M'Clyde's window after we've fixed the explosive in the mine,' Hall explained. 'On that note I'm goin' t'tell him that the gal has bin kidnapped and taken down the mine as a reprisal — an' that there's nothin' M'Clyde or anybody else c'n do about it. M'Clyde bein' th' sort uv sucker he is he'll dash off down the mine pronto to find her — an' everythin' will be nicely timed so that when he gits down there the soup'll blow up and seal him in. If that don't take care uv him I don't know what will.'

'Yeah, it's a nice idea,' Lefty agreed. 'An' we do it tonight, did y'say?'

'To-night — you an' me. Any more uv us would cause too much disturbance. Best thing y'can do is get those two cases of soup from our arms stores and load 'em one each to a horse. An' take care you pack 'em tight. If either of 'em drop we're finished.'

'Yore tellin' me,' Lefty commented, with a grimace. 'Yuh mean two separate horses to our own?'

'Uh-huh. They'll be heavy — too heavy to carry with us as well. So fix that up, Lefty, an' meet me outside the saloon an hour after sundown.'

Lefty nodded and went from the office, leaving Hall to begin the task of writing the note which, he hoped, would take Rex M'Clyde straight to his doom. He wrote it several times before he was satisfied; then he pushed the finished copy in his wallet and turned to other matters.

He found killing time throughout the rest of the day an irksome job. Once settled on a plan he had not the patience to wait before he could put it into action — but it had to be done. He only began to feel happy again when, at the appointed time, an hour after sunset, he went to the Double Nickel saloon and found Lefty waiting. Beside him stood his own horse, two mares loaded with a case apiece, and Hall's sorrel which he had brought from the livery stable.

'Everythin' ready, boss,' he announced. 'Just like you ordered.'

Hall nodded. 'Nothin' more t'wait fur, then. Let's be movin'.'

He climbed into the saddle, used his spurs viciously, and began the journey out of town. Lefty kept close behind him, tailing the two pack horses at a six foot distance.

'Bring a candle and an oil lamp?' Hall asked suddenly. 'I forgot t'mention them.'

'In my saddle bag,' Lefty told him. 'An' I got matches too. Nothin' bin forgotten.'

'Good.'

'An' th' sooner we git rid of this dynamite th' better I'll like it,' Lefty added anxiously. 'Tailin' it along behind us makes me kinda nervous.'

Hall did not answer, but he was certainly every bit as scared as his henchman. The thought that worried him most was the possibility of some hidden lookout suddenly firing, and if his bullet went wide and landed in the explosive anything could happen. So Hall looked about him constantly in the starlight as he rode, but he and Lefty came within seeing distance of M'Clyde's Town — as much of it as had been rebuilt at least — without any interruption.

'This is goin' t'be easier than I'd figgered,' Hall remarked, drawing his sorrel to a halt and surveying the scene. 'Look at it — only half a town so fur. I guess it'll come down like a pack of cards once we get dynamite under it.'

'How d'yuh know y'*can* get under it?' Lefty asked. 'The mine's a good mile from the centre uv th' town.'

'Plenty uv underground tunnels, though — always are to mines uv that size. We take the longest one travelling north an' plant the soup at th' fur end of it. That won't be so hard.'

Lefty said nothing. In silence he gazed at the town from the half-mile distance. There were lights in most of the windows, and some in the main street, still under the job of reconstruction after the fire. Further away still, faintly outlined against the stars, were the new props of the shaft gear which had been reared in place of those destroyed by the earlier fire.

'They're all up an' about right now,' Lefty commented. 'Not time t'start yet, boss, is it?'

'Our first job's to load th' mine. By that time it's more'n likely the folks there will have gone t'bed — an' if they haven't we'll wait 'til they do, that's all.'

'There's sump'n else too,' Lefty said. 'How'd we know where M'Clyde, the gal, and Atkinson hang out? You ain't had no boys in this town since it were rebuilt, to learn things, have yuh?'

'The guards at the mine can tell us all we want t'know,' Hall answered. 'Let's go — an' follow me carefully. I know this territory backwards: you don't. Bring those cayuses with yuh.'

Hall urged his horse forward again, keeping well away from the town and following the desert track. Lefty kept up with him. In a wide detour they finally reached a point where they were perhaps half a mile from the rear of the mine. Here Hall dismounted.

'Stay here an' watch the horses and cases,' he ordered, drawing his guns. 'I'll take care uv the rest fur myself.'

Silently, his feet making no noise in the loose sand, he crept in the direction of the mine. Around it were many wooden buildings, all used in connection with the area, and these he used as cover to mask his advance. So he came finally to a vantage point where he could see the main shaft opening of the mine. The cage was at the top of its winding gear, the gates drawn across it, whilst on either side of it, betrayed by the glow of their cigarettes as they stood talking, were two guards.

Hall grinned to himself, picked up a fair-sized stone from the rubble at his feet, and flung it away to his right. The noise of it falling brought both men to attention immediately. They swung round, seemed to speak to each other for a moment — then they hurried off in the direction of the sound. Instantly Hall sped across the intervening space and concealed himself in the wilderness of wooden props near the cage. After a while the two men returned.

'Must'a been a chunk uv rock or somethin' failin',' one of them was saying. 'Best t'look, though: anythin' c'n happen at any time, I guess.'

'How right you are, feller,' Hall murmured, suddenly appearing and jabbing his gun in the man's back. 'An' take it easy,' he added. 'Both of yuh. One move th' wrong way an' yuh'll soak in plenty uv lead.'

Hall reached out, whipped the men's guns from their holsters, and threw them away. They stood with upraised hands, unwilling to risk sudden death in an effort to do battle with the gunman behind them.

'Right now I only need one of yuh,' Hall added — and without further hesitation he crashed his gun down on the skull of the left-hand man. He flattened and lay still. His colleague's head moved as he looked down at him, then he half turned.

'Keep lookin' frontwards,' Hall advised. 'Now start t'talk. Where does M'Clyde hang out in town?'

'I'll see yuh in hell afore I'll —'

'*Where*?' Hall demanded, jabbing his gun harder. 'Yore brain's in low gear, feller, if yuh think I'm kiddin'.'

'Okay, I'll tell yuh. He lives in a small buildin' which is also his headquarters. On the right uv the main street at the corner. It sez "Office" on a plank outside it.'

'He lives in an *office*? What yuh tryin' t'pull?'

'Only place he's got since his other place was burned down. He usta stay with the Atkinsons.'

'I know he did. Where do I find them while I'm 'bout it?'

'Right next door. There's a newly built place they've turned into a home.'

'Do they sleep there?'

'Sure they do.'

'An' M'Clyde sleeps in his office place? That it?'

'Yeah.'

Hall's revolver came down with blinding impact. His late informant dropped soundlessly beside his companion. Smiling to himself Hall turned on his heel and began running through the rubble until he had regained the waiting Lefty and the horses.

'I got everythin' I wanted,' Hall said. 'Bring the horses along. I'll go ahead with this rope' — he tugged it from his saddle horn — 'and make sure them two guards don't give us away if they recover.'

In a few moments he had returned to where he had left the unconscious guards. Rolling them back to back he secured them immovably with the lariat, their arms and legs tethered together — then with Lefty's help the two men were rolled to the edge of the cage shaft.

'Just room,' Hall said. 'The cage's stopped two feet above ground level. Okay — shove 'em over.'

'Down the shaft yuh mean?' Lefty asked, startled for the moment.

'Why in heck not? We don't want these two blabbermouths sayin' anythin' any time, do we?'

So the two bodies were given a shove and vanished over the shaft edge. After what seemed an infinity of time there came a faint sloshy thud from the depths.

'Okay — now we go down too,' Hall decided. 'Get the cases unpacked while I unfasten this cage gate.'

He turned to the task, using the muzzle of his gun to prise open the padlock which held the wooden cage gate in place. By the time he had completed the job Lefty had the cases unfastened and with tremendous care he brought them across one after the other and laid them on the cage floor.

'Just the candle,' he said, and went over to his horse's saddle-bag. In a moment or two he returned, tucking the candle in his pocket, and Hall operated the rope which controlled the winch pulleys. Slowly the cage began descending into utter darkness.

The blackness suddenly vanished before the light of Hall's lamp and the view became one of rock walls, glistening with the inevitable moisture of the depths … For quite a hundred and fifty feet the shaft went down before it left the imprisoning walls and descended instead into a huge, man-made cavern in the midst of which was the mining equipment, most of it standing against yellow-veined walls.

'If ever there was a bonanza, this is it,' Hall breathed, the glint of avarice in his eyes as he brought the cage to a stop and slammed back the guarding gate. 'I don't even blame M'Clyde an' his crowd fur stickin' around as they do when they've got this to work on.'

Still holding his lamp ahead of him he stepped out of the cage and then glanced down briefly at the two men who had been hurled down from above. They lay motionless, still bound. Hall kneeled for a moment and examined them; then he stood up again.

'I guess these critters won't be givin' anybody much trouble frum here on,' he said; then he turned to give Lefty a hand with the cases.

He and his henchman, each carrying a case, they crossed the giant main cavern and searched round until they found one of the many natural honeycomb tunnels in the rock. Hall selected the largest and swung his lamp into it.

'This goes in the right direction,' he said, 'but for how far I don't know. Guess we'd better look.'

Lefty nodded and followed him into the depths, the light of the lamp casting on the roughly circular walls, reflecting back from the endless film of moisture. After they had been making steady progress for nearly fifteen minutes — and in an upward direction from the feel of things — the tunnel narrowed so suddenly it was impossible to get any further.

'Couldn't be better,' Hall decided in satisfaction, putting down his case with extreme gentleness. 'We can load the cases in this narrow part here, and set the candle burning in the tunnel where we're standin' now.'

'Yeah,' Lefty agreed. 'But 'spose that M'Clyde, when he comes down here t'look fur the gal — if he comes — should come along this tunnel and find the candle burnin'?'

'Try usin' some brains, y'lunkhead,' Hall retorted. 'It's taken us nearly fifteen minutes to get this fur. D'yuh think that M'Clyde would waste fifteen minutes comin' along here when he's searchin' for the gal? Anyways, there are six tunnel openings in th' main cavern, an' it's an odds-on chance that he'd pick this tunnel particularly. Y'can bet he knows these tunnels by heart — so he must know this one ends in a blank wall. It'll be okay. Let's get the cases fixed.'

'Yeah — okay,' Lefty agreed, uneasily, and though both he and Hall were inwardly terrified of the slightest slip or movement, they set about the task, sweating freely, and moving the cases as though they were as fragile as egg-shells.

When at last they were in position in the narrow neck of the tunnel's continuation Lefty breathed a trifle more freely and drew the back of his hand over his streaming face.

'I s'pose we're under the town?' he questioned.

'Should be — near as I can tell. An' it's only a hundred an' fifty feet to the surface with the helluva lot of blow holes through which the explosion can tear its way. Don't furget, Lefty, we've enough soup in these boxes to blow M'Clyde's Town to Kingdom Come if things go as we figgered — an' naterally if M'Clyde's down here somewheres — as he will be — he'll be sealed up fur good, even if he isn't killed …'

'Yeah … How's about the fuse trail? Who's fixin' it?'

'You are,' Hall said dryly.

'How?' Lefty licked his lips and glanced towards the cases.

'Make a small hole with your knife in the top of the side of the case — doesn't matter which — and collect the powder that falls out. Use yuh hat t'catch it in.'

'An' s'pose the penknife sets the stuff off?'

'No reason why it should if y'work carefully — an' by God yuh'd better. In fact,' Hall said, 'I'll do it meself. I c'n see yuh've gone yeller an' yuh might fumble it.'

Rather than look scared himself, he snatched out his jack-knife and snapped open the smallest blade, then he went to work on the top corner of the upper case, gently drilling through the woodwork until suddenly his knife blade shot inwards as the last fragment of wood was eaten away. He gulped and sweated as the case shifted slightly — but nothing happened beyond the sudden pouring of an inky powder around his feet. Instantly he whipped off his hat and caught the cascade in it until it had levelled off inside the case and no more came forth.

'This should be enough,' he said, and began to very carefully lay a dark stream of the powder along the tunnel floor. By the time he had finished it stretched perhaps eight feet, leaving a trail to the boxes.

'Yeah, that's okay,' Lefty agreed, tugging the candle from his pocket as Hall returned his hat to his head.

'No thanks t'you,' Hall growled, and snatched the candle from him.

Once again using exquisite care he scooped out a hole for the candle so it could not possibly fall over and bedded it down for a quarter of its length.

'I reckoned it up in my office this mornin',' he said, as Lefty watched him, round-eyed. 'Three quarters of a candle this length takes forty minutes to burn down — so we've got to figger it so that M'Clyde's down here forty minutes frum now … So let's get outa here.'

He struck a match, lighted the candle wick, and then beat a quick retreat with Lefty hurrying behind him.

Seven

Many of the lights in the main street of M'Clyde's Town had been extinguished when Hal and Lefty returned to the surface. Mounted on their horses and trailing the two pack animals beside them, they kept well to the rear of the buildings until they found a convenient side opening from where they could survey.

'I guess that'll be where M'Clyde hangs out,' Lefty said, nodding to a semi-completed building at the opposite corner. 'An' from the look o' that light in the lower room he's still not gone t'bed. Hope t'heck he gets a move on.'

'Don't matter whether he does or not,' Hall responded. 'An' in fact he probably won't 'cos I s'pose he's the sort uv sheriff around here an' probably has plenty t'do.'

'Don't matter?' Lefty repeated, staring in the gloom. 'But I thought yuh said we'd got forty minnits to —'

'Sure I did — but look next door where th' Atkinsons hang out. There's lights in two o' them upstairs rooms, so I reckon Atkinson an' his gal are hittin' th' hay. The *main* thing, Lefty, is t'be sure the gal isn't on view — so's M'Clyde'll jump to the obvious conclusion. If he saw a light in the lower room at Atkinson's he'd naturally go an' look if the gal was there. If he sees th' place in darkness th' odds are that he'll head straight fur th' mine. Don't partic'larly matter whether he does or not: th' town'll be wrecked anyways, but I want M'Clyde trapped down there if I can manage it.'

Lefty became silent, waiting anxiously. He kept his eyes fixed on the corner building with its board saying 'Office' fixed over the doorway. Then his gaze switched presently to the upper windows of the adjoining building as one of the lamps went out. After a while the second did likewise and the place was dark. Up and down the street, in the half-completed dwellings, other lights began to extinguish too.

'Keep them blasted cayuses still,' Hall breathed fiercely; and Lefty gave a start. He had not noticed, so intent had he been on watching the windows and mentally counting the seconds, that the two pack horses beside him were getting restive.

'Shurrup, blast you!' he commanded, hoarsely.

'I reckon we might risk it now,' Hall said, taking the ready written message from his pocket. He got down from the saddle, found a suitable-sized stone, and wrapped the message round it — then returning to the saddle he hurled the stone dead true to the lower lighted window of Rex M'Clyde's abode.

The tinkle of glass died away. Hall drew his horse back into the deeper shadows. Lefty moved too, dragging on the reins of the recalcitrant pack horses.

'Here he comes,' Hall breathed, as Rex became vaguely visible hurrying through the doorway of his headquarters. He stopped when he reached the street and stood gazing about him.

'Yuh'll never have a better chance than now to plug him, boss,' Lefty whispered.

'An' awake th' whole town with the shots? Don't be more blamed crazy than yuh haveta.'

Abruptly Rex wheeled round and started off at a run in the direction of the mine. Hall watched him go and grinned.

'Simple, ain't it?' he asked dryly. 'I guess a guy's reasonin' powers go completely haywire when he's in love with a gal. He'll go through fire an' water t'try and find her.'

'An' we'd best get outa here quick,' Lefty said, anxiously. 'I ain't hankerin' to hang around with that soup buried under our feet.'

'Okay — let's go,' Hall agreed.

He swung his horse round, but in doing so his spurs accidentally caught one of the pack animals. Already impatient and fractious, the creature let out a frantic whinny and lashed out his back feet. They slammed into the half-completed wooden wall of the nearby building and knocked the planks and the props out.

'Shut *up*, you damned fool!' Hall panted. 'D'yuh want t'wake up the whole tarnation place?'

He stopped in alarm as with a sudden cascading roar the flimsy building began to break up, crumbling in a snapping and cracking of timbers and thin beams.

'Move!' Lefty yelled, lashing at the pack horses. 'Git goin', damn yuh!'

Confused and bewildered with the tails of the whip and the collapsing building, the pack horses kicked out blindly, whinnied furiously, and then bucked up and down. Hall tore his own whip out and added his quota of savage lashes, tearing brutally on the pack horses' reins with his free hand. Somehow he and Lefty dragged the frightened animals clear of the chaos — but the noise they made had been heard by more than one inhabitant of the town.

Louise Atkinson was one of those who got up quickly from bed and went to the window. She had not been asleep and the sudden outburst demanded investigation. She was just in time to see two dim horsemen and two riderless horses vanishing in the starlight. Instantly she swung round, hurried into shirt and riding pants, dragged on her half-boots and then went to find her father. He, too, was half dressed in the dim light of his room when she broke in on him.

'What's goin' on?' he demanded, blundering over to her. 'What was all that racket outside jus' now? Sounded like a buildin' came down.'

'I've more than an idea that Sherman Hall, or some of his boys, are up to something,' the girl answered. 'I'm going right now to tell Rex — unless he's heard the noise already.'

She swept out of the room and down the stairs to the outdoors. To her surprise, as she came out into the open, there was no sign of Rex, even though the light was still on in the lower room of his office living quarters. Across the road the fallen building had subsided into a crumpled mass of props and smashed timbers.

Loo's surprise was even greater when she found the door of Rex's abode swinging open. She hurried into the place quickly, calling as she went, then brought up short in puzzlement when she found the office living room empty. There was a litter of papers on the desk, the oil lamp burning steadily — and a crumpled piece of paper lying on the floor.

Frowning, the girl stooped and picked it up, smoothed it out. Then her eyes widened. She swung as her father came in.

'Gone to look for me.' Louise handed the note across. 'I don't like this, dad: some funny business is going on somewheres. This note's a deliberate decoy to take Rex away from the town so something can be attempted.'

'Yeah ...' Atkinson scratched his jaw and scowled at the note. 'Sure looks like it.'

'Lend me one of your guns,' the girl said, holding out her hand.

'Huh?' Her father unstrapped one of his cross-over belts. 'Why? What are y'figgerin' on doin'?'

'I'm going to find Rex, of course. If trouble breaks out we're going to need him. You collect the men and see if you can find Sherman Hall or his people anywheres. I'll swear I saw two of them at least, with a couple of riderless horses. I'll be back with Rex as quickly as I can.'

'Okay — an' look after yuhself, gal.'

Louise patted the buckle of the gun-belt significantly and then raced from the room and out into the street again. As she went she had time to notice that men and women were hurrying down the street, obviously intent on finding Rex. Since she had no time to give them information she continued at a run towards the mine. Once there she paused and looked about her in surprise. There were no guards — unless they had gone down into the mine with Rex. Yes, that was probably it. The cage was at the bottom of the shaft. Moving to the opening she megaphoned her hands and shouted down.

'Hey, Rex! You down there?'

A multitude of echoes came whispering back to her, and that was all; so she turned her attention to the winch pulleys and dragged on the ropes which started the cage moving upwards again. It occurred to her when the cage reached the top and she climbed into it that she had not brought a lamp with her — but now there was no time to go back for one.

Working the ropes again she sent herself speeding down into the darkness. It had no particular terrors for her since on numerous occasions she had been down here with Rex and knew the layout of the mine in detail. She could tell almost to a yard where the shaft ended and was prepared for the bump when it hit bottom.

'Rex!' she shouted hoarsely into the void. 'Rex! You down here?'

There was still no response save from the echoes. With rising fears that something might already have happened to Rex she felt her way out of the cage and relying purely on her memory of the major cavern, worked her way across the great space, calling as she went.

'Rex! *Rex, where are you?*'

And on the fifth occasion she received an answer, remote and far away, muffled with echoes.

'Right here, Loo! Fourth tunnel. Where are *you?*'

'I'm in the main cavern.'

'Stay there! I'll come to you.'

So Loo waited, until at last there came the distant glow of Rex's bobbing lamp. It changed after a while into a full circle of brilliance, becoming brighter as he hurried towards her.

'So here you are!' he exclaimed in relief. 'I was worried sick as t'what those swine had done t'you —'

'That was a trick, Rex. I never was down here. I came to fetch you. I found that note in your office —'

'A trick?' Rex gripped her arm tightly. 'How'd you mean?'

She gave him the facts. 'Something's going on,' she finished urgently. 'I don't know what; but it seems to me that Hall deliberately got you down here out of the way so he can do something up above.'

'Seems like it,' Rex admitted. 'He killed off both the mine guards, too. I found their bodies, roped together, and both men dead. We'd best get back to th' surface quickly.'

He seized the girl's arm and they began the journey back across the cavern. Hardly had they covered a dozen feet, however, before the explosive left behind by Sherman Hall suddenly disintegrated. From the tunnel where the gelignite was hidden there came the buried reverberation of the upheaval, then something approaching the effect of an earthquake hit the cavern. It rocked from side to side as though at the end of a giant pendulum. Rex and the girl were both thrown from their feet, but Rex had the presence of mind to keep the lamp from hitting the floor. Its light still shone on the small rocks which came down from the roof.

The commotion lasted perhaps a minute, rising to a roar at times as tremendous rock falls occurred ... then gradually everything settled into a common haze of dust, through which the lamplight shone diffusedly.

'That seems to be that,' Rex muttered, helping the girl up beside him. 'An' things are takin' rather better shape at last. Now I guess we can see why Hall wanted me down here. He'd got some soup planted. That you came too must ha' made him laugh like hell — grantin' he knew about it.'

'It's what's going on up above that worries me,' the girl said quickly. 'That explosion can't have improved our town — and from the sound of it it must have been about under the buildings we've so painstakingly rebuilt.'

'Yeah ... we'd better see how we get out of here.'

Keeping close to each other they headed in the direction of the cage, and received their first shock when they reached it. The vibration of the explosion had caused the shaft props and underpinnings to collapse, allowing the rock to fall inwards. Now the cage lay buried under incalculable tons of boulders and rubble.

'Not very pretty, is it?' Rex turned a grim face in the lamplight. 'The way out's jammed — an' if, as I suspect, the whole shaft is bottled up it would take months to get through it. In those months our health wouldn't exactly improve, I'm afraid.'

Loo was silent, trying to hide the fear she certainly felt. Rex turned and made an examination of the cavern walls — not with any particularly high hopes, for knowing the cavern as intimately as he did he knew only too well that the only means of communication to the surface was via the shaft. He turned at last as the girl caught his arm.

'Rex — don't try and hide things from me,' she insisted. 'It means we're — entombed, doesn't it?' She tried to say the word steadily.

'Right now,' Rex said quietly, putting his arm about her shoulder, 'it looks that way. Our only hope is that the explosion also weakened other parts of the cavern so that there may be a way to the surface somewheres which didn't exist before.'

'Where, for instance?'

'Mebbe in one of the tunnels. I've never thoroughly explored them. It's possible there might be a way out and —'

Rex's voice had been slowing down, and now it suddenly stopped. Loo knew why. There was a queer sound in these buried depths — a sound that had terror in it, rumbling and growling and becoming ever louder as though the very earth were going to fold up.

'Dis-distant rock fall?' the girl suggested shakenly.

'Mebbe.'

They both remained motionless. Rex's lamp light shining steadily through the haze. The devouring, tumbling din increased — then suddenly then saw it … a surging torrent of water sweeping out of the tunnel where the explosion had occurred. In the space of seconds it covered the cavern floor, rising above the ankles of the two as they stood watching.

'That adds joy to the proceedings,' Rex said bitterly. 'It isn't spending itself, either: it just keeps on coming. The explosion must have split through a rock skin covering an underground river, or something.'

'Which means we can't explore any of the tunnels?'

'I reckon not.'

Silence, save for the lapping, surging water. Rex flashed his torch around and upwards to where the shaft rubble had fallen. He turned, the water bubbling round his knees.

'We can climb up these rocks,' he said. 'Might delay things. No telling whether or not the water mightn't cease flowin' after a while.'

'Supposing it does?' the girl asked hopelessly. 'We're still stuck down here and no possible way of getting aid.'

'As long as we're alive we c'n still figger things out,' Rex told her. 'Let's get up on the rocks.'

Refusing any further argument he gripped her arm and helped her to climb upwards. Then he followed her to the highest point. They sat down, looking at the lamplight reflecting back from the muddy, swirling scum which still crept up towards them, niche by niche.

'Better put my lamp out,' Rex decided. 'We may need it later.'

The lamp extinguished, there was nothing but the darkness, the slap of the water against the cavern walls and, far away, a dull, distant rumbling which bespoke the point where this underground river was cascading through.

'I'd have preferred almost any death but this,' the girl said at last.

'Who's talkin' about dyin'?' Rex growled.

'I am. What's the use of trying to deny it, Rex?' Loo's hand gripped his unseen arm. 'We're stuck — and the only decent thing in it all is that we are at least together. It counts for a lot — to me. I'm hoping it does to you.'

'Sure it does.' There was a moment's pause, then Rex made a sound like a chuckle. 'Y'know, it's kinda funny. When everythin' was free an' easy up above I could never screw up enough nerve t'tell you what I thought of you: best I could do 'til I got courage up was spend as much time as possible with you an' your dad. Yet now we're shut down here in the dark, with this blasted river aimin' to get us I'm just in th' mood t'ask you to marry me ... Queer, ain't it?'

'Not queer, Rex: it's wonderful — and if only things were different I would marry you, on the spot ... If only it were anything but *this*!' the girl went on, with a desperate movement. 'To be bottled up down here! I'd sooner have a bullet in my back, just as long as it happened in the fresh air, under the sky.'

'Yeah ... Yeah, I know how y'feel, Loo.'

Rex lit his lamp on momentarily and watched the water. It had risen about a foot, and was still coming upwards. He extinguished the lamp and stared in all directions in the total dark. If there were any crack in the roof which gave access to the surface it would be visible. Even the night sky or starlight would reveal itself in such utter blackness. But there was nothing. Just the water, ever rising, ever spreading, and the dense, impenetrable, void.

'My feet are getting wet,' Loo said at last, with a shaken laugh. 'Second time in the last hour.'

Rex, slightly higher up, felt water surge into his own boots at the moment the girl spoke. He lit the lamp again. The flood was over their ankles and still coming up — and to climb any higher away from it was impossible. This time Rex kept his lamp on and the reflected glow shone on the girl's set features.

'Time we faced it,' Rex said, patting her arm. 'This flood isn't goin' t'subside. In half an hour it'll have gotten to the roof. We can either wait for it to do that — an' drown. Or there is a quicker way ...' And he glanced down at his guns.

'I prefer the quicker way,' Loo said, setting her jaw.

'All right ...' Rex watched her pull out her gun and study it pensively. 'The only thing I ask is that you don't ask me to do it for you.'

She said nothing. She still played with the gun in her fingers and watched the water dancing in the lamplight. Her eyes strayed presently to Rex's right hand. A gun was in it, held steadily. The lamp was in his other hand.

'Tough thing to have t'do,' he said. 'Leastways, until every spark of hope's gone.'

The girl nodded. The water rose. It was swirling round their waists now as they still sat on. They raised their hands above the level of the flood.

'You first,' Rex said, and he kissed the girl gently. 'Happy landings, Loo. Knowing you has bin one of the nicest things that ever happened to me.'

The girl raised the gun — then abruptly the unexpected happened. She was torn clean off the rock by a sudden tremendous, surging current in the flood. Rex made a frantic grab at her and missed; then the water, swirling round his waist, dragged on him too and in total darkness, his lamp extinguished, he was hurled along in something approaching a cataract. Where he was going he had not the slightest notion. He and Loo — he hoped — were as much at the mercy of the roaring waters as insects swept down a sluice.

Time and again he was forced under, to rise to the surface gasping for breath and striving to see something in the utter dark. The water was roaring round his ears now, telling him that he was in a confined space, possibly a tunnel. His speed too was tremendous. Though now and again he brushed against rocks in the darkness, he did not dare make an effort to catch at them for fear in doing so he might severely lacerate himself. There seemed to be no alternative but to keep going ... And he did, until at length he felt himself thrown over the edge of some kind of rock lip. He dropped perhaps twenty feet and landed in filthy ooze, the water here extremely shallow hut making plenty of noise as it boiled out somewhere to his left. Dazed, half drowned, he staggered to his feet.

'Louise!' he yelled. '*Loo!* Are you there?'

'Omigosh — yes!' he heard her cry, not very far away. 'How'd you enjoy the sleigh ride?' Far from sounding depressed there was almost a laugh of relief in her voice. There came the sound of sloshing in the water, then Rex realized that she was beside him.

'Thank heaven,' he breathed, gripping her saturated shoulders. 'What d'you suppose happened?'

'Up to now I've been too busy looking after myself to think — but now I can attempt a guess. I think one of the tunnels must have given way at one end when the water pressure became too powerful. Outwent the water as through a sluice, and we were carried with it — but where to I don't know. From the sound of things we're in a pretty large-sized cavern.'

'Yeah ...' Rex listened to the bubbling of the water and the echo of their voices. 'Does sound that way. But I've never known of any big cavern, 'cept the one where the gold is.'

'We know of it now. If only we could see something. You lost your lamp, I suppose?'

'Uh-huh. An' our guns are ruined — for the moment anyway.'

'What about matches?'

Rex gave a low whistle. 'Forgot that!' He felt at his sodden shirt pocket. 'Mebbe they'll work. They're in an oilskin bag with my tobacco.'

He was busy for some moments dragging the pouch out of his wet shirt. Then taking two of the matches, since there was nowhere dry where he could strike them, he ground their heads together. They flared instantly, the pouch having kept them perfectly in condition.

The flame was brief and only weak in the vast space, but it did at least reveal to the two that they were not very far from the cavern wall and that the huge flood of water had dropped to a mere trickle and drained itself off somewhere through the underground rock honeycomb. Apparently they had fallen through a twelve-foot hole in the rock wall.

'Say,' Loo breathed, in an incredulous voice, as the match flames expired. 'Did you notice something just now? The wall of the cavern there?'

'Huh? I saw th' wall, sure. What about it?'

'Go right up to it and strike some more matches.'

'Okay — but we've got to conserve. I've only about a dozen.'

Loo was insistent nevertheless, so they advanced until they were touching the wall with their fingers. Then Rex struck two more matches and the wavering glow revealed something that took his breath away too this time. The rocks, swilled clean by the sweeping waters of the flood, were sandwiched with deep yellow seams.

'*Gold*!' Rex breathed, and the expired matches sizzled in the wet at his feet. 'Countless tons of it! Why, great heavens, that other cavern we were workin' on is just breadcrumbs compared t'this lot … It's — it's a super-bonanza!' he finished, excitedly.

'So I thought,' Loo responded. 'This cavern is infinitely richer than the other one, and but for that explosion would probably never have been located. Rex, we've got to get out. We *must* get out! What could be more frightful than to have found this colossal fortune, enough to build an entire city instead of a town, and then die amidst it without anybody else being the wiser?'

'We're not goin' t'die.' Rex's voice was determined, even though he had not the least idea what to do next.

'Wonder where the water went to? Outside someplace?'

'I don't think so. Underground, if you ask me.'

They were silent for a space, then presently the girl gripped Rex's arm out of the void.

'Rex — take a look over there, a bit to our right. Is it phosphorescence, a glow of some sort, or even volcanic gas? Or am I just seeing things?'

Rex looked and saw what the girl meant. There was an area about a foot long by one wide not very far away, mysteriously translucent in the darkness.

'Probably underground gas,' he said, 'but there's no harm in looking.'

Holding on to each other they advanced towards it, and as they did so it lost the appearance of phosphorescence and became instead a solid thing — oblong, rather after the shape of an irregular eclipse.

'It's —' Rex started to say — then he stopped and stared over his head. He gave a yell. '*Look!*'

In that moment the mystery was a mystery no longer. Overhead was a rent in the rocks, the night sky with the stars riding clear and high plainly visible. It was reflecting into the water lying in pools on the cavern floor from when the first flood had passed through it.

'Way out,' Loo breathed, giving a little dance in the dim light. 'Our luck's still holding, Rex. Maybe you're going to have to take up that offer to marry me, after all.'

'Good job I was in earnest,' Rex responded, a grin vaguely discernible on his shadowy features. 'The problem is going to be how to get out. That hole's about twenty feet above us. I've no lariat or anything, either.'

After a moment Loo snapped her fingers. 'Got it! Look, when that flood was suddenly released a rock wall gave way, didn't it?'

'Must ha' done.'

'All right, then. We climb back into that tunnel and find the rocks that gave way — then we pile them up in a cairn until we're near enough to that opening to make a jump for it and get out. It'll take time, of course — but we'll make it finally.'

'What are we waitin' for?' Rex demanded, and with the girl beside him they sped back across the cavern.

To clamber up the rough rock into the tunnel through which they had been swept was not a particularly difficult matter, then continuing to grope their way forward in the darkness they came at length to a wilderness of rocks and stones which had clearly been torn away by the force of the flood. Striking two more of his precious matches, Rex looked around him on the rubble.

'Perfect,' he breathed. 'You go back t'the cavern, Loo, and I'll carry the rocks that far and throw 'em down to you. Then you start the buildin' up. We'll be outa here before we know it.'

'Okay.' The girl turned and hurried away.

Rex was somewhat optimistic in his calculations, however. In all it took him and Loo some three or four hours to complete their task, then, aching in every joint, they had a slender pile of balanced stones and wedges towering some thirteen or fourteen feet high in the cavern centre. The top was by no means secure, but they were prepared to risk it.

'I'll go first,' Rex said, as they surveyed from halfway down the cairn, and he began to climb gingerly, pausing whenever the pyramid showed signs of swaying Loo far out of the perpendicular.

Reaching the top of it he remained poised on his knees for a moment or two, then he gradually straightened up, raising his arms over his head. Tensing himself, he sprang suddenly, and his hands caught against the edges of the fracture. In another moment he was out in the fresh night air with the impersonal stars glowing far overhead.

'Okay,' he called down, throwing himself on his face. 'Up you come.'

There were movements below, then after a while a dim vision of Loo springing upwards. He caught hold of her arms, helped her to gain a grip, then dragged her out beside him. Breathing hard they stood up together, feeling the cold of the night wind striking through their still only half-dried clothes.

'For the love of Pete!' Rex breathed suddenly.

'What?' The girl looked about her sharply.

'Take a look!' Rex pointed in the starlight. 'That's Gold Point town over there — that dim mass of buildings about a mile away. That means we're in Gold Point territory here … It also means that super-bonanza is on *Hall's land*!' If he finds it and works it there's nothing to stop him doing so. Since the Government have a claim they'll take a percentage, of course, but even at that Hall will be able to build a city if he wants and we shan't be able to do a thing about it!'

Eight

'We've *got* to do something about it!' Loo declared flatly. 'It's not to be thought of that after the way he tried to murder us Hall should benefit to the extent of a super-bonanza.'

'Yeah, that would be too unkind,' Rex admitted. 'But th' moment this fissure's seen — an' that might quite easily happen as soon as it's daylight — Hall's bound to investigate, and that'll settle everything as far as we're concerned.'

'The only alternative to that one is to act to-night,' Loo said. 'Don't ask me *what*, but that's the obvious answer.'

Rex thought for a moment or two, then seemed to come to a decision.

'First thing we do is get home — if there's anythin' left of our town, that is. Then I've got a proposition to put before the folks. An' this time it should have the sort of action they're wantin'. We've got to settle this issue right now. Either I'm having control of this territory — all of it, I mean — or Hall is. The attacks on either side have got to cease … Let's start walkin'.'

Rex set the pace, striding swiftly through the coarse grass, the girl beside him. By contemplating the stars Rex calculated their direction so they could reach the desert trail — and also roughly estimated the hour.

'Be round about one in the mornin',' he said. 'An' from the look of things we must ha' bin carried the devil of a way underground. Not that that matters now. Considerin' what we found in the finish it was well worth it.'

'Just what sort of a plan have you got for dealing with Hall?' Loo asked. 'Outside the obvious one of shooting him up, that is.'

'Shooting him up wouldn't do us any good, Loo. It wouldn't give us the mine … I've got to work it so that Hall gives his town and land over to me, *legally*, which — all unknown to him — will include that super-bonanza.'

'I can see him doing it,' the girl sighed.

'He may be forced to. Depends on how things work.'

More than this Rex would not say, but he was obviously turning plans over in his mind as he and the girl continued their long walk back to their own town. Though they were fatigued after their experiences they were none the less glad of the exercise. It at least prevented them catching a chill.

As near as they could estimate, it was about three in the early hours when at last they came within sight of their town. They were fully prepared to find it in ruins, but instead it seemed in the main to be still standing. Lights were flaring in all directions as the populace moved about busily, evidently repairing what damage had been done. Then, the moment Rex and the girl were sighted entering the main street, things happened. They found themselves mobbed by a delighted crowd of men and women, foremost amongst them being Atkinson himself.

'What in heck happened t'you two?' he demanded. 'I'd given th' pair of you up fur lost in the mine! How'd you get out?'

'Lucky,' Rex said. 'Tell you more later. What happened here?'

'Nothin' much. I figger that Hall planted dynamite to try and wreck our town. All that happened was that some of the partly constructed buildings fell down while the rest remained okay. Nobody was hurt … Jus' the same,' Atkinson finished grimly, 'this sort o'thing has got to stop! It's time Hall wus taught a lesson once an' for all, whether it's legal or it ain't.'

'With that I entirely agree,' Rex said. 'An' if you folks will listen for a moment I'll tell you what I've got in mind. First, let me explain what happened to Loo an' me. Amongst other things, we've found more gold than any of us ever dreamed of — which is just as well considerin' th' shaft to our own mine has bin blocked.'

'Gold!' somebody shouted. 'Where?'

Using the porch of the Atkinson house to raise himself above crowd level Rex explained in every particular just what had happened to himself and the girl. Without a word the men and women listened.

'I'm all fur goin' right now, before daylight comes, and shootin' up Hall an' his crowd,' Atkinson declared. 'It's th' only way there'll ever be peace around here, Rex.'

'There's another way,' Rex said. 'All of us will go to his town, sure — but unless we're compelled we won't shoot. What we *will* do if we can is drive Sherman Hall and his satellites into the saloon — the Double Nickel — an' there pin 'em. We'll be there too — the two opposing sides under one roof.'

'Yeah?' Atkinson looked dubious in the lamplight. 'Then what?'

'Hall is a born gambler,' Rex said. 'We all know that. I'm not a bad gambler myself when it comes to it. I'm willing to play a game of poker with him, the stakes being his town and land against mine. Winner take all. Loser gets out — and stops out.'

'Too big a risk,' Atkinson decided flatly. 'If you lost we'd have t'vamoose. An' if you won yuh don't s'pose Hail'd let you alone and just hit the trail with the rest of his townsfolk d'yuh?'

'No. I fully expect he'd come back an' try and shoot me up — which is exactly what I want him to do. That, though, is part of a future plan. The present idea is to *legally* win his town and land and secure a transfer of the deeds to myself. With so many witnesses to prove I won it as a stake in a poker game the authorities can't touch me. Once I've got the deeds transferred I've got the land, the town, and the bonanza.'

Rex waited for a while as the men and women talked amongst themselves, then one of them shouted.

'Hall'll trick you somehow, Mr M'Clyde. Yore stickin' your neck out a mile.'

'I'd stick it out much further if I just tried to shoot him an' his people up,' Rex answered. 'He could bring the authorities down on us for that — an' don't forget we'd have no defence because we can't prove he tried to blow us up to-night.'

'Your aim then is to sneak in on the town whilst they're all asleep and force 'em into the saloon for a showdown?' Loo asked.

'That's it. We've got to act before dawn, else that bonanza may be found and that'll finish everythin'. Naturally, if Hall knew of that bonanza he'd never play a poker game for the stakes I have in mind. As it is I think he'll gamble because if he wins he'll become undisputed boss of this entire state.'

'Let's go,' Atkinson decided promptly. 'No use hangin' around here talkin'.'

'I'm not doin' a thing for two hours,' Rex stated. 'Y'seem t'forget what Loo an' I have bin through — an' the walking we've done. We're both taking two hours' sleep an' followin' it up with a meal. Even then it'll only be about half past five, 'bout an hour an' a half ahead of the dawn. We can be in Gold Point in thirty minutes from here — even less. That's the way it is — an' that's the way it's going to be.'

*

Rex kept rigidly to his schedule, snatching two hours of heavy sleep, at the end of which time he was awakened by Atkinson, who had prepared a meal for himself, Loo, and Rex in the living room. At the table the girl herself appeared, refreshed from slumber.

During the early breakfast Rex had little to say. He had quite enough on his mind without indulging in needless gossip. When the meal was over he put aside his water-logged guns and strapped on a pair which Atkinson loaned him. The girl too provided herself with a fresh bandolier of cartridges and a spare .38.

'Which makes us 'bout ready,' old man Atkinson said, putting a massive .45 in its holster and then buckling it round his waist. 'I'm ready to give that skunk Hall all we've got, feller — an' so are the folks, I reckon. I told 'em to arm themselves, get their hosses, and wait outside fur us.'

Rex nodded and made his way outdoors. The men and women of the town had followed out orders completely. Close on two hundred of them were assembled on their horses, every one of them armed and itching to be off.

'Your horses are at the tie-rail there,' Atkinson said to Rex and the girl, and nodded to them.

'Okay.' Rex looked over the assembled crowd, then raised his voice: 'All right, folks — on our way! An' remember — no shootin unless we have to. The main purpose of this is surprise — an' leave Sherman Hall exclusively to me. I know where he'll be. His living quarters are next door to th' sheriff's office, an' I s'pose they'll still be there if they escaped the fire when we burned the place down.'

'An' the rest of us get as many of Gold Point's inhabitants into the saloon as possible?' Atkinson asked. 'That it?'

'That's it.' Rex helped Loo to her horse, then vaulted to his own beside her. A touch of the spurs and he started to the head of the gathering, thereafter sweeping out of the main street and presently hitting the desert trail.

Swiftly, silently in the sand, the avenging horde swept onward under the stars, none of them speaking, all of them getting the utmost out of their mounts ... the miles flew by. In under half an hour they had reached the rebuilt town of Gold Point and Rex called a halt for a moment whilst he surveyed.

'Pretty much as it used to be,' he said. 'They've had time to straighten things out, of course. They seem t'have taken a lot fur granted too. No look-outs. Evidently they don't think we'll be in any shape to make reprisal after havin' our town blown up.'

'Hall should ha' planted his explosives less deep,' Atkinson growled. 'If he hadn't stuck 'em so far down nothin' could have saved us, I guess.'

'Looks like everythin's all set for us,' Rex added, gazing down the empty main street. 'And fur those of you who don't know this place, the Double Nickel's over there — on the right. That's where we drive everybody. Do it how you like. I'm goin' after Hall. Now get busy … You stay with your dad, Loo: I want t'take care of Hall in my own way.'

The girl started to protest, but Rex did not stay to continue the argument. Spurring his horse forward, he raced down the high street and round the side of the sheriff's office. This in turn brought him presently to the rear of the building, the upper windows of which belonged to Hall's living quarters.

Using the horse to help him, Rex stood on the saddle and leapt upwards lightly, landing on the small veranda roof. Silently he moved up the slope, his right hand gun drawn, and gained the window. The upper and lower sashes were slightly open. He raised the lower one swiftly, stepped into the room beyond, and without pause strode across in the gloom to the bed.

'Get up!' he snapped, and dug his gun into the dimly visible form under the blanket.

The sleeper turned, muttered something, and then broke it off into an oath. In the filtering light of the brilliant stars the startled features of Sherman Hall were plainly visible.

'Surprised?' Rex enquired dryly. 'I know I oughta be at th' bottom of the gold mine, dead — an' Loo Atkinson as well, only it didn't work out.'

Hall gazed fixedly, plainly unable to realize what had happened to blow his plans sky high.

'I said get up,' Rex repeated in a deadly voice. 'An' get dressed — quick!'

Hall slid out of the bed on the opposite side — and at the same instant he made a sudden dive for his gun holsters on the dresser near the bedside. Rex fired. The bullet went clean through the dresser mirror not an inch from Hall's head.

'I'm not jokin',' Rex explained. 'Try that again, Hall, an' you'll fall on the floor — an' never get up ag'in.'

Swearing under his breath, Hall turned to his shirt and pants and began to scramble into them. He was not such a fool as to again risk Rex's gun. He knew only too well that he was dealing with one of the fastest marksmen in the territory.

'What are yuh aimin' t'do?' he demanded, buttoning up his shirt. 'If it all adds up t'yuh just killin' me why don't yuh get on with it? I'm not scared.'

'I don't play the game your way, feller,' Rex told him. 'An' I don't figger on killin' you either … yet. Now go in front of me and do as I tell you.'

Hall had no choice. He left the room, went down the stairs, and to the outdoors, Rex immediately behind him. On the boardwalk Hall stopped and stared at the gathered crowd of mounted men and women in the main street, and amidst them a goodly majority of Gold Point's inhabitants.

'What gives?' Hall snapped, swinging round on Rex.

'It's a showdown,' Rex said coldly. 'Not before it's time, is it? You've bin asleep on the job to-night, Hall — no doubt thinkin' we were all cleaned up. You've another think coming. One thing I will tell you. I'm not aimin' to have any gun play on either side. My folks have orders only to fire if your folks do. An' if they do yore mighty near to me and unarmed. Figger it out for yourself.'

'Yuh mean yuh'd shoot me down in cold blood?'

'If any of your people shoot at *my* people — yes.'

Hall licked his lips and gazed again at the crowd in the waxing light of dawn. As usual his own safety had — to him at least — first priority.

'No shootin', you folks!' he ordered. 'Let's see what M'Clyde has t'say first.'

'That's better,' Rex said. 'Now get into that saloon — all of you. Loo — go ahead and light the lamps, will you?'

The girl withdrew her horse from the mob and rode it further down the street. Rex waited until lights appeared behind the saloon windows. Then he frowned.

'How'd she get in?' he demanded. 'I forgot it'd be locked.'

'I smashed the door in earlier,' Atkinson grinned. 'Don't think Hall'll mind, in the circumstances.'

''Fore I'm finished,' Hall breathed, 'I'm goin' t'even the score for this night's work!'

'Y'can think about that later,' Rex told him. 'Right now you can get in that saloon of yours.'

The gun jabbing in his back, Hall sullenly began to obey, stepping down into the street. Behind him, covered by the guns of the men and women of M'Clyde's town, came the rest of Gold Point's inhabitants — or at least the majority of them who mattered.

Rex kept his gun in Hall's back until they had reached the centre of the saloon — then he turned.

'Set out the chairs,' he ordered. 'This is goin' t'be conducted peacefully, near as we can make it. Any shooting from you folks of this town and you can count Hall here as finished ... Now find seats, all of you.'

There was a shuffling and scrambling as orders were obeyed. Following out their previous instructions, Rex's own fellow townspeople remained standing, their weapons ready, their eyes fixed on the assembly. Finally Rex was satisfied and pulled up a table, putting a chair at each side of it. He sat on one and motioned to Hall to sit on the other.

Very slowly Hall sank down, his eyes on the gun levelled at him on the table edge.

'What's the idea uv all this monkey business?' he snapped.

Rex cuffed up his hat on to his forehead and then felt in his shirt pocket. From it he withdrew a deck of cards, still in its original wrapper. He dropped it on the table with an emphatic slap.

'You pride yourself on bein' a gambler, Hall, don't you?' he enquired.

'Sure I am: yuh've known me long enough to know that.'

'I've known you *too* long: that's what worries me ... Right here's a deck of unwrapped cards. No trickery, no anythin'. You an' I are goin' t'play poker — the game of our lives — an' the stake's a high one.'

Hall fished a cheroot out of his pocket and lit it. His dark eyes were commencing to gleam in sinister satisfaction. Rarely had he lost a game of poker — playing it in his own subtle way.

'I'll back any stake yuh care to name,' he said.

'Good enough.' Rex watched him levelly. 'You an' me are sworn enemies, Hall. We always have bin. As long as both of us stay in this State there'll never be peace for either of us. Right?'

'Right!'

'Okay then. The stake is winner take all. If you win you get my town and everything belonging it — including the gold mine — an' I'll hit the trail along with the folks by sundown to-morrow night. They're agreed on that.'

Hall nodded, waiting. Rex continued to gaze at him.

'If you lose I get this town and the land and the deeds that go with it — and you and your folks get out by sunset, and *stop* out. Simple enough, ain't it?'

'What yuh really mean is a poker game showdown?'

'That's what it's come to. I could have shot this place up to-night, but it would only have meant that you'd have come an' done th' same thing to us sooner or later. We get nowheres doin' that ... This game is goin' t'settle it once an' for all.'

Hall grinned. 'Suits me, feller, but I think yore crazy. I never lose at poker — or had yuh forgotten?'

'You've never played me,' Rex said calmly. 'I couldn't have grown up in this town without learning how to play poker like a master ...' He glanced about him. 'An' these folks are witnesses, particularly Cawley over there, that lawyer of yours.'

'Surprises me yuh trust him,' Hall commented.

'I don't. I just want him t'see what goes on so he can start rememberin' where the deeds for this land and property are when he has to transfer your land and town to me ...' Rex reached out and slapped the cards again. 'Tear off the wrapper,' he ordered.

Hall did so. Rex laid his gun on the table at his elbow.

'Cut for dealer,' Rex said — and the cut fell to Hall. He distributed five cards to Rex and five to himself and put the remainder of the pack on the table.

'Invisible ante,' he said. 'Your town against mine.'

'Uh-huh,' Rex acknowledged. 'Start playing ...'

Nobody spoke as the game began. The denizens of Gold Point were as interested in this method of settling a dispute as those who watched relentlessly over them.

Hall discarded three of his cards, picked up three more, and sat motionless with his cheroot smouldering. His dark eyes aimed at Rex across the table as he considered his own hand.

'A flush,' Rex said at length, and laid down his five cards on the table, all of the same suit but not in sequence.

'Fours,' Hall said, grinning widely, and threw down four cards of the same rank. 'Looks like yuh'd better be thinkin'; about getting' outa town, M'Clyde.'

Beaten, Rex looked at the cards, set his lips, and then gave a shrug. He got to his feet slowly.

'Okay, that's the way it is,' he said. 'I'll keep to my word, Hall, and get out. There aren't any deeds t'hand over as far as my town's concerned, because it isn't legalized as yet —'

'Better be certain first, M'Clyde, that Hall *did* win,' said Cawley, the lawyer, in his placid voice.

Rex glanced at him. 'Four ranks higher than a flush, Cawley. I'm satisfied.'

'I'm not ... If you examine that deck on the table you'll find that it's been shuffled into sequences so that Hall couldn't help but bid higher than you. It's sleight-of-hand. I've seen him do it too often not to know. As luck had it it fell to him to deal so he could fix things.'

'You low-down blasted snake,' Hall breathed, getting on his feet slowly and glaring at the lawyer. 'What the blue hell are yuh talkin' about —?'

Rex snatched up the pack from the table and riffled through it quickly; then he threw it down again, his eyes glinting.

'You're right, Cawley,' he breathed. 'How come you tell me? I thought you were supposed t'be behind Hall in everythin' he does?'

'I hate the sight of the skunk,' Cawley said, shrugging. 'If there's anythin' I can do to kick the props from under him I'll do it — an' gladly.'

Hall divided his attention for a moment between the cynical legal man in his seedy black suit and Rex's grim face — then abruptly Hall dived, his hand snatching at the gun Rex had laid on the table for his own protection. Rex lashed out in an endeavour to stop the movement, but he was not quick enough — so instead he upended the table so the edge of it struck Hall violently in the stomach.

He fired at that moment, but the bullet struck the wooden roof of the saloon. Immediately Rex had dived upon him, tore the gun out of his fingers, and then planted a right-hander. Swearing and panting, Hall tottered backwards, collided with the chairs behind him and somehow slewed up on his feet again.

'We set out to play this game the straight way,' Rex told him, seizing his coat lapel and swinging him round. 'Seems you didn't grasp the idea. Mebbe that means you need softenin' up.'

Hall flung up his hands to protect his face, so instead Rex hit hard for the midriff. Utterly winded Hall doubled up; then he kneeled sideways at a hammer blow on the ear which started the blood flowing.

'On your feet!' Rex roared at him, and dragged him upwards to land a merciless right clean in his face. 'I've bin owin' you this, Hall, ever since you sent me out into the desert and had your folks throw garbage at me. Now seems as good a time as any to clean up that little account.'

Hall kept on his feet even though he rocked. He lashed a blow back and missed. Iron knuckles smote him across the nose. Behind him the assembly broke up hastily and made room as Rex lashed out time and again, battering the struggling man across the saloon.

Here and there Hall managed to make a comeback and struck out with vicious jabs. Rex jolted, but he did not fall. He was aware of a trickle of blood from his nose, of a dull ache in the side of the jaw, but neither impaired his hitting power. Without mercy he pounded Hall across the face, over the heart, in the stomach, and finally delivered an uppercut which lifted the dazed and winded man momentarily off his feet. He fell backwards against the bar counter, lurched forward, and Rex brought down his right with the force of a sledgehammer. It hit Hall across the back of the neck and flattened him into the sawdust.

'Satisfied?' Rex panted, tossing the dishevelled hair out of his face. 'Now get up and start playin' square!'

Hall stirred helplessly on his face, but did not rise. Tightlipped, Rex swung round, snatched up a whisky bottle and broke off the top on the side of the counter. The spirit he threw on Hall's head and he gasped and choked as it seared into the cuts and scratches on his face.

'C'm on, damn you, get up!' Rex reached down and dragged him to his feet. 'Now get over there and we'll start playin' again — the *straight* way!'

He shoved. Hall, nearly too dazed to see where he was going, reeled across the saloon and half fell at the table. Steadying himself, he sank down and rubbed his hand over his damaged features.

'One uv these days, M'Clyde, I'll —'

'Shut up!' Rex cut him short and sat down opposite him. He dabbed his own troublesome nose and then glanced across at Cawley. 'Come here,

Cawley — You can deal for a change. I reckon there won't be no question about that. Since you ain't on Hall's side, or mine either if it comes t'that, it sorta makes you neutral.'

The legal man nodded and went on his knees to pick up the fallen cards. Straightening again he counted them out placidly, satisfied himself and the watchers that there were fifty-two, then he shuffled them vigorously, finally setting them on the table.

'Cut them!' Rex snapped — and Hall did so, his eyes glowing with fury.

'Deal!' Rex ordered, glancing at the lawyer — and he gave five cards to each man and then stood back with folded arms to watch results.

This time the silence was deadly as each man took up his cards and studied them. It seemed that nobody was even breathing. Finally Hall set his cards on the table and grinned crookedly. He had four cards of the same rank. Rex looked at them fixedly for a moment, then returned his attention to his own hand. He had four cards in sequence — the two, three, four and five of hearts. Hall had played high. Only one more trick, the straight flush, could beat him. Rex bit his lip. He was one short of a straight flush. Either the ace or the six of hearts could give it to him, discarding the useless queen of clubs he possessed.

'You've lost anyways if you don't,' Atkinson breathed, watching over his shoulder. 'Risk it ...'

Rex nodded and threw down his useless queen of clubs. He picked up the topmost card from the pack and hardly dared to look at it as he turned it over. Then he felt himself sweating suddenly ... it was the ace of hearts.

'Straight flush,' he said, and laid the five cards on the table.

Hall gazed as though he could not believe it. He made a sudden dive at the remainder of the pack and searched through it; then he hurled it down in a shower of cards.

'Nothing wrong with that deck, Hall,' Cawley told him. 'I made sure of that.'

'Yuh mean you fixed it for M'Clyde t'get a straight flush!' Hall yelled at him. 'By God, Cawley, one day I'll put a slug through your belly fur this night's work ...'

'Shut up and sit down!' Rex ordered.

Hall hesitated and then did as he was told. Rex's cold eyes fixed him.

'Hall, in front of all these people — who are witnesses — I've beaten you fair an' square. I want those land deeds handin' over right now, an' the transfer makin' legal. That's a job for you to do, Cawley.'

'Glad to,' he said, shrugging. 'I'd rather have you as the boss of this town than Hall any time … The guy's gun-crazy. I'll go get the deeds.'

He went off swiftly and not a word was spoken until he returned. He put the deeds on the table together with a blank transfer-of-property deed.

'That's already Government-stamped,' he said. 'All you've got to do, Hall, is sign on this top line here — an' you, M'Clyde, sign down here. That makes the thing legal. Tomorrow I'll file it with the authorities in Washington an' that'll settle that.'

Cawley went across to the bar counter, found a bottle of ink and a pen, and came back with them. Rex signed swiftly and pushed the deed over to Hall. With vindictiveness in every line of his face he added his own signature.

'Thanks,' Rex said curtly, and handed the folded deed up to Cawley. Then he added, 'I'm trustin' you with it, Cawley, becos I don't see how a guy could do as you did tonight an' not be on the level. But if you try and gyp me, watch out. That's all.'

The lawyer gave his humourless smile. 'You needn't worry, Mr M'Clyde. I've waited all my life for a night like this. I've stayed in this town because my roots are in it, but I've always wanted to see the place run properly. I'd hoped in the old days before you got ran out that you'd take over — but at that time it just didn't happen. Now it has … and I aim to help you to keep it that way.'

'It won't work,' Hall breathed, glaring. 'I'll damned well see it doesn't!'

'There's one thing you can remember, Hall,' Cawley told him. 'This town and land is now owned by Mr M'Clyde, and the law is on *his* side. Raise one finger against him or his followers, damage one little scrap of property, and he has the power to bring in the State to make you suffer for it.'

'Jus' the same I'll get even!' Hall vowed.

'All *you'll* do,' Rex told him, getting to his feet, 'is get out of this town as fast as you can go — an' not come back. You've got till sunset — an' no longer. I'm stayin' in town here 'til you and your stinking crowd are on your way. Now I reckon the lot of you had better start packin', hadn't you?'

316

Hall looked about him at the array of guns and relentless faces, the cowed looks on the faces of the men and women who were his townsfolk. He got up slowly.

'Okay,' he said, his mouth setting. 'But I'll be back ...'

Nine

'I think,' lawyer Cawley said, as the saloon emptied of Hall and his followers, followed by Rex's own guardian gunmen and women, 'that Hall means exactly what he says. He *will* return. It isn't to be expected that he'll just walk out and stop out. He has no respect for law — never has had. He'll have even less now.'

Rex mused for a moment and then glanced up at the lawyer's lean face.

'It may surprise you, Cawley, but that's the very thing I want Hall to do.'

The legal man stared — and so did Loo and her father.

'*What?*' Atkinson demanded. 'Y'mean you ain't satisfied even yet, Rex?'

'I'm satisfied as far as gainin' possession of this town's concerned — along with our own — but there's another outstanding issue. Since the Government have taken over this land and town they must also have copies of all its statistics and legal records. Right, Cawley?'

'That's right.'

'So they must have it on record that I was convicted of murder.' Rex clenched his fist. 'They must also know that Judge Barrow passed sentence on me ... though I'm quite sure they don't know that Judge Barrow was murdered afterwards.'

'Yeah, but ... dammit, man, you're innocent!' Atkinson protested. 'Everybody knows it.'

'The authorities don't. They'd be in their rights if they walked in here to arrest me because Judge Barrow outlawed me from Gold Point for all time. That puts me in a spot, and the only way I can get out of it is for Hall to come back here an' try and wreak vengeance.'

Lawyer Cawley gave Atkinson a puzzled glance. 'How does that help?' Loo asked, mystified.

'We all know,' Rex said, 'that the murder charge was a frame-up — that the real murderer was Hall himself. What I mean to do is to make him say so in front of witnesses who matter.'

'Couldn't y'have done that tonight when you beat him up?' Atkinson demanded.

'Sure I could — but I said witnesses who *matter*. The law wouldn't take much notice of these townsfolk, or any of you. They must hear it for *themselves.* That's why, when Hall has gone, I intend to get some law officers down here, explain the position, and then have them wait until such time as Hall tries to strike again, as inevitably he will. Once he does that I'll make him talk — before the right people.'

'An' if he *doesn't* come back?' Atkinson asked. 'There's just a chance he mightn't, I reckon.'

'If he doesn't within a reasonable time I'll take the law with me an' go on the prod for him, Rex said. 'But he'll come back: I'm sure of it … An' I'll tell you why. 'Cos just before he goes I'm goin' to let it slip that he's traded me a super-bonanza without knowing it. That'll fetch him!'

'Super-bonanza?' Cawley repeated, shaken for once. 'Where?'

'You'll find out, Cawley, in good time — same as the rest of the folks …' Rex got to his feet. 'I think it's about time we all had something to eat. Sun's up an' it's around breakfast time. Once we've had it you'd better ride to Denver, Mr Atkinson, and from there get in touch with the authorities and tell 'em to send some law officers over here quick. There's no knowin', once he's left, how soon Hall will hit back.'

'I'll do that,' Atkinson promised.

Rex led the way out of the saloon, the girl beside him. When they reached the boardwalk they paused, surveying the men and women in the main street. Most of them were packing their belongings on to horses or throwing them in buckboards. Others, belonging to M'Clyde's Town, were standing watching, their guns ready for any infraction of orders.

'We'll take Ma Cassell's place for a meal,' Rex decided. 'She's one who needn't go. Good woman right through: far too good for a gun-ridden town like this. She'll sure have plenty to cater for with us lot in relays.'

Rex stepped down into the street and Loo followed him. There was no difficulty in making catering arrangements with Ma Cassell. Everything went off perfectly, the men and women having their meals in shifts so that at no time was the town left unguarded. Immediately after he had had his breakfast, Atkinson set off for Denver. For Rex and the girl there came then a period of quiet, and they spent most of the day watching the unwanteds of Gold Point departing in pairs, groups, and families. Here and there, where he knew certain people were completely reliable, Rex gave permission for them to stay: upon the others he had no mercy. So, towards sundown, there was only Hall himself and his immediate retinue of gunmen left.

'I meant what I said, M'Clyde, about comin' back,' he snapped, as Rex and the girl watched him from the boardwalk. 'An' when I do I'll make yuh blamed sorry for ever getting this town.'

'If yore anxious t'eat lead, come back by all means,' Rex invited, shrugging. 'For th' moment you'd best think about getting on your way — and when you've hit the trail there's somethin' y'can think over. You didn't just trade me a town last night when I won that poker game.'

'Meanin' what?'

'Meanin' that if you hadn't tried to blow up my layout I wouldn't ha' found a super-bonanza, along with Miss Loo here. An' that super-bonanza's on *this* land ...' Rex grinned at the look of consternation on Hall's swarthy face. 'Tragic, ain't it?' he asked dryly.

'I don't believe it!' Hall snapped.

'No? You will, feller, when you get to hearin' how this state's prosperin' once yore out of it.'

Hall set his mouth, scowled, then jerked his head to his followers. They began moving and soon they had vanished from the high street in a cloud of dust. The girl gave a contented sigh.

'Air smells a lot sweeter already,' she commented.

Rex nodded, then as he was about to turn away, he paused as a lone horseman came riding in from the other end of the street. It was old man Atkinson, trail-filthy, but grinning.

'I guess that's all fixed up, Rex,' he said, drawing to a halt at the rail. 'I got through to the authorities okay and by mornin' three law officers will be down here — a Captain Gregory and two of his men. They'll talk things over with you.'

'Good enough,' Rex acknowledged.

And the next morning the three law officers rode into town. There was Captain Gregory, a tall, square-jawed man with the rank of U.S. Marshal besides his official title, and two other men who rated as either his deputies or subalterns. Rex saw all three men in the sheriff's office — formerly Hall's headquarters — and there made the situation clear.

'Naturally,' Captain Gregory said, 'it's irregular, Mr M'Clyde. You realize that?'

'Sure I do — but I guess one has t'be irregular sometimes to get at the truth, 'specially in a lawless region like this.'

'True ...' Gregory reflected for a moment. 'Hall's wanted, of course, for quite a few crimes, murder amongst them, but we've never been able to get the necessary evidence. If we can pink him on only one charge — such as admitting he committed the murder for which you were wrongfully convicted — we might be able to bring the other charges against him too.'

'Possible,' Rex agreed. 'What I want to know is: will you co-operate with me? Give me a chance to try and prove my innocence?'

Gregory smiled. 'Sure we will. What sort of a plan have you in mind?'

Rex hunched forward confidentially across the desk and began explaining. It took him fifteen minutes to outline in detail.

For eight weeks there was no sign of any return visit from Sherman Hall — but during that time Rex never once relaxed his vigilance. The three law officers stayed in Gold Point, waiting, waiting, until that moment when Rex could put his plan into operation. Now and again the law officers wondered if Hall ever would return — but Rex's faith in his own judgement never once wavered. Knowing the kind of mind Hall possessed, and knowing too how the thought of a lost bonanza must have increased his avarice and viciousness a hundred-fold, Rex was supremely sure that one day — or night — Hall would strike back.

And in the ninth week the thing happened. Hidden look-outs reported to Rex that Hall had been sighted, with his six closest friends, heading down trail towards Gold Point. Immediately Rex contacted the law officers and then sprang into action himself. At top speed he changed into black shirt and pants, as were always worn by Hall's gunmen, saddled his horse, and rode out on a detour trail to find the approaching avengers.

He sighted them half a mile from the town, drew to the side of the trail, and there remained in the starlight with his lariat noosed ready for action. As the last of the seven horsemen came thundering by the rope whirled soundlessly, noosed round the rearmost man, and brought him down into the dust with a crash. Instantly Rex hurtled out of his hiding place, snatched the dazed man's hat and kerchief, and then tore after the still scampering horse. He had just vaulted into the saddle when the others glanced round in the gloom.

'What did yuh have to fall back fur?' Hall demanded. 'Didn't I say we'd all got t'keep together?'

'Me saddle slipped,' Rex growled, through the folds of the kerchief drawn up to his eyes.

'Should fasten it better,' Hall said sourly. 'An' look, you mugs. We've only 'bout quarter uv a mile t'go. Y'know what we do. Ride straight through th' town an' throw these bombs we've got as we go. Th' place'll go up in smoke 'fore anybody has even had a chance t'do anythin'. Later we'll come back an' see what's doin', then call the rest of th' folks t'follow us. That'll be your job, Curly.'

Realizing that *he* was Curly, Rex growled an assent.

'What's the *matter* with you?' Hall demanded. 'Gone deaf or loco, or sump'n? Once we're through the town you ride back t'Arrow Head an' get the rest of the folks who's waitin' there. We'll take Gold Point by force, or else — Okay, time to get them bombs out. Git busy on your saddle bags.'

The riders slowed their pace and whilst Rex only fumbled his saddle bag as he rode, he watched what the others were doing. There was quite a stock of small home-made bombs in each bag. Evidently Hall intended sheer audacity and speed to give him the initiative in opening his range war.

As they neared the town Rex spoke, disguising his voice as well as he could.

'Say, boss, mebbe we're makin' a mistake all goin' through th' main street in the same direction.'

'Mistake? How'd yuh mean, mistake?'

'Well, if we're spotted, M'Clyde an' his boys have only gotta follow us — but if we came in at opposite ends we'd confuse 'em an' they wouldn't know which way t'go first. I reckon you an' me should go in from this end, an' the rest uv the boys oughta detour round the back of the buildings and come in frum the other end. We'd pass in the middle and join each other later — say at Fallow's Pasture, or some place.'

'Yeah,' Hall mused, as he jogged his horse along. 'Yeah, mebbe you've got somethin' there, Curly. Okay, you fellers,' he called. 'Detour! Go in frum the opposite end.'

The other men nodded and broke away, hurrying ahead. Rex grinned to himself and remained at Hall's side as they came to the further end of the lighted main street.

'Gotyuh bombs ready?' Hall snapped.

'Sure have. I'm reachin' behind me as I go along —'

'Okay. Let's step on it … '

Hall spurred his horse and Rex followed him — but before a dozen yards had been covered Hall found a gun in his back. He paused with a bomb in his hand.

'What in thunder's th' idea?' he demanded. 'Git that blasted rod out uv my back!'

'Put that bomb down,' Rex ordered.

'You gone crazy, Curly?' Hall yelled.

'Nope, but I want t'be sure where yore aimin' t'throw the durned thing. Might benefit yuh a lot if *I* got that bomb instead of th' town.'

Hall dragged his horse to a standstill. Above his face-mask he gazed round on the emptiness.

'What in blue thunder are yuh talkin' about?' he breathed. 'Why should I want t'wipe *you* out?'

''Cos I'm 'bout the only one who knows it were you who killed Morton Ringer, an' not M'Clyde. Kinda dangerous havin' witnesses lyin' around, ain't it?' 'S'posin' yuh do know?' Hall demanded. 'This ain't no time t'talk about it! We'll be seen any minnit. For God's sake, man, get wise to yuhself. Come on —'

'I don't feel like riskin' it,' Rex said stubbornly. 'Yuh've got a swell chance right now t'take care of me as yuh did Morton Ringer —'

'I fixed Morton Ringer so I could fix M'Clyde,' Hall retorted, 'it's nothin' t'do with what we're doin' now — an' yore quite safe frum —'

'Get down from that horse,' Rex ordered, in his own voice, and pulled down his face mask.

Hall stared for a moment, trying to take the situation in, then he raised the bomb he was still holding. At the moment his hand rose over his head, however, a lariat flashed out from the boardwalk and tightened on his wrist. Rex reached forward and snatched the bomb, laid it gently in his own saddle bag.

'Guess I ain't lost my touch with a rope,' Atkinson commented, grinning as he straddled the tie rail.

His wrist tethered, Hall had no possible chance of breaking free. Rex twisted in his saddle.

'Four more of the skunks are comin' from the opposite end of town, dad,' he said quickly. 'Fix it, will you?'

323

'Sure will!' And Atkinson thrust two fingers in his mouth and gave a piercing whistle. Instantly, before Hall's dazed eyes, the street seemed to sprout men and women, all of them armed and waiting.

'They're comin' in from the far end!' Rex yelled at them. 'They've got bombs — so nail 'em. Shoot to kill if you have to.'

'What is this?' Hall demanded savagely.

'Curtains, far as yore concerned, Hall ...'

Hall looked up again to the boardwalk, where Captain Gregory and his two men stood with their guns levelled.

'More plainly,' Gregory said, 'it's a plant. M'Clyde here took a long chance and impersonated one of your men in the dark. At a given spot — right here — where we could hear, he made you admit you killed Morton Ringer, which frees M'Clyde from all blame. You couldn't have made a better confession if you'd learned it beforehand ... As for the rest of the folks in this town they've been waiting for you coming back. Day after day, week after week. Now they're rewarded.'

Hall breathed hard, but there was nothing he could say. He sat watching dumbly as further up the street he saw the rest of his men run straight into the ambush prepared for them.

'It's all yours, Captain,' Rex said, sliding from the saddle and holstering his gun. 'And thanks for cooperating.'

'I guess that works both ways,' Gregory said. 'Now we c'n be on our way with these men ...'

Rex nodded and clambered up to the boardwalk. In silence, Loo and Atkinson and several of the townsfolk beside him, he watched the law officers mount their horses, draw their guns, and then gather the six gunmen into their midst. This done they began to make their way out of town.

'Good riddance,' murmured lawyer Cawley, spitting casually over the rail.

Rex turned at last to where Loo was standing. He gave an awkward grin.

'Mebbe we'd better go down a gold mine in the dark so's I can get up nerve to propose all over again,' he said.

The girl smiled. 'Why do that when I accepted long ago? Besides, I've already tipped off Mr Cawley here that he might have to perform a legal ceremony before long. He *can*, y'know, as a lawyer.'

'Yeah?' Rex looked at him in surprise.

Not that Cawley looked surprised. No expression at all was on his saturnine face. From his inside pocket he took a legal document and unfolded it.

'Sign here,' he said briefly. 'I reckon there won't be much more needed t'make you man and wife ... And we've certainly got all the witnesses we need.'

'Here's pen and ink,' Atkinson said, handing them over. 'I've bin carryin' 'em around. Figgered we might need 'em any time.'

Printed in Great Britain
by Amazon

81418001R00192